# Union Pacific

# Union Pacific

## A WESTERN STORY

# Zane Grey®

**FIVE STAR**
*A part of Gale, Cengage Learning*

GALE
CENGAGE Learning™

Detroit • New York • San Francisco • New Haven, Conn • Waterville, Maine • London

**GALE**
CENGAGE Learning™

**LIBRARY OF CONGRESS CATALOGING-IN-PUBLICATION DATA**

Grey, Zane, 1872–1939.
    Union Pacific : a western story / by Zane Grey. — 1st ed.
        p. cm. — (Five star western)
    ISBN-13: 978-1-59414-743-2 (alk. paper)
    ISBN-10: 1-59414-743-4 (alk. paper)
    1. Railroads—Design and construction—Fiction. 2. Union Pacific Railroad Company—Fiction. 3. Kidnapping victims—Fiction. 4. Surveyors—Fiction. 5. Wyoming—Fiction. I. Grey, Zane, 1872–1939. U.P. trail. II. Title.
PS3513.R654U18 2008
813'.52—dc22

First Edition. First Printing
Published in 2009 in con

Printed in the United States
1 2 3 4 5 6 7 12 11 10 09

*. . . When I think how the railroad has been pushed through this unwatered wilderness and haunt of savage tribes,—how at each stage of the construction roaring, impromptu cities, full of gold and lust and death, sprang up and then died away again, and are now but wayside stations in the desert; how in these uncouth places Chinese pirates worked side by side with border ruffians and broken men from Europe, gambling, drinking, quarrelling and murdering like wolves;—and then when I go on to remember that all this epical turmoil was conducted by gentlemen in frocks, and with a view to nothing more extraordinary than a fortune and a subsequent visit to Paris, it seems to me as if this railway were the one typical achievement of the age in which we live, as if it brought together into one plot all the ends of the world and all the degrees of social rank, and offered to some great writer the busiest, the most extended, and the most varied subject for an enduring literary work. If it be romance, if it be contrast, if it be heroism that we require, what was Troy to this?*

*Robert Louis Stevenson*

# FOREWORD
# BY JON TUSKA

It was stories that Zane Grey heard told by his friend and guide, Al Doyle, about the building of the Union Pacific Railroad that inspired him in late 1916 to attempt what would be his first historical novel. He worked out an elaborate outline of the book he intended to write, detailing characters, events, and the themes he wanted to incorporate. For all of his enthusiasm for the subject, he was constrained by an ambivalence about the triumphalism usually attached to narrating epic historical events from American frontier history. Early on he noted about his character, the mountain man and trapper, Slingerland: "the beginning and end of book, his point of view. Beauty, lonesomeness, silence, wildness!" He also reminded himself at the beginning of the outline: "Last page—the Indian's setting sun."

Contrasting this outline with his holographic manuscript, Grey appears to have written disparate scenes having to do with various parts of the story somewhat out of linear sequence, then added new scenes and changed others. The problem for him became that under the inspiration and emotion of writing these scenes they did not always adhere closely to his narrative outline, so that transitions between scenes became awkward. Also in the writing of his story, the book became much longer than he had anticipated it would be. So it was a large, diffuse, and even at times confusing manuscript that he sent to Ripley Hitchcock, his editor at Harper & Bros. From his home in Lackawaxen,

Pennsylvania, accompanying his submission, Grey wrote to Hitchcock:

*My dear Critic and Friend:*

*In the light of my quotation from Stevenson it may be presumptuous for me to aspire to tell the story of the building of the Union Pacific Railroad.*

*But many a night by the camp-fire on the starlit desert have I listened to my old guide, Al Doyle, while he recounted his experiences as teamster, grader, spiker, and fighter during the construction of that great work. It is as though I had lived through the blood and lust and death, the "epical turmoil," the labor of giants, the heroism and sacrifice of this wildest time in the opening of the West.*

*Your love of the West and your early travels there and your study of historical frontier days, from which I have profited, have been strong factors in my undertaking this book; and they, like Stevenson's noble words, have made me see the wonder, the dignity, the importance of the subject.*

*For the romance, for the inspiration, I have my own love of the wild desert, plain, and mountain; I have Doyle's stories of sudden death and terrible lust and alluring gold—unforgettable stories; and it seems as though all the labor and violence and havoc of those years have become embodied in my imagination.*

*So here I give you my book—for which I have written all the others—and I do it with hope and dread and fear and yet with joy.*

*Faithfully,*
*Zane Grey*

As was usual with Ripley Hitchcock, given a Zane Grey manuscript, he set about rewriting whole sections, altering the sequence of events and what happened to characters. To give but one example. In Grey's manuscript Warren Neale fights with the reprobate gambler Durade and brutally kills him. Hitchcock altered this scene and had Durade survive the fight, although fundamentally maimed. Grey accepted these many changes, although they made the story almost as much Hitchcock's as his own, because it was his objective to rise to a higher plane of literature and he was convinced that Hitchcock's editorial contribution could help him do it. After all, Ripley Hitchcock had been Stephen Crane's editor. Harper & Bros. sold a condensed section of the Hitchcock version of the novel to *Blue Book,* a prestigious monthly pulp fiction magazine, where it appeared under the title "The Roaring U.P. Trail" in eight installments, from May, 1917 to December, 1917.

Grey's ambition to write strictly psychological fiction in the future, rather than Western stories, would be altered by the critical praise in response to what Harper & Bros. titled *The U.P. Trail.* Grey wrote in his diary:

> *My power and my study and passion shall be directed to that which already I have written best—the beauty and color and mystery of great spaces, of the open, of Nature in her wild moods. This decision has been a relief.*

To Ripley Hitchcock he wrote on February 20, 1918:

> *Much good has come to me, in the way of significant appreciation, since The U.P. Trail was published. It is like wine.*

I do not know what the critical reception would have been had Harper & Bros. published Grey's historical novel as he wrote it. One thing is certain. His version contains scenes of unique power and images that will stay with you long after reading it. There is also a psychological depth to several of the characters that was not customary in Grey's fiction prior to this novel, especially in the depiction of Allie Lee, following her survival of an attack by Sioux Indians and in her captivity with Durade and her later relationship with her biological father. Moreover, despite the occasional awkwardness in transitions, there is an elemental power in this narrative that was compromised, if not lost altogether, in the Ripley Hitchcock version. For his part Grey would not revise his view of editorial intervention in his stories until the conflict erupted over the censorship imposed by Harper & Bros. on *The Vanishing American*. From that point forward, everything changed. Yet, thanks to the existence of Zane Grey's holographic manuscript at the Library of Congress of what now is titled *Union Pacific*, as readers of today we are able to put aside all such controversy and experience directly what Zane Grey wrote and what he himself described so aptly as "the blood and lust and death, the 'epical turmoil,' the labor of giants, the heroism and sacrifice of this wildest time in the opening of the West."

# CHAPTER ONE

In the early 'Sixties a trail led from the broad Missouri, swirling yellow and turgid between its green-groved borders, for miles and miles out upon the grassy Nebraska plains—westward over the undulating prairie, with its swales and billows and long winding lines of cottonwoods, to a slow vast heave of rising ground, Wyoming, where the herds of buffalo grazed and the wolf was lord and the campfire of the trapper sent up its curling blue smoke from beside some lonely stream—on and on over the barren lands of eternal monotony, all so gray and wide and solemn and silent under the endless sky—on and ever up to the bleak black hills and into the waterless gullies and through the rocky gorges where the deer browsed and the savage lurked—slowly rising to the pass between the great bold peaks, and across the windy uplands into Utah, with its verdant valleys, green as emeralds, and its haze-filled cañons and wonderful wind-worn cliffs and walls, and its pale salt lakes, veiled in the shadows of stark and lofty rocks, dim, lilac-colored, austere, and isolated—and ever onward and ever westward, up from desert to mountain, up into California where the white streams rushed and roared and the stately pines towered, and seen from craggy heights, deep down, the little blue lakes gleamed like gems—and so on to the great descent, where the mountain world ceased, and where out beyond the golden land, asleep and peaceful, stretched the illimitable Pacific, vague and grand beneath the setting sun.

# CHAPTER TWO

In 1865, just after the war, a party of engineers was at work in the Black Hills on a survey as hazardous as it was problematical. They had charge of the laying of the Union Pacific Railroad.

This party, escorted by a company of U.S. troops under Colonel Dillon, had encountered difficulties almost insurmountable. And now, having penetrated the wild hills to the eastern slope of the Rockies, they were halted by a seemingly impassable barrier—a gorge too deep to fill, too wide to bridge.

General Lodge, chief engineer for the corps, gave an order to one of his assistants.

"Put young Neale on the job. If we ever survey a line through this awful place, we'll owe it to him."

The assistant, Baxter, told an Irishman standing by to find Neale. This individual, Casey by name, was smoking a short black pipe in the presence of his superiors. Casey was rawboned, red-faced, hard-featured, a man inured to exposure and rough life. His expression seemed to be a fixed one of extreme good-humor, as if his face had set, mask-like, during a grin. He removed the pipe.

"Gineral, the flag I've bin holdin' fer that domn' young surveyor is the wrong color. I want a green flag."

Baxter waved the Irishman to his errand, but General Lodge looked up from the maps and plans before him with a faint smile. He had a dark stern face and the bearing of a soldier.

"Casey, you can have any color you like," he said. "Maybe

green would change our luck."

"Gineral, we'll niver git no railroad built, an' if we do, it'll be the Irish that builds it," responded Casey, and went his way.

Only one hope remained, and it was that the agile and daring Neale, with his eye of a mountaineer and his genius for estimating distance and grade, might run a line around the gorge. They sent for him back to the troop camp, and, while waiting, they went over the maps and drawings, again and again, with the earnestness of men who could not be beaten.

Lodge had been a major-general in the Civil War just ended, and before the war he had traveled that part of the West many times, with the mighty project of the building of the railroad fermenting in his mind. It had taken years to evolve the plan to build that road, and it came at last through many new and devious ways, plots, and counter-plots. The wonderful idea of the uniting of East and West by a railroad originated in one man's brain and he lived for it. Later, one by one, other men divined and believed despite doubt and fear, until the day arrived when Congress put the government of the U.S., the Army, and a group of frock-coated directors with gold back of General Lodge, and bade him build the road.

In all the length and breadth of the land no men but the chief engineer and his assistants knew the difficulty, the peril of that undertaking. The outside world was interested; the nation waited, mostly in doubt. But Lodge and his engineers had been grasped by the spirit of some great thing to be, in the making of which were adventure, fortune, fame, and that strange call of life which saw a heritage for those to come. They were grim; they were indomitable.

Warren Neale came hurrying up. He was a New Englander of poor family, self-educated, wild for adventure, keen for achievement, eager, ardent, bronze-faced, and keen-eyed, under six feet in height, built like a wedge, but not heavy—a young man of

13

twenty-three with strong latent possibilities of character.

General Lodge himself undertook to explain the difficulties of the situation, and what was hoped for from the young surveyor. Neale flushed with pride; his eyes flashed; his jaw set. But he said little while the engineers led him out to the scene of the latest barrier. It was a rugged gorge, old and yellow and crumbled, cedar-fringed at the top, bare and white at the bottom. The approach to it was through a break in the walls, so that the gorge was really both above and below this vantage point.

"This is the only passage through these foothills," said Engineer Henney, the eldest of Lodge's corps.

The passage mentioned ended where the break in the walls fronted abruptly on the gorge. It was a wild scene. Only inspired and implacable men could have entertained any hope of building a railroad through there. The mouth of the break was narrow; a rugged slope led up to the left; to the right a huge buttress of stone wall bulged over the gorge; across stood out the seamed and cracked cliffs, and below yawned the abyss. The nearer side of the gorge could only be guessed at.

Neale crawled to the extreme edge of the precipice and, lying flat, tried to see what was beneath. Evidently he did not see much, for, upon getting up, he shook his head. Then he gazed at the bulging wall.

"The side of that can be blown off," he muttered.

"But what's around the corner? If it's straight stone wall for miles and miles, we are done," said Boone, another of the engineers.

"The opposite wall is that," added Henney. "You can see a long way."

General Lodge gazed at the baffling gorge. His face worked grimmer, harder. "It seems impossible to go on, but we *must* go on," he said.

A short silence ensued. The engineers faced each other like men confronted by a last and crowning hindrance. Then Neale laughed. He appeared cool and confident.

"It only looks bad," he said. "We'll climb to the top and I'll go down over the wall on a rope."

Neale had been let down over many precipices in those stony hills. He had been the luckiest, the most daring and successful of all the number of men put to perilous tasks. One spoke of the accidents that had happened, or even of the fatal fall of a lineman, who a few weeks before had ventured once too often. Every rod of road surveyed made the engineers sterner at their task, just as it made them keener in realization of the tragedy that must attend this work.

The climb to the top of the bluff was long and arduous. The whole corps went, and also some of the troopers.

"I'll need a long rope," Neale had said to King, his lineman.

It was this order that made King take so much time in ascending the bluff. Besides, he was a cowboy, used to riding, and could not climb well.

"Wal . . . I . . . shore . . . rustled . . . all the line . . . aboot heah," he drawled pantingly, as he threw lassoes and coils of rope at Neale's feet.

Neale picked up some of the worn pieces. He looked dubious. "Is this all you could get?" he asked.

"Shore is. An' thet includes what Casey rustled . . . from the soldiers."

"Help me knot these," went on Neale.

"Wal, I reckon this heah time I'll go down before you," drawled King.

Neale laughed, and looked curiously at his lineman. Back somewhere in Nebraska this cowboy from Texas had attached himself to Neale. They worked together and became friends. Larry Red King made no bones of the fact that Texas had grown too hot for him. He had been born with an itch to shoot. To Neale it seemed that King made too much of a service Neale had rendered—the mere matter of a helping hand. Still there had been danger.

"Go down before me!" Neale exclaimed.

"I reckon," replied King.

"You will not," rejoined the other bluntly. "I may not need you at all. What's the sense of useless risk?"

"Wal, I'm goin' . . . else I throw up my job."

"Oh, hell!" burst out Neale, as he strained hard on a knot. Again he looked at his lineman, this time with something warmer than curiosity in his glance.

Larry Red King was tall, slim, round, hard as iron, yet somehow graceful in line—a singularly handsome and picturesque cowboy with flaming red hair and smooth face as red, and eyes of flashing blue. From his belt swung a sheath holding a heavy gun.

"Wal, go ahaid," added Neale, mimicking his comrade. "An' I shore hope that this heah time you-all get aboot enough of your job."

One by one the engineers returned from different points along the wall, and they joined the group around Neale and King.

"Test that rope," ordered General Lodge.

The long rope appeared to be amply strong. When King fastened one end around his body under his arms, the question arose among the engineers, just as it had arisen for Neale, whether or not it was needful to let the lineman down before the surveyor.

"I reckon I'll go ahaid," said King. Like all Texans of his type, Larry Red King was slow, easy, cool, careless. Moreover he gave a singular impression of latent nerve, wildness, violence.

There seemed all assurance of a deadlock, when General

Lodge stepped forward, and addressed his inquiry to Neale.

"Red thinks the rope will break. So he wants to go first," replied Neale.

There were broad smiles forthcoming, yet no one laughed. This was one of the thousands of strange human incidents that must be enacted in the building of the railroad. It might have been humorous, but it was big. It fixed the spirit and it foreshadowed events. All this shone in General Lodge's stern face.

"Obey orders," he admonished King.

The loop was taken from King's waist and transferred to Neale's, and then all was made ready to let the daring surveyor with his instrument down over the wall.

Neale took one more look down the rugged front of the cliff. When he straightened up, the ruddy bronze had left his face.

"There's a bulge of rock. I can't see what's below it," he said. "No use for signals. I'll go down the length of the rope and trust to find a footing. I can't be hauled up."

They all conceded this, silently. Then Neale sat down, let his legs dangle over the wall, firmly grasped his instrument, and said to the troopers who held the rope: "All right."

They lowered him foot by foot.

It was windy up there. The dust flew up from under the wall. Black cañon swifts, like swallows, darted with wildly rustling wings, uttering frightened twitterings. The engineers leaned over, watching Neale's progress. Larry Red King did not look over the precipice. He seemed uncertain, waiting. He watched the slowly slipping rope as knot by knot it passed over. It fascinated him.

"He's reached the bulge of rock!" called Baxter, craning his neck.

"There, he's down . . . out of sight!" exclaimed Henney.

Casey, the flagman, leaned farther out than any other.

"Phwat a domn' strange way to build a railroad, I sez," he remarked.

The gorge lay asleep in the westering sun, silent, full of blue haze. Seen from this height, far above the break when the engineers had first halted, it had the dignity and dimensions of a cañon. Its walls had begun to change color in the sunset light.

Foot by foot the soldiers let the rope slip until probably two hundred feet had been let out, and there were scarcely a hundred left. By this time all that part of the cable that had been made of lassoes had passed over; the remainder consisted of pieces of worn and knotted and frayed rope at which the engineers began to gaze fearfully.

"I don't like this," said Henney nervously. "Neale surely ought to have found a ledge or bench or slope by now."

Instinctively the soldiers held back, reluctantly yielding inches when before they had slacked feet. But intent as was their gaze, it could not rival that of the cowboy.

"Hold!" he yelled, suddenly pointing to where the strained rope curved over the edge of the wall.

The troopers held hard. The rope ceased to pay out. The strain seemed to increase. Larry Red King pointed with a lean hand.

"It's a-goin' to break!"

His voice, hoarse and swift now, checked the forward movement of the engineers. He plunged to his knees before the rope and reached clutchingly, as if he wanted to grasp it, yet dared not.

"Ropes was my job! Old an' rotten! It's breakin' . . . !"

Soon as he spoke the rope snapped. The troopers, thrown off their balance, fell backward. Baxter groaned; Boone and Henney cried out in horror; General Lodge stood aghast, dazed. Then they all froze right in the position of intense listening.

A dull sound puffed up from the gorge, a low *crash,* then a

18

slow-rising roar and *rattle* of sliding earth and rock. It diminished and ceased with the hollow *cracking* of stone against stone.

Casey broke the silence among the listening men with a curse. Larry Red King rose from his knees, holding the end of the snapped rope, which he threw from him with passionate violence. Then with action just as violent he unbuckled his belt and pulled it tighter and buckled it again. His eyes seemed blazing with blue lightning and they accused the agitated engineers of murder. But he turned away without speaking and hurried along the edge of the gorge, evidently searching for a place to go down.

General Lodge ordered the troopers to follow King and, if possible, recover Neale's body.

"That lad had a future," said old Henney sadly. "We'll miss him."

Boone's face expressed sickness and horror. Baxter choked. "Too bad    but what's to be done?"

The chief engineer looked away from the shadowy gorge where the sun was burning the ramparts red. To have command of men was hard, bitter. Death stalked with his orders. He foresaw that the building of this railroad was to resemble the war in which he had sent so many lads and soldiers and officers to their graves.

The engineers descended the long slope and returned to camp a mile down the narrow valley. Fires were blazing; columns of smoke were curling aloft; the merry song and reckless laugh of soldiers were ringing out, so clear in the still air; horses were neighing and stamping.

Colonel Dillon reported to General Lodge that one of the scouts had sighted a large band of Sioux Indians encamped in a valley not far distant. This tribe had gone on the warpath and had begun to harass the engineers. Neale's tragic fate was forgotten in the apprehension of what threatened when the

Sioux discovered the significance of that surveying expedition.

"The Sioux could make the building of the U.P. impossible," said Henney, always nervous and pessimistic.

"No Indians . . . nothing can stop me," declared his chief.

The troopers sent to follow Larry Red King came back to camp saying that they had lost him and that they could not find any place where it was possible to get down into the gorge.

In the morning King had not returned.

Detachments of troopers were sent in different directions to try again. And the engineers went out once more to attack their problems. Success did not attend the efforts of either the troopers or the engineers. And at sunset, when all had wearily returned to camp, Larry Red King was still absent. Then he was given up for lost.

But before dark the tall cowboy limped into camp, dusty and torn, carrying Neale's long tripod and surveying instrument. It looked the worse for a fall, but apparently was not badly damaged. King did not give the troopers any satisfaction. Limping on to the tents of the engineers, he set down the instrument and called. Boone was the first to come out, and his call brought Henney, Baxter, and younger members of the corps. General Lodge, sitting at his campfire some rods away and bending over his drawings, did not see King's arrival.

No one detected any difference in the cowboy, except that he limped. Slow, cool, careless, he was yet somehow vital and impelling.

"Wal, we run the line around . . . five miles up the gorge whar crossin' is easy . . . an' only ninety feet grade to the mile."

The engineers looked at him as if he were crazy.

"But Neale! He fell . . . he's dead!" exclaimed Henney.

"Daid? Wal, no, Neale ain't daid," drawled King.

"Where is he, then?"

"I reckon he's comin' along back heah."

"Is he hurt?"

"Shore. An' hungry, too, which is what I am," replied Larry, and he limped away.

Some of the engineers hurried out in the gathering dusk to meet Neale while the others went to General Lodge with the good news.

The chief received this quietly with intent eyes.

"Bring Neale and King here . . . as soon as their needs have been seen to," he ordered. Then he called after Baxter: "Ninety feet to the mile . . . you said?"

"Ninety foot grade, so King reported."

"By all that's lucky," breathed the chief, as if his load had been immeasurably lightened. "Send those boys to me."

Some of the soldiers had found Neale down along the trail and were helping him into camp. He was crippled and almost exhausted. He made light of his condition, yet he groaned when he dropped into a seat before the fire, and appeared grateful for the service tendered him.

Someone approached Larry Red King to inform him that the general wanted to see him.

"Wal, I'm hungry . . . an' he ain't my boss," replied King, and went on with his meal. It was well known that the Southerner would not talk.

But Neale talked—he blazed in eloquence about his lineman—and before an hour had passed everyone in camp knew that King had saved Neale's life. Then the loquacious Casey, intruding upon the cowboy's reserve, got roundly cursed for his pains.

"Go whan out among thim Sooz Injuns, an' be a dead hero, then," retorted Casey as the cowboy stalked off to be alone in the gloom. Evidently Casey was disappointed not to get another cursing, for he turned to his comrade McDermott, an axe-man.

"Say, Mac, whot do you make of cowboys?"

"I tell ye, Pat, I make of thim thet you'll be full of bullet holes before this railroad's built."

"Thin, b'gosh, I should drink fer a long time yit," replied Casey.

Later General Lodge visited Neale and received the drawings and figures that made easy solution to what had been a formidable problem.

"It was easy, once I landed under that bulge of cliff," said Neale. "There's a slope of about forty-five degrees . . . not all rock. And four miles up, the gorge peters out. We can cross. I got to where I could see the divide . . . and, oh, there is where our troubles begin. The worst is all to come."

"You've said it," replied the chief soberly. "We can't follow the trail and get the grade necessary. We've got to hunt up a pass."

"We'll find one," said Neale hopefully.

"Neale, you're ambitious and you've the kind of spirit that never gives up. I've watched you work from the start. You'll make a big position for yourself with this railroad, if you only live through the building of it."

"Oh, I'll live through it all right," replied Neale, laughing. "I'm like a cat . . . always land on my feet . . . and have nine lives besides."

"You sure must. How far did you fall this time?"

"Not far. I landed in a tree, where my instrument stuck. But I crashed down, and got a hard knock on the head. When Red joined me, I was unconscious and sliding for another precipice."

"That Texan seems attached to you."

"Well, if he wasn't before, he will be now, for I'll make him attached," said Neale feelingly. "I'll tell you, General, King's red-headed, a droll lazy Southerner, and he's made fun of by the men. But they don't understand him. They certainly can't

see how dangerous he is. Only I don't mean that. I do mean . . .
he's true."

"Yes, he showed that. When the rope snapped, I was sure
he'd pull a gun on us. . . . Neale, I would have liked to have you
and Larry Red King with me through the war."

"Thank you, General Lodge. . . . But I like the prospects
now."

"Neale, you're hungry for wild life?"

"Yes," replied Neale simply.

"I said as much. I felt . . . somewhat of that when I was your
age. . . . And you like our prospects? Well, you've thought things
out. Neale, the building of the U.P. will be hell."

"General, I can see that. It sort of draws me . . . two ways . . .
the wildness of it and then to accomplish something."

"My lad, I hope you accomplish something more . . . for you
have already a thousand soldiers in one wild camp out here in
these wild hills . . . and thousands of others . . . honest
merchants and dishonest merchants, whiskey men, gamblers,
desperadoes, bandits, and bad women. Niggers, greasers,
Indians, all together moving from camp to camp, where there
can be no law."

"It will be great!" exclaimed Neale, with shining eyes.

"It will be terrible," muttered the elder man gravely. Then, as
he got up and bade his young assistant good night, the somber-
ness had returned to his eyes and the weight to his shoulders.
He did not underestimate his responsibility or the nature of his
task, and he sensed nameless and unknown events, beyond all
divining, that inevitably must grow out of the colossal enterprise.

Henney was the next to come to see Neale. The old engineer
appeared elated about something, which for the moment he apparently forgot in his solicitation for the young man's welfare.
Presently, after he had been reassured, the smile came back to
his face, and he said: "The chief has promoted you."

"What?" exclaimed Neale, starting up.

"It's a fact. He just talked it over with Baxter and me. This last job of yours pleased him mightily . . . and so you go up."

"Go up! To what?" queried Neale eagerly.

"Well, that's why he consulted me, I guess." Henney laughed. "You see we sort of had to make something to promote you to, for the present."

"Oh, I see. I was wondering what job there could be," replied Neale, and he laughed, too. "What did the chief say?"

"He said a lot. Seems to have you figured both as to your work . . . and desire to see this wild life out here. He said you'd land at the top if the U.P. is ever built. . . . Chief engineer. Superintendent of maintenance of way!"

"Good Lord," breathed Neale. "You're not in earnest?"

" 'Wal, I shore am,' as your cowboy pard says," returned Henney. And then he shifted to earnestness. "Listen, Neale. Here's the matter in a nutshell. You will be called up to run those particular and difficult surveys, as that of yesterday. But no more of the routine for you. Added to that you will be sent forward and back, inspecting, figuring. You can make your headquarters with us or in the construction camps, as suits your convenience. All this of course presently, when we get farther on. So you will be in a way free . . . your own boss a good deal of the time. And fitting yourself for that maintenance of way job. In fact the chief said that . . . called you Maintenance of Way Neale. . . . I congratulate you. And my advice is, keep on as you've begun . . . go straight . . . look out for your wildness and temper. . . . That's all. Good night."

Then he went out, leaving Neale speechless.

Neale had many callers that night and the last was Larry Red King. The cowboy stooped to enter the tent.

"Wal, how aboot you-all?" he drawled.

"Not so good, Red," replied Neale. "My head's hot and I've got a lot of pain. I think I'm going to be a little flighty. Would you mind getting your blankets and staying with me tonight?"

"I reckon I'd be glad," answered King. He put a hand on Neale's face. "You shore have fever." He left the tent, to return presently with a roll of blankets and a canteen, which he carried awkwardly. Then he began to bathe Neale's face with cold water. There was a flickering campfire outside that threw shadows on the wall of the tent. By its light Neale saw that King's left hand was bandaged and that he used it clumsily.

"What's wrong with your hand?" he queried.

"I reckon nawthin'."

"Why is it bound up, then?"

"Wal, someone sent thet fool Army doctor to me an' he said I had two busted bones in it."

"He did? I had no idea you were hurt. You never said a word. And you carried me and my instrument all day . . . with a broken hand!"

"Wal, I ain't so shore it's broke."

Neale swore at his friend, and then he fell asleep. King watched beside him, ever and anon re-wetting the hot brow.

The campfire died out and at length the quietness of late night set in. The wind mourned and lulled by intervals; a horse *thudded* his hoofs now and then; there were soft steady footsteps of the sentry on guard, and the wild cry of a night bird.

# CHAPTER THREE

Across the Black Hills some miles from the camp of the engineers lay a valley watered by a stream that ran down from Cheyenne Pass.

A band of Sioux Indians had an encampment there. Viewed from the summit of a grassy ridge the scene was colorful and idle and quiet, in keeping with the lonely beautiful valley. Cottonwoods and willows showed a bright green; the course of the stream was marked in dark where the water ran, and light where the sand had bleached; brown and black dots scattered over the valley were grazing horses; lodge-pole tents gleamed white in the sun, and tiny bits of red stood out against the white as lazy wreaths of blue smoke rose upward.

The Black Hills were split by many such valleys and many bore grassy ridges sloped up toward the mountains. Upon the side of one ridge, the highest that rose boldly between the camp of the white men and that of the red men, there stood a solitary mustang, haltered with a lasso. He was a ragged, shaggy wild beast, and there was no saddle or bridle on him, nothing but the halter. He was not grazing, although the grass bleached white grew long and thick under his hoofs. He looked up the slope, in a direction indicated by his pointing ears, and he watched a wavering movement of the long grass.

It was wild up on that ridge, bare of everything except grass, and the strange wavering had a nameless wildness in its motion. No stealthy animal accounted for that trembling—that forward undulating quiver. It wavered on to the summit of the ridge.

What a wide and wonderful prospect opened up to view from this lofty point! Ridge after ridge sloped up to the Black Hills and these in turn raised their bleak dark heads toward the mountains, looming pale and gray, with caps of snow, in the distance. Out beyond the ridges, indistinct in the glare, stretched an illimitable expanse, gray and dull, that was the prairie land. An eagle, lord of all he surveyed, sailed around and around in the sky.

Below this grassy summit yawned a valley, narrow and long, losing itself by turns to distant east and west, and through it ran a faint white winding line that was the old St. Vrain and Laramie Trail.

There came a moment when the wavering in the grass ceased on the extreme edge of the slope. Then it parted to disclose the hideous visage of a Sioux Indian in war paint. His dark piercing malignant glance fixed upon the St. Vrain and Laramie Trail. His half-naked body rested at ease; a rifle lay under his hand.

There he watched while the hours passed. The sun moved on in its course until it tipped the peaks with rose. Far down the valley black and white objects appeared, crawling round the bend. The Indian gave an almost imperceptible start, but there was no change in his expression. He watched as before.

These moving objects grew to be oxen and prairie schooners—a small caravan traveling east. It wound down the trail and halted in a circle on the bank of a stream.

The Indian scout slid backward, and the parted grass, slowly closing, hid from his dark gaze the camp scene below. He wormed his way back well out of sight, then, rising, he ran over the summit of the ridge to leap upon the mustang and ride wildly down the slope.

# CHAPTER FOUR

Bill Horn, leader of the caravan, had a large amount of gold that he was taking back East. No one in his party except a girl knew he had the fortune.

Horn had gone West at the beginning of the gold strikes, but it was not until 1853 that any success attended his labors. Later he struck it rich, and in 1865, as soon as the snow melted on the mountain passes, he got together a party of men and several women and left Sacramento. He was a burly miner, bearded and uncouth, of rough speech and taciturn nature, and absolutely fearless.

At Ogden, Utah, he had been advised not to attempt to cross the Black Hills with so small a party, for the Sioux Indians had gone on the warpath.

Horn was leading his caravan and finding the trail eastward. He did not have a scout or hunter with him. Eastward traveling caravans were wont to be small and poorly outfitted, for only the homesick, the failures, the wanderers, and the lawless turned their faces from the Golden State. At the start Horn had eleven men, three women, and the girl. On the way he had killed one of the men, and another, with his wife, had yielded to persuasion of friends at Ogden, and had left the party. So when Horn halted for camp one afternoon in a beautiful valley in the Black Hills, there were only nine men with him.

On a long journey through wild country strangers grew close together or far apart. Bill Horn did not think much of the men who had accepted the chance he offered them, and daily he grew more aloof. They were not a responsible crowd, and the best he could get out of them was the driving of oxen and camp chores indifferently done. He had to kill the meat and find the water and keep the watch. Upon entering the Black Hills, Horn had shown a restlessness and hurry and anxiety. This in no wise affected others. They continued to be aimless and careless as men who had little to look forward to.

This beautiful valley offered everything desirable for a campsite except any natural cover or protection in case of attack. But Horn had to take the risk. The oxen were tired, the wagons had to be greased, and it was needful to kill meat. Here was an abundance of grass, a clear cold brook, wood for campfires, and sign of game on all sides.

"Haul around . . . make a circle," Horn ordered the drivers of the oxen.

This was the first time he had given an order like that, and the men guffawed or grimaced as they hauled the great clumsy prairie schooners into a circle. The oxen were unhitched; the camp duffle piled out; the ring of axes broke the stillness, and fires were started.

Horn took his rifle and strode away up the brook to disappear in the green brush of a ravine.

It was early in the afternoon with the sun not yet out of sight behind a lofty ridge that topped the valley slope. High grass, bleached white, shone brightly on the summit. Soon several columns of blue smoke curled lazily aloft until, catching the wind high up, they were swept away.

The men talked while at their tasks.

"Say, pard, did you come along this here Laramie Trail goin' west?" asked one.

"Nope. I hit the Santa Fé Trail," was the reply.

"How about you, Jones?"

"Same fer me."

"Wal," said another, "I went 'round to California by ship, an' I'd hev been lucky to drown."

"An' now we're all goin' back poorer than when we started," remarked a third.

"Pard, you've said somethin'."

"Wal, I seen a heap of gold, if I didn't find any."

"Jones, has this here Bill Horn any gold with him?"

"He acts like it," answered Jones. "An' I heered he struck it rich out thar."

Then they appeared divided in their opinions of Bill Horn. From him they drifted to talk of possible Indian raids and scouted the idea, and then wondered if the famous Pony Express had been over this Laramie Trail, and, finally, got on the subject of a rumored railroad to be built from East to West.

"No railroad can't be built over this trail," said Jones bluntly.

"Sure not. But couldn't more level ground be dug?" asked another.

"Dug? Across them Utah deserts an' up them mountains? Hell! Men sure hev more sense than thet!" exclaimed the third.

And so they talked and argued at their tasks.

The women, however, had little to say. One, the wife of the loquacious Jones, lived among past associations of happy years that would not come again—a sober-faced, middle-aged woman. The other woman was younger, and her sad face showed traces of a former comeliness. They called her Mrs. Durade. The girl was her daughter Allie. She appeared about fifteen years old, and was slight of form. Her face did not seem to tan. It was pale. She had long rich chestnut-colored hair that she wore in a braid. She looked tired, and was shy and silent, almost ashamed. Her eyes were singularly large and dark, and violet in color.

"It's a long long way we are from home yet," sighed Mrs. Jones.

"You call East home," replied Mrs. Durade bitterly.

"For land's sake! Yes, I do," exclaimed the other. "If there was a home in that California, I never saw it. Tents and log cabins and mud holes! Such places for a woman to live. Oh! I hated that California. A lot of wild men all crazy over gold. Gold that only a few could find and none could keep! I pray every night to live to get back home."

Mrs. Durade had no reply; she gazed away over the ridges toward the east with a haunting shadow in her eyes.

Just then a rifle shot sounded from up in the ravine. The men paused in their tasks, and looked at each other. Then reassured by this exchange of glances they fell to work again. But the women cast apprehensive eyes around. There was no life in sight except the grazing oxen. Presently Horn appeared carrying a deer slung over his shoulders.

Allie ran to meet him. She and Horn were great friends. To her alone was he gentle and kind. She saw him pause at the brook, then drop the deer carcass and bend over the ground, as if to search for something. When Allie reached his side, he was on his knees examining a moccasin print in the sand.

"An Indian track!" exclaimed Allie.

"Allie, it sure ain't anythin' else," he replied. "Thet is what I've been lookin' fer. . . . A day old . . . mebbe more."

"Uncle Bill, is there danger?" she asked, fearfully gazing up the slope.

"Lass, we're in the Black Hills, an' I wish to the Lord we was out," he answered. Then he picked up the deer carcass, a heavy burden, and slung it, hoofs in front, over his shoulders.

"Let me carry your gun," said Allie.

They started toward camp.

"Lass, listen," began Horn earnestly. "Mebbe there's no need to fear. But I don't like Injun tracks. Not these days. Now I'm goin' to scare this lazy outfit. Mebbe thet'll make them rustle.

But don't you be scared."

In camp the advent of fresh venison was hailed with satisfaction.

"Wal, I'll gamble the shot thet killed this meat was heered by Injuns," blurted out Horn as he deposited his burden in the grass and whipped out his hunting knife. Then he glared at the outfit of men he had come to despise.

"Horn, I reckon you 'pear more set up about Injuns than usual," remarked Jones.

"Fresh Sioux track right out thar along the brook."

"No!"

"Sioux!" echoed another.

"Go an' look fer yourself."

Not a man of them moved a step. Horn snorted his disdain and without more talk began to dress the deer.

Meanwhile the sun set behind the ridge and the day seemed far spent. The evening meal of the travelers was disrupted when Horn suddenly leaped up and reached for his rifle.

"Thet's no Injun, but I don't like the looks of how he's comin'."

All gazed in the direction in which Horn pointed. A horse and rider were swiftly approaching down the trail from the west. Before any of the startled campers recovered from their surprise, the horse reached the camp. The rider hauled up short, but did not dismount.

"Hello!" he called. The man was not young. He had piercing gray eyes and long hair. He wore fringed gray buckskin, and carried a long heavy muzzle-loading rifle. "I'm Slingerland . . . trapper in these hyar parts," he went on, with glance swiftly taking in the group. "Who's boss of this caravan?"

"I am . . . Bill Horn," replied the leader, stepping out.

"Thar's a band of Sioux redskins on your trail."

Horn lifted his arms high. The other men uttered exclamations of amaze and dread. The women were silent. "Did you see them?" asked Horn.

"Yes, from a ridge back hyar ten miles. I saw them sneakin' along the trail an' I knowed they meant mischief. I rode along the ridges or I'd been hyar sooner."

"How many Injuns?"

"I counted fifteen. They were goin' along slow. Like as not they've sent word for more. There's a big Sioux camp over hyar in another valley."

"Are these Sioux on the warpath?"

"I saw dead an' scalped white men a few days back," replied Slingerland.

Horn grew as black as a thundercloud and he cursed the group of pale-faced men who had elected to journey eastward with him. "You'll hev to fight," he ended brutally, "an' thet'll be some satisfaction to me."

"Horn, there's soldiers over hyar in camp," went on Slingerland. "Do you want me to ride after them?"

"Soldiers!" ejaculated Horn.

"Yes. They're with a party of engineers surveyin' a line fer a railroad. Reckon I could git them all hyar in time to save you . . . *if* them Sioux keep comin' slow. . . . I'll go or stay hyar with you."

"Friend, you go . . . an' ride thet hoss!"

"All right. You hitch up an' break camp. Keep goin' hard down the trail, an' I'll fetch the troops an' head off the red-skins."

"Any use to take to the hills?" queried Horn sharply.

"I reckon not. You've no hosses. You'd be tracked down. Hurry along. Thet's best. . . . An' say, I see you've a young girl hyar. I can take her up behind me."

"Allie, climb up behind him," said Horn, motioning to the girl.

"I'll stay with Mother," she replied.

"Go, child . . . go!" entreated Mrs. Durade.

Others urged her, but she shook her head. Horn's big hand trembled as he held it out and for once there was no trace of hardness about his face.

"Allie, I never had no lass of my own. . . . I wish you'd go with him. You'd be safe . . . an' you could take my. . . ."

"No!" interrupted the girl.

Slingerland gave her a strange admiring glance, then turned his quick gray eyes upon Horn. "Anythin' I can take?"

Horn hesitated. "No. It was jest somethin' I wanted the girl to hev."

Slingerland touched his shaggy horse and called over his shoulder. "Rustle out of hyar!" Then he galloped down the trail, leaving the travelers standing aghast.

"Break camp!" thundered Horn.

A scene of confusion followed. In a very short while the prairie schooners were lumbering down the valley. Twilight came just as the flight got under way. The tired oxen were beaten to make them run. But they were awkward and the loads were heavy. Night fell. And the road was difficult to follow. The wagons rolled and bumped and swayed from side to side, and camp utensils and blankets dropped from them. One wagon broke down. The occupants, frantically gathering together their few possessions, ran ahead to pile into the wagon in front.

Horn drove on and on, at a gait cruel to both men and beasts. The women were roughly shaken. Hours passed—and miles were gained. That valley led into another with an upgrade, rocky and treacherous. Horn led on foot and ordered the men to do likewise. The night grew darker. By and by further progress became impossible, for the oxen failed and a wild place of trees and rocks barred the way.

Then the fugitives sat and shivered and waited for dawn. No

one slept. All listened intently to the sounds of the lonely night, magnified now by their fears. Horn strode to and fro with his rifle—a grim dark silent form. Whenever a wolf mourned or a cat squalled or a night bird voiced the solitude or a stone rattled off the cliff, the fugitives started up quiveringly alert, expecting every second to hear the screeching yell of the Sioux. They whispered to keep up a flickering courage. And the burly Horn strode to and fro, thoughtful, as if he were planning something, and always listening.

Allie sat in one of the wagons close to her mother. She was wide awake and not so badly scared. Her mother had acted strangely. All through this dreadful journey her mother had not seemed natural to Allie and the farther they traveled eastward, the stranger she grew. During the ride that night she had moaned and shuddered and clasped Allie close, but when the ride had come to a forced end, she grew silent.

Allie was young and hopeful. She kept whispering to her mother that the soldiers would come in time.

"That brave fellow in buckskin . . . he'll save us," said Allie.

"Child, I feel I'll never see home again," finally whispered Mrs. Durade.

"Mother!"

"Allie, I must tell you . . . I *must*," cried Mrs. Durade, very low and fiercely. She clung to her daughter.

"Tell me what?" whispered Allie.

"The truth . . . the truth! Oh, I've deceived you all your life."

"Deceived me? Oh, Mother! Then tell me . . . now."

"Child . . . you'll forgive me . . . and never . . . hate me?" cried the mother brokenly.

"Mother, how can you talk so? I love you." And Allie clasped the shaking form closer. Then followed a silence during which Mrs. Durade recovered her composure.

"Allie, I ran off with Durade before you were born," began

the mother swiftly, as if she must hurry out her secret. "Durade is not your father. . . . Your name is Lee. Your father is Allison Lee. I've heard he is a rich man now. . . . Oh! I want to get back . . . to give you to him . . . to beg his forgiveness. . . . We were married in New Orleans in Eighteen Forty-Seven. My father made me marry him. I never loved Allison Lee. He was not a kind man . . . not the sort I admired. . . . I met Durade. He was a Spaniard . . . a blue-blooded adventurer. . . . I ran off with him. We joined the gold seekers traveling to California. You were born out there in Eighteen Fifty. . . . It has been a hard life. But I taught you . . . I did all I could for you. I kept my secret from you . . . and his! Lately I could endure it no longer. I've run off from Durade."

"Oh, Mother, I knew we were running off from him!" cried Allie breathlessly. "And I know he will follow us!"

"Indeed I fear he will," replied the mother. "But Lord spare me his revenge!"

"Mother. . . . Oh, it is terrible. . . . He is not my father. I never loved him. I couldn't. . . . But Mother, *you* must have loved him."

"Child, I was Durade's slave," she replied sadly.

"Then why did you run away? He was kind . . . good to us."

"Allie, listen. Durade was a gambler . . . a man crazy to gamble. He did not love gold. But he loved games of chance. It was a terrible passion with him. Once he meant to gamble my honor away. But that other gambler was too much of a man. There *are* gamblers who are men. I think I began to hate Durade from that time. . . . He was a crooked gambler. He made me share in his guilt. My face lured miners to his dens. . . . My face . . . for I was beautiful once. Oh, I sunk low. But he forced me. . . . Thank God I left him . . . before it was too late . . . for you!"

"Mother, he will follow us!" cried Allie.

"But he will never have you. I'll kill him before I'd let him get you," replied the mother.

"He'd never harm me, Mother, whatever he is," murmured Allie.

"Child, he would use you exactly as he used me. He tried to make me let him have you . . . already. He wanted to train you . . . he said you'd be beautiful someday."

"Mother!" gasped Allie. "Is *that* what he meant?"

"Forget him, child. And forget your mother's guilt. I've suffered. I've repented. . . . All I ask of God is to take you safely home to Allison Lee . . . the baby he never saw."

The night hour before dawn grew colder and blacker. A great silence seemed wedged down between the ebony hills. The stars were wan. No cry of wolf or moan of wind disturbed the stillness. And the stars grew warmer. The black east changed and paled. Dawn was at hand. An opaque and obscure grayness filled the world, and all changed, except that strange oppressive and vast silence of the wild.

That silence was broken by the shrill screeching blood-curdling yell of the Sioux.

Sometimes those bloody savages attacked without warning, in a silence of the grave; again they sent out their war cries chilling the hearts of the bravest. Perhaps that warning yell was given only when doom was certain.

Horn realized, and accepted it. He called all of the fugitives to him and, choosing the best protected spot among the rocks and wagons, put the women in the center.

"Now men . . . if it's the last for us . . . let it be fight. Mebbe we can hold out till the troops come."

Then in the gray gloom of dawn he took a shovel, and prying up a piece of sod, he laid it aside and began to dig. And while he dug he listened for another war screech and gazed often into the gloom. But there was no sound and nothing to see. When he had dug a hole several feet deep, he carried an armful of heavy leather bags and deposited them in it. Then he went back to the wagon for another armful. The men, gray-faced in the gloom, watched him fill up the hole, carefully replace the sod, and stamp it down.

He stood an instant gazing down, as if he had buried the best of his life. Then he laughed, grim and hard. "There's my gold! If any man lives through this, he can have it!"

Bill Horn divined that he would never live through it. He who had slaved for gold and had risked all for it cared no more. Gripping his rifle, he turned to await the inevitable.

Moments of awful suspense passed. Nothing but the sodden beating of hearts came to the ears of the fugitives—ears that strained to hear the stealthy approach of the red foe—ears that throbbed prayerfully for the tramp of troopers' horses. But only silence ensued—a horrible silence, more nerve-racking than the sight of swift sure death.

Then out of the gray gloom burst jets of red flame, and rifles *cracked,* and the air suddenly filled with hideous clamor. The men began to shoot at gliding shadows, grayer than the gloom, and every shot brought a volley in return. Smoke mingled with the gloom. In the slight intervals between rifle shots there were swift rustling sounds and sharp *thuds* from arrows. Then a shrill strife of sound became continuous, from all around, and closed in upon the doomed caravan. It swelled and rolled away, and again there was silence.

# CHAPTER FIVE

Neale had not been wrong when he told the engineers that once they had a line surveyed across the gorge and faced the steep slopes of the other side, their troubles would be magnified. They found themselves deeper in the Black Hills, a range of mountains that had given General Lodge great difficulty upon former exploring trips, and over which a pass had not yet been discovered. The old St. Vrain and Laramie Trail wound along the base of these slopes and through the valleys. But that trail was not possible for a railroad. A pass must be found—a pass that would give a grade of ninety feet to the mile. These mountains had short slopes and they were high.

It turned out that the line as surveyed through ravines and across the gorge had to be abandoned. The line would have to go over the hills. To that end the camp was moved east again to the first slopes of the Black Hills; from there the engineers began to climb. They reached the base of the mountains where they appeared to be halted for good and all. The second line, as far as it went, overlooked the Laramie Trail, which fact was proof that the old trail finders had as keen eyes as engineers.

With a large band of hostile Sioux watching their movements, the engineer corps found it necessary to have the troops close at hand all the time. The surveyors climbed the ridges while the soldiers kept them in sight from below. Day after day this futile search for a pass went on. Many of the ridges promised well, only to end in impassable cliffs or breaks or ascents too steep.

There were many slopes and they all looked alike. It took hard riding and hard climbing. The chief and his staff were in despair. Must their great project fail because of a few miles of steep ascent? They would not give up.

The vicinity of Cheyenne Pass seemed to offer encouragement. Camp was made in the valley on a creek. From here observations were taken. One morning the chief with his subordinates and a scout ascended the creek, and then the pass to the summit. Again the old St. Vrain and Laramie Trail lay in sight. And again the troops rode along it with the engineers above.

The chief with his men rode on and up farther than usual and farther than they ought to have gone unattended.

Once the scout halted and gazed intently across the valley. "Smoke signals over thar," he said.

The engineers looked long, but none of them saw any smoke. They moved on. But the scout called them back.

"Thet bunch of redskins has split on us. Fust thing we'll run into some of them."

It was Neale's hawk eye that first sighted Indians. "Look! Look!" he cried, in great excitement, as he pointed with shaking finger.

Down a grassy slope of a ridge Indians were riding, evidently to head off the engineers, to get between them and the troops.

"Wal, we're in fer it now," declared the scout. "We can't git back the way we come up."

The chief gazed coolly at the Indians, and then at the long ridge sloping away from the summit. He had been in tight places before.

"Ride!" was his order.

"Let's fight!" cried Neale.

The band of eight men was well mounted and well armed, and, if imperative, could have held off the Sioux for a time. But

General Lodge and the scout headed across a little valley and up a higher ridge, from which they expected to sight the troops. They rode hard and climbed fast, but it took a quarter of an hour to gain the ridge top. Sure enough, the troops were in sight, but far away. And the Sioux were cutting across to get in front.

It was a time for quick judgment. The scout said they could not get down over the ridge and the chief decided they would follow along it. So they did. The going got to be hard and rough. One by one the men dismounted to lead their horses. Neale, who rode a mettlesome bay, could scarcely keep up.

"Take mine!" called Larry Red King as he turned to Neale.

"Red, I'll handle this stupid beast or. . . ."

"Wal, you ain't handlin' him," interrupted King. "Hosses is my job, you know." Red took the bridle from Neale and in one moment the balky horse recognized a master arm.

"By heaven, we've got to hurry!" called Neale.

It did seem that the Indians would head them off at least. Neale and King labored over the rocky ground as best they could and by dint of hard effort came up with their party. The Indians were quartering the other ridge, riding as if on level ground. The ridge grew rougher. Baxter's horse slipped and lamed his right foreleg. Henney's saddle turned, which accident lost valuable time. All the men drew their rifles. And at every dip of ground they expected to come to a break that would make a stand inevitable.

From one point on the ridge they had a good view of the troops.

"Signal!" ordered the chief.

They yelled and shot and waved hats and scarves. No use— the soldiers kept moving in at snail's pace far below.

"On . . . down the ridge!" was the order.

"Wal, General, thet way looks bad to me," objected the scout.

King shoved his lean brown hand between them. There was a flame in his flashing blue glance as it swept the slowly descending ridge.

"Judgin' the lay of land is my job," he said in his cool way. "We'll git down heah or not at all."

Neale was sore, lame, and angry as well. He kept gazing across at the Sioux. "Let's stop . . . and fight," he panted. "We can . . . whip . . . that bunch."

"We may have to fight, but not yet," replied the chief. "Come on."

They scrambled on over rocky places, up and down steep banks. Here and there were stretches where it was possible to ride, and over these they made better time. The Indians fell out of sight under the side of the ridge and this fact was disquieting, for no one could tell how soon they would show up again or where. This spurred the men to sterner efforts.

Meanwhile the sun was setting and the predicament of the engineers grew more serious. A shout from Neale, who held up the rear, warned all that the Indians had come up on the ridge behind them and now were in straightaway pursuit. Thereupon General Lodge ordered his men to face about with rifles ready. This move checked the Sioux. They halted out of range.

"They're waitin' fer dark to set in," said the scout.

"Come on! We'll get away yet," said the chief grimly.

They went on, and darkness began to fall about them. This increased both difficulty and danger. On the other hand it enabled them to try to signal the troops with fire. One of them would hurry ahead and build a signal fire while the others held back to check the Indians if they appeared. And at length their signals were answered by the troops. Thus encouraged, the little band of desperate men plunged on down the slope, and just when night set in black—an hour that would have precipitated the Indian attack—the troops met the engineers on the slope.

The Indians faded away into the gloom without firing a shot. There was a general rejoicing. Neale, however, complained that he would rather have fought them.

"Wal, I shore was achin' fer trouble," drawled his faithful ally, King.

The flagman Casey removed his black pipe to remark: "All thet cloimb without a foight!"

General Lodge's first word to Colonel Dillon of the troops was evidently inspired by Casey's remark.

"Colonel, did you have steep work getting up to us?"

"Yes, indeed, straight up out of the valley," was the rejoinder.

But General Lodge did not go back to camp by this short cut down the valley. He kept along the ridge and it led for miles slowly down to the plain. There in the starlight he faced his assistants with singular fire and earnestness.

"Men, we've had a bad scare and a hard jaunt, but we've found our pass over the Black Hills. Tomorrow we'll run a line up that long ridge. We'll name it Sherman Pass. . . . Thanks to those red devils!"


On the following morning Neale was awakened from a heavy dreamless sleep by a hard dig in the ribs.

"Neale . . . air you daid?" Larry Red King was saying. "Wake up! An' listen to thet."

Neale heard the clear ringing notes of a bugle call. He rolled out of his blankets. "What's up, Red?" he cried, reaching for his boots.

"Wal, I reckon them Injuns," drawled King.

It was just daylight. They found camp astir—troopers running for horses, saddles, guns.

"Red, you get our horses and I'll see what's up!" cried Neale.

The cowboy lumbered away, hitching at his belt. Neale ran forward into camp. He encountered Lieutenant Leslie, who he knew well, and who told him a scout had come in with news of a threatened raid, and Colonel Dillon had ordered out a detachment of troopers

"I'm going!" shouted Neale. "Where's that scout?" Neale soon descried a buckskin-clad figure and he made toward it. The man, evidently a trapper or hunter, had a long brown rifle, and he had a powder horn and bullet pouch slung over his shoulder. There was a knife in his belt. Neale liked this type of Westerner, having met a good many since his advent beyond the Missouri. He went directly up to the man.

"My name's Neale," he said. "Can I be of any help?"

Then he encountered penetrating gray eyes.

"My name's Slingerland," replied the other, and he offered his hand. "Are you an officer?"

"No. I'm a surveyor. But I can ride and shoot. I've a cowboy with me . . . a Texan. He'll go. What's happened?"

"Wal, I ain't sure yet. But I fear the wust. I got wind of some Sioux thet was trailin' some prairie schooners up in the hills. I warned the boss . . . told him to break camp an' run. Then I came fer the troops. But the troops had changed camp an' I jest found them. Reckon we'll be too late."

"Was it a caravan?" inquired Neale, intensely interested.

"Six wagons. Only a few men. Two wimmen. An' one girl."

"Girl!" exclaimed Neale.

"Yes. I reckon she was about sixteen. A pretty girl with big soft eyes. I offered to take her up behind me on my hoss. An' they all wanted her to come. But she wouldn't. . . . I hate to think. . . ."

Slingerland did not finish his thought aloud. Just then King rode up leading Neale's horse. Slingerland eyed the lithe cowboy.

"Howdy," drawled King. He did not seem curious or eager, and his cool easy reckless air was a sharp contrast to Neale's fiery daring.

"Red, you got the rifles, I see," said Neale.

"Shore, an' I rustled some biscuits."

In a few moments the troops were mounted and ready. Slingerland led them up the valley at a rapid trot and soon started to climb. When he reached the top, he worked up for a mile, and then, crossing over, went down into another valley. Up and down he led, over ridge after ridge, until a point was reached where the St. Vrain and Laramie Trail could be seen in the valley below. From here he led along the top of the ridge, and, just as the sun rose over the hills, he pointed down to the spot where the caravan had been encamped when he had warned them. Soon he descended into this valley. There in the trail were fresh tracks of horses.

"We ain't fur behind, but I reckon fur enough to be too late," he said. And he clenched a big fist.

On this level trail he led at a gallop with the troops behind in a clattering roar. They made short work of that valley. Then rougher ground hindered speedy advance.

Presently Slingerland sighted something that made him start. It proved to be a charred skeleton of a prairie schooner. The oxen were nowhere to be seen. And not far beyond blankets and camp utensils littered the trail. Still farther on, the broad wheel tracks sheered off the road, where the hurried drivers had missed the way in the dark. This was open undulating ground, rock-strewn and overgrown with brush. A ledge of rock, a few scraggy trees, and more black charred remains of wagons marked the final scene of the massacre.

Neale was the first man who dismounted and King was the second. They had outstripped the more cautious troopers.

"My Gawd," breathed Larry.

Neale gripped his rifle with fierce hands and strode forward between two of the burned wagons. Naked mutilated bodies, bloody and ghastly, lay in horrible positions. They had been scalped.

Slingerland rode up with the troops, and all dismounted, cursing and muttering.

Colonel Dillon ordered a search for anything to identify the dead. There was nothing. All had been burned or taken away. Of the camp implements, mostly destroyed, there were two shovels left, one with a burned handle. These were used by the troopers to dig graves.

Neale had at first been sickened by the ghastly spectacle. He walked aside a little way and sat down upon a rock. His face was wet with clammy sweat. A gnawing rage seemed to affect him in the pit of his stomach. This was his first experience with the fiendish work of the savages. A whirl of thoughts filled his mind. Suddenly he fancied he heard a low moan. He started violently.

"Well, I'm hearing things," he muttered soberly. It made him so nervous that he got up and walked back to where the troopers were digging. He saw the body of a woman lowered into a grave and the sight reminded him of what Slingerland had said. He saw the scout searching around and he went over to him. "Have you found the girl?" he asked.

"Not yet. I reckon the devils made off with her. They'd take her, if she happened to be alive."

"God! I hope she's dead."

"Wal, son, so does Al Slingerland."

More searching failed to find the body of the girl. She was given up as lost.

"I'll find out if she was took captive," said Slingerland. "This Sioux band has been friendly with me."

"Man, they're on the warpath," rejoined Dillon.

"Wal, I've traded with them same Sioux when they was on the warpath. . . . This massacre sure is awful, an' the Sioux will hev to be exterminated. But they hev their wrongs. An' Injuns is Injuns."

Slingerland's talk was not appreciated by his listeners.

Slabs of rock were laid upon the graves. Then the troopers rode away.

Neale and Slingerland and King were the last to mount. And it was at this moment that Neale either remembered the strange low moan or heard it again. He reined in his horse. "I'm going back!" he called.

"What fer?" Slingerland rejoined.

King wheeled his mount and trotted back to Neale.

"Red, I'm not satisfied," said Neale, and told his friend what he thought he had heard.

"Boy, you're out of yur haid!" expostulated King.

"Maybe I am. But I'm going back. Are you coming?"

"Shore," replied King, with his easy good nature.

Slingerland sat his horse and watched while he waited. The dust cloud that marked the troops drew farther away.

Neale dismounted, threw his bridle, and looked searchingly around. But King, always more comfortable on horseback than on land, kept his saddle. Suddenly Neale felt inexplicably drawn. Still he heard nothing except the wind in the few scraggy trees. All the ground in and around the scene of the massacre had been gone over; there was no need to go over it again. Neale had no tangible thing upon which to base his strange feeling. Yet absurd or not he refused to admit it was fancy or emotion. He knew he had extremes of emotion. But this matter was different. Some voice had called him. He swore it. If he did not make sure, he would always be haunted. So with clear deliberate eyes he surveyed the scene. Then he strode for the ledge of rock.

Tufts of sage grew close at its base. He advanced among them. The surface of the rock was uneven—and low down a crack showed. At that instant a slow sobbing gasping intake of breath electrified Neale.

"Red . . . come here!" he yelled in a voice that made the cowboy jump.

Neale dropped to his knees and parted the tufts of sage. Lower down the crack opened up. On the ground just inside that crack he saw the gleam of a mass of chestnut hair. His first flashing thought then, before he even considered possible life saved, was that here was a scalp the red devils did not get.

Then King was kneeling beside him—bending forward. "It's a girl!" he ejaculated.

"Yes . . . the one Slingerland told me about . . . the girl with big eyes," replied Neale. He put a hand softly on her head. It was warm. Her hair felt silky and the touch sent a quiver over him. Probably she was dying.

Slingerland came riding up. "Wal, boys, what hev you found?" he asked curiously.

"That girl," replied Neale.

This reply brought Slingerland sliding out of his saddle.

Neale hesitated a moment, then, reaching into the aperture, he got his hands under the girl's arms and carefully drew her out upon the grass. She lay face down, her hair a tumbled mass, her body inert. Neale's quick eyes searched for bloodstains, but found none.

"I remember thet hair," said Slingerland. "Turn her over."

"I reckon we'll see then . . . where she's hurt," muttered Red King.

Evidently Neale thought the same, for he was plainly afraid to turn her over on her back. "Slingerland, she's not such a little girl," he said irrelevantly. Then he slipped his hands under her arms again. Suddenly he felt something wet and warm and sticky. He pulled a hand out. It was bloodstained.

"*Aw!*" exclaimed Red.

"Son, what'd you expect?" demanded Slingerland. "She got shot or cut, an' in her fright she crawled in thar. Come over with her. Let's see. She might live."

This practical suggestion acted quickly upon Neale. He turned the girl over so that her head lay upon his knees. The face thus exposed was deathly pale, set like stone in horror. The front of her dress was a bloody mess and her hands were red.

"Stabbed in the breast!" exclaimed King.

"No," replied Slingerland. "If she'd been stabbed, she'd been scalped, too. Mebbe thet blood comes from an arrow an' she might hev pulled it out."

Neale bent over her with swift scrutiny. "No cut or hole in her dress."

"Boys, thar ain't no marks on her . . . only thet blood," added Slingerland hopefully.

Neale tore open the front of her blouse and slipped his hand in upon her breast. It felt round, soft, warm under his hand, but quiet. He shook his head.

"Those moans I heard must have been her last dying breaths," he said.

"Mebbe. But she shore doesn't look daid to me," replied King. "I've seen daid people. Put your hand on her heart."

Neale had been feeling for heart pulsations on her right side. He shifted his hand. Instantly through the soft swell of her breast throbbed a beat-beat-beat. They were regular and not at all faint. "Good Lord, what a fool I am!" he cried. "She's alive. Her heart's going. There's not a wound on her."

"Wal, we can't see any, thet's sure," replied Slingerland.

"She might hev a fatal hurt, all the same," suggested King.

"No!" exclaimed Neale. "That blood's from someone else . . . most likely her murdered mother. . . . Red, run for some water. Fetch it in your hat. Slingerland, ride after the troops."

Slingerland rose and mounted his horse. "Wal, I've an idee.

Let's take the girl to my cabin. Thet's not far from hyar. It's a long ride to the camp. An' if she needs the troop doctor, we can fetch him to my place."

"But the Sioux?"

"Wal, she'd be safer with me. The Injuns an' me are friends."

"All right. Good. But you ride after the troops anyhow and tell Dillon about the girl . . . that we're going to your cabin."

Slingerland galloped away after the dust cloud down the trail.

Neale gazed strangely down at the face of the girl he had rescued. Her lips barely parted to make again the low moan. That was what had called him. No—not all. There was something more than a feeble cry that had turned him back to search. A strong and nameless and inexplicable impulse. Neale believed in his impulses—in those strange ones that came to him at intervals. So far in his life girls had been rather negative influences. But this girl or the fact that he had saved her or both together struck deeply into him, fixing the wildness and the nature of this West upon an impelling and romantic and tragical incident. The expression of her face made him dread her return to consciousness.

King came striding back with a sombrero full of water.

"Take your scarf and wash that blood off her hands and dress, before she comes to and sees it," said Neale.

The cowboy was awkward at the task, but infinitely gentle. "Poor kid! I'll bet she's alone in the world now."

Neale wet his scarf and bathed the girl's face. This did not give any immediate result, still he kept doing it. "If she's only fainted, she ought to be reviving now. I'm afraid. . . ."

Then suddenly her eyes opened. They were large, violet-hued, covered with a kind of veil or film, like eyes opened before sleep had wholly gone, and they were unseeingly, staringly set with horror. Her breast heaved with a sharply drawn breath; her hands groped and felt for something to hold; her body trembled.

Suddenly she sat up. She was not weak. Her motions were violent. The dazed horror-stricken eyes roved around and did not fasten upon anything.

"*Aw!* Gone crazy," muttered King pityingly.

It did seem so. She put her hands to her ears as if to shut out a horrible sound. And she screamed. Neale grasped her shoulders, turned her around, and forced her into such a position that her gaze must meet his.

"You're safe!" he cried sharply. "The Indians have gone. I'm a white man!"

It seemed his piercing voice stirred her reason. She stared at him. The face changed. Her lips parted and her hand, shaking like a leaf, covered them, clutched at them. The other hand waved before her as if to brush something aside.

Neale held that gaze with all the dominance the moment gave him. He repeated what he had said. Then it became a wonderful and terrible sight to watch her—to divine in some little way the dark and awful state of her mind. The lines, the tenseness, the shade, the age faded out of her face; the deep-set frown smoothed out of her brow, and it became young. Neale looked into her eyes as strongly fascinated himself as he was determined to compel her to realization. He saw those staring eyes fix upon his; he saw a dull opaque blackness of horror, hideous veils let down over the windows of a soul, images of hell limned forever on a mind. Then that film, that unseeing cold thing, like the shade of sleep or death, passed from her eyes. They suddenly were alive, great dark-violet gulfs, full of shadows, dilating, changing, so that Neale saw the spirit of youth, a life of hope suddenly dawn in exquisite and beautiful lights.

"I'm a white man," he said tensely. "You're saved. The Indians are gone."

She understood him. She realized. With a low agonized and

51

broken cry she shut her eyes tightly and reached blindly out with both hands. Then she screamed. Shock claimed her again. Horror and fear convulsed her, and it must have been fear that was uppermost. She clutched Neale with fingers of steel, in a grip he could not have loosened without breaking her bones.

"Red, you saw . . . she was right in her mind for a moment . . . you saw!" burst out Neale.

"Shore, I saw. She's only scared now," replied King. "It must hev been hell fer her."

At this juncture, Slingerland came riding up to them. "Did she come around?" he inquired, curiously gazing at the girl as she clung to Neale.

"Yes, for a moment," replied Neale.

"Wal, thet's good. . . . I caught up with Dillon. Told him. He was mighty glad we found her. Cursed his troopers some. Said he'd explain your absence, an' we could send over fer anythin'."

"Let's go, then," said Neale. He tried to loosen the girl's hold on him, but had to give it up. Taking her in his arms, he rose and went toward his horse. King had to help him mount with his burden. Neale did not imagine he would ever forget that spot, but he took another long look to fix the scene indelibly on his memory. The charred wagons, the graves, the rocks over which the naked gashed bodies had been flung, the three scraggly trees close together, and the ledge with the dark aperture at the base—he gazed at them all, and then turned his horse to follow Slingerland.

# CHAPTER SIX

Some ten miles from the scene of the massacre and perhaps fifteen from the line surveyed by the engineers, Slingerland lived in a wild valley in the heart of the Black Hills.

The ride there was laborious and it took time, but Neale scarcely noted either fact. He paid enough attention to the trail to fix landmarks and turnings in his mind so that he would remember how to find the way there again. He was, however, mostly intent upon the girl he was carrying.

Twice, that he knew of, her eyes opened during the ride. Then it was to see nothing, and only to grip him tighter, if that were possible. Neale began to imagine that he had been too hopeful. Her body was a dead weight and cold. Those two glimpses he had of her opened eyes hurt him. What could he do when she did come to herself? She would be frantic with horror and grief and he would be helpless. In a case like hers it might have been better if she had been killed.

The last mile to Slingerland's lay in a beautiful green valley with steep sides, almost like a cañon, trees everywhere, and a swift clear brook running over a bed of smooth rock. The trail led along this brook, up to where the valley boxed, and the water boiled out of a great spring in a green glade, overhung by bushy banks and gray rocks above. A rude cabin with a red stone chimney and clay-chinked cracks between the logs, with furs and pelts and horns and traps everywhere, marked the home of the trapper.

"Wal, we're hyar," sung out Slingerland, and in the cheery tones was something that told that the place was indeed home to him.

"Shore is a likely lookin' camp," drawled King, throwing his bridle. "Been heah a long time, thet cabin."

"Me and my pard was the first white men in these hyar hills. He's gone now," replied Slingerland, and then he turned to Neale. "Son, you must be tired. Thet was a ways to carry a girl nigh onto dead. . . . Look how white. Hand her down to me."

The girl's hands slipped nervelessly and limply from their hold of Neale. Slingerland laid her in the grass in a shady spot. Then the three men gazed down upon her, all sober, earnest, doubtful.

"I reckon we can't do nothin' but wait," said the trapper.

King shook his head as if the problem was beyond him.

Neale did not voice his thought which was that he wanted to be the first person her eyes beheld upon her return to consciousness.

"Wal, I'll set to work, an' clean out a place fer her," said Slingerland.

"We'll help," rejoined Neale. "Red, you have a look at the horses."

"I'll slip the saddles an' bridles," replied King, "an' let 'em go. Horses couldn't be chased out of heah."

Slingerland's cabin consisted really of two cabins built adjoining one another with a door between, one part being larger and of later construction. Evidently he used the older one as a storeroom for his pelts. When all these had been removed, the room was seen to be small, with two windows, no table, and a few other crude articles of homemade furniture. The men cleaned this room and laid a carpet of deer hides, fur side up. A bed was made of a huge roll of buffalo skins, flattened and shaped, and covered with Indian blankets. When all this had been accomplished, the trapper removed his fur cap and scratched his grizzled head and appealed to Neale and King.

"I reckon you can fetch over some comfortable-like necessaries . . . fer a girl," he suggested.

King laughed, his cool easy droll way. "Shore, we'll rustle fer a lookin' glass, an' hairbrush, an' sich as girls hev to hev. Our camp is full of them things."

But Neale did not see any humor in Slingerland's perplexity or in the cowboy's facetiousness. It was the girl's serious condition that worried him, not her future comfort.

"Run out thar!" called Slingerland sharply.

Neale, who was the nearest to the door, bolted outside, to see the girl sitting up, her hair disheveled, her manner wild in the extreme. At sight of him she gave a start so sudden and violent that it seemed unnatural, and she uttered a cry. When Neale reached her, it was to see her shaking all over. Terrible fear had never been more vividly shown, yet Neale believed she saw in him a white man, a friend. It was that fear in her that was stronger than reason.

"Who are you?" she asked.

"My name's Neale . . . Warren Neale," replied Neale, sitting down beside her. He took one of the shaking hands in his. He was glad that she talked rationally.

"Where am I?"

"This is the home of a trapper. I brought you here. It was the best . . . in fact the only place."

"You saved me . . . from . . . from those devils?" she queried hoarsely, and that cold and horrible shade veiled her eyes.

"Yes . . . yes . . . but don't think of them. They're gone," replied Neale hastily. The look of her distressed and frightened him. He did not know what to say.

The girl fell back with a poignant cry and covered her eyes as if to shut out a hateful and appalling sight.

"My mother," she moaned, and shuddered with agony. "They . . . murdered . . . her! Oh, those terrible yells . . . shot fire. . . . I saw . . . killed . . . every man . . . Missus Jones! My mother . . . she fell . . . she never spoke! Her blood was on me . . . ! I crawled away . . . I hid. . . . The Indians . . . they . . . tore . . . hacked . . . scalped . . . burned! I couldn't die! I saw . . . Oh . . . oh . . . oh!"

Then she fell to moaning.

Slingerland and King came out and looked down at the girl.

"Wal, the life's strong in her," said the trapper. "I reckon I know when life is strong in any critter. She'll get over thet. All we can do now is to watch her an' keep her from doin' herself harm. Take her in an' lay her down."

For two days and nights Neale watched over her, except for the few hours she slept and during which he divided his watch with King. She had periods of consciousness in which she knew Neale, but most of the time she raved or tossed or moaned, or lay like one dead. On the third day, however, Neale was encouraged. She awoke weak and somber, but quiet and rational. Neale talked earnestly to her, in as sensible a way as he knew how, speaking briefly of the tragic fate that had been hers, bidding her force it out of her mind by taking interest in her new surroundings—to be active in some way—to think of the time when he surely would get her back to civilization. She heard him, but did not seem impressed. It was a difficult matter to get her to eat. She did not want to move. At length Neale told her that he must go back to the camp of the engineers, where he had work to do, and he would return to see her soon and often. She did not speak or raise her eyes when he left her.

Outside, when King brought up the horses, Slingerland said to Neale: "See hyar, son, I reckon you needn't worry. She'll come around all right."

"Shore she will," corroborated the cowboy. "Time'll cure her.

I'm from Texas, whar sudden death is plentiful in all families."

Neale shook his head. "I'm not so sure. That girl's more sensitively and delicately organized than you fellows see. I doubt that she'll ever recover from the shock. It'll take a mighty great influence. . . . But let's hope for the best. Now, Slingerland, take care of her as best you can. Shut her in when you leave camp. I'll ride over as often as possible. If she gets so she will talk, then we can find out if she has any relatives, and, if so, I'll take her to them. If not, I'll do whatever else I can for her."

"Wal, son, I like the way you're makin' yourself responsible fer thet kid," replied the trapper. "I never had no wife nor daughter. But I'm thinkin' . . . wouldn't it jest be hell to be a girl . . . tender an' young, an' like Neale said . . . sudden hev all you loved butchered before your eyes?"

"It shore would," said King feelingly. "An' thet's what she sees all the time."

"Slingerland, do we run any chance of meeting Indians?" queried Neale.

"I reckon not. Them Sioux will git far away from hyar after thet massacre. But you want to keep sharp eyes out an', if you meet any, jest ride an' shoot your way through. You've the best hosses I've seen. Whar'd you git them?"

"They belong to King. He's a cowboy."

"Hosses was my job. An' we can shore ride away from any redskins," replied King.

"Wal, good luck, an' come back soon," was Slingerland's last word.

So they parted. The cowboy led the way with the steady easy trotting walk that saved a horse yet covered distance, and in three hours they were hailed by a trooper outpost, and soon were in camp.

Shortly after their arrival the engineers returned tired, dusty, work-stained, yet in unusually good spirits. They had run the line up over Sherman Pass and now it seemed their difficulties were to lessen as the line began to descend from the summit of the divide. Neale's absence had been noted for his services were in demand. But all the men rejoiced in his rescue of the little girl and were sympathetic and kind in their inquiries. It seemed to Neale that his chief looked searchingly at him or through him, as if somehow the short absence had made a change. Neale himself grew conscious of a strange something that was puzzling, and once curiously certain of it, he pondered over the idea. It was, then, the girl and that about her—her helplessness and pathetic plight—that made the difference.

"Well, it's curious," he soliloquized, as soon as he re-analyzed it. "But . . . it's not, either. I'm sorry for her." And he remembered the strange change in her eyes when he had watched the shadow of horror and death and blood fade away before the natural emotions of youth and life and hope.

Next day he showed more than ever his value to the engineering corps and again won a word of quiet praise from his chief. Neale gathered from a new impetus in the way he went at things that he found the work more fascinating as the achievements grew behind him. He liked the praise of his superiors. He was heart and soul in the belief of the greatness of the railroad. And that week he drove his faithful lineman King to complaint, which fact was so unusual that it amazed Neale.

King tugged at his boots and groaned as he finally pulled them off. They were full of holes, at which he gazed ruefully. "Shore I'll be done with this heah job when they're gone," he said.

"Why do you work in high-heeled boots?" inquired Neale. "You can't walk or climb in them. No wonder they're full of holes."

"Wal, I couldn't weah no boots like yours," declared King.

"You'll have to. Another day will about finish them and your feet, too."

King eyed his boss with interest. "You-all cussed me today because I was slow," he complained.

"Red, you always are slow, except with a horse or gun. And lately you've been . . . well, you don't move out of your tracks."

Neale often exaggerated out of a desire to tease his friend. Nobody else dared to banter King.

"Wal, I didn't sign up with this heah outfit to run uphill all day," replied King.

"I'll tell you what. I'll get Casey to be my lineman . . . no . . . I've a better idea . . . Casey is slow, too. I'll use one of the niggers."

King gave a hitch to his belt and a cold gleam chased away the lazy blue warmth from his eyes. "Go ahaid," he drawled, "an' they'll bury the nigger tomorrow night."

Neale laughed. He knew Red hated darkies—he suspected the Texan had thrown a gun on more than a few—and he knew there surely would be a funeral in camp if he changed his lineman.

"All right, Red, I don't want blood spilled," he said cheerfully. "I'll be a martyr and put up with you. . . . What do you say to a day off? Let's ride over to Slingerland's."

The cowboy's red face slowly wrinkled into a smile. "Wal, I shore was wonderin' what in the hell made you rustle so lately. I reckon nothin' would suit me better. I've been wonderin', too, about our little girl."

"Red, let's wade through camp and see what we can get to take over."

"Man, you mean jest steal?" queried King in mild surprise.

"No. We'll ask for things. But if we can't get what we want that way, why . . . ," replied Neale thoughtfully. "Slingerland did not have even a towel over there. Think of that girl. She's been used to comfort, if not luxury. I could tell. . . . Let's see, I've a mirror and an extra brush. Red, come on."

Eagerly they went over their scant belongings, generously approximating whatever might be made of possible use to an unfortunate girl in a wild and barren country. Then they fared forth into the camp. Everyone in the corps contributed something. The chief studied Neale's heated face and a smile momentarily changed his stern features—a wise smile, a little sad, and full of light.

"I suppose you'll marry her," he said.

Neale blushed like a girl. "It . . . that hadn't occurred . . . to me, sir," he stammered.

Henney laughed, but his glance, too, was kind. "Sure you'll marry her," he said. "You saved her life. And, boy, you'll be a big man of the U.P. someday. Chief engineer or some big job. What could be finer? Romance, boy! The little waif of the caravan . . . you'll send her back to Omaha to school . . . she'll grow into a beautiful woman! She'll have a host of admirers, but you'll be the. . . ."

Neale got out of that tent with tingling ears. He was used to the badinage of the men and had always retaliated with a sharp and ready tongue. But here this half kind and half humorous talk encroached upon what he felt to be the secret side of his nature—the romantic and the dreamful side—to which just such fancies as he had heard were unconsciously dear. He could have had them without ever a conscious realization of any sense or seriousness in them.

Early the next morning Neale and King rode out on the way to Slingerland's.

The sun was warm when they reached the valley through which ran the stream that led up to the cabin. Spring was in the air. The leaves of cottonwood and willow added their fresh green to the darker green of pine. Bluebells showed in the grass along the trail; there were lavender and yellow flowers unfamiliar to Neale; trout rose and splashed on the surface of the pools, and the way was melodious with the *humming* of bees and the singing of birds.

Slingerland saw their coming and strode out to meet them with hearty greeting.

"Is she all right?" queried Neale abruptly.

"No, she ain't," replied Slingerland, shaking his shaggy head. "She won't eat or move or talk. She's wastin' away. She just sits or lays with thet awful look in her eyes."

"Can't you make her talk?"

"Wal, she'll say no to most anythin'. There was three times she asked when you was comin' back. Then she quit askin'. I reckon she's forgot you. But she's never forgot that bloody massacre. It's there in her eyes."

Neale dismounted, and, untying the pack from his saddle, he laid it down, removed saddle and bridle, and turned the horse loose. He did this automatically, while his mind was busy.

"Where is she?" he asked.

"Over thar under the pines whar the brook spills out of the spring. Thet's the only place she'll walk to. I believe she likes to listen to the water. An' she's always afraid."

"I've fetched a pack of things for her," said Neale. "Come on, Red."

"Shore you go alone," replied the cowboy, hanging back. "Girls is not my job."

So Neale approached alone. The spot was green, fragrant, shady, bright with flowers, musical with murmuring water. Presently he spied her—a drooping forlorn little figure. The instant he saw her, he felt glad and sad at once. She started quickly at his step and turned. He remembered the eyes, but hardly the face. It had grown thinner and whiter than the one he had in mind.

*My Lord, she's going to die,* thought Neale. *What can I do . . . what can I say?* He walked directly, but slowly up to her, aware of her staring eyes, and confused by them. "Hello, little girl, I've brought you some things," he said, and tried to speak cheerfully.

"Oh . . . is . . . it you?" she said.

"Yes, it's Neale. I hope you've not forgotten me."

There came a fleeting change over her, but not in her face, he thought, because not a muscle moved and the white stayed white. It must have been in her eyes, although he could not tell. He bent over to untie the pack.

"I've brought you a lot of things," he said. "I hope you'll find them useful. Here. . . ."

She did not look at the open pack or pay any attention to him. The drooping posture had been resumed and the somber staring at the brook. Neale watched her in despair, and, watching, he divined that only the most infinite patience and magnetism and power could bring her out of her brooding long enough to give Nature a chance. He recognized how unequal he was to the task. But the impossible or the unattainable had always roused Neale's spirit. Defeat angered him. This girl was alive—she was not hurt physically—he believed she could be made to forget that tragic night of blood and death. He set his teeth, and swore he would find the tact of a woman, the patience of a saint, the skill of a physician, the love of a father—anything to hold back this girl from the grave into which she was fading.

Reaching out he touched her. "Can you understand me?" he asked.

"Yes," she murmured. Her voice was thin, faraway, an effort.

"I saved your life."

"I wish you had let me die."

Her reply was quick with feeling, and it thrilled Neale because it was proof that he could stimulate or aggravate her mind.

"But I *did* save you. Now you owe me something."

"What?"

"Why, gratitude . . . enough to want to live, to try to help yourself."

"No . . . no," she whispered, and faded back into the somber apathy.

Neale could scarcely elicit another word from her, and by way of change he held out different articles he had brought— scarves, a shawl, a mirror—and made her look at them. Her own face in the mirror did not interest her. He tried to appeal to a girl's vanity. She had none.

"Your hair is all tangled," he said, bringing forth comb and brush. "Here, smooth it out."

"No . . . no . . . no," she moaned.

"All right. I'll do it for you," he stated. Surprised at finding her passive when he had expected resistance, he began to comb out the tangled tresses. In his earnestness he did not perceive how singular or ludicrous his action might be. And she had a mass of hair that began to smooth out and brighten under his hand. He became absorbed in his task, and failed to see King approach.

The cowboy was utterly amazed, and presently he grinned his delight. Silently he took this to be an indication that the girl was all right and no longer to be feared.

"Wal, shore thet's fine," he drawled. "Neale, I always knowed you was a lady's man." And King sat down beside them. The girl's face was half hidden under the mass of hair and her head was lowered. Neale gave King a warning glance, meant to convey that he was not to be funny.

"This is my cowboy friend, Larry Red King," said Neale. "He was with me when I . . . I found you."

"Larry . . . Red . . . King," murmured the girl. "My name is . . . Allie."

Again Neale had penetrated into her somber locked mind. What she said astounded him so that he dropped the brush and stared at King. As for King—his name spoken that way seemed to affect him strangely. He lost his grin. He caught a glimpse of her face, and then his own grew troubled.

"Allie . . . I shore . . . am glad to meet you," he said, and there was more feeling in his voice than Neale had ever heard. King was not slow of comprehension. He began to talk in his drawling way. Neale heard that talk with a smile he tried to hide, but he liked King the better for his simplicity. This gun-throwing cowboy had a big heart.

King, however, did not linger for long. His attempts to get the girl to talk grew weaker and ended, and, after another glance at the tragic wan face, he got up and thoughtfully slouched away with his cowboy's gait.

"So your name is Allie," said Neale. "Well, Allie what?"

She did not respond to one in a hundred questions and this was one that found no lodgment in her mind.

"Will you braid your hair now?" he asked.

The answer was the low and monotonous negative, but, nevertheless, her hands sought her hair and parted it and braided it mechanically. This encouraged Neale more than anything else and taught him that there were habits of mind into which he could turn her. In this way he got her to walk along the brook and likewise made her eat and drink.

At the end of that day he was more exhausted than he would have been after a hard climb. It had developed that he could now and then draw her out of her strange clamped state—and that he could get some kind of passive unconscious obedience from her.

"Reckon you'd better stay over tomorrer," suggested Slingerland. His concern for the girl could not have been greater had she been his own daughter. "Allie . . . thet was her name, you said. Wal, it's pretty an' easy to say."

Next day Allie showed an almost imperceptible improvement. It might have been Neale's imagination making him believe what he hoped. He was sure of one thing, however, and that was that, although the trapper and the cowboy could not get any response from her, there was proof that he could. It affected him as a way new to him. There was a stir of emotion deep within him—a feeling that seemed old, but had never before been called up.

An hour before sunset Neale decided to depart, and told King to get the horses. Then he went to Allie, undecided what to say, feeling that he must have tortured her this day with his ceaseless importunities. How small the chance that he might strike interest from her once more. Yet the desire was strong within him to try.

"Allie!" He repeated her name before she heard him. Then she looked up. The depths—the tragic lonesomeness of her eyes haunted Neale. "I'm going back. I'll come again soon."

She made a quick movement—seized his arm. He remembered the close tight grip of her hands. "Don't go!" she implored. Black fear stared out of her eyes.

Neale was thunderstruck at the suddenness of her speech—at its intensity. Also, he felt an unfamiliar kind of joy that seemed selfish—not concerned with this new and surprising sign of her sanity. He began to explain that he must return to work, that he would soon come to see her again, and, even as he talked, she faded back into that dull and somber apathy.

Neale rode away with only one conviction gained from the developments of the two days, and it was that he would be restless and haunted until he could go to her again. Something big and moving—something equal to his ambition for his work on the great railroad—had risen in him.

# CHAPTER SEVEN

Neale rode to Slingerland's cabin twice during the ensuing fortnight, and did not note any improvement in Allie's condition or demeanor. The trapper, however, assured Neale that she was gradually gaining a little, taking slight interest in things, and he said that, if Neale could only spend enough time there, the girl might recover. This made Neale thoughtful.

General Lodge and his staff had decided to station several engineers in camp along the line of the railroad for the purpose of studying the drift of snow in winter. It was important that all information possible should be obtained during the next several winters. There would be severe hardship attached to this work, but Neale volunteered to serve, and the chief complimented him warmly. He was to study the action of snow drift along Sherman Pass.

Upon his next visit to Slingerland he had the project soberly in mind and meant to broach it upon the first opportunity.

This morning when Neale and King rode up to the cabin Allie did not appear as she had on the last occasion of their arrival. Neale missed her.

Slingerland came out with his usual welcome.

"Where's Allie?" asked Neale.

"Wal, she went in jest now. She saw you comin' an' then run in to hide, I reckon. Girls is queer critters."

"She watched for me . . . for us . . . and then ran?" queried Neale curiously.

"Wal, she ain't done nuthin' but watch fer you since you went away last. An' son, thet's a new wrinkle fer Allie. An' run? Wal, like a skeered deer."

"Wonder what that means," pondered Neale. Whatever it meant it sent a little tingle of pleasure along his pulses. "Red, I want to have a serious talk with Slingerland," he announced thoughtfully.

"Shore, go ahaid an' talk," drawled the Southerner as he slipped his saddle and turned his horse loose with a slap on the flank. "I reckon I'll take a gun an' stroll off fer a while."

Neale led the trapper aside to a shady spot under the pines and there unburdened himself of his plan for the winter.

"Son, you'll freeze to death!" ejaculated the trapper.

"But I must build a cabin, of course, and prepare for severe weather," replied Neale.

Slingerland shook his shaggy head. "I reckon you ain't knowin' these winters hyar as I know them. But thet long ridge you call Sherman Pass . . . it ain't so far we couldn't get thar on snowshoes except in the wurst weather. I reckon you can stay with me hyar."

"Good!" exclaimed Neale. "And now about Allie."

"Wal, what about her?"

"Shall I leave her here or send her back to Omaha with the first caravan or send her back to Fort Fetterman with the troops?"

"Son, she's your charge, but I say leave her hyar, 'specially now you can be with us. She'd die or go crazy if you sent her. Why, she won't even say if she's got a livin' relation. I reckon she hasn't. She'd be better hyar. I've come to be fond of Allie. She's strange. She's like a spirit. But she's more human lately."

"I'm glad you say that, Slingerland," replied Neale. "What to do about her has worried me. I'll decide right now. I'll leave here with you and I hope to heaven I'm doing best by her."

"Wal, she ain't strong enough to travel far. We didn't think of that."

"That settles it, then," said Neale, in relief. "Time enough to decide when she is well again. . . . Tell me about her."

"Son, thar's nuthin' to tell. She's done jest the same, except fer thet takin' to watchin' fer you. Reckon thet means a good deal."

"What?"

"Wal, I don't figger girls as well as I do other critters," answered Slingerland reflectively. "But I'd say Allie shows interest in you."

"Slingerland! You don't mean she . . . she cares for me?" demanded Neale.

"I don't know. Mebbe not. Mebbe she's beyond carin'. But I believe you an' that red memory of bloody death air all she ever thinks of. An' mostly of it."

"Then it'll be a fight between me and that memory?"

"So I take it, son. But recollect I ain't no . . . no mind doctor. I jest feel you could make her fergit thet hell if you tried hard enough."

"I'll try . . . hard as I can," replied Neale resolutely, yet with a certain softness. "I'm sorry for her. I saved her. Why shouldn't I do everything possible?"

"Wal, she's alone."

"No, Allie has friends. You and Red and me. That's three."

"Son, I reckon you don't figger me. Listen. You're a fine strappin' young feller an' good-lookin'. More'n thet, you've got some . . . some quality like an Injun's . . . thet you can feel but can't tell about. You needn't be insulted fer I know Injuns thet beat white men holler fer all thet's noble. Anyway, you attract. An' now if you keep on with all thet . . . thet . . . wal, usin' yourself to make Allie fergit the bloody murder of all she loved . . . to make her mind clear again, why sooner or later she's a-goin' to breathe an' live through you. Jest as a flower lives offen the sun. Thet's all, I reckon."

Neale's bronze cheek had paled a little. "Well, if that's all, that's easy," he replied with a cool bright smile that showed the latent spirit in him. "If it's only that . . . why she can *have* me. . . . Slingerland, I've no ties now. The last one was broken when my mother died . . . not long ago. I'm alone, too. . . . I'd do more for any innocent girl . . . and for this poor child Allie . . . whose life I saved . . . I'd do anything."

Slingerland shoved out a horny hand and made a giant grip express what evidently just then he could not express in speech.

Upon returning to the cabin they found Allie had left her room. From appearances Neale concluded that she had made little use of the things he had brought her. He was conscious of something akin to impatience. He was not sure what he did feel. The situation had subtly changed and grown, all in that brief talk with Slingerland. Neale slowly walked out toward the brook where he expected to find her. It struck him suddenly that, if she had watched for him all week and had run when he came, then she must have wanted to see him but was afraid or shy or perverse. How like any girl! Possibly in the week past she had unconsciously grown a little away from her grief and if so . . . what might not have come into her head?

"I'll try something new on you, Allie," he muttered, and the boy in him that would never grow into a man meant to be serious even in fun.

Allie sat in the shady place under the low pine where the brook spilled out of the big spring. She drooped and appeared oblivious to her surroundings. A stray gleam of sunlight, touching her hair, made it shine brightly. Neale's quick eye took note of the fact that she had washed the bloodstain from the front of her dress. He was glad. What hope had there been for her as long as she sat hour after hour with her hands pressed to that great black stain on her dress—that mark where her mother's head had rested? Neale experienced a renewal of hope. He began to whistle, and, drawing his knife, he went into the brush to cut a fishing pole. The trout in this brook had long tempted his fisherman's eye, and upon this visit he had brought a line and hooks. He made a lot of noise all for Allie's benefit, and, tramping out of the brush, he began to trim the rod within twenty feet of where she sat. He whistled; he even hummed a song while he was rigging up the tackle. Then it became necessary to hunt for some kind of bait, and he went about this with pleasure, both because he liked it and because out of the corner of his eye he saw that Allie was watching him. Therefore he redoubled his efforts at pretending to be oblivious of her presence, and at keeping her continually aware of his. He found crickets, worms, and grubs under the dead pine logs, and with variety of bait he approached the brook.

The first cast Neale made fetched a lusty trout and right there his pretension vanished as did his awareness of Allie's proximity. Neale loved to fish. He had not yet indulged his favorite pastime in the West. He saw trout jumping everywhere. It was a beautiful little stream, rocky, swift here and eddying there, clear as crystal, and murmurous with tiny falls; all about was a freshness of green and gold; there were birds singing in the trees, but over all seemed to hang the quiet of the lonely hills. Neale forgot Allie—forgot that he meant to see if she could be susceptible to a little neglect. The brook was full of trout, voracious and tame; they had never been angled for. He caught three in short order.

When his last bait, a large and luscious grub, struck the water there was a swirl, a splash, a tug—and Neale excitedly realized that he had hooked a whale of a trout. It leaped. That savage leap—the splash—the amazing size of the fish inflamed in Neale the old boyish desire to capture, and, forgetting what little skill he possessed, he gave a mighty pull. The rod bent double. But with a vicious splash lunged the huge glistening trout—to dangle heavily for an instant in the air. Neale thought he heard a cry behind him. He was sitting down, in awkward posture. But he lifted and swung. The line snapped. The fish dropped in the grass and began to thresh. Frantically Neale leaped to prevent the escape of the hugest trout he had ever seen. There was a dark flash—a commotion before him. Then it seemed he was staring in bewilderment at Allie who held the wriggling trout by the gills.

"You don't know how to fish!" she exclaimed with great severity.

"I don't . . . eh?" ejaculated Neale blankly.

"You should play a big trout. You lifted him right out. He broke your line. He'd have . . . gotten . . . away . . . but for me."

She ended panting a little from her exertion and quick speech. A red spot showed in each white cheek. Her eyes were resolute and flashing. It dawned upon Neale that he had never before seen a tinge of color in her face, nor any of the ordinary feelings of life glancing in her eyes—and now she seemed actually pretty. He had made a discovery—and perhaps he had another means to distract her from herself. Then the squirming trout drew his attention and he took it from her.

"What a whopper! Oh, say, Allie, isn't he a beauty? I could hug . . . I . . . you bet I'm thankful. You were quick. . . . He certainly is slippery."

Allie dropped to her knees and wiped her hands on the grass while Neale killed the fish and strung it upon a willow with the others he had caught. Then turning to Allie, he meant to tell her how glad he was to see her again—to ask her if she was glad to see him. But upon looking at her, he decided to keep her mind from herself. She was different then and he liked this difference. He feared he might frighten it away.

"Will you help me get more bait?" he asked.

Allie nodded and got up. Then Neale noticed she was in her bare feet. Poor child! She had no shoes and he did not know how to procure any in that wilderness.

"Have you ever fished for trout?" he asked, as he began to dig under the rotting log.

"Yes. In California," she replied, with a sudden shadowing of her eyes.

"Let's go down the brook," said Neale hastily, fearful that he had been tactless. "There are some fine holes below."

She walked beside him, careful of the sharp stones that showed here and there. Presently they came to a likely-looking pool.

"If you hook another big one, don't try to pull him right out," admonished Allie.

Neale could scarcely conceal his delight and in his effort to appear natural made a poor showing at this pool, losing two fish and scaring others so they would not rise.

"Allie, won't you try?" he asked, offering the rod.

"I'd rather look on. You like it so much."

"How do you know that?" he asked, more to hear her talk than from curiosity.

"You grow so excited," she said.

Thankfully he accepted the realization that, after all these weeks of silence, it was possible to make her speak. But he must exercise extreme caution. One wrong word might send her back into that apathy—that senseless, voiceless trance.

In every pool where Neale cast, he caught or lost a trout. He was enjoying himself tremendously while at the same time feeling a warmth in his heart that was not entirely the exhilaration of fishing. Below the boxing of the valley, where the stream began and the cabin nestled, the ground was open, like a meadow, with grass and flowers growing to the edge of the water. In curves there were deep swirling pools running under the banks and in these Neale hooked fish he could not handle with his poor tackle, and they broke away. But he did not care. There was a brightness, a beauty, a fragrance along the stream that seemed to enhance the farther down he went. Presently they came to a place where the water rushed over a rocky bed, and here Neale wanted to cross. He started to wade, curious and eager to see what Allie would do.

"I can't wade that!" she called.

Neale returned to her side. "I'll carry you," he said. "You hold the rod. We'll leave the fish here." Then he lifted her in his arms. How light she was—how much lighter than upon that first occasion of his carrying her! He slipped in the middle of the brook and nearly fell with her. Allie squealed. That filled Neale with glee. After all she had gone through, she was feminine—she was a girl—she was squeamish. Thereupon he slipped purposely and made a heroic effort to save himself. She clasped his neck convulsively with her free arm, and, as he recovered his balance, he had bumped into her and her hair got into his eyes. He laughed. This was great fun. But it could scarcely have been the exertion that made his heart beat out of time. At last he gained the opposite bank.

"You nearly fell with me," she said.

"Well, I'd have got wet, too," he replied, wondering if it was possible to make her laugh or even smile. If he could do that today, even in the smallest degree, he would be assured that happiness might come back to her. Then he went on.

Soon they met King, who came stooping along, burdened with a deer carcass on his shoulder. Relieving himself, he hailed them. "How air you-all?" he drawled, addressing himself mostly to Allie.

"What's your name?" she asked.

"Allie, he's my friend and partner," replied Neale. "Larry

Red King. But I call him Red . . . for obvious reasons."

"Wal, Miss Allie, I reckon no tall kick would be a-comin' if you was to call me Red," drawled King. "Or better . . . Reddy. No other lady ever had thet honor."

Allie looked at him steadily, as if this was the first time she had seen him, but she did not reply. And King, easily disconcerted, gathered up his burden, and turned toward camp.

"Wal, I'm shore wishin' you-all good luck!" he called significantly.

Neale shot a quick glance at Allie to see if the cowboy's good-humored double-meaning had occurred to her. She might never have heard. She seemed to be tiring. Her lips were parted and she panted.

"Are you tired? Shall we go back?" he asked.

"No . . . I like it," she returned slowly, as if the thought was strange to her.

They fished on, and presently came to a wide shallow place, with smooth rock bottom, where the trail crossed. Neale waded across alone, and he judged that the water in the middle might come up to Allie's knees. "Come on!" he called.

Allie hesitated. She gathered up her faded skirt and slowly waded in and halted, uncertain of her footing. She was not afraid, Neale decided, and neither did she seem aware that her slender shapely legs gleamed white against the dark water.

"Won't you come and carry me?" she asked.

"Indeed I won't," replied Neale. "Carry a big girl like you!"

She took him seriously and moved a little farther. "My feet slip so," she said.

It became fascinating to watch her. The fun of it—the pleasure of seeing a girl wade a brook, innocently immodest, suddenly ceased for Neale. There was something else. He had only meant to tease; he was going to carry her; he started back. And then he halted. There was a strange earnestness in Allie's face—a deliberation in her intent out of all proportion to the exigency of the moment. It was as if she must cross that brook. But she kept halting. "Come on!" Neale called. And she moved again. Every time this happened she seemed to be compelled to go on. When she got into the swift water nearly to her knees, then she might well have faltered. Yet she did not falter. All at once Neale discovered that she was weak. She did not have the strength to come on. It was that which made her slip and halt. What then made her try so bravely? How strange that she tried at all! Stranger than that was her peculiar attitude toward the task—earnest, sober, grave, forced.

Neale was suddenly seized with surprise and remorse. That which actuated this girl Allie was merely the sound of his voice—the answer to his demand. He plunged in and reached her just as she was slipping. He carried her back to the side from which she had started. It cost him an effort not to hold her close. Whatever she was—orphan or waif—left alone in the world by a murdering band of Sioux—an unfortunate girl to be cared for, succored, pitied—none of these accounted for the change that his power over her had wrought in him.

"You're not strong," he said as he put her down.

"Was that it?" she asked with just a touch of wonder. "I used to wade . . . anywhere."

He spoke little on the way back up the brook, for he hesitated to tell her that he must return to his camp so as to be ready for important work on the morrow, and not until they were almost at the cabin did he make up his mind. She received the intelligence in silence, and upon reaching the cabin she went into her room.

Neale helped King and Slingerland with the task of preparing a meal that all looked forward to having Allie share with them. However, when Slingerland called her, there was no response.

Neale found her sunk in the old hopeless, staring, brooding

mood. He tried patience at first and gentleness but without avail. She would not come with him. The meal was eaten without her. Later Neale almost compelled her to eat a little. He felt discouraged again. Time had flown all too swiftly and there was King coming with the horses and sunset not far off. It might be weeks, even months before he would see her again.

"Allie, are you *ever* going to cheer up?" he demanded.

"No . . . no," she sighed.

He put his hand under her chin, and, forcing her face up, he studied it earnestly. Strained, white, bloodless, thin, with drooping lips and tragic eyes, it was not a beautiful, not even a pretty face. But it might have been very easily. The veiled mournful eyes did not evade his; indeed they appeared to stare deeply, hopelessly, yearningly. Neale imagined he saw something thick and turgid between what he might call the past and future as revealed there. If he could only say and do the right thing he might kill that melancholia. She needed to be made alive. Suddenly he had an impulse to kiss her. That no doubt was owing to the proximity of her lips. But he must not kiss her. She might care for him someday—it was natural to imagine she would but she did not care now, and that made kisses impossible.

"You just won't cheer up?" he went on.

"No . . . no."

"But you were so different out there by the brook!"

She made no reply. The veil grew darker, more shadowy over her eyes. Neale divined a deadness in her.

"I'm going away," he said sharply.

"Yes."

"Do you care?" he went on, with greater intensity.

She only stared at him.

"You *must* care!" he exclaimed.

"Why?" she asked dully.

"Why . . . ? Because . . . because," he stammered, angry with himself. After all why should she care?

"I wish . . . you'd . . . left me . . . to die!" she moaned.

"Oh! Allie! Allie," began Neale, in distress. Then he caught the different quality in her voice. It carried feeling. She was thinking again. He *swore* he could overcome this malady of hers. And he grew keen, subtle, on fire with his resolve. He watched her. He put his hands on her shoulders and pulled her gently. She slid off the pile of buffalo robes to her knees before him. Then she showed the only hint of shyness he had ever noted in her. Perhaps it was fear. At any rate she half averted her face, so that her loosened hair hid it.

"Allie! Allie! Listen! Have you nothing to *live* for?" he asked.

"No!"

"Why, yes you have."

"What?"

"Why I . . . the thing is . . . Allie . . . you have *me*," he said a little hoarsely. Then he laughed. How strange his laugh sounded. He would always remember that rude room of logs and furs and the kneeling girl in the dim light.

"*You!*"

"Yes, me," he replied, with a ring in his voice. Never before had she put wonder in a word. He had struck the right chord at last. Swiftly then it seemed he held a live creature under his hands, as if the deadness and dread apathy had quivered out in that one syllable. He felt surer now that he was on the right track. This was a big moment. If he only could make up to her for what she had lost. He felt his throat swell and speech difficult.

"Allie, do you understand me now? You . . . have something . . . to live for. . . . Do you hear?"

When his ear caught the faint—"Yes."—he suddenly grew glad and strong with what he felt to be a victory over her gloom and despair. "Listen. I'm going to my work," he began swiftly.

"I'll be gone weeks . . . maybe more. *But I'll come back.* . . . Early in the fall. I'll be with you all winter. I'm to work here on the pass. . . . Then . . . then. . . . Well, I'll be a big man on the U.P. Someday. You're all alone . . . maybe you'll care for me someday. I'll work hard. It's a great idea . . . this railroad. When it's done . . . and I've my big job . . . will you . . . you'll marry me then?"

Neale heard her gasp and felt her quiver. He let go of her and stood up, for fear he might suddenly take her in his arms. His words had been shock enough. He felt remorse, anxiety, tenderness, and yet he was glad. Some delicate and fine consciousness in him told him he had not done wrong, even if he had been dominating. She was alone in the world; he had saved her life. His heart beat, quick and heavy.

"Good bye, Allie. I'll come back. Never forget!"

She stayed motionless on her knees with the mass of hair hiding her face, and she neither spoke nor made a sign.

Neale went out. The air seemed to wave in his face, cool and relieving. King was there with the horses. Slingerland stood by with troubled eyes. Both men stared at Neale. He was aware of that and conscious of his agitation. And suddenly, as always at a climax of emotion, he swiftly changed and grew cool.

"Red, old pard, congratulate me. I'm engaged to marry Allie," he said with a low laugh that had pride in it.

"Wal, damn me!" ejaculated King. Then he shot out the hand that was so quick with rope and gun. "Put her thar! Shore if you hadn't made up to her, I'd have! An', Neale, if you say pard, I'm yours till I'm daid."

"Pard," replied Neale as he met the outstretched hand.

Slingerland's hard and wrinkled face softened. "Strange how we all cottoned to thet girl. No . . . I reckon it ain't so strange. Wal, it's as it oughter be. You saved her. May you both be happy, son!"

Neale slipped a ring from his little finger. "Give Allie this. Tell her it's my pledge. I'll come back to her. And she must think of that."

# CHAPTER EIGHT

That summer the engineers crossed the Black Hills and ran the line into Utah where they met the surveying party working in from the Pacific.

The initial step of the great construction work was done, the engineers had with hardship and loss of life proved that a railroad across the Rockies was a possibility. Only, they had little conception of the titanic labor involved in the building.

For Neale the months were hard, swift, full. It came to him that love of the open and the wild was incorporated in his ambition for achievement. He wondered if he would have felt the one without the other. Camp life and the daily climbing over the ridges made of him a lithe and strong and sure-footed mountaineer. They made even the horse-riding cowboy a good climber, although nothing, Neale averred, would ever straighten King's bowlegs.

Only two incidents or accidents marred the work and pleasure of those fruitful weeks. The first happened in camp. There was a surly stake-driver by the name of Shurd who was lazy and otherwise offensive among hard-working men, and he, having been severely handled by Neale, had nursed a grievance and evidently had only waited for an opportunity for revenge. Neale was quick-tempered, and prone to sharp language and action when irritated or angered. Shurd, passing through the camp, either drunk or unusually surly, kicked Neale's instrument out of his way. Someone saw him do it and told Neale. Thereupon

Neale, in high dudgeon, sought out the fellow. And King, always Neale's shadow, came slouching after with his cowboy's gait. They found Shurd at the camp of the teamsters and other laborers. Neale did not waste many words. He struck Shurd a blow that staggered him and would have followed it up with more had not the man, suddenly furious, plunged away to pick up a heavy stake with which he made at Neale to bean him.

Neale could not escape. He yelled at Shurd, trying to intimidate him. Then came a shot from behind. It broke Shurd's arm. The stake fell and the man began to bawl curses.

"Get out of heah!" called King, advancing slowly. The maddened Shurd tried to use the broken arm, perhaps to draw on King. Thereupon the cowboy, with gun low and apparently not aiming, shot again, this time almost tearing Shurd's arm off. Then he prodded Shurd with the cocked gun. The man turned ghastly. He seemed just to have realized the nature of this gaunt flaming-eyed cowboy.

"Shore your mind ain't workin'," said King. "Get out of heah. Mosey over to thet camp doctor or you'll never need one."

Shurd backed away, livid and shaking, and presently he ran.

"Red!" expostulated Neale. "You . . . you shot him all up! You might . . . you nearly killed him."

"Why in the hell don't you pack a gun?" drawled King.

"Red, you're . . . you're . . . I don't know what to call you. I'd have licked him, club and all!"

"Mebbe," replied the cowboy as he sheathed the big gun. "Neale, I'm used to what you ain't. Shore I can see death a-comin'. Wal, every day the outfit grows wilder. A little whiskey'll burn hell loose along this heah U.P. line."

King strode on in the direction Shurd had taken. Neale pondered a moment, perplexed, impressed, and grateful to his comrade. He heard remarks among the laborers and he saw the flagman Casey remove his black pipe from his lips—an unusual occurrence.

"Mac, it was that red-headed cowboy, wot oncet pinted his gun at me!" burst out Casey.

"Did yez see him shoot?" replied Mac, with round eyes. "Niver aimed an' yit he hit."

Mike Shane, the third of the trio of Irish laborers in Neale's corps, was a little runt of a sandy-haired weazened man, and he spoke up: "B'gorra, he's wan of thim Texas Jacks. He'd loike to kill yez, Pat Casey, an' if he ever throwed thot cannon at yez . . . why, runnin'd be slow to phwat yez'd do."

"I never run in my loife," declared Casey doggedly.

Neale went his way. It was noted that from that day he always carried a gun, preferably a rifle when it was possible. In the use of the long gun he was an adept, but when it came to King's kind of a gun, Neale needed practice. King could draw his gun and shoot twice before Neale could get his hand on his own. And it was through Neale's habit of carrying his rifle out in his surveying trips that the second incident came about.

One day in early summer Neale was waiting near a spring for King to come with the horses. On this occasion the cowboy was long in coming. Neale fell asleep in the shade of some bushes and was awakened by the *thud* of hoofs. He sat up to see King in the act of kneeling at the brook to drink. As the same instant a dark moving object just above King attracted Neale's quick eye. It was an Indian sneaking along with a gun ready to level. Quick as a flash Neale raised his own weapon and fired. The Indian fell and lay still.

King's drink was rudely disturbed by plunging horses. When he had quieted them, he turned to Neale. "So you-all was heah. Shore you scared me. What'd you shoot at?"

Neale stared and pointed. His hand shook. He felt cold, sick, hard, yet he held the rifle ready to fire again. King dropped the bridles, and, pulling his gun, he climbed the bank with unusual

Zane Grey

quickness for him. Neale saw him stand over the Indian.

"Wal, plumb center!" he called, with a new note in his usually indolent voice.

"Come heah!" shouted Neale violently. "Is he dead?"

"Daid! Wal, I should smile. . . . An' mebbe he ain't alone."

The cowboy ran down to his horse and Neale followed suit. They rode up on the ridge to reconnoiter, but saw no moving objects.

"I reckon thet redskin was shore a-goin' to plug me," drawled King as they trotted homeward.

"He certainly was," replied Neale with a shudder.

King reached a long hand to Neale's shoulder. He owed his life to his friend. But he did not speak of that. Instead he glanced wisely at Neale and laughed. "Kinda weak in the middle, eh?" he said. "I felt thet way once. . . . Pard, if you ever get riled, you'll be shore bad."

For Neale shooting at an Indian was strikingly different from boyish dreams of doing it. He had acted so swiftly that it seemed it must have been instinctive. Yet thinking back, slowly realizing the nature of the repellant feeling within him, he remembered a bursting gush of hot blood, a pantherish desire to leap, to strike—and then cool, stern watchfulness. The thing was unpleasant.

Upon arriving at camp they reported the incident, and they learned Indians had showed up at various points along the line. Troopers had been fired upon. Orders were once more given that all work must be carried on under the protection of the soldiers, so that an ambush would be unlikely. Meanwhile, a detachment of troops would be sent out to drive back the band of Sioux.

These two hard experiences made actuality out of what Neale's chief had told him would be a man's game in a wild time. This work on the U.P. was not play or romance. But the

84

future unknown called alluringly to him. In his moments of leisure, by the campfire at night, he reflected and dreamed and wondered, and these reflections always turned finally to memory of Allie.

The girl he had saved seemed far away in mind as well as distance. He tried to call up her face—to see it in the ruddy embers. But he could visualize only her eyes. They were unforgettable—the somber haunting shadows of thoughts of death. He remembered that once or twice they had changed— had become wonderful, with promise of exceeding beauty, if only the dark veils vanished.

It seemed incredible that he had pledged himself. He had no regrets. Time had not made any difference, only it had shown him that his pity and tenderness were not love. Still there had been another emotion connected with Allie—a strange thing too subtle and brief for him to analyze—for when away from her he lost it. Could that have been love? He thought of the day she waded the brook, the picture of her then; he thought of the feel of her as he carried her in his arms, and of that last sight of her, on her knees in the cabin, her face hidden, her slender form still as a statue, all so significant of a girl, young and helpless, alone and heart-broken. His own heart was touched. Yet this was not love. It was enough for Neale to feel that he had done what he would have applauded in another man, that he seemed the better for his pledge, that the next meeting with Allie was one he looked forward to with strange new interest.

September came and half sped by before Neale, with King and an engineer named Service, arrived at the head of Sherman Pass with pack burros and supplies, ready to begin the vigil of watching the snow drift over the line in winter.

They were to divide the pass between them—Service to range the upper half and Neale the lower. As there were but few trees up in that locality, and these necessary for a large supply of firewood, they decided not to attempt building a cabin for Service, but to dig instead a dug-out. This was a hole hollowed out in a hillside, and covered with a roof of branches and earth.

No small job indeed was it to build a satisfactory dug-out— one that was not conspicuous from every ridge for Indian eyes to spy out—and warm and dry and safe. They started several before they completed one.

"It'll be lonesomer for you . . . and colder," observed Neale.

"I won't mind that," replied the other.

"We'll see each other before the snow flies, surely?"

"Not unless you come up. I'm no climber. I've got a bad leg."

"I'll come, then. We may have weeks of fine weather yet. I'm going to hunt some."

"Good luck to you."

So these comrades parted. They were only two of the intrepid engineers selected to brave the peril and hardships of that wild region in winter, to serve the great cause.

The golds and purples of autumn mingled with the predominating green of Slingerland's valley. In one place beaver had dammed the stream, forming a small lake, and here cranes and other aquatic birds had congregated. Neale saw beaver at work, and deer on the hillside.

"It's been three months," he soliloquized as he paused at the ford where Allie had so bravely and weakly tried to cross at his bidding. "Three months! So much can have happened. But Slingerland is safe from Indians. I hope . . . I believe I'll find her well."

Nevertheless he was prey to dread and he did not hurry. King, driving the pack train, drew on ahead and passed out of sight in a green bend of the brook. At length Neale saw a column of blue smoke curling up above the trees and that sight relieved him. If the trapper was there, the girl would be with him. Unless!—but she had been in no ill health.

At this juncture, when he was about to hurry on and make a certainty in his mind of whatever was, his horse shot up his long ears and snorted.

A gray form glided out of the green—began to run down the trail toward him—a lithe swift girl in buckskin.

"An Indian girl!" ejaculated Neale.

But her face was white—her hair tawny, flying in the wind. Could that be Allie? It must be she. It was!

"Lord . . . I'm in for it," muttered Neale, dismounting, and he gazed with eager eyes.

"Neale! You've come!" she cried, and ran straight upon him.

He hardly recognized her face or her voice, but what she said proclaimed her to be Allie. She enveloped him. Her arms, strong, convulsive, clasped him, and lifted herself. Up came her face, white, gleaming, joyous, strange to Neale, but he knew somehow that it was held up to be kissed. Dazedly he kissed her—felt cool sweet lips touch him—then his cheek—again—again.

"Allie! I . . . I hardly knew you," was his greeting. Then he was holding her, and felt her press her head close to his breast, felt the intensity of what must have been her need of physical contact to make sure he was there in the flesh. And as he held her, looking down upon her, he recognized the little head and the dull gold and ripple of chestnut hair. Yes—it was Allie. But this Allie was taller—up to his shoulder—and lithe and full-bosomed and strong. This was not the frail girl he had left.

"I thought . . . you'd . . . never, never come," she murmured, clinging to him.

"It was . . . pretty long," he replied unsteadily. "But I've come. . . . And I'm very glad to see you."

"You didn't know me," she said shyly. "You looked . . . it."

"Well, no wonder. I left a thin pale little girl, all eyes . . . and what do I find? Let me look at you."

She drew back and stood before him, shy and modest, but without a trace of embarrassment—surely the sweetest and loveliest girl he had ever beheld. Some familiar trace he found in her features, perhaps the looks—the shape of her eyes. All else was unfamiliar. And that all else was a white face, blue-veined, with rich blood slowly mantling to the broad brow, with sweet red lips haunting in their sadness, with glorious eyes, like violets drenched in dew, shadowy, exquisite, mournful, and deep, yet radiant, with beautiful light.

Neale realized her beauty at the instant he realized her love, and he was so utterly astounded at the one and overwhelmed with the other that he was mute. A powerful reaction of some kind took place within him, so strong that it helped free him from the other emotions. He found his tongue and controlled his glance.

"I took you for an Indian girl in all this buckskin," he said.

"Dress, leggings, moccasins I made all myself," she replied, sweeping a swift hand from fringe to beads. "Not a single button! Oh, it was hard . . . so much work! But they're more comfortable than any clothes I ever had."

"So you've not been . . . altogether idle since I left?"

"Since that day"—and she blushed exquisitely at the words—"I've been doing everything under the sun except that grieving you disliked. . . . Everything! Cooking, sewing, fishing, bathing, climbing, riding, shooting . . . *and* watching for you."

"That accounts," he replied musingly.

"For what?"

"Your . . . your improvement. You seem happy . . . and well."

"Do you mean all the activity accounts for that . . . or my watching for you?" she queried archly. She was quick, bright, roguish. Neale had no idea what qualities she might have had before that fateful massacre that had left her alone, but she was bewilderingly different from the sick-minded girl he had tried so hard to interest and draw out of her gloom. He was so amazed, so delighted with her, and so confused with his own peculiar state that he could not be natural. Then, as always in difficulty, his mood shifted and a little heat at himself roused his wits.

"Allie, I want to realize what's happened," he said. "Let's sit down here. We sat here once before, if you remember. Slingerland can wait to see me."

Neale's horse grazed along the green border of the brook. The water ran with low swift rush, there were bees *humming* around the autumn flowers, and a fragrance of wood smoke wafted down from the camp; over all lay the dreaming quietness of the season and of the wild.

Allie sat down upon the rock, but Neale, changing his mind, stood beside her. Still he did not trust himself to face her yet. He was unsettled, uncertain. All this was like a dream.

"So you watched for me?" he asked gently.

"For hours and days and weeks." She sighed.

"Then you . . . cared . . . care a little for me?"

She kept silence. And he, wanting intensely to look up, did not.

"Tell me," he insisted, with a limit of the old dominance. He remembered again the scene at the crossing of the brook. Could he control this wonderful girl now?

"Of course," she replied.

"But . . . how do you care?" he added more forcibly. He felt ashamed, yet he could not resist it. What was happening to him?

"I . . . I love you." Her voice was low, almost unfaltering, rich with sweetness, and full of some unutterable emotion.

Neale sustained a shock. He never could have told how that

affected him, except in his sudden fury at himself for he knew not what. Then he stole a glance at her, and knew as he did it that, if she manifested any signs of duty or gratitude to him, he would lose some strange feeling that must have been joy or elation. Her eyes were downcast, hidden under long lashes; her face was soft and sweet, dreaming and spiritual, singularly pure, her breast heaved under the beaded buckskin. Neale divined she had never dreamed of owing him anything except her love, which quivered on her tremulous lips and hovered in the exquisite light of her countenance. And here he received, if not another shock, then a great and impelling change in his spirit, an uplift, a splendid and beautiful consciousness of his good fortune. But what could he say to her? If only he could safely pass over this moment, so he could have time to think, to find himself! Another glance at her encouraged him. She expected nothing—not a word—she took all for granted. She was lost in dreams of her soul.

He looked down again to see her hand—small, shapely, strong, and brown, and upon the third finger he espied his ring. He had forgotten to look to see if she wore it. Then softly he touched it and drew her hand in his.

"My ring. Allie . . . ," he whispered. The response was a wonderful purple blaze of her eyes. He divined then that his ring had been the tangible thing upon which she had reconstructed her broken life—had found something to live for.

"You rode away . . . so quietly . . . I had no chance to . . . to . . . ," she replied haltingly and low-voiced. All was sweet shame about her now and he had to fight himself to keep from gathering her to his breast. Verily this meeting between Allie and him was not what he had anticipated.

He kissed her hand. "You've all the fall . . . and all the winter to tell me . . . such sweet things," he said. "Perhaps tomorrow . . . soon . . . I'll find my tongue and tell you something."

"Tell me now," she said quietly in response.

"Well, you're beautiful," he replied, with strong feeling.

"Really?" She smiled, and that smile was the first he had ever seen upon her face. It brought out the sadness—that thing that perhaps was the soul of her beauty. "I used to be pretty," she went on naïvely. "But, if I remember how I used to look I'm . . . not pretty any more."

Neale laughed. He had begun to feel freer, to accept this unparalleled situation. "Tell me," he said with gentle voice and touch, "tell me your name. Allie . . . what?"

"Didn't you ever know?" she asked.

"You said Allie. That was all." He feared this call to her memory, yet he wanted to put her to a test, all about her seemed too good to be true. Her eyes dilated—the light shaded—they grew sad, dark, humid gulfs of thought. But the old somber veil—the insane brooding stare did not return.

"Allie what?" he repeated.

Then the tears came, softening, dimming the pain. "Allie . . . Lee," she said.

# CHAPTER NINE

Slingerland appeared younger to Neale. The burden of loneliness did not weigh upon him and the habit of silence had been broken. Neale guessed why and was actually jealous.

"Wal, it's beyond my calculatin'," the trapper said, out by the spring, where Neale followed him. "She jest changed, thet's all. Not so much at first, though she sparked up after I give her your ring. I reckon it came little by little. . . . An' one day, why the cabin was full of sunshine! Since then, I've seen how she's growed an' brightened. Workin', runnin' after me . . . an' always watchin' fer you, Allie's changed to what she is now. Oncet, far back, I recollect she said she had you to live for. Mebbe thet's the secret. Anyhow she loves you as I never seen any man loved. . . . An', son, I reckon you oughter be somewhar's near the kingdom of heaven!"

Neale stole off by himself and walked in the twilight. The air was warm and sultry, full of fragrance, and the low *chirp* of crickets. Within his breast was a full uneasy sensation of imminent catastrophe. It was as if he must prepare to feel his heart burst presently. Something was rising in him—great—terrible—precious. It bewildered him to try to think of himself, of his strange emotions, when his mind seemed to hold only Allie.

What then had happened? After a long absence up in the mountains he had returned to Slingerland's valley home and to the little girl he had rescued and left there. He had left her frail,

92

sick-minded, silent, somber, a pale victim to a horrible memory. He had found her an exceedingly amazing contrast to all she had been. She had grown strong, active, swift. She was as lovely as a wild rose. No dream of his idle fancy, but a fact! Then last—stirring him even as he tried intelligently to clarify and arrange this magic, this mystery—came the unbelievable and momentous and dazzling fact that she loved him. It was so plain that it seemed unreal. While near her he saw it, yet could not believe his eyes, felt it, but doubted his sensibilities. Still, now away from the distraction of her presence, with Slingerland's eloquent words ringing in his ears, he realized the truth. Love of him had saved the girl's mind and had made her beautiful and wonderful. He had heard of the infinite transforming power of love; here in Allie Lee was its manifestation. Whether or not he deserved such a blessing was not the question. It was his and he felt unutterably grateful and swore he would be worthy.

Neale shirked the resurging thrilling intimation of what was happening within himself. It made him tremble. It seemed great and uplifting and terrible like the spirit that was driving him and his engineer comrades to build the railroad.

Darkness had set in when Neale returned to the cabin, the interior of which was lighted by blazing sticks in the huge stone fireplace.

Slingerland was in the shadow, busy as usual, but laughing at some sally of King's. The cowboy and Allie, however, were in plain sight. Neale needed only one look at King to divine what had come over that young man. Allie appeared perplexed.

"He objects to my calling him Mister King . . . and even Larry," she said.

King suddenly looked sheepish.

"Allie, this cowboy is a bad fellow with guns, ropes, horses . . . and, I suspect, with girls," replied Neale severely.

"Neale, he doesn't look bad," she rejoined. "You're fooling me. . . . He wants me to call him Reddy!"

"Ahuh," grunted Neale. He had a grim laugh on himself, for again he had felt a pang of jealousy. He knew what to expect from King or any other young man who ever had the wonderful good luck to get near Allie Lee. "All right, call him Reddy. I guess I can allow my future wife so much familiarity with my pard."

This confused Allie out of her sweet gravity and she blushed.

"Shore you're mighty kind," drawled King, recovering. "More'n I reckoned on, from a fellar who's shore lost his haid."

"I've lost more than that," retorted Neale, "and I'm afraid a certain wild young cowboy I know has lost as much."

"Wal, I reckon somethin' aboot this heah place of Slingerland's draws on a fellar," admitted King resignedly.

Allie did not long stay confused by their sallies.

"Neale, tell me. . . ."

"See heah, Allie, if you call me Reddy an' him only Neale . . . why he's a-goin' to pitch into me," interrupted King, with twinkling eyes. "An' he's shore a bad customer when he's riled."

"Only Neale? What does he mean?" inquired Allie.

"Beyond human conjecture," replied Neale, laughing.

"Wal, don't you know his front name?" asked King.

"Neale. I called him that," she replied.

"Haw! Haw! But it ain't thet."

"Allie, my name is Warren," said Neale. "You've forgotten."

"Oh? Well, it's always been Neale . . . and always will be."

King rose and stretched his long arm for the pipe on the rude stone chimney. "Slingerland," he drawled, "these heah young people need to find out who they are. An' I reckon we'd do wal to go out an' smoke an' talk."

The trapper came forth from the shadows, and, as he filled his pipe, his keen bright gaze shifted from the task to his friends.

"It's good to see you an' hyar you," he said. "I was a youngster oncet. I missed . . . but thet's no matter. . . . Live while you may. Red, come with me. I've got a trap to set yit."

Allie flashed a glance at them. "It's not so. You never set traps after dark."

"Wal, child, any excuse is better'n none. Neale wouldn't never git to hyar you say all thet sweet talk as is comin' to him . . . if two old fools hung 'round."

"Slingerland, I've throwed a gun fer less'n thet," drawled King. "Aboot the fool part I ain't shore, but I was twenty-five yesterday . . . an' I'm sixteen today."

They lit their pipes with red embers scraped from the fire and, with wise nods at Neale and Allie, passed out into the dark.

Allie's eyes were on Neale, with shy eloquent intent, and directly the others had departed she changed her seat to one close to Neale, and nestled against his shoulder, her face to the fire.

"They thought we wanted to make love, didn't they?" she said dreamily.

"I guess they did," replied Neale. He was intensely fascinated. Did she want him to make love to her? A look at her face was enough to rebuke him for the thought. The shadows from the flickering fire played over her.

"Tell me all about yourself," she said. "Then about your work."

Neale told all that he thought would interest her about his youth in the East with a widowed mother, and the home that was broken up after she died, and his working his way through a course at civil engineering.

"I was twenty when I first read about this U.P. railroad project," he went on. "That was more than three years ago. It decided me on my career. I determined to be an engineer and be in the building of the road. No one had any faith in the railroad. I used to be laughed at. But I stuck. And . . . well, I had to steal some rides to get as far west as Omaha.

"That was more than a year ago. I stayed there . . . waiting. Nothing was sure, except that the town grew like a mushroom. It filled with soldiers . . . and the worst crowd I ever saw. You can bet I was shaky when I finally got an audience with General Lodge and his staff. They had an office in a big storehouse. The place was full of men . . . soldiers . . . tramps. It struck me right off what a grim and discouraged bunch those engineers looked. I didn't understand then, but I do now. . . . Well, I asked for a job. Nobody appeared to hear me. It was hard to make yourself heard. I tried again . . . louder. An old engineer, who I know now . . . Henney . . . waved me aside. Just as if a job was unheard of."

Neale quickened and warmed as he progressed, aware now of a little hand tight on his, of an interest that would have made any story-telling a pleasure.

"Well, I felt sick. Then mad. When I get mad, I do things. I yelled at that bunch . . . 'Here, you men. I've walked and stole rides to get here. I'm no surveyor. You're going to build a railroad. I want a job and I'm going to get it.'

"My voice quieted the hubbub. The old engineer Henney looked queerly at me.

" 'Young man, there's not going to be any railroad.'

"Then I blurted out that there *was* going to be a railroad. Someone spoke up . . . 'Who said that? Fetch him here.' Pretty soon I was looking at Major-General Lodge. He was just from the war and he looked it . . . stern and dark, with hard lines and keen eyes. He glanced me over.

" 'There *is* going to be a railroad?' he questioned sharply.

" 'Of course there is,' I replied. I felt foolish, disappointed.

" 'You're right,' he said, and I'll never forget his eyes. 'I can use a few more young fellows like you.' And that's how I got on the staff.

"Well, we ran a quick survey west to the badlands . . . for it was out here that we must find success or failure. And, Allie, it's all been like . . . like an adventure. The troops and horses and camps and trails . . . the Indian country with its threats from out of the air, it seemed . . . the wild places out here, deer, buffalo, panthers, trappers like Slingerland, scouts, and desperadoes . . . all began to get such a hold on me that I was wild. That might have been bad for me but for my work. I did well. Allie, I ran lines for the U.P. that no other engineer could run!"

Neale paused, as much from the squeeze Allie suddenly gave him as for an instant's rest.

"I mean I had the nerve to tackle cliffs and dangerous slopes," he went on. Then he told how Larry Red King had saved his life, and that recollection brought back his service to the cowboy, and then naturally followed the two dominating incidents of the summer.

Allie lifted a blanched face and darkening eyes. "Neale! You were in danger!"

"Oh, not much, I guess. But Red thought so."

"He saved you again! I . . . I'll never forget that."

"Anyway, we're square, for he'd have got shot sure the day the Indian sneaked up on him." Allie shuddered here and shrank back to Neale, and he hastily resumed his story: "We're great pards now, Red and me. He doesn't say much, but his acts tell. He will not let me alone. He follows me everywhere. It's a joke among the men. Well, Allie, it seems unbelievable that we have crossed the mountains and the desert . . . grade ninety feet to the mile. The railroad can . . . and will be built. I wish I could tell you how tremendously all this has worked upon me . . . upon all the engineers. But somehow I can't. It chokes me. The idea is big. But the work . . . what shall I call that? Allie, if you can, imagine some spirit seizing hold of you and making you see difficulties as joys . . . impossible tasks as only things to strike fire from genius, perils of death as merely incidents of daring adventure to treasure in memory. The idea of the U.P. has got me. I believe in it. I shall see it accomplished. . . . I'll live it all."

Allie moved her head on his shoulder, and, looking up at him with eyes that made him ashamed of his egotism, she said: "Then, when it's done, you'll be chief of engineers?" She had remembered his very words.

"Allie, I hope so," he replied, thrilling at her faith. "I'll work . . . I'll get some big position."

Next day ushered in for Neale a well-earned rest that was a delight to spend any way he chose. The fall had always been Neale's favorite season. Here as elsewhere the aspect of it was flaming and golden, but different from what he had known. Dreaming silence of autumn here held the wildness and loneliness of the Black Hills. The sage showed gray and purple, the ridges yellow and gold, the valleys green and amber and red. No dust, no heat, no wind—a clear blue cloudless sky—sweet odors in the still air—it was a beautiful time.

Days passed and nights passed, as if on wings. Every waking hour drew him closer to this incomparable girl who had arisen upon his horizon like a star. He knew that hour was imminent when he must read his heart. He fought it off; he played with his bliss. Allie was now his shadow instead of the faithful King, although he was often with them, adapting himself to the changed condition, too big and splendid to be envious or jealous. They fished down the brook, and always at that never to be forgotten ford he would cross first and turn to see her follow. She could never understand why Neale would delight in carrying her across at other points, yet made her ford this one herself.

"It's such a bother to take off moccasins and leggings," she would say.

They rode horseback up and down the trails that Slingerland assured them were safe. And it was the cowboy who lent his horse and taught her a flying mount and said she would make a rider.

In the afternoon they would climb the high ridge and on the summit sit in the long whitening grass and gaze out over the dim and purple vastness of the plains. In the twilight they walked under the pines. When night set in and the air grew cold, they would watch the ruddy fire on the hearth and see pictures of the future there and feel a warmth on hand and cheek that was not all from the cheerful blaze.

Strange to Neale was it to realize one day how his attachment for King had changed to love. All Neale's spiritual being was undergoing a great and vital change, but this was not the reason he loved King. It was because of Allie. The cowboy was a Texan and he had inherited the Southerner's fine and chivalrous regard for women. Neale never knew whether King had ever had a sister or a sweetheart or a girl friend. But at sight King had become Allie's arm; not a brother or friend or a lover— something bigger and higher. The man expanded under her smiles, her teasing, her playfulness, her affection. Neale had no pang in divining the unconscious love King bore Allie. The cowboy grew. Drifter, gun-thrower, man-killer, whatever he had been, the light of this girl's beautiful eyes, her voice, her touch had worked the last marvel in man—forgetfulness of self. And so Neale loved him.

It made Neale quake inwardly to think of the havoc being wrought—perhaps already wrought in himself. It made him thoughtful of many things. There was much in life utterly new to him. He had listened to a moan in his keen ear—he had felt a call of something helpless—he had found a gleam of chestnut hair—he had stirred two other men to help him befriend a poor broken-hearted half-crazed orphan girl—and, lo, the world had changed, his friends had grown happier in their unloved lives, a strange strength had come to him, and sweetest, most wonderful of all, in the place of the helpless and miserable waif appeared a woman, lovely of face and form, with only a ghost of sadness haunting her eyes, a woman adorable and bright, with the magic of love on her lips.

October came. In the early morning and late afternoon a keen cold breath hung in the air. Slingerland talked of a good prospect for fur. He chopped great stores of wood. King climbed the hills with his rifle. Neale walked the trails hand in hand with Allie.

He had never sought to induce her to speak of her past, although at times the evidence of refinement and education and mystery around her made strong appeal to him. She could tell her story whenever she liked or never—it did not greatly matter.

Then, one day, quite naturally, but with a shame she did not try to conceal, she told him part of the story her mother had told her that dark night when the Sioux were creeping upon the caravan.

Neale was astounded, agitated, intensely concerned.

"Allie! Your father lives!" he exclaimed.

"Yes."

"Then I must find him . . . take you to him!"

"Do what you think best," she replied sadly. "But I never saw him. I've no love for him. And he never knew I was born."

"Is it possible? How strange. . . . If any man could see you now. . . . Allie, do you resemble your mother?"

"Yes, we were alike."

"Where is your father?" Neale went on curiously.

"How should I know? It was in New Orleans Mother ran off

100

from him. I . . . I never blamed her . . . since she said what she said. . . . Do you? Will this . . . make any difference to you?"

"My God, no! But I'm so . . . so thunderstruck. . . . This man . . . this Durade . . . tell me more of him."

"He was a Spaniard of high degree. . . . An adventurer . . . a gambler. He was mad to gamble. He forced my mother to use her beauty to lure men to his gambling . . . hell . . . ! Oh, it's terrible to remember. . . . She said he meant to use me for that purpose. That's why she left him. But in a way he was good to me. I can see so many things now to prove he was wicked. . . . And Mother said he would follow her . . . track her to the end of the world."

"Allie! If he should find you someday!" exclaimed Neale hoarsely.

She put her arms up around his neck. And that, following a terrible pang of dread in Neale's breast, was too much for him. The tide burst. Love had long claimed him, but its utterance had been withheld. He had been happy in her happiness. He had trained himself to spare her.

"But someday . . . I'll be . . . your wife," she whispered.

"Soon? Soon?" he returned, trembling.

The scarlet fired her temples, her brow, darkening the skin under her bright hair.

"That's for you to say."

She held up her lips, tremulous and sweet.

Neale realized the moment had come. There had never been but the one kiss between them—that of the meeting upon his return in September. If there were to be another now—nay— when that other happened it must be followed by hundreds, thousands, millions of kisses, it seemed to him, in his utter surrender, and he was afraid.

"Allie, I love you."

"I love you," she replied quickly.

"This news you've told . . . this man Durade," he went on hoarsely. "I'm suddenly alive . . . stinging . . . wild! If I lost you."

"Dear, you will never lose me . . . never in this world or any other," she replied tenderly.

"My work, my hope, my life . . . all get spirit now from you. . . . Allie! You're sweet. . . . Oh, so sweet. . . . You're glorious!" he rang out passionately.

Surprise momentarily checked the rising response of her feeling. "Neale! You've never before said . . . such . . . such things . . . and the way you look!"

"How do I look?" he queried, seeing the joyousness of her surprise.

Then she laughed and that was new to him—a sound low, unutterably rich and full, sweet-toned like a bell, and all of youth. "Oh, you look like Durade when he was gambling away his soul . . . you should see him."

"Well, how's that?"

"So white . . . so terrible . . . so piercing."

Neale drew her closer, slipped her arms farther up around his neck. "I'm gambling my soul away now," he said. "If I kiss you, I lose it . . . and I must."

"Must what?" she whispered, with all a woman's charm.

"I must kiss you."

"Then hurry."

So their lips met.

In the sweetness of that embrace, in the simplicity and answering passion of her kiss, in the overwhelming sense of her gift of herself, heart and soul, he found a strength, a restraint, a nobler fire that gave him peace.

Allie was to amaze Neale again before the sun set on that memorable day.

"I forgot to tell you about the gold!" she exclaimed, her voice fading.

"Gold!" Neale ejaculated.

"Yes. He buried it . . . there . . . under the biggest of the three trees together. Near a rock. . . . Oh, I can see him now."

"Him? Who? Allie, what's this wild talk?"

She pressed his hand to enjoin silence. "Listen. Horn had gold. How much I don't know. But it must have been a great deal. He owned the caravan with which we left California. Horn grew to like me. But he hated all the rest. . . . That night we ended the awful ride! The wagons stalled! The grayness of dawn . . . in the stillness. . . . Oh, I feel them now! That terrible Indian yell rang out. All my life I'll hear it! Then Horn dug a hole. He buried his gold. . . . And he said whoever escaped could have it. He had no hope."

"Allie, you're a mine of surprises. Buried gold! What next?"

"Neale, I wonder . . . did the Sioux find that gold?" she asked.

"It's not likely. There certainly isn't any hole left open around that place. I saw every inch of ground under those trees. . . . Allie, I'll go there tomorrow . . . hunt for it."

"Let me go," she implored. "Ah! I forgot! No . . . no! There must be my mother's grave."

"Yes, it's there. I saw. I will mark it. . . . Allie, how glad I am that you can speak of her . . . of her past . . . her grave there without weakening. You are brave. But forget. . . . Allie, if I find that gold, it'll be yours."

"No. Yours."

"But I was not one of that caravan. He did not give it to any outsider. You escaped. Therefore it will belong to you."

"Dearest, I am yours."


Next day, without acquainting Slingerland or King with his purpose, Neale rode down the valley trail. He expected the trail to cross the old St. Vrain and Laramie Trail, but if it did cross, he could not find the place. It was easy to lose bearings in these hills. Neale had to abandon the hunt for that day, and, turning back with some annoyance at his failure, he decided it would be best to take King and Slingerland into his confidence.

Allie was waiting for him at the brook ford. "Oh, it was gone!" she cried.

"Allie, I couldn't find the place. Come, ride back and let me walk beside you. . . . We'll have fun telling Red and Slingerland."

"Neale, let me tell them," she begged.

"Go ahead. Make it a strong story. Red always had leanings toward gold strikes."

And that night, after supper, when the log fire had begun to blaze and all were comfortable before it, Allie glanced demurely at King and said: "Reddy, if you had known that I was heiress to great wealth would you have proposed to me?"

Slingerland roared. King seemed utterly stricken.

"Wealth," he echoed feebly.

"Yes. Gold! Lots of gold!"

Slingerland's merry face suddenly grew curious and earnest.

King struggled with his discomfiture. "I reckon I'd . . . done that anyhow . . . without knowin' you was rich . . . if it hadn't been fer this heah U.P. surveyor fellar!"

And then the joke was on Allie as her blushes proved. Neale came to her rescue and told the story of Horn's buried gold, and of his own search that day for the place.

"Shore I'll find it," declared King. "We'll go tomorrow. . . ."

Slingerland stroked his beard thoughtfully. "If there's gold been buried thar, it's sure an' certain thar yet," he said. "But I'm afraid we won't get thar tomorrow."

"Why not? Surely you or Red can find the place?"

"Listen."

Neale listened while he was watching Allie's parted lips and speaking eyes. A low whining wind swept through the trees and over the roof of the cabin.

"Thet wind says snow," declared the trapper.

Neale went outside. The wind struck him, cold and keen, with a sharper edge to it. The stars showed, pale and dim, through hazy atmosphere. Assuredly there was a storm brewing. Neale returned to the fire, shivering and holding his palms to the heat.

"Cold, you bet, with the wind rising," he said. "But, Slingerland, suppose it does snow. Can't we go anyhow?"

"It ain't likely. You see it snows up hyar. Mebbe we'll be snowed in fer a spell. An' thet valley is open down thar. In deep snow what could we find? We'll wait an' see."

On the morrow a storm raged and all was dim through a ghostly whirling pall. The season of drifting snow had come and Neale's winter work had begun.

Five miles by short cut over the ridges curved the long survey over which Neale must keep watch, and the going and coming were Neale's hardest toil. It was laborious to trudge up and down in soft snow.

That first snow of winter, however, did not last long, except in the sheltered places. Fortunately for Neale almost all of his section of the survey ran over open ground. But this fact augured seriously for his task when the dry and powdery snow of midwinter began to fall and sweep before the wind and drift over the lee side of the ridge.

During the first week of tramping he thoroughly learned the lay of the land, the topography of his particular stretch of Sherman Pass. And one day, taking an early start from camp, he set forth to make his first call upon his nearest associate in this work, the engineer, Service. Once high up on the pass he found the snow had not all melted, and still higher it lay white and unbroken as far as he could see. The air was keener up there. Neale gathered that Service would have a colder job than his own, if it was not so long and hard.

He found Service at home in his dug-out, warm and comfortable, and in excellent spirits. They compared notes and, even in this early work, decided it would be a wise plan for the engineering staff to study the problem of drifting snow.

Neale enjoyed a meal with Service, and then early in the afternoon he started back on his long tramp homeward. He gathered from his visit that Service did not mind the loneliness but he did suffer from the cold more than he had expected. Service was not an active full-blooded man, and Neale had some misgivings. Judging from the trapper's remarks, winter high up in the Black Hills was something to dread.

November brought the real storms—the gray banks of rolling clouds—the rain and sleet and snow and ice—and the wind. Neale concluded he had never before faced a real wind, and, when one day on a ridge top he was blown off his feet, he was sure of it. Some days he could not go out at all. Other days it was not imperative, for it was only during and after snowstorms that he could make observations. He learned to travel on snowshoes, and ten miles of such traveling up and down the steep slopes was the most killing hard toil he had ever attempted. After such trips he would reach the cabin utterly fagged out, too tired to eat, too weary to talk, almost too dead to hear the solicitations of his friends, or to appreciate Allie's tender anxious care. If he had not been strong and robust and in good training to begin with, he would have failed under the burden. Gradually he became used to the strenuous toil and grew hardened, tough, and enduring.

Although Neale hated the cold and the wind, there were moments when an exceedingly keen exhilaration uplifted him.

These experiences visited him while on the heights looking far over the snowy ridges to the white monotonous plain or up toward the shining peaks. All seemed barren and cold. The old wildness did not strike him up there. He never saw a living creature or a track upon those slopes. When the sun shone, all was so dazzlingly, glaringly white that his eyes were struck by blindness.

Upon one of the milder days, which were getting rarer in mid-December, Neale again visited his comrade on the summit. He found Service in bad shape. In falling down a slippery ledge he had injured or broken his lame leg. Neale with great concern tried to ascertain the nature and extent of the harm done, but he was unable to do so. Service was practically helpless, but not suffering any great pain. The two of them decided at length that he had not broken any bones, but that it was necessary to move him to where he could be waited upon and treated, or else have someone with him there for that purpose.

Neale deliberated a moment.

"I'll tell you what," he said finally. "You can be moved down to Slingerland's cabin without pain to you. I'll get Slingerland and his sled. You'll be more comfortable there. It'll be better all around."

So that was decided upon. And Neale, after doing all he could for Service, and assuring him that he would return in less than twenty-four hours, turned his steps for the valley.

The sunset that night struck him as singularly dull, pale, menacing. He understood its meaning later when Slingerland said they were in for another storm. Before dark the wind began to moan through the trees like lost spirits. The trapper shook his shaggy head ominously. "Reckon that sounds bad to me," he said. And from moan it rose to wail and from wail to roar.

That alarmed Neale. He went outside and Slingerland followed. Snow was sweeping down—light, dry, powdery. The wind was piercingly cold. Slingerland yelled something, but Neale could not distinguish what. When they got back inside, the trapper said: "Blizzard."

Neale grew distressed.

"Wal, no use to worry about Service," argued the trapper. "If it is a blizzard, we can't git up thar, thet's all. Mebbe this'll not be so bad. But I ain't bettin' on thet."

Even Allie could not cheer Neale that night. Long after she and the others had retired, he kept up the fire and listened to the roar of wind. When the fire died down a little, the cabin grew uncomfortably cold, and this fact attested to a continually dropping temperature. But he hoped against hope, and finally sought his blankets.

Morning came, but the cabin was almost as dark as by night. A blinding, swirling snowstorm obscured the sun.

A blizzard raged for forty-eight hours. When the snow finally ceased falling, the cold increased until Neale guessed the temperature was forty degrees below zero. The trapper claimed sixty. It was necessary to stay indoors till the weather moderated.

On the fifth morning Slingerland was persuaded to attempt the trip up to aid Service. King wanted to accompany them, but Slingerland said he had better stay with Allie. So, muffled up, the two men set out on snowshoes, dragging a sled. A crust had frozen on the snow, otherwise traveling would have been impossible. Once up on the slope the northwest wind hit them squarely in the face. Heavily clad as he was, Neale thought the very marrow in his bones would freeze. That wind blew through him. There were places where it took both men to hold the sled to keep it from blowing away. They were blown back one step for every two steps they made. On the exposed heights they could not walk upright. At last after hours of desperate effort they got over the ridge to a sheltered side along which they labored up to Service's dug-out.

Up there the snow had blown away in places leaving bare spots, bleak, icy, barren, stark. No smoke appeared to rise above the dug-out. The rude habitation looked as if no man had been there that winter. Neale glanced in swift dismay at Slingerland.

"Son, look fer the wust," he said. "An' we haven't got time to waste."

They pushed open the canvas framework of a door and, stooping low, passed inside. Neale's glance saw first the fireplace, where no fire had burned for days. Snow had sifted in the dug-out and lay in little drifts everywhere. The blankets on the bunk covered Service, hiding his face. Both men knew before they uncovered him what his fate had been.

"Frozen to death!" gasped Neale.

Service lay white, rigid, like stone, with no sign of suffering upon his face.

"He jest went to sleep . . . an' never woke up," declared Slingerland.

"Thank God for that!" exclaimed Neale. "Oh, why did I not stay with him!"

"Too late, son. An' many a good man will go to his death before thet damn' railroad is done."

Neale searched for Service's notes and letters and valuables that could be turned over to the engineering staff.

Slingerland found a pick and shovel, which Neale remembered to have used in building the dug-out, and with these the two men toiled at the frozen sand and gravel to open up a grave. It was like digging in stone. At length they succeeded. Then, rolling Service in the blankets and tarpaulin, they lowered him into the cold ground, and hurriedly filled up his grave.

It was a grim gruesome task. Another nameless grave! Neale had already seen nine graves. This one was up the slope not a hundred feet from the line of the survey.

"Slingerland!" exclaimed Neale. "The railroad will run along there. Trains will pass this spot. In years to come travelers will look out of the train windows along here. Boys riding away to seek their fortunes. Bride and groom on their honeymoon. Thousands of people going . . . coming . . . busy, happy at their own affairs, full of their own lives, will go by poor Service's grave and never know it's there."

"Wal, son, if people must hev railroads, they must kill men to build them," replied the trapper.

Neale conceived the idea that Slingerland did not welcome the coming of the steel rails. The thought shocked him. But then, he reflected, a trapper would not profit by the advance of civilization.

With the wind at their backs Neale and Slingerland were practically blown home. They made it up between them to keep knowledge of the tragedy from Allie. So ended the coldest and hardest and grimmest day Neale had ever known.

The winter passed, the snows melted, the winds quieted, and spring came.

Long since, Neale had decided to leave Allie with Slingerland that summer. She would be happy there and wished to stay until Neale could take her with him. That seemed out of the question for the present. A construction camp full of troopers and laborers was no place for Allie. Neale dreaded the idea of taking her to Omaha. Always in his mind were haunting fears of this Spaniard Durade who had ruined Allie's mother, and of the father whom Allie had never seen. Neale intuitively felt that these men were to crop up somewhere in his life, and, before they did appear, he wanted to marry Allie. She was little more than sixteen years old.

Neale's plans for the summer could not be wholly known until he had reported to the general staff, which might be at

Fort Fetterman or North Platte, or all the way back in Omaha. But it was probable that he would be set to work with the advancing troops and trains and laborers. Engineers had to accompany both the grading gangs and the rail gangs.

Neale, in his talks with King and Slingerland, had dwelt long and conjecturingly upon what life was going to be in the construction camps. To King what might happen was of little moment. He lived in the present. But Neale was different. He had to be anticipating events; he lived in the future, his mind centered on future work, achievement, and what he might go through in attaining his end. Slingerland was his appreciative listener.

"Wal," he would say, shaking his grizzled head, "I reckon I don't believe all your General Lodge says is goin' to happen."

"But, man, can't you imagine what it will be?" protested Neale. "Take thousands of soldiers . . . the riff-raff of the war . . . and thousands of laborers of all classes, niggers, greasers, pig-tailed chinks . . . and Irish. Take thousands of men who want to earn an honest dollar in trade, following the line. And thousands who want dollars, but not honestly. All the gamblers, outlaws, robbers, murderers, criminals, adventurers in the States, and perhaps many from abroad will be on the trail. Think, man, of the money . . . the gold! Millions spilled out in these wilds! And last and worst . . . the bad women!"

Slingerland showed his amaze. This feature was a new one in his conception of the construction work.

"Wal, I reckon thet's all guff, too," he said. "A lot of bad women out in these wilds ain't to be feared. Supposin' thar was a lot of them . . . which ain't likely . . . how'd they ever git out to the camps?"

"Slingerland, the trains . . . the trains will follow the laying of the rails."

"Oho! An' you mean thar'll be towns grow up overnight . . .

all full of bad people who ain't workin' on the railroad . . . jest followin' the gold?"

"Exactly. Now, listen. Remember all these mixed gangs . . . the gold . . . and the bad women . . . out here in the wild country . . . no law . . . no restraint . . . no fear, except of death . . . drinking hells . . . gambling hells . . . dancing hells! What's going to happen?"

The trapper meditated a while, stroking his beard, and then he said: "Wal, thar ain't enough gold to build thet railroad . . . an', if thar was, it couldn't never be done."

"Ah!" cried Neale, raising his head sharply. "It's a matter of gold first. Streams of gold . . . and then . . . *can* it be done?"

One day, as the time for Neale's departure grew closer, Slingerland's quiet and peaceful valley was violated by a visit from four rough-looking men.

They rode in without packs. It was significant to Neale that King swore at sight of them, and then in his cool easy way sauntered between them and the cabin door, where Allie stood with astonishment fixed in her beautiful face. The Texan always packed his heavy gun and certainly no Western men would mistake his quality. These visitors were civil enough, asked for a little tobacco, and showed no sign of evil intention.

"Way off the beaten track up hyar," said one.

"Yes. I'm a trapper," replied Slingerland. "Whar do you hail from?"

"Ogden. We're packin' east."

"Much travel on the trail?"

"Right smart fer wild country. An' all goin' east. We haven't met an outfit headin' west. Hev you heerd any talk of a railroad buildin' out of Omaha?"

Here King put a word in. "Shore. We've had soldiers campin' around aboot all heah."

"Soldiers!" ejaculated one of the gang.

"Shore, the road's bein' built by soldiers."

The men made no further comment and turned away without any good byes.

Slingerland called out for them to have an eye open for Indians on the warpath. "Wal, I don't like the looks of them fellars," he declared.

Neale likewise took unfavorable view of the visit, but King scorned the idea of there being any danger in a gang like that.

"Shore, they'd be afraid of a man," he declared.

"Red, can you look at men and tell whether or not there's danger in them?" inquired Neale.

"I shore can. One man could bluff thet outfit. . . . But I reckon I'd hate to have them find Allie aboot heah alone."

"I can take care of myself," spoke up Allie spiritedly.

Neale and Slingerland, for all their respect for the cowboy's judgment, regarded the advent of these visitors as a forerunner of an evil time for lonely trappers.

"I'll hev to move back deeper in the mountains, away from the railroad," said Slingerland.

This incident also put a different light upon the intention Neale had of hunting for the buried gold. Just now he certainly did not want to risk being seen digging up the gold or packing it away, and Slingerland was just as loath to have it concealed in or near the cabin.

"Wal, seein' we're not sure it's really thar, let's wait till you come back in summer or fall," he suggested. "If it's thar, it'll stay thar."

All too soon the dawn came for Neale's departure with King. Allie was braver than he. At the last he was white and shaken. She kissed King.

"Reddy, you'll take care of yourself . . . and him," she said.

"Allie, I shore will. Good bye." And King rode down the trail

113

in the dim gray dawn.

"Watch sharp for Indians," she breathed, and her face whitened momentarily. Then the color returned. Her eyes were full of sweet soft light.

"Allie, I can't go," said Neale hoarsely. The clasp of her arms unnerved him.

"You must. It's your work. Remember the big job. . . . Dearest . . . dearest! Hurry . . . and . . . go!"

Neale could no longer see her face clearly. He did not know what he was saying. "You'll . . . always . . . love me?" he implored.

"Do you need to ask? All my life. I promise."

"Kiss me then," he whispered hoarsely, blindly leaning down. "It's hell . . . to leave you. . . . Wonderful girl . . . treasure . . . precious. Allie! Kiss me . . . enough. . . . I. . . ."

She held him with strong and passionate clasp and kissed him again and again.

"Good bye." Her last word was low, choked, poignant—and had in it a mournful reminder of her old tragic woe.

Then he was alone. Mounting clumsily, with blurred eyes, he rode into the winding trail.

# CHAPTER TEN

Neale and King traveled light, without pack animals, and at sunrise reached the main trail. It bore evidence of considerable use and was no longer a trail but a high road. Fresh tracks of horses and oxen, wagon-wheel ruts, dead campfires, and scattered brush that had been used for windbreaks—all attested to the impetus of that movement that was to become extraordinary.

All this was Indian country. Neale and his companion had no idea whether or not the Sioux had left their winter quarters for the warpath. But it was a vast region, and the Indians could not be everywhere. Neale and King took chances, as had all these travelers, although perhaps the risk was not so great because they rode fleet horses. Their watchfulness did not discover to them any signs of Indians, and it appeared as if they were alone in a wilderness.

They covered sixty miles from early dawn to dusk, with a short rest at noon, and reached Fort Fetterman safely without incident or accident. Troops were there, but none of the U.P. engineering staff. Neale did not meet any soldiers with whom he was acquainted. Orders were there for him, however, to report at North Platte as soon as it was possible to reach there. Troops were moving soon, Neale learned, and the long overland journey could be made in comparative safety.

Here Neale received the tidings that forty miles of railroad had been built during the last summer and trains had been run that distance west from Omaha. His heart swelled. Not for many

115

a week had he heard anything favorable to the great U.P. project, and here was news of rails laid, trains run. Already this spring the graders were breaking ground far ahead of the rail layers. Report and rumor there at the fort had it that lively times had attended the construction work. But the one absorbing topic was the Sioux Indians who were expected to swarm out of the hills that summer and give the troops hot work.

In due time Neale and King arrived at North Platte, which was little more than a camp. The construction gangs were not expected to reach there until late in the fall. Baxter was at North Platte, with a lame surveyor, and no other helpers, and he hailed Neale and King with open arms. A summer's work in the hot monotonous plains stared Neale in the face, and all he could do was to resign himself to the inevitable. He worked, as always, with that ability and energy that had made him invaluable to his superiors. Here, however, the labor was a hot grind, without any thrills. Neale filled the long glaring days with duty, and seldom let his mind wander. In leisure hours, however, he dreamed of Allie and the future. There was no trouble passing time that way. Also, he watched for arrivals from the west, who he questioned about Indians in the Black Hills, and from troops or travelers coming from the east, he heard all the news of the advancing railroad construction. It was absorbing, interesting, yet Neale could credit so few of the tales. Nowhere on earth had things happened as rumor brought them.

The summer and early fall passed.

Neale was ordered to Omaha. The news stunned him. He had built all his hopes on another winter out in the Black Hills, and this disappointment was crushing. It made him ill for a day. He almost threw up his work. It did not seem possible at all to live that interminable stretch without seeing Allie Lee. The nature of his commission, however, brought once again to mind the opportunity that knocked at his door. Neale had run all the difficult surveys for bridges in the Black Hills and now he was needed in the office of the staff, where plans and drawings were being made. Again he bowed to the inevitable. But he determined to demand in the spring that he be sent ahead to the foremost of the construction work.

Another disappointment seemed in order. King refused to go any farther back east. Neale was also exceedingly surprised.

"Do you throw up your job?" he asked.

"Shore not. I can work heah," replied King.

"There won't be any outside work on these bleak plains in winter."

"Wal, I reckon I'll loaf then," he drawled.

Neale could not change him. King vowed he would take his old place with Neale next spring, if it would be open to him.

"But why? Red, I can't figure you," protested Neale.

"Pard, I reckon I'm far enough back east right heah," said King significantly.

A light dawned upon Neale. "Red! You've done something bad!" exclaimed Neale, in genuine dismay.

"Wal, I don't know jest how bad it was . . . but it shore was hell," replied King, with a grin.

"Red, you aren't afraid," asserted Neale positively.

The cowboy flushed and looked insulted. "If anyone but you said thet to me, he'd hev to eat it."

"I beg your pardon, old man. But I am surprised. It docsn't seem like you. . . . And then . . . Lord, I'll miss you."

"No more'n I'll miss you, pard," replied King.

Suddenly Neale had a happy thought. "Red, you go back to Slingerland's and help take care of Allie. I'd feel she was safer."

"Wal, she might be safer, but I wouldn't be," declared the cowboy bluntly.

"You red-head! What do you mean?" demanded Neale.

"I mean this heah. If I stayed around another winter near Allie Lee . . . with her alone, fer thet trapper never set up before thet fire . . . I'd . . . why, Neale, I'll ambush you like an Injun when you come back."

"You wouldn't," rejoined Neale. He wanted to laugh, but had no mirth. King did not mean that, but neither did he mean to be funny.

"I'll be hangin' round heah waitin' fer you. It's only a few months. Go on to your work, pard. You'll be a big man on the road someday."

Neale left North Platte with a wagon train.

After a long slow journey the point was reached where the graders had left off work for that year. Here had been a huge construction camp, and the bare and squalid place looked as if it once had been a town of crudest make, suddenly wrecked by a cyclone and burned by prairie fire. Fifty miles farther on—ten more long tedious and unendurable days—and Neale heard the whistle of a locomotive. It came from far off. But it was a whistle. He yelled and the men journeying with him joined in.

Smoke showed on the horizon and a wide low uneven line of shacks and tents.

Neale was all eyes when he rode into that construction camp. The place was a bedlam. A motley horde of men appeared to be doing everything under the sun but work, and most of them seemed particularly eager to board a long train of boxcars and little old passenger coaches. Neale made a dive for the train, and his sojourn in that camp was a short and exciting one of ten minutes.

He felt utterly proud. He had helped swing the line along which the train was now *rattling* and *creaking* and swaying. All that swiftly passed under his keen eyes was recorded in his memory—the uncouth crowd of laborers, the hardest lot he had ever seen; the talk, noise, smoke; the rickety old *clattering* coaches; the wayside dumps and heaps and wreckage. But they all seemed parts of a beautiful romance to him. Neale saw through the eyes of ambition and dreams.

And not for a moment of another endless ride, with interminable stops, did he weary of the two hundred and sixty miles of rails laid that year, and the forty miles of the preceding year. Then Omaha, a beehive—the making of a Western metropolis!

Neale plunged into the thickest of the bewildering turmoil of plans, tasks, schemes, land grants, politics, charters, inducements, liens and loans, government and Army and state and national interests, grafts and deals and bosses, all that mass of selfish and unselfish motives, all that cunning and noble aim, all the congested assembly of humans that went to make up the building of the Union Pacific.

Neale was a dreamer, like the few men whose minds had first given birth to the wonderful idea of a railroad from East to West. Neale found himself confronted by a singularly disturbing fact. However grand this project was, the political and mercenary end of it was not going to be beautiful to him. Why could not all men be right-minded about a noble cause and work for the development of the West and the future generations? It was a melancholy thing to learn that men of sincere and unselfish purpose had spent their all trying to raise the money to build the Union Pacific, just as it was a satisfaction to learn that many capitalists with greedy claws had ruined themselves in like effort.

The President of the United States and Congress had their troubles at the close of the war, and the government could do but little with their land grants and loans to raise the money. But they offered a great bonus to the men who would build the road.

The first construction company subscribed over a million

119

and a half dollars and paid in one quarter of that. The money went so swiftly that it opened the company's eyes to the insatiable gulf beneath that enterprise, and they quit.

Thereupon what was called the Crédit Mobilier was inaugurated, and it became both famous and infamous. It was a type of the construction company by which it was the custom to build railroads at that time. The directors, believing that whatever money would be made out of the Union Pacific would be made during the construction, organized a clever system for just this purpose, an extravagant sum was to be paid to the Crédit Mobilier for the construction work, thus securing for stockholders of the Union Pacific, who now controlled the Crédit Mobilier, the bonds loaned by the U.S. government.

The operations of the Crédit Mobilier finally gave rise to one of the most serious political scandals in the history of the U.S. Congress. The cost of all material was high and rose with leaps and bounds until it was prodigious. Omaha had no railroad entering it, and so all the supplies, materials, engines, cars, machinery, and laborers had to be transported from St. Louis up the swift Missouri on boats. This in itself was a work calling for the limit of practical management and energy. Out in the prairie land, for hundreds of miles, were to be found no trees, no wood, scarcely any brush. That prairie land was beautiful ground for buffalo, but it was the most barren desert for the exigencies of railroad men. Moreover, not only did wood and fuel and railroad ties have to be brought from afar, but all stone for bridges and abutments. Then thousands of men had to be employed, and those who hired out for reasonable money soon learned the fact that others were getting more, and, having the company at their mercy, they demanded exorbitant wages.

One of the peculiar features of the construction so far, and one over which Neale grew impotently furious, was the law that when a certain section of so many miles had been laid and equipped as required, the government of the United States would send out expert commissioners, who would go over the line and pass judgment upon the construction and finished work. No two groups of commissioners seemed to agree. Those experts, who had to hold up their bid in the bewildering and labyrinthine magic of men's contrary plans and plots, reported that certain sections had to be done over again.

The fault found with one of these purported to be in the grade, which was too steep, and as Neale had surveyed that section he soon heard of his poor work. He went over his figures and notes with the result that he called on Henney and absolutely and irrevocably swore that the grade was right. Henney swore, too, in a different and more forcible way, agreed with Neale, and advised him to call on the expert commissioners.

Neale did so, and found them, with one ex-captain, open to conviction. The exception was a man named Allison Lee. The name Lee gave Neale a little shock. He was a gray-looking man, with lined face, and that concentrated air Neale learned to associate with those who were high in the affairs of the U.P.

Neale stated that his business was to show that his work had been done right and he had the figures to prove it. Mr. Lee replied that the survey was poor and would have to be done over.

"Are you a surveyor?" queried Neale sharply, with the blood beating in his temples.

"I have some knowledge of civil engineering," replied the commissioner.

"Well, it can't be very much," declared Neale, whose temper was up.

"Young man, be careful what you say," replied the other.

"But Mister . . . Mister Lee . . . listen to me, will you?" burst out Neale. "It's all here in my notes. You've hurried over the line . . . and just slipped up on a foot or so in your observations

121

of that section."

Mr. Lee refused to look at the notes and waved Neale aside.

"It'll hurt my chance for a big job," Neale said stubbornly.

"You probably will lose your job, judging from the way you address your superiors."

That finished Neale. He grew perfectly white. "All this expert commissioner business is rot!" he flung at Lee. "Rot! Lodge knows it. Henney knows it. We all do. And so do you. It's a lot of damn' red tape! Every last man who can pull a stroke with the government runs in here to annoy good efficient engineers who are building the road. It's an outrage. It's more. It's not honest. . . . That section has forty miles in it. Five miles you claim must be resurveyed . . . regraded . . . relaid. Forty-six thousand dollars a mile! That's the secret! Two hundred and thirty thousand dollars for a construction company!"

Neale left the office and, returning to Henney, reported the interview to him word for word. Henney complimented Neale's spirit, but deplored the incident. It could do no good and might do harm. Many of these commissioners were politicians, working in close touch with the directors, and not averse to bleeding the Crédit Mobilier.

All the engineers, including the chief, although he was non-committal, were bitter about this expert commissioner law. If a good roadbed had been surveyed, the engineer knew more about it than anyone else. They were the pioneers of the work. It was exceedingly annoying and exasperating to have a number of men travel leisurely in trains over the line and criticize the labors of engineers who had toiled in heat and cold and wet, with brains and heart in the task. But so it was.

In May, 1866, a wagon train escorted by troops rolled into the growing camp of North Platte, and the first man to alight was Warren Neale, strong, active, eager-eyed as ever, but older, and with face pale from his indoor work and hope long deferred.

The first man to greet him was Larry Red King, in whom time did not make changes.

They met as long-separated brothers.

"Red, how're your horses?" was Neale's query following the greeting.

"Wintered well, but cost me all I had. I'm shore busted," replied King.

"I've plenty of money," said Neale, "and what's mine is yours. Come on, Red. We'll get light packs and hit the trail for the Black Hills."

"Wal, I reckoned so. . . . Neale, it's shore goin' to be risky. The Injuns are on the rampage already. You see how this heah camp has growed. Men ridin' in all since the winter broke. An' them from west tell some hard stories."

"I've got to go," replied Neale, with emotion. "It's nearly a year since I saw Allie. Not a word between us in all that time. . . . Red, I can't stand it longer."

"Shore, I know," replied King hastily. "You ain't reckonin' I wanted to craw fish? I'll go. We'll pack light, hit the trail at night, an' hide up in the daytime."

Neale had arrived in North Platte before noon and before sunset he and King were far out on the slow-rising bulge of plain land toward the west.

Traveling by night, camping by day, they soon left behind the monotonous plains of Nebraska. The Sioux had been active for two summers along the southern trails of Wyoming. The Texan's long training on the ranges stood them in good stead here. His keen eye for tracks and smoke and distant objects, his care in hiding trails and selecting camps, and his skill and judgment in all pertaining to the horses—these made the journey possible. For they saw Indian sign more than once before the Black Hills loomed up in the distance. More than one flickering campfire they avoided by a wide detour.

Slingerland's valley showed all the signs of early summer. The familiar trail, however, bore no tracks of horse or man or beast. A heavy rain had fallen recently, and it would have obliterated tracks.

Neale's suspense sustained the added burden of dread. In the oppressive silence of the valley he read some nameless reason for fear. The trail seemed the same, the brook flowed and murmured as of old, the trees shone soft and green, but there was a difference Neale sensed. He dared not look at King for confirmation of his fears. The valley had not of late been lived in!

Neale rode hard up the trail under the pines. A blackened heap lay where once the cabin had stood! Neale's heart gave a terrible leap, and then seemed to cease beating. He could not breathe or speak or move. His eyes were wide on the black remains of Slingerland's cabin.

"God almighty!" gasped King, and he put out a shaking hand to clutch Neale. "The Injuns! I always feared this . . . spite of Slingerland's talk."

The feel of King's fierce fingers, like hot stinging arrows in his flesh pierced Neale's mind and made him realize his stunned faculties. It seemed to loosen the vise-like hold upon his muscles—to liberate his tongue.

He fell off his horse. "Red! Look . . . look around!"

Allie was gone! The disappointment at not seeing her was crushing and the fear of utter loss was terrible. Neale lay on the ground, blind, sick, full of agony, with his fingers tearing the grass. The evil presentiments that had haunted him for months had not been groundless fancies. Perhaps Allie had called to him again in another hour of calamity, and this time he had not responded. She was gone! That idea struck him cold. It meant the most dreadful of all happenings possible for him. For a while he lay there, prostrate under the shock. He was aware when King came and sat down beside him.

"No sign of anyone," he said huskily. "Not even a track! Thet fire must hev been aboot two weeks ago. Mebbe more, but not much. There's been a big rain an' the ground's all washed clean an' smooth. . . . Not a track."

It was the cowboy's habit to calculate the past movements of people and horses by the nature of the tracks they left.

Then Neale awoke to violence. He sprang up and rushed to the ruins of the cabin, frantically tore and dug around the burnt embers, and did not leave off until he had overhauled the whole pile. There was nothing but ashes and embers. Whereupon he ran to the empty corrals, to the sheds, to the woodpile, to the spring, and all around the space once so habitable. There was nothing to check his fierce energy—nothing to scrutinize. Already the grass was springing up in the trails and the spots that had once been bare.

Neale halted, sweating, hot, wild, before his friend. King avoided his gaze.

"She's gone . . . she's gone!" Neale panted.

"Wal, mebbe Slingerland moved camp and burned this place," suggested King. "He was sore after them four road agents rustled in heah."

"No . . . no. He'd have left the cabin. In case he moved . . . Allie was to write me a note . . . telling me how to find them. I remember . . . we picked out the place to hide the note. . . . Oh, she's gone! She's gone!"

"Wal then, mebbe Slingerland got away . . . an' the cabin was burned after."

"I can't hope that. . . . I tell you . . . it means hell's opened up before me."

"Wal, it's tough, I know, Neale, but mebbe. . . ."

Neale wheeled fiercely upon him. "You're only saying those things! You don't believe them! Tell me what you *do* believe."

"Lord, pard, it couldn't be no wuss," replied King, his lean face working. "I figger only one way. This heah Slingerland has left Allie alone. . . . Then . . . she was made away with an' the cabin burned."

"Indians?"

"Mebbe. But I lean more to the idee of an outfit like thet one what was heah."

Neale groaned in his torture. "Not that, Red . . . not that! The Indians would kill her . . . scalp her . . . or take her captive into their tribe. . . . But a gang of cut-throat ruffians like those. . . . My God, if I *knew* that had happened, it'd kill me."

King swore at his friend. "It can't do us any good to go to pieces. Let's do somethin'."

"What . . . in heaven's name!" cried Neale in despair.

"Wal, we can rustle up every trail in these heah Black Hills. Mebbe we can find Slingerland."

Then began a search—frantic, desperate, and forlorn on the part of Neale—faithful and dogged and keen on the part of King. Neale was like a wild man. He heeded no advice or caution. Only the cowboy's iron arm saved Neale and his horse. It was imperative to find water and grass, and to eat—which things Neale seemed to have forgotten. He seldom slept or rested or ate. They risked meeting the Sioux in every valley and on every ridge. Neale would have welcomed the sight of Indians; he would have rushed into peril in the madness of his grief. Still, there was hope! He lived all the hours utterly hopelessly, but his heart did not give up. Nor did his spirit receive visitation from Allie's.

They coursed far and near, always keeping to the streambeds, for if Slingerland had made another camp, it would be near water. More than one trail led nowhere; more than one horse track roused hopes that were futile. The Black Hills country was surely a lonely and wild one, singularly baffling to the searchers, for in two weeks of wide travel it did not yield up a sign or track of man. Neale and King used up all their scant supply of food, threw away all their outfit except a bag of salt, and went on, living on the meat they shot.

Then one day, unexpectedly, they came upon two trappers by a beaver dam. Neale was overcome by his emotion; he sensed that from these men he would learn something. The first look from them told him that his errand was known.

"Howdy," greeted King. "It shore is good to see you men . . . the first we've seen in an awful hunt through these heah hills."

"Thar ain't any doubt thet you look it, friend," replied one of the trappers.

"We're huntin' fer Slingerland. Do you happen to know him?"

"Knowed Al fer years. He went through hyar a week ago, jest after the big rain, wasn't it, Bill?"

"Wal, to be exact, it was eight days ago," replied the comrade Bill.

"Was . . . he . . . alone?" asked King thickly.

"Sure, an' lookin' sick. He lost his girl not long since, he said, an' it broke him bad."

"Lost her! How?"

"Wal, he was sure it wasn't redskins," rejoined the trapper reflectively. "Slingerland stood in with the Sioux . . . traded with 'em. He. . . ."

"Tell me quick!" hoarsely interrupted Neale. "What happened to Allie Lee?"

"Fellars, my pard heah is hurt deep," said King. "The girl you spoke of was his sweetheart."

"Young man, we only know what Al told us," replied the trapper. "He said the only time he ever left the lass alone . . .

was the time she was taken. Al come home to find the cabin red-hot ashes. Everythin' gone. No sign of the lass. No sign of murder. She was jest carried off. There was tracks . . . hoss tracks an' boot tracks, to the number of three or four men an' horses. Al trailed 'em. But thet very night he had to hole up to keep from bein' drowned, as we had to hyar. . . . Wal, next day he couldn't find any tracks. But he kept on huntin' fer a few days, an' then gave up. He said she'd be dead by then . . . said she wasn't the kind that could have lived more'n a day, with men like them. . . . Some hard customers are driftin' by from the gold fields. An' Bill an' I, hyar, ain't in love with this railroad idee. It'll ruin the country fer trappin' an' livin'!"

Some weeks later a gaunt and ragged cowboy limped into North Platte, walking beside a broken horse, upon the back of which swayed and reeled a rider tied in the saddle. It was not a sight to interest any except the lazy or the curious, for in that day such things were common in North Platte. The horse had bullet creases on his neck; the rider wore a bloody shirt; the gaunt pedestrian had a bandaged arm.

Neale lay ill of a deeper wound while the bullet hole healed in his side. Day and night King tended him or sat near him in a shack on the outskirts of the camp. Shock, grief, starvation, exhaustion, loss of blood and sleep—all these laid Warren Neale close to death. He did not care to live. It was the patient loyal friend who fought fever and heart-break and the ebbing tide of life.

Baxter and Henney visited North Platte and called to see him, and later the chief came and ordered King to take Neale to the tents of the corps. Everyone was kind, solicitous, earnest. He had been missed. He could not be spared. The members of his corps knew of the rescue of Allie Lee—they guessed the romance—and grieved over the tragedy. They did all they could do; the troop doctor added his attention, but it was the nursing, the presence, and the spirit of King that saved Neale.

He got well and he went back to work with the cowboy for his helper.

In that camp of toil and disorder no one but the few with whom Neale was brought in close touch noted anything singular about him. The engineer, however, observed that he did not work so well, nor so energetically, nor so accurately. His enthusiasm was lacking. The cowboy, always with him, was the one who saw the sudden spells of somber abstraction, and the poignant hopeless sleepless pain, the eternal regret. And as Neale slackened in his duty, King grew more faithful.

Neale began to drink and gamble. For long the cowboy fought, argued, appealed against this order of things, and then, failing to change or persuade Neale, he went to gambling and drinking with him. But then it was noted that Neale never got under the influence of liquor or lost materially at cards. The cowboy spilled the contents of Neale's glass and played the game into his hands.

Both of them shrunk from the women of the camp with a strange and unalterable mien. The sight of anything feminine hurt.


North Platte stirred with the quickening stimulus of the approach of the rails and the trains, and the army of soldiers whose duty was to protect the horde of toilers, and the army of tradesmen and parasites who lived off them.

The construction camp of the graders moved on westward, keeping ahead of the camps of the layers.

The first train that reached North Platte brought directors of the U.P.R., among them Warburton and Rudd and Roger—and commissioners Lee and Dunn—and a host of followers on a tour of inspection.

The five miles of Neale's section of road that the commissioners had judged at fault had been torn up and resurveyed and relaid.

Neale rode back over the line with Baxter, surveyed the renewed part, and, returning to North Platte, precipitated consternation among directors and commissioners and engineers, as they sat in council, by throwing on the table figures of the new survey identical with his old figures.

"Gentlemen, the five miles of track torn up and rebuilt has precisely the same grade, to an inch," he declared, with ringing scorn.

Baxter corroborated his statement. The commission men roared and the director demanded explanations.

"I'll explain it!" shouted Neale. "Forty-six thousand dollars a mile! Five miles . . . two hundred and thirty thousand dollars! Spent twice! Taken twice by the same construction company!"

Warburton, a tall white-haired man in a frock coat, got up and pounded the table with his fist.

"Who is this young engineer?" he thundered. "He has the nerve to track his work instead of sneaking to get a bribe. And he tells the truth. We're building twice . . . spending twice when once is enough."

An uproar ensued. Neale had cast a bomb into the council. Every man there and all the thousands in camp knew that railroad ties cost several dollars each, that wages were abnormally high, often demanded in advance and paid twice, that parallel with the great spirit of the work ran a greedy and cunning graft. It was inevitable considering the nature and proportions of the enterprise. An absurd law sent out the commissioners—the politicians appointed them—and both had fat pickings. The directors likewise played both ends against the middle— they received the money from stock sales and loans, then paid it out to construction companies, and, as they employed and owned these companies, the money returned to them. But more than one director was fired by the spirit of the project—the good to be done—the splendid achievement—the trade to come from across the Pacific. The building of the road meant more to some of them than a fortune.

Warburton was the lion of this group and he roared down the dissension. Then with a whirl he grasped Neale around the shoulders and shoved him face to face with the others.

"Here's the kind of men we want on this job!" he shouted, with red face and bulging jaw. "His name's Neale. I've heard of some of his surveys. You've all seen him face this council. . . . That only, gentlemen, is the spirit which can build the U.P.R.. . . . Let's push him up. Let's send him to Washington with these figures. Let's break this damned idiotic law for appointing commissioners to undo the work of efficient men!"

Opportunity was again knocking at Warren Neale's door.

Allison Lee arose in the flurry, and his calm cold presence, the steel of his hard gray eyes, and the motion of his hand, entitled him to a voice.

"Mister Warburton . . . and gentlemen," he said, "I remember this young engineer Neale. When I got here today, I inquired about him, remembering that he had taken severe exception to the judgment of the commissioners about that five miles of roadbed. I learned he is a strange, excitable young fellow, who leaves his work for long wild trips, and who is a drunkard and a gambler. It seems to me somewhat absurd to consider the false report with which he has excited this council."

"It's not false," retorted Neale, with flashing eyes. Then he appealed to Warburton and he was white and eloquent. "You directors know better. This man Lee is no engineer. He doesn't know a foot grade from a forty-five degree slope. Not a man in that outfit had the right or the knowledge to pass judgment on our work. It's political. It's a damned outrage. It's graft."

Another commissioner bounced up with furious gesture. "We'll have you fired!" he shouted.

Neale looked at him and back at Allison Lee and then at Warburton. "I quit," he declared with scorn. "To hell with your rotten railroad!"

Another hubbub threatened in the big tent. Someone yelled for quiet.

And suddenly there was quiet, but it did not come from that individual's call. A cowboy had detached himself from the group of curious onlookers and had confronted the council with two big guns held low.

"Red! Hold on!" cried Neale.

It was King. One look at him blanched Neale's face.

"Everybody sit still an' let me talk," drawled King, with the cool reckless manner that now seemed so deadly over those two heavy guns.

No one moved and the silence grew unnatural. The cowboy advanced a few strides. His eyes with a singular piercing intention were bent upon Allison Lee, yet seemed to hold all the others in sight. He held one gun in direct alignment with Lee, low down, and with the other he rapped on the table. The gasp that went up from around that table proved that someone saw the guns were both cocked.

"Did I understand you to say Neale lied about them surveyin' figgers?" he queried gently.

Allison Lee turned white as a corpse. The cowboy radiated with some dominating force, but the chill in his voice was terrible. It meant that life was nothing to him—or death. What was the U.P.R. to him or its directors or its commissioner or the law? There was no law in that wild camp but the law in his hands. And he knew it.

"Did you say my pard lied?" he repeated.

Allison Lee struggled and choked over a halting: "No."

132

The cowboy backed away slowly, carefully, with soft step, and he faced the others as he moved. "I reckon thet's aboot all," he said, and, slipping into the crowd, he was gone.

# CHAPTER ELEVEN

After Neale and King left, Slingerland saw four seasons swing around, in which no visitors violated the loneliness of his valley. All this while he did not leave Allie Lee alone or, at least, out of hearing. When he went to tend his traps or to hunt, to chop wood or to watch the trail, Allie always accompanied him. She grew strong and supple; she could walk far and carry a rifle or pack; she was keen of eye and ear, and she loved the wilds; she not only was of help to him, but she made the time pass swiftly.

When a year passed after the departure of Neale and King, it seemed to Slingerland that they would never return. There was peril in the trails these days. He grew more and more convinced of some fatality, but he did not confide his fears to Allie. She was happy and full of trust; every day, almost every hour, she looked for Neale. The long wait did not drag her down; she was as fresh and hopeful as ever and the rich bloom mantled her cheek. Slingerland had not the heart to cast a doubt into her happiness. He let her live her dreams.

There came a day that spring when it was imperative for him to visit a distant valley, where he had left traps he now needed, and, as the distance was long and time short, he decided to go alone.

Allie laughed at the idea of being unsafe at the cabin. "I can take care of myself," she said. "I'm not afraid."

Slingerland scarcely doubted her. She had nerve, courage; she knew how to use a gun, and underneath her softness and tenderness was a spirit that would not flush at anything. Still he did not feel satisfied with the idea of leaving her alone, and it was with a wrench that he did it now.

Moreover, he was longer at the journey than he had anticipated being. The moment he turned his face homeward a desire to hurry, an anxiety, a dread fastened upon him. A presentiment of evil gathered. But encumbered as he was with heavy traps, he could not travel swiftly. It was late afternoon when he topped the last ridge between him and home.

What Slingerland saw caused him to drop his traps and gaze aghast. A heavy column of smoke rose above the valley. His first thought was of Sioux. But he doubted that the Indians would betray his friendship. The cabin had caught on fire by accident or else wandering desperadoes had happened along to ruin him. But he was not one to conjecture or to make despair over he knew not what. He ran down the slope, stole down around to the group of pines, and, under cover, cautiously approached the spot where his cabin had stood.

It was a heap of smoking logs and probably had burned for hours. There was no sign of Allie or of anyone. Then he ran into the glade. Almost at once he saw boot tracks and hoof tracks; pelts and hides and furs lay scattered around, as if they had been discarded for choicer ones.

"Robbers," muttered Slingerland. "An' they've got the lass."

He shook under the roughest blow he had ever been dealt; his conscience flayed him; his distress over Allie's fate was so keen and unfamiliar that, used as he was to prompt decision and action, he remained there, staring at the ruins of his home.

Presently he roused himself. He had no hopes. He knew the nature of men who had done this deed. But it was possible that he might overtake them. In the dust he found four sizes of boot tracks and he took the trail down the valley.

Then he became aware that a storm was imminent and that

the air had become cold and raw. Rain began to fall, and darkness came quickly. Slingerland sought the shelter of a nearby ledge, and there, hungry, cold, wet, and unhappy, he waited for sleep that would not come.

It rained hard all night and by morning the brook had become a yellow flood and the trail was under water. Toward noon the rain turned to a drizzly snow and finally ceased. Slingerland passed on down the valley searching for tracks. The ground everywhere had been washed clean and smooth. When he reached the old St. Vrain and Laramie Trail, it looked as if a horse had not passed there in months. He spent another wretched night, and next day awoke to the necessities of life. Except for his rifle, and his horses, and a few traps back up in the hills, he had nothing to show for years of hard and successful work. But that did not matter. He had begun with as little and he could begin again. He killed meat, satisfied his hunger, and cooked more that he might carry with him. Then he spent two more days in that locality, until he had crossed every outlet from his valley. Not striking a track he saw nothing but defeat.

That moment was bitter.

"If Neale'll happen along hyar now he'd kill me . . . an' sarve me right," muttered the trapper.

But he believed Neale, too, had gone the way of so many who braved these wilds. Slingerland saw in the fate of Neale and Allie the result of civilization marching westward. If before he had disliked the idea of the railroad entering his wild domain, he hated it now. Before that survey the Indians had been peaceful, and no dangerous men rode the trails. What right had the government to steal land from the Indians—to break treaties—to run a steam track down the plains and mountains? Slingerland foresaw the bloodiest period ever known in the West, before that work should be completed. It had struck him deep—this white man movement across the Black Hills, and it was not the loss of all he had worked for that he minded. For years his life had been lonely, and then suddenly it had been full. Never again would it be either.

Slingerland turned his back to the trails made by the advancing march of the empire builders and he sought the seclusion of the more inaccessible hills.

"Someday I'll work out with a load of pelts," he said. "An' then . . . mebbe I'll hyar what become of Neale . . . an' her."

He found, as one of his kind knew how to find, the valleys where no white man had trod—where the game abounded and was tame—where if the red man came he was friendly—where the silent days and lonely nights slowly made bearable his memory of Allie Lee.

# CHAPTER TWELVE

Allie Lee possessed a mind twice as active and dreamy. While she dreamed of Neale and their future, she busied herself with many tasks and many activities, and a whole year blew by without a lagging or melancholy hour.

Neale had been detained or sent back to Omaha, or given more important work than formerly. She divined Slingerland's doubt, but it would not stay before her consciousness. Her heart told her that all was well with Neale and that sooner or later he would return for her.

In Allie love had worked magic. It had freed her from a horrible black memory. Her state had been one of wretchedness; she had been alone; she had wanted to die to forget those awful yells and screams—the murder—the blood—the terror and her anguish; she had nothing to want to live for; she had almost hated those two kind men who tried so hard to make her forget. Then suddenly, she never remembered when, she had seen Neale with different eyes. A few words, a touch, a gift, and a pledge—and life was transformed for Allie Lee. Like a flower blooming overnight her heart had opened to love, and all the distemper in her blood and the blackness in her mind were dispelled. The relief from pain and dread was so great that love became a beautiful and all-absorbing passion. Freed then, and strangely happy, she took to the life around her as naturally as if she had been born there, and she grew like a wildflower. Neale returned to her that autumn to make perfect the realization of her dreams. When he went away, she could not be unhappy. She owed it to him to be perfect in joy, faith, love, and duty, and her adversity had discovered to her a courage and a will. She lived for Neale.

Summer, autumn, winter passed, short days, full of solitude, beauty, thoughts, and anticipations, and always achievement, for she could not stay idle. When the first green brightened the cottonwoods and willows along the brook, she knew that before their leaves had attained full growth Neale would be on his way to her. A strange and inexplicable sense of the heart told her he was coming.

More than once that spring had she bent over the mossy rock to peer down at her face mirrored in the crystal spring. Neale had made her aware of her beauty, and proud of it, since it seemed to be such a strange treasure for him. She marveled at her value to Neale and she accepted it as a fact because he had told her she was precious. At a word of his it seemed all the forces of her nature were drawn upon to fulfill his wish.

On the May morning that Slingerland left her alone, a few hours after his departure she was startled by a *clip-clop* of horses trotting up the trail. Her first thought was that Neale and King had returned. All her being suddenly radiated with rapture. She flew to the door.

Four horsemen rode into the clearing, but Neale was not among them.

Allie's joy was short-lived. The reaction to disappointment seemed a violent agonizing wrench. She lost all control of her muscles for a moment and had to lean against the cabin to keep from falling.

By this time the foremost rider pulled in his horse near the door. He was a young giant with hulking shoulders—ruddy-faced, bold-eyed, ugly-mouthed. He reminded Allie of someone she had seen in California. He stared hard at her.

"Hullo! Ain't you Durade's girl?" he asked in gruff astonishment.

Then Allie knew she had been seen out in the gold fields. "No, I'm not," she replied.

"A-huh! You look uncommon like her. . . . Anybody home 'round here?"

"Slingerland went over the hill," replied Allie. "He'll be back presently."

The fellow brushed her aside and went into the cabin. Then the other three riders arrived.

" 'Mornin', miss," said one, a grizzled veteran who might have been miner or trapper or bandit. The other two reined in behind him. One wore a wide-brimmed black sombrero from under which a dark sinister face gleamed. The last had sandy hair and light roving eyes.

"Whar's Fresno?" asked this last individual.

"I'm inside," replied the man called Fresno, and he appeared at the door. He stretched out a long arm and grasped Allie before she could avoid him. When she began to struggle, the huge hand closed on her wrist until she could have screamed in pain.

"Hold on, girl! It won't do you no good to jerk . . . an', if you holler, I'll choke you," he said. "Fellers, get inside the cabin an' rustle around lively."

With one pull he hauled Allie toward his horse, and, taking a lasso off his saddle, he roped her arms to her sides and tied her to the nearest tree.

"Keep mum now or it'll be the wuss fer you," he ordered, then went into the cabin.

They were a bad lot. Slingerland's reason for worry had at last been justified. Allie did not realize this until she found herself bound to the tree. Then she was furious and she strained with all her might to slip free of the rope. But the efforts were useless, she only succeeded in bruising her arm for nothing. And when she desisted, she was ready to succumb to despair. Until a flashing thought of Neale, of the agony that must be his if he lost her or if harm befell her, drew her up sharply, thrillingly. A girl's natural and instinctive fear was vanquished by her love. And love in that desperate strait became all which was humanly possible of courage and spirit.

She heard the robbers knocking things about in the cabin. They threw bales of beaver pelts out of the door. Presently Fresno reappeared carrying a buckskin sack in which Slingerland kept his money and few valuables, and the others followed, quarreling over a cane-covered demijohn in which there had once been liquor.

"Nary a drop!" growled the one who got possession of it. And with rage he threw the thing back into the cabin where it crashed into the fire.

"Sandy, you've scattered the fire," protested the grizzled robber as he glanced into the cabin. "Them furs is catchin'."

"Let 'em burn!" called Fresno. "We got all we want. Come on."

"But what's the sense burnin' the feller's cabin down?"

"Nothin'll burn," said the dark-faced man, "an', if it does, it'll look like Indian work. Savvy, Old Miles."

They shuffled out together. Evidently Fresno was the leader or at least the strongest force. He looked at the sack in his hand, and then at Allie.

"You fellers fight over that," he said, and, throwing the sack on the ground, he strode toward Allie.

The three men all made a rush for the sack and Sandy got it. The other two pressed around him, not threateningly, but aggressively, sure of their rights.

"I'll divide," said Sandy, as he mounted his horse. "Wait till we make camp. You fellers pack the beavers."

Fresno untied Allie from the tree, but he left the lasso around her, and, holding to it and her arm, he rudely dragged her to his horse.

"Git up, an' hurry," he ordered.

Allie mounted. The stirrups were too long.

"You fellers clear out!" called Fresno. "An' ketch me one of them hosses we seen along the brook."

While he re-adjusted the stirrups, Allie looked down upon him. He was an uncouth ruffian and his touch gave her an insupportable disgust. He wore no weapons, but his saddle holster contained a revolver and the sheath a Winchester. Allie could have shot him and made a run for it, and she had the nerve. The others, however, did not get out of sight before Fresno had the stirrups adjusted. He strode after them, leading the horse. Allie glanced back to see a thin stream of smoke coming out of the cabin door. Then she faced about, desperately resolved to take any chance to get away. She decided these men would not be safe for very long. Whatever she was to do, she must do that day, and she only awaited her chance.

At the ford Sandy caught one of Slingerland's horses—a mustang and a favorite of Allie's, and one she could ride. He was as swift as the wind. Once upon him she could run away from any horse these robbers rode. Fresno put the end of the lasso around the mustang's neck.

"Can you ride bareback?" he asked Allie.

Allie lied. Her first thought was to lead them astray as to her skill with a horse, and then it occurred to her that, if she rode Fresno's saddle, there might be an opportunity to use the gun.

Fresno leaped astride the mustang and was promptly bucked off. The other men guffawed. Fresno swore and, picking himself up, tried again. This time the mustang behaved better, but it was plain he did not like the weight. Then Fresno started off, leading his own horse, and at a trot that showed he wanted to cover ground.

Allie heard the others quarrelling over something, probably the gold Slingerland had been so many years in accumulating.

They rode on to where the valley opened into another, along which wound the old St. Vrain and Laramie Trail. They kept to this, traveling east for a few miles, and then entered an interesting valley, where some distance up they had a camp. They had not taken the precaution to hide either packs or mules, and so far as Allie could tell they had no fear of Indians. Probably they had crossed from California, and being dishonest, and avoiding caravans and camps, they had not become fully acquainted with the perils of that region.

It was about noon when they arrived at this place. The sun was becoming blurred and a storm appeared brewing. Fresno dismounted, dropping the halter of the mustang. Then he let go his own bridle. The eyes he bent on Allie made her turn hers away as from something that could scorch and stain. He pulled her off the saddle, rudely, with coarse and meaning violence.

Allie pushed him back and faced him. In a way she had lived among such men as this man, and she knew that resistance or pleadings were useless—would only inflame him. She was not ready yet to court death.

"Wait," she said.

"A-huh," he grunted, breathing heavily. He was an animal, slow-witted and brutal.

"Fresno, I am Durade's girl," she went on.

"I thought I knowed you. But you've grown to be a woman an' a damn' pretty one."

Allie drew him aside, farther from the others, who had renewed a loud altercation.

"Fresno, it's gold you want," she affirmed, rather than asked.

"Sure. But no small stake like thet'd be my choice . . . ag'in' you." He leered, jerking a thumb back at his companions.

"You remember Horn?" went on Allie.

"Horn! The miner who made thet big strike out near Sacramento?"

"Yes, that's who I mean," replied Allie hurriedly. "We . . . we left California in his caravan. He brought all his gold with him."

Fresno began to lean down in great interest.

"We were attacked by Sioux. . . . Horn buried all that gold . . . on the spot . . . where he . . . all . . . all the others were killed . . . except me. . . . And I know where." Allie shuddered with what the words brought up. But no memory could weaken her.

Fresno opened his huge mouth to bawl this unexpected news to his comrades.

"Don't call them . . . don't tell them," Allie whispered. "There's only one condition . . . I'll take you . . . where that gold's hidden."

"Girl, I can make you tell," he replied menacingly.

"No, you can't."

"You ain't so smart you think I'll let you go . . . jest fer some gold?" he queried. "Gold'll be cheap along this trail soon. An' girls like you are scarce."

"No . . . that's not what I meant. . . . Get rid of the others . . . and I'll tell you where Horn buried his gold."

Fresno stared at her. He grinned. The idea evidently surprised and flattered him, and grew perplexing.

"But Frank . . . he's my pard . . . thet one with the black hat," he protested. "I couldn't do no dirt to Frank. . . . What's your game, girl? I'll beat you into tellin' me where that gold is."

"Beating won't make me tell," replied Allie with intensity. "Nothing will . . . if I don't want to. . . . My game is for my life. You know I've no chance among four men like you."

"*Aw,* I don't know about thet," he blustered. "I can take care of you. . . . But say, if you'd stand fer Frank . . . mebbe I'll take you up. . . . Girl, are you lyin' about thet gold?"

"No."

"Why didn't the trapper dig it up? You must hev told him."

"Because he was afraid to keep it in or near his cabin. We meant to leave it until we were ready to get out of the country."

That appeared plausible to Fresno and he grew more thoughtful.

Meanwhile the altercation among the other three ruffians assumed proportions that augured a fight.

"I'll divide this sack when I git good an' ready," declared Sandy.

"But, pard, thet's no square deal," protested Old Miles. "I'm a-gittin' mad. I seen you meant to keep it all."

The dark-faced ruffian shoved a grasping hand under Sandy's nose. "When do I git mine?" he demanded.

Fresno wheeled and called: "Frank, you come here!"

The other approached sullenly. "Fresno . . . thet Sandy is whole hog or none!" he exclaimed.

"Let 'em fight it out," replied Fresno. "We've got a bigger game. . . . Besides, they'll shoot each other up. Then we'll hev it all. Come on, give 'em elbow room."

He led Allie and his horse away a little distance. "Fetch them packs, Frank!" he called.

The mustang followed, and presently Frank came with one of the packs. Fresno slipped the saddle from his horse, and, laying it under a tree, he pulled a gun and rifle from their sheaths. The gun he stuck in his belt, the rifle he leaned against a branch.

"Sandy'll plug Old Miles in jest another minnit," remarked Fresno.

"What's this other game?" queried Frank curiously.

"It's gold . . . Frank . . . gold," replied Fresno, and in few words he told his comrade about Horn's buried gold. But he did not mention the condition under which the girl would reveal its hiding place. Evidently he had no doubt that he could force her to tell.

"Let's rustle!" cried Frank, his dark face gleaming. "We want to get out of this country quick."

"You bet. An' I wonder when we'll be fetchin' up with them railroad camps we heered about. . . . Camp full of gold an' whiskey an' wimmen!"

"We've enough on our hands now," replied Frank. "Let's rustle fer thet. . . ."

A gunshot interrupted him. Then a hoarse curse rang out— and then two more shots from a different gun.

"Them last was Sandy's," observed Fresno coolly. "An' of course they landed. . . . Go see if Old Miles hit Sandy."

Frank strode off under the trees.

Allie had steeled herself to anything, and those shots warned her that perhaps she had two less to contend with and that she must be quick to seize the first opportunity to act. She could leap upon the mustang and, if she was lucky, could get away. She could jump for the Winchester and surely shoot one of these villains, perhaps both of them. But the spirit that gave her the nerve to attempt either plan bade her wait, not too long, but longer, in the hope of a more favorable moment.

Frank returned to Fresno and he carried the sack of gold that had caused dissension. Fresno laughed. "Sandy's plugged hard . . . low down," said Frank. "He can't live. An' Old Miles is croaked."

"A-huh! Frank, I'll go git the other packs. An' you see what's in this sack," said Fresno.

When he got out of sight, Allie slipped the lasso from her waist. "I don't need that hanging to me," she said.

"Sure you don't, sweetheart," replied the ruffian Frank. "Thet man Fresno is rough with ladies. Now I'm gentle. . . . Come an' let me spill this sack in your lap."

"I guess not," replied Allie.

"Wal, you're sure a cat. Look at her eyes! All right, don't get mad at me." He spilled the contents of the sack out on the sand and bent over it.

What had made Allie's eyes flash was the recognition of her opportunity. She did not hesitate an instant. First she looked to see just where the mustang stood. He was near, with the rope dragging, half coiled. Allie suddenly was struck with the head and ears of the mustang. He heard something. She looked up the valley slope and saw a file of Indians riding down. Some were silhouetted against the sky. They were coming fast. For an instant Allie's senses reeled. Then she rallied. Her situation was desperate—almost hopeless. But here was the issue of life or death, and she met it.

In one bound she had the rifle. Long before, she had ascertained that it was loaded. The man Frank heard the click of the raising hammer.

"What're you doin'?" he demanded fiercely.

"Don't get up!" warned Allie. She stepped backward nearer the mustang. "Look up the slope. . . . Indians!"

But he paid no heed. He jumped up and strode toward her.

"Look, man!" cried Allie piercingly.

He came on.

Then Fresno appeared running, white of face.

Allie, without leveling the rifle, fired at the furious fool, even as his clutching hands struck the weapon. He halted, with sudden gasp, sank to his knees, fell against the tree, and then staggered up. Allie had to drop the rifle to hold the frightened mustang. She got on him, urged him away, and hauled in the dragging lasso. Once free of brush and stones he began to run. Allie saw a clear field ahead, but steep rocky slopes boxing the valley. She would be hemmed in there. She got the mustang turned, and ran among the trees, keeping far over to the left. She heard beating hoofs off to her right, crashings in brush, and then yells. An opening showed her the slope alive with Indians riding down hard. Some were heading down the valley to cut off escape, others up, and the majority were coming straight for the clumps of trees.

Fresno burst out of cover mounted on Sandy's bay horse. He began to shoot. And the Indians fired in reply, all along the slope rose white puffs of smoke, and bullets clipped dust from the ground in front of Allie. Fresno drew ahead. The bay horse was swift. Allie pulled her mustang more to the left, hoping to get over the ridge, which on that side was not high. To her dismay Indians appeared there, too. She wheeled back to the first course and saw that she must try what Fresno was trying.

Then the robber Frank appeared riding out of the cedars. The Indian riders closed rapidly in on him, shooting all the time. His horse was hit and, stumbling, almost threw the rider. Then he ran wildly—could not be controlled. The Indian was speeding from among the others. He had a bow bent double, and suddenly it straightened. Allie saw dust fly from Frank's back. He threw up his arms and slid off under the horse, the saddle slipping with him. The horse, wounded and terrorized, began to plunge, dragging man and saddle.

In that direction Allie looked no more.

Ahead, far to the right, Fresno was gaining on his pursuers. He was out of range now, but the Indians kept shooting. Then Allie's situation became so perilous that she saw only the Indians to the left, with mustangs stretched out to intercept her before she got out into the wider valley. Her mustang did not need to be goaded. The yells behind, on all sides, and the whistling bullets, drove him to his utmost. Allie had all she could do to ride him. She was nearly blinded by the stinging wind, yet she saw those lithe half-naked savages dropping back gradually, and knew she was gaining. Her hair became loose and streamed in the wind. She heard the yells then. No more rifles cracked. Her pursuers had discovered that she was a girl, and were bent on capture.

Fleet and strong the mustang ran, sure-footed, leaping the washes, and out-distanced the pursuers on the left. Allie thought she could turn into the big valley and go down the main trail, before the Indians chasing Fresno discovered her. But vain hope! Across the width of the valley, where it opened out, a string of Indians stretched, riding back to meet her.

A long dust line, dotted with bobbing objects, to the right! Behind a close-packed bunch of hard riders! In front an opening trap of yelling savages! She was lost. And suddenly she remembered the fate of her mother. Her spirit sank—her strength fled. All blurred around her. She lost control of the mustang. She felt him turning, slowing. The yells burst hideously in her ears. Like her mother's—her fate! A roar of speedy hoof beats seemed to envelop her and her nostrils were filled with dust. They were upon her. She prayed for a swift stroke—then for her soul. All darkened— her senses were failing. Neale's face glimmered there—in space—was lost. She was slipping—slipping. . . . A rude and powerful hold fastened upon her. Then all faded.

# CHAPTER THIRTEEN

When Allie Lee came back from that black gap in her consciousness, she was lying in a circular tent of poles and hides. For a
second she was dazed. But the Indian designs and trappings in
the tent brought swift realization—she had been brought a captive to the Sioux encampment. She raised her head. She was lying on a buffalo robe; her hands and feet were bound; there was
no one else in the tent; the floor was littered with blankets and
beaded buckskin garments. Through a narrow opening she saw
that the day was far spent; Indians and horses passed to and
fro; there was a bustle outside and jabber of Indian jargon; the
wind blew hard and drops of rain pattered on the tent.

Allie could scarcely credit the evidence of her own senses.
Here she was alive! She tried to see and feel if she had been
hurt. Her arms and body appeared bruised and they ached, but
she was not in any great pain. Her hopes arose. If the Sioux
meant to kill her, they would have done it at once. They might
intend to reserve her for torture, but more likely it was to make
her a captive in the tribe. In that case Slingerland would find
her and get her freedom.

Rain began to fall more steadily. Allie smelled smoke and saw
the reflection of fires on the wall of the tent. Presently a squaw
entered. She was a huge woman, evidently old, very dark of
face, and wrinkled. She carried a bowl and platter that she set
down, and, grunting, she began to untie Allie's hands. Then she
gave the girl a not ungentle shake. Allie sat up.

150

"Do you . . . do they mean . . . to harm and kill me?" she asked.

The squaw shook her head to indicate she did not understand and she spoke in Indian language. Her gestures toward the things she had brought were easy to interpret. Allie partook of the Indian food, which was coarse and unpalatable, but satisfied hunger. When she had finished, the squaw laboriously tied the thongs around Allie's wrists and, pushing her back on the robe, covered her up and left her there.

After that it grew dark rapidly and the rain increased to a torrent. Allie, hardly realizing how cold she had been, began to warm up under the woolly robe. The roar of the rain drowned all the sounds outside. She wondered if Slingerland had returned to his cabin, and, if so, what he had done. She felt sorry for him. He would take the loss hard. But he would trail her; he would hear of a white girl captive in the Sioux camp and she would soon be free. How fortunate she was. A star of Providence watched over her. The prayer she had breathed had been answered. She thought of Neale. She would live; she would pray and fight off harm; she would find him if he could not find her; she was his utterly. And lying there bound and helpless in an Indian camp, captive of the relentless Sioux, for all she knew in peril of death, with the roar of wind and rain around her and the darkness like pitch, she yet felt her pulses throb and thrill and her spirit soar at remembrance of the man she loved. In the end she would find Neale, and it was with his name trembling on her lips, his face there in the blackness that she fell asleep.

More than once during the night she awoke in the pitchy darkness to hear the wind blow and the rain roar. The dawn broke cold and gray, and the storm gradually diminished. Allie lay alone for hours, beginning to suffer by reason of her bonds and cramped limbs. The longer she was left alone, the more hopeful her case seemed.

In the afternoon she was visited by the squaw, released, and fed as before. Allie made signs that she wanted to have her feet free, to get up and move. The squaw complied with her wishes. Allie could scarcely stand; she felt dizzy; a burning, aching sensation filled her limbs.

Presently the old woman led her out. Allie saw a great number of tents, many horses and squaws and children, but few braves. The encampment lay in a wide valley, similar to all the valleys of that country, except that it was larger. A stream in flood swept, yellow and noisy, along the edge of the encampment. The children ran at sight of Allie and the women stared. It was easy to see they disapproved of her. The few braves looked at her with dark steady unfathomable eyes. The camp appeared rich in color, in horses, trappings; evidently this tribe was not poor. Allie saw utensils, blankets, clothing—many things never made by Indians.

She was led to a big lodge with tent adjoining. Inside an old Indian brave, grizzled and shrunken, smoked before a fire, and, as Allie was pushed on into the tent, a young Indian squaw appeared. She was small, with handsome scornful face and dark proud eyes, gorgeously clad in elaborate braided and fringed and ornate buckskin—evidently an Indian princess or a chief's wife. She threw Allie a venomous glance as she went out. Allie heard the old squaw's grunting voice and the young one's quick and passionate answers.

There was nothing for Allie to do but await developments. She rested, rubbing her sore wrists and ankles, thankful she had been left unbound. She saw that she was watched, particularly by the young woman who often walked to the opening to glance in. The interior of this tent presented a contrast to the other in which she had been confined. It was dry and clean, with floor of rugs and blankets, and all around hung beaded and painted and feathered articles, some for wear, and some for what purpose she could not guess.

The afternoon passed without further incident until the old squaw entered, manifestly to feed Allie, and tie her up as heretofore. The younger squaw came in to watch the tying process.

Allie spoke to her—held out her bound hands appealingly. This elicited no further response than an intent look.

Night came. Allie lay awake a good while, and then she fell asleep. Next morning she was awakened by an uproar. Whistling and trampling of mustangs, whoops of braves, the babble of many voices, barking of dogs, movement, bustle, sound all about attested to the return of the warriors. Allie's heart sank for a moment; this would be the time of trial for her. But the clamor subsided without any disturbance near her tent. By and by the old squaw returned to attend to her needs. This time, on the way out, she dropped a blanket curtain between the tent and lodge.

Soon Indians entered the lodge, quite a number, with squaws among them, judging by their voices, and a harangue lasting an hour or more interested Allie, especially because at times she heard and recognized the quick passionate utterance of the young squaws.

Soon Allie's old attendant shuffled in, lifting the curtain and motioning Allie to come out. Allie went into the lodge. An early sun, shining into the wide door, lighted the place brightly. It was full of Indians. In the center stood a striking figure, probably a chief, tall and lean, with scars on his naked breast. His face was bronze, with deep lines, somber and bitter, and cruel thin lips, and eyes that glittered like black fire. His head had the poise of an eagle.

His piercing glance scarcely rested an instant upon Allie. He motioned for her to be taken away. Allie, as she was led back, got a glimpse of the young squaw. Sullen, with bowed head and dark rich blood thick in her face, with heaving breast and clenched hands she seemed a picture of outraged pride and jealousy. Allie gathered that she was probably to be the captive of the chief and the young bride fiercely resented it.

The camp quieted down after that. Allie peeped through a slit between the hides of which her tent was constructed, and she saw no one but squaws and children. The mustangs appeared worn out. Evidently the braves and warriors were resting after a hard ride or fight or foray.

Nothing happened. The hours dragged. Allie heard the breathing of heavy sleepers. About dark she was fed again and bound.

That night she was awakened by a gentle shake. A hand moved from her shoulder to her lips. A pale moonlight filtered into the tent. Allie saw a figure kneeling beside her and she heard a: *"Sh-s-s-sh."* Then her hands and feet were freed. She divined then that the young squaw had come to let her go, in the dead of night. Her heart throbbed high as her liberator held up a side of the tent. Allie crawled out. A bright moon soared in the sky, the camp was silent. The young woman slipped after her, and, with a warning gesture to be silent, she led Allie away toward the slope of the valley. It was a goodly distance.

Not a sound disturbed the peace of the beautiful night. The air was cold and still. Allie shivered and trembled. This was the most exciting adventure of all. She felt a softness and warmth for this Indian girl. Once, the squaw halted, with ear turned, listening. Allie's heart stopped beating. But no bark of dog, no sound of pursuit justified alarm. At last they reached the base of the slope.

The Indian pointed high toward the ridge top. Then she made undulating motions of her hand as if to picture the topography of the ridges, and valley between, and then, kneeling, she made a motion with her finger on the ground that indicated a winding trail. Whereupon she stealthily glided away.

Allie was left alone—free—with directions how to find the trail. What use was it for her to find it in that wilderness? But her star kept drawing her spirit. She began to climb. The slope was grassy, and her light feet left little trace. She climbed and climbed until she thought her heart would burst. Once upon the summit she fell in the grass and rested.

Far below in the moon-blanched valley lay the white tents and the twinkling campfires. The bay of a dog floated up to her. It was a tranquil, beautiful, scene. Rising, she turned her back upon it, with an unuttered prayer for the Indian girl whose jealousy and generosity had freed her, and faced the ridge top and the unknown before her.

A wolf mourned, and the sound, clear and sharp, startled her. But remembering Slingerland's word that no beast would be likely to harm her in the warm season, she was reassured. Soon she had crossed the narrow back of the ridge, to see below another valley like the one she had left but without the tents and fires. Descent was easy and she covered ground swiftly. She feared to come to a stream in flood. Again she mounted a slope, zigzagging up, going slowly, reserving her strength, pausing often to rest and to listen, and keeping a straight line with the star she had marked. Climbing was hard work, however slowly she went, just as going down was a relief.

In this manner she climbed four ridges and crossed three valleys before a rest became imperative. Besides, dawn was near, as evidenced by the paling stars and the gray in the east. It would be well for her to remain on high ground while day broke. So she rested, but soon, cooling off, she suffered with the cold. Huddling down in the grass against a stone, facing the east, she waited for dawn to break.

The stars shut their eyes; the dark blue of sky turned gray; a pale light seemed to suffuse itself throughout the east. The valley lay asleep in shadow, the ridges awoke in soft gray mist. Far down over the vastness and openness of the plains appeared a ruddy glow. It warmed, it changed, it brightened. A sea of cloudy vapors, serene and motionless, changed to rose and pink, and a red curve slid up over the distant horizon. All that world of plain and cloud and valley and ridge quickened as with the soul of day while it colored with the fire of sun. Red, radiant, glorious the sun rose.

It was the dispeller of gloom, the bringer of hope. Allie Lee, lost in the heights, held out her arms to the east and the sun, and she cried: "Oh God! Oh! Neale . . . Neale!"


When she turned to look down into the valley below, she saw the white winding ribbon-like trail and with her eye she followed it to where the valley opened wide upon the plains.

She must go down the slope to the cover of the trees and brush, and there work along eastward, ever with eye alert. She must meet with travelers within a few days or perish of starvation or again fall into the hands of the Sioux. Thirst she did not fear, for the recent heavy rain had left water holes everywhere.

With action her spirit arose and the numbness of hands and feet left her. Time passed swiftly. The sun stood straight overhead before she realized she had walked miles, and it declined westward as she skulked like an Indian from tree to tree, from bush to bush, along the first bench of the valley floor.

Night overtook her at the gateway of the valley. The vast monotony of the plains opened before her, like a gulf. She feared it. She found a mound of earth with a wind-worn shelf in its side and overgrown with sage, and into this she crawled, curled in the sand and prayed and slept.

Next day she took up a position some few hundred yards from the trail and followed its course, straining her eyes to see before and behind her, husbanding her strength with frequent rests, and drinking from every pond.

That day, too, like its predecessor, passed swiftly by, and left her out upon the huge, billowy, heaving bosom of the plains. Again she sought a hiding place, but none offered. There was no warmth in the sand and the night wind arose, cold, moaning. She could not sleep. The whole empty world seemed haunted. Rustlings of the sage, seeping of the sand, gusts of the wind, and the night, and the loneliness, and the faithless stars and a treacherous moon that sank, and the wailing of wolves— all worked upon her mind and spirit until she lost her courage. She feared to shut her eyes or cover her face, for then she could not see the stealthy forms stalking her out of the gloom. She prayed no more to her star.

"Oh, God! Have you forsaken me?" she moaned.

The answer was there in the great silence, so much more striking because of the raw and puny little ghosts of sounds in the vast lonely empty hall of the night, so terrible now in its reality.

How relentless the grip of the endless hours! The black night held. And yet when she had grown nearly mad waiting for the dawn, it broke, ruddy and bright, with the sun as always a promise.

Allie found no water that day. She suffered from the lack of it, but hunger appeared to have fled. Her strength diminished, yet she walked and plodded miles on miles, always gazing hopelessly and hopefully along the winding trail.

At the close of the short and merciful day, despair seized upon part of Allie's mind. With night came gloom—the old somber spirit—memory of her mother's fate. It impinged upon that later spirit and at intervals thrust aside the face of the man that had almost become to her the face of God. She clung to a strange faith. But all reason, all fact, all reality, all present pointed to her doom—starvation—death by thirst—or Indians!

A thousand times she imagined she heard the fleet hoof beating of many mustangs. Only the tiny pats of the broken sage leaves in the wind!

It was a dark and cloudy night, warmer and threatening rain. She kept continuously turning around and around to see what it was that was creeping up behind her so stealthily. How horrible was the dark—the blackness that showed invisible things. A wolf sent up his hungry, lonely cry. She did not fear this reality as she feared the intangible. If she lived through this night, then another like it would return the horror. She would rather not live. Yet like a creature beset by foes all around she watched, she faced every little sound, she peered into the darkness, shaking and cold, instinctively unable wholly to give up, to end the struggle, to lie down and die.

Neale was with her. He was alive. He was thinking of her at that moment. He would expect her to overcome self and accident and calamity. He spoke to her out of the distance and his voice had the old power, stranger than fear, exhaustion, hopelessness, insanity. He could call her back from the grave.

And so the night passed.

In the morning, when the sun lit the level land, far down the trail westward gleamed a long white line of moving wagons. Allie uttered a wild and broken cry, in which all the torture shuddered out of her heart. Again she was saved! That black doubt was shame to her spirit. She prayed her thanksgiving and vowed in her prayers that no adversity, however cruel, could ever shake her faith or conquer her spirit.

She was going on to meet Neale. Life was suddenly sweet again, unutterably full, blazing like the sunrise. He was there— somewhere to the eastward.

She waited. The caravan was miles away. But no mirage—no trick of the wide plain! She watched. If the hours of night had been long, what were these hours of day with life and happiness for her creeping along in that caravan?

At last she saw the scouts riding in front and alongside, and the plodding oxen. It was a large caravan, well equipped for defense.

She left the little rise of ground and made for the trail. How uneven the walking. She staggered. Her legs were weak. But she gained the trail and stood there. She waved. They were not so far away. Surely she would be seen. She staggered on—waved again.

There! The leading scout had halted. He pointed. Other riders crowded around him. The caravan halted.

Allie heard voices. She waved her arms and tried to run. A scout dismounted—advanced to meet her—rifle ready. The caravan feared a Sioux trick. Allie descried a lean gray old man—now striding rapidly.

"It's a white gal!" she heard him shout.

Others ran forward, then came on as she staggered to meet them.

"I'm alone . . . I'm . . . lost . . . ," she faltered.

"A white gal in Injun dress," said another.

And then kind hands were outstretched to her.

"I'm . . . running . . . away. . . . Indians," panted Allie.

"Whar?" asked the lean old scout.

"Over the ridges . . . miles . . . twenty miles . . . more. They had me. I got . . . away. . . . Four . . . three days ago."

The group around Allie opened to admit another man.

"What's this . . . who's this?" called a quick voice, soft and liquid, yet with a quality of steel in it.

Allie had heard that voice. She saw a tall man in long black coat and wide black hat and flounced vest and flowing tie. Her heart contracted.

"*Allie!*" rang the voice.

159

She looked up to see a dark handsome face—a Spanish face with almond eyes, sloe-black and magnetic—a face that suddenly blazed.

She recognized the man with whom her mother had run away . . . who she had long believed her father . . . the adventurer Durade! Then she fainted.

# CHAPTER FOURTEEN

Allie recovered to find herself lying in a canvas-covered wagon and being worked over by several sympathetic women.

She did not see Durade. But she knew she had not been mistaken. The wagon was rolling along as fast as oxen could travel. Evidently the caravan had been alarmed by the proximity of Sioux and was making as much progress as possible.

Allie did not answer many questions. She drank thirstily, but was too exhausted to eat.

"Whose caravan?" was the only query she made.

"Durade's," replied one woman, and it was evident from the way she spoke that this was a man of consequence.

As Allie lay there, slowly succumbing to weariness and drowsiness, she thought of the irony of fate that had led her to escape the Sioux only to fall into the hands of Durade. Still there was hope. Durade was traveling toward the East. Out there somewhere he would meet Neale, and then blood would be spilled. She had always regarded Durade strangely, wondering that, in spite of his kindness to her, she could not really care for him. She understood now and hated him passionately. And if there was anyone she feared, Durade was he. Allie lost herself in the past, seeing the stream of mixed humanity that passed through Durade's gambling halls. No doubt he was on his way now, first to search for her mother, and secondly to profit by the building of the railroad. But he would never find her mother. Allie was glad.

At length she fell asleep and slept long, then dozed at intervals. The caravan halted. Allie heard the familiar singsong calls to the oxen. Soon all was bustle about her, and this fully awakened her. In a moment or more she must expect to be face to face with Durade. What should she tell him? How much should she let him know? Not one word about her mother. He would be less afraid of her if he found out that her mother was dead. Durade had always feared Allie's mother.

The women with whom Allie had ridden helped her out of the wagon, and, finding her too weak to stand, they made a bed for her on the ground. The campsite appeared to be just the same as any other part of that monotonous plain land. Evidently there was a stream or water hole nearby. Allie saw her companions were the only women in the caravan, and were plain persons, blunt yet kind, used to hard honest work, and probably wives of defenders of the wagon train.

They could not conceal their curiosity in regard to Allie, nor their wonder. She had heard them whispering together whenever they came near.

Presently Allie saw Durade. He was approaching. How well she remembered him! Yet the lapse of time and the change between the childhood when she had been with him and the present seemed incalculable. He spoke to the women, motioning in her direction. His bearing and action was that of a man of education, and a gentleman. Yet he looked what her mother had called him—a broken man of class—an adventurer, victim to some passion.

He came and knelt by Allie. "How are you now?" he asked. His voice was gentle and courteous, different from that of other men. It was as if he had learned to speak that way before he had come among rough Western men.

"I can't stand up," replied Allie.

"Are you hurt?"

"No . . . only worn out."

"You escaped from Indians?"

"Yes . . . a tribe of Sioux. They intended to keep me captive. But a young squaw freed me . . . led me off."

He paused as if it was an effort to speak and a long thin shapely hand went to his throat. "Your mother?" he asked hoarsely. Suddenly his face had turned white.

Allie gazed straight into his eyes, with wonder, pain, suspicion. "My mother! I've not seen her for nearly two years."

"My God! What happened? You lost her? You became separated? Indians . . . bandits . . . ? Tell me!"

"I have . . . no . . . more to tell," said Allie. His pain revived her own. She pitied Durade. He had changed—aged—there were lines new to her.

"I spent a year in . . . and around Ogden . . . searching," went on Durade. "Tell me . . . more."

"No!" cried Allie.

"Do you know . . . then?" he asked very low.

"I'm not your daughter . . . and Mother ran off from you. Yes, I know that," replied Allie bitterly.

"But I brought you up . . . took care of you . . . helped educate you," protested Durade with agitation. "You were my own child, I thought. I was always kind to you. I . . . I loved the mother in the daughter."

"Yes, I know. . . . But you were wicked."

"If you won't tell, it must mean she's still alive," he replied swiftly. "She's not . . . dead! I'll find her. I'll make her come back to me . . . or kill her. . . . After all these years . . . to leave me!"

He seemed wrestling with mingled emotions. The man was proud and strong, but defeat in life, in the crowning passion of life, showed in his white face. The evil in him was not manifest then.

"Where have you lived all this time?" he asked presently.

"Back in the hills with a trapper."

"You have grown. When I saw you, I thought it was the ghost of your mother. You are just as she was . . . when we met."

He seemed lost in sad retrospection. Allie saw streaks of gray in his once jet-black hair.

"What will you do?" asked Allie.

He was startled. The softness left him. A blaze seemed to leap under skin and eyes, and suddenly he was different—he was Durade the gambler, instinct with the lust for gold and life.

"Your mother left me for *you*," he said with terrible bitterness. "I'll keep you. I'll hold you to get even with her."

Allie felt stir in her the fear she had had of him in her childhood when she disobeyed. "But you can't keep me against my will . . . not any more . . . among people we'll meet eastward."

"I can . . . and I will!" he declared softly but implacably. "We're not going East. We'll be in rougher camps than gold camps of California. There's no law except gold and guns out here. . . . But . . . if you speak of me to anyone . . . if you try to get away . . . may your God have mercy on you."

The blaze of him then was the Spaniard. He meant more than dishonor, torture, and death. The evil in him was rampant. The love that had been the only good in an abnormal and disordered mind had turned to hate.

Allie knew him. He was the first who had ever dominated her through sheer force of will. Unless she abided by his command, her fate would be worse than if she had stayed captive among the Sioux. This man was not American. His years among men of later mold had not changed the old-world cruelty of his nature. She recognized the fact in utter despair. She had not strength left to keep her eyes open.

After a while Allie grew conscious that Durade had left her. She felt like a creature that had been fascinated by a deadly snake, and left, only to await its return. Shudderingly, mournfully she resigned herself to the feeling that she must stay under Durade's control until a dominance stronger than his released her. Neale seemed suddenly to have retreated far into the past in her consciousness. A call of his voice—the sight of his face would make that spirit of hers—his spirit—leap like a tigress in her defense. But where was Neale? The habits of life were allpowerful, and all her habits had been formed under Durade's magnetic eye. Neale retreated—and so did spirit, courage, hope. Love remained, despairing, yet unquenchable.

Allies's resignation established a return to normal feelings. She ate and grew stronger; she slept and was refreshed.

The caravan moved on twenty-five miles a day. At the next camp Allie tried walking again, to find her feet were bruised, her legs cramped, and action awkward and painful. But she persevered, and the tingling of revived circulation was like needles pricking her flesh. She limped from one campfire to another, and all the rough men had a kind word or question or glance for her. Allie did not believe they were all honest men. Durade had employed a large force and apparently he had taken all who applied. Miners, hunters, scouts, and men of no hallmark except that of wildness composed the mixed caravan. It spoke much for Durade that they were under control. Allie well remembered hearing her mother say that he had a genius for drawing men to him and managing them.

One, during her walk, when everyone appeared busy, a big fellow, with hulking shoulders, and bandaged head, stepped beside her.

"Girl," he whispered, "if you want a knife slipped into Durade . . . tell him about me."

Allie recognized the whisper before she did the heated red face with its crooked nose and bold eyes and ugly mouth.

Fresno! He had escaped from the Sioux and had fallen in with Durade.

Allie shrank from him. Durade, compared to this kind of ruffian, was a haven of refuge. She passed on without a sign. But Fresno was safe from her. This meeting made her aware of an impulse to run back to Durade, instinctively, as she had when a child. He had ruined her mother; he had meant to make a lure of her, the daughter; he had showed what his vengeance would be to that mother, as he had showed Allie her doom should she betray him. But notwithstanding all this, Durade was not Fresno, nor like any of those men whose eyes seemed to burn her.

She returned to the wagon, and to the several women and men attached to it, with the assurance that there were at least some good persons with the caravan. The women, naturally curious and sympathetic, questioned her in one way and another, about who she was, what had happened to her, where her people or friends were, how she had ever escaped robbers and Indians in that awful country, and they asked if she was really Durade's daughter.

Allie did not tell much about herself, and finally she was left in peace.

The lean old scout, who had first seen Allie as she staggered into the trail, told her it was over a hundred miles to the first camp of the railroad builders.

"Downhill all the way," he concluded. "An' we'll make it in a jiffy."

Nevertheless it took nearly all of four days to sight the camp of the graders—the advance guard of the great construction work.

In those four days Allie had recovered her bloom, her health, her strength, all except the wonderful assurance that had been hers. Durade had spoken daily with her, and had been kind, watchful, like a guardian.

It was with a curious thrill that Allie gazed out as she rode into the construction camp. Horses and men and implements all following the line of Neale's work! Could Neale be there? If so, how dead was her heart to his nearness?

White and soiled and ragged tents stretched everywhere; huge tents belched smoke and resounded with the *ring* of hammers on anvil; soldiers stood on guard; men, red-shirted and blue-shirted, swarmed as thick as ants; in a wide hollow a long line of horses, in double row, heads together, pulled hay from a rack as long as the line, and they pulled and snorted and bit at each other; a strong smell of hay and burning wood mingled with the odor of hot coffee and steaming beans; fires blazed on all sides; inside another huge tent, or many tents without walls, stretched wooden tables and benches; on the scant sage and rocks and brush and everywhere upon the tents lay in a myriad of colors and varieties the late washed clothes of the toilers, and through the wide street of the camp *clattered* teams and swearing teamsters, dragging plows with *clanking* chains and huge scoops turned upside down. Bordering the camp, running east as far as eyes could see, stretched a high flat yellow lane, with the earth hollowed away from it, so that it stood higher than the level plain—and this was the work of the graders, the roadbed of the U.P.R.

This camp appeared to be Durade's destination. His caravan rode through and halted on the outskirts of the far side. Preparations began for what Allie concluded was to be permanent halt. And here there was at once a significant disintegration of Durade's party. One by one the scouts received payment from their employer and with horse and pack disappeared toward the camp. The lean old fellow who had taken kindly interest in Allie looked in at the opening of the canvas over her wagon and, wishing her luck, bade her good bye. The women likewise said good bye, informing her that they were going on home. Not one man among those left would Allie have trusted.

During the hurried settling of camp Durade came to Allie.

"Allie, you don't have to keep cooped up in there unless I tell you," he said. "But don't talk to anyone . . . and don't go that way." He pointed toward the humming camp. "That place beats any gold diggings I ever saw," he concluded.

The tall scant sage afforded Allie some little seclusion and she walked there until Durade called her to supper. She ate alone on a wagon seat, and, when twilight fell, she climbed into her wagon, grateful that it was high off the ground and enclosed her from all except sound.

Darkness came; the fire died down; the low voices of Durade and his men, and of callers who visited them, flowed continuously. Then, presently, there arose a strange murmur, unlike any sound Allie had ever heard. It swelled into low distant roar. She was curious about it. Peeping out of her wagon cover, she saw where the darkness flared to yellow with a line of lights, torches or lanterns or fires. Crossing and recrossing these lights were black objects, in twos and threes and dozens. And from this direction floated the strange low roar. Suddenly she realized. It was the life of the camp. Hundreds and thousands of men were there together—and as the night advanced the low roar rose and fell, lulled away to come again—strange, sad, hideous, mirthful. For a long time Allie could not sleep.

Next morning Durade called her. When she unlaced the canvas flaps, it was to see the sun high and to hear the bustle of work all about her.

Durade brought her breakfast, and gave her instructions. While he was about in the daytime, she might come out and do what she could to amuse herself, but when he was absent, or at night, she must be in her wagon tent, laced in, and was not to answer any call. She would be guarded by Stitt, one of his men, a deaf mute, faithful to his interests and who had orders to handle her roughly should she disobey. Allie would not have been inclined to disobey even without the fear and abhorrence she felt of this ugly and deformed mute.

That day Durade caused to be erected tents, canopies, tables, benches, and last a larger tent, into which the tables and benches were carried. Fresno worked hard, as did all the men except Stitt, who had nothing to do but watch Allie's wagon.

Wearily the day passed for her. How many more days must she spend thus, watching idly, because there was nothing else to do? Still, back in her consciousness, there was a vague and growing thought. Sooner or later Neale would appear in the flesh. As he appeared in her dreams.

That night, Allie, peeping out, saw by the fire and torchlight, men drawn to Durade's large tent. Mexicans, Negroes, Irishmen—all kinds of men passed, loud and profane, careless and reckless, quarrelsome and loquacious. Soon there arose in her ears the long-forgotten but now familiar sounds of a gambling hall in full blast. The rolling rattle of the wheel, sharp between the lulls of many voices, strident and keen, intermingled with the strange rich false *clink* of gold.

It needed only a few days and nights for Allie Lee to divine Durade's retrogression. He had been a gambler for the sake of gambling; now in addition he was possessed of an unscrupulous intent, a strange cold devouring passion to get gold that he might gamble with it. Allie divined evidence of this, saw it, heard it. The man had struck the descent, and he was all the more dangerous for that breaking of his career.

Not a week had elapsed before his gambling hall roared all night. Allie got most of her sleep during the day. She shut out what sound she could and tried to be deaf to the rest. But she had to hear the pistol shots, and shrill cries, and the trample of heavy boots, as men dragged a dead gamester out to the ditch.

Day was a relief, a blessing. Allie was frequently cooped up in her narrow canvas-covered wagon, but she saw from there that life of the grading camp.

There were various bosses—boarding boss, who fed the laborers, and stable boss, who had charge of the teams, and grading boss, who ruled the diggers and scrapers, and the timekeeper boss, who kept track of the work of all.

In the early morning, a horde of hungry men stampeded the boarding tents where the cooks and waiters made mad haste to satisfy loud and merry demands. At sunset the same horde drooped in, dirty and hot and lame, and fought for seats while others waited.

Out on the level plain stretched the hundreds of teams, moving on and returning, the drivers shouting, the horses bending. The hot sun glared, the wind whipped up the dust, the laborers spurred to the shout of the boss—and on westward crept the low level yellow bank of sand and gravel—the roadbed of the U.P.R.

Thus the daytime had its turmoil, too, but splendid, like the toil of heroes united to gain some common end, and the army of soldiers was there, ever keen-eyed, for the skulking Sioux.

Mull, the boss of the camp, became a friend of Durade's. The wily Spaniard could draw any class of man. This Mull had been a driver of truck horses in New York and now he was a driver of men.

He was huge, like a bull, heavy-lipped and red-cheeked, hairy and coarse, with big sunken eyes. A brute—a cave man! He drank; he gambled. He was at once a bully and a pirate. Responsible to no one but his contractor, he hated the contractor and hated his job. He was great in his place, brutal with fist and foot, a gleaner of results from hard men at a hard time.

He won gold from Durade, or, as Fresno guffawed to a comrade, he had been allowed to win it. Durade picked his man. He had big schemes and he needed Mull.

Benton was Durade's objective point—Benton, the great and growing camp city, where gold and blood were spilled in the dusty streets and life roared like a blast from hell.

All that Allie heard of this Benton increased her dread, and at last determined her that she would run any risk rather than be taken there.

That night, as soon as it grew dark, she slipped out of the wagon and, under cover of the darkness, made her escape.

# CHAPTER FIFTEEN

The building of the U.P.R. as it advanced westward, caused many camps and towns to spring up and flourish, like mushrooms in a single night. Therefore towns and communities were born, for the strangeness and the like of which there was no analogy.

Warren Neale did not get away from the fascination of the work and life, even though, instead of being important and strenuous, he was now insignificant and idle. He began to drink and gamble in North Platte, more in a bitter defiance than from any real desire. Then he drifted to Kearney and afterward to Cheyenne.

At Kearney, King answered to the violence growing more unrestrained in him. In a quarrel with a construction boss named Smith, King accused Smith of being the crooked tool of the crooked commissioners who had forced Neale to quit his job. Smith grew hot and profane. The cowboy promptly slapped his face. Then Smith, like the fool he was, went after his gun. He never got it out.

It distressed Neale greatly that King had badly shot up a man—and a railroad man. No matter what King said, Neale knew the shooting was on his account. His deed made the cowboy a marked man. It changed him, also, toward Neale, inasmuch as that he saw his wildness was making small Neale's chances of returning to work. King never ceased importuning Neale to go back to his job. After shooting Smith, the cowboy made one more eloquent appeal to Neale, then left for Cheyenne. Neale followed him.

Cheyenne was just emancipating itself from the end of a reign as a headquarters town, and although depleted and thin it had made a bid for permanency. But the sting and wildness of life had gone on with the rails and the operation of the next and most famous town—Benton.

Neale boarded a train for Benton and watched with bitterness the familiar landmark he had learned to know so well while surveying the line and now saw again under hateful circumstance. He was no longer connected with the great project—no more a necessary part of the great movement.

Beyond Medicine Bow the grass and the green failed, and the immense train of freight cars and passenger coaches, loaded to capacity, *clattered* on into arid country. Gray and red, the drab and fiery colors of the desert lent the ridges character, forbidding and barren.

From a car window Neale got his first glimpse of the wonderful terminus city and for once his old thrills returned. He recalled the distance—seven hundred—no, six hundred and ninety-eight miles from Omaha—so far westward was Benton.

It lay in the heart of barrenness, alkali, desolation, in the face of windswept desert with dust devils sweeping along, yellow and funnel-shaped—a huge blocked-out town set where no town could ever live. Benton was prey for sun, wind, dust, drought—and the wind was terrible and insupportably cold. No sage, no cedars, no grass, not even a cactus bush, nothing green or living relieved the eye, which swept across the gray and the white, through the dust, to the distant bare and desolate hills of drab. The hell that was reported to abide at Benton was in harmony with its setting. The immense train *clattered* and jolted to a stop. A roar of wind, a cloud of powdery dust, a discordant and unceasing din of voices, came through the open windows of the

173

car. The heterogeneous mass of humanity with which Neale had traveled jostled out, struggling with packs and bags.

Neale, carrying his bag, stepped off into half a foot of dust. He saw a disintegrated crowd of travelers that had just arrived, of travelers ready to depart, and soldiers, Indians, Mexicans, Negroes, loafers, merchants, tradesmen, laborers—changing and remarkable spectacle of humanity. He saw stagecoaches with hawkers bawling for passengers to Salt Lake, Ogden, Montana, Idaho; he saw a white street—white with dust where it was not thronged with moving men and women, and lined by tents and canvas houses and clapboard structures, and the strangest conglomeration of painted and printed signs that ever advertised anything in the world.

A woman, well clad, young, not uncomely, but with hungry eyes like those of a hawk, accosted Neale. He drew away. In the din he had not heard what she said. A boy likewise spoke to him; a Mexican tried to take his baggage; a man jostling him felt of his pocket, and, as Neale walked on, he was leered at, importuned, grasped, accosted, and all but mobbed.

So this was Benton.

A pistol shot pierced the din. Someone shouted. A wave of the crowd indicated commotion somewhere, and then the action and noise were precisely as before. Neale crossed five intersecting streets, and evidently the wide street he was on was the main one. In that walk of five blocks he saw thousands of persons, but they were not the soldiers who protected the line nor the laborers who made the road. These were the travelers, the business people, the stragglers, the nondescripts, the parasites, the criminals, the desperadoes, and the idlers—all who must by hook or crook live off the builders.

Neale was conscious of a sudden exhilaration. The spirit was still in him. After all, his defeated ambition was nothing in the great sum of this work. How many had failed! He thought of the nameless graves already dotting the slopes along the line and already forgotten. It would be something to live through the heyday of Benton.

Under a sign, *Hotel,* he entered a door in a clapboard house. The place was as crude as an unfinished barn. Paying in advance for lodgings, he went to the room shown him—a stall with a door and a bar, a cot and a bench, a bowl and a pitcher. Through cracks he could see out over an uneven stretch of tents and houses. Toward the edge of town stood a long string of small tents and several huge ones, which might have been the soldiers' quarters.

Neale went out in search of a meal and entered the first restaurant. It was merely a canvas house stretched over poles, with compartments at the back. High wooden benches served as tables, low benches as seats. The floor was sand. At one table sat a Mexican, an Irishman, and a Negro. The Irishman was drunk. The Negro came to wait on Neale, and, receiving an order, went darting to the kitchen. The Irishman sidled over to Neale.

"Say, did yez hear about Casey?" he inquired, very friendly.

"No, I didn't," replied Neale. He remembered Casey, the flagman, but probably there were many Caseys in that camp.

"There was a foight . . . out on the line . . . yisteddy," went on the fellow, "an' the domn' redskins chased the gang to the troop train. Phurst do you think? A bullet knocked Casey's pipe out of his mouth . . . as he was runnin' . . . an' b'gorra, Casey stopped fer it an' was all shot up."

"Is he dead?" inquired Neale.

"Not yit. No bullets can't kill Casey."

"Was his pipe a short black one?"

"It was that."

"And did Casey have it everlastingly in his mouth?"

"He shlept in it."

Neale knew that particular Casey, and he examined this loquacious Irishman more closely. He recognized him as Pat Shane, one of the trio he had known during the survey in the Black Hills two years ago. The recognition was a stab to Neale. Memory of the Black Hills—of the lost Allie Lee—was a flayed and exquisite surface on his mind. Shane had aged greatly. There were scars on his face that Neale had not seen before.

"Mister, don't I know yez?" leered Shane, studying Neale with bleary eyes.

Neale did not care to be remembered. The waiter brought his dinner, which turned out to be a poor one at a high price. After eating, Neale went out and began to saunter along the walk. The sun had set and the wind had gone down. There was no flying dust. The street was again crowded with men but nothing like it had been after the arrival of the train. No one paid much attention to Neale. On that wall he counted nineteen saloons, and probably some of the larger places were of like nature, but not so wide open to the casual glance.

Neale strolled through the town from end to end, and across the railroad outside of the limits, to a high bank where he sat down. The desert was beautiful away to the west, with its dull mottled lines backed by gold and purple, and its sweep and heave and notched horizon. Near at hand it seemed drab and bare, like his life, unproductive and desolate. He watched a long train of flat and boxcars come in, and saw that every car swarmed with soldiers and laborers. The train discharged its load of thousands and steamed back for more.

Twilight fell. All hours were difficult for Neale, but twilight was the most unendurable, for it had been the hour Allie Lee loved best and during which she and Neale had walked hand in hand along the brook, back there in the lonely and beautiful valley in the Black Hills. Neale could not sit still long; he could not rest, nor sleep well, nor work, nor be of any use to himself or anyone, because he was haunted and driven by the memory of Allie Lee. He drifted to find new scenes, he drank so that he would gamble, and he gambled to forget. And at such quiet hours as this one, in the midst of the turmoil he had sought for weeks, a sadness filled his soul and an eternal remorse. Then the love that had changed him and life that had failed him seemed utterly unrelated.

To and fro he paced over the bare ridge while twilight shadowed. A star twinkled in the west, a night wind began to seep the sand. The desert, vast, hidden, mysterious, yet so free, so untrammeled, darkened.

Lights began to flash up along the streets of Benton. And presently Neale became aware of a low and mounting *hum*, like a first stir of angry bees.

Loud and challenging strains of a band drew Neale toward the center of the main street where men were pouring into a big tent. He halted outside and watched. It took no more now than this strident business-like quick-step music and sight of the men and women attracted thereby to make Neale realize that Benton had arisen in a day, would die out in a night, and its life would be swift, vile, and deadly.

When the band ceased, a subdued roar came from inside the big tent—a commingling of rough voices of men and *humming* of wheels and *clinking* of glasses and gold, and *rattling* of dice, the hoarse call of a croupier or dealer, the shuffling of feet—a roar pierced now and then by a shrill, vacant, soulless laugh of a woman.

It was that last sound that almost turned Neale away from the door. He shunned women. But this place fascinated him. Tonight he was not in one of his violent moods when he must have drinking, gambling—both of which for him were attended by violent action. He went in under the flaming lamps.

The place was crowded—a huge tent stretched over a

framework of wood, and it was full of people, din, smoke, movement. The floor was of good planking covered with sand. Walking was possible only around the narrow aisles between groups at tables.

Neale's sauntering brought him to the bar. It had to him a familiar look, and afterward he learned it had been brought complete from St. Louis where he had seen it in a saloon. It seemed a huge glittering magnificent monstrosity in that coarse bare setting: wide mirrors, glistening bottles, paintings of nude women, row after row of polished glasses, a brawny villainous bartender with three attendants all working fast, a line of roughhouse men five deep before the bar—all constituted a scene with the aspects of a city and yet with an atmosphere no city ever knew. The drinkers were not all rough men. There were elegant black-hatted frock-coated men of leisure in that line—not directors and commissioners and traveling guests of the U.P.R. but gentlemen of chance. Gamblers!

The band now began a different strain—dance music. Neale slowly worked his way around. At the end of the big tent a wide door opened into another big room—a dance hall, full of dancers. Neale had seen nothing like this in the other construction camps. A ball was in progress. Just now it was merry, excited, lively—the first dance of the evening. Neale got inside and behind the row of crowded benches where he stood up against a post to watch. Probably two hundred people were in the hall, most of them sitting. How singularly it struck Neale to see good-looking bare-armed and bare-necked young women dancing there and dancing well! There were other women—painted—hollow-eyed—sad wrecks of womanhood. The male dancers were young men, as years counted, mostly unfamiliar with the rhythmic motion of feet to a tune, and they bore the rough stamp of soldiers and laborers. But there were others, as there had been before the bar, who wore their clothes differently, who had a different poise and swing—young men, like Neale, whose earlier years had known some of the graces of society. They did not belong there; the young women did not belong there. The place seemed unreal. This was a merry scene, apparently with little sign at that moment of what it actually meant. Neale sensed its undercurrent.

He left the dance hall. Of the gambling games, he liked best to watch and to play poker. It had interest for him. The winning or losing of money was not of great moment. Poker was not all chance or luck, such as the roll of a ball, the turn of a card, the facing-up of dice. Presently he became one of an interested group around a table watching four men play poker.

One, a gambler in black, immaculate in contrast to his companions, had a white, hard expressionless face, with eyes of steel and thin lips. His hands were wonderful. Probably they never saw the sunlight, certainly no labor. They were as swift as light, too swift for the glance of an eye. But when he dealt the cards, he was slow, careful, deliberate. The stakes were of gold and the largest heap lay in front of him. One of his opponents was a giant of a fellow, young, with hulking shoulders, heated face, and broken nose—a desperado if Neale ever saw one. The other two players called this strapping brute Fresno. Of these, the little man with a sallow face like a wolf was evidently too intent on the game to look up. He appeared to be losing—beside his small pile of gold stood an empty tumbler. The other and last player was a huge bull-necked man who Neale had seen before. It was difficult to place him, but, after studying the red cheeks and heavy black drooping mustache, and hearing the loud voice, he recognized him as a boss of graders—a head boss. Presently the sallow-faced player called him Mull, and then Neale remembered him well.

Several of the watchers around this table lounged away, leaving a better vantage place for Neale.

"May I sit in the game?" he inquired, during a deal.

"Certainly," replied the gambler.

"Now we gotta 'nough," said the sallow man, and he glanced from Neale to the gambler as if he suspected them. Gamblers often worked in pairs.

"I just came to Benton," added Neale, reading the man's thought. "I never saw the gentleman in black before."

"What'n hell?" rumbled Mull, grabbing up his cards.

Fresno leered.

The gambler leaned back and his swift white hands flashed. Neale believed he had a Derringer up each sleeve. A wrong word now would precipitate a fight.

"Excuse me," said Neale hastily. "I don't want to make trouble. I just said I never saw this gentleman before."

"Nor I him," returned the gambler courteously. "My name is Place Hough and my word is not doubted."

Neale had heard of this famous Mississippi River gambler. So evidently had the other three players. The game proceeded, and, when it came to Hough's deal, Mull bet hard and lost all. His big hairy hands shook. He looked at Fresno and the other fellow, but not at Hough.

"I'm broke," he said gruffly, and he got up from the bench. He strode past Hough, behind him, and then as if suddenly, instinctively answering to fury, he whipped out a gun.

Neale, just as instinctively, grasped the rising hand. "Hold on, there!" he called. "Would you shoot a man in the back?" And Neale, whose grip was powerful, caused the other to drop the gun. Neale kicked it aside.

Fresno got up. "Whar's your head, Mull?" he growled. "Git out of this!"

Attention had been attracted to Mull. Someone picked up the gun. The sallow-faced man rose, holding out his hand for it. Hough did not even turn around.

"I was goin' to hold him up," said Mull. He glared fiercely at Neale, wrenched his hand free, and, with his comrades, disappeared in the crowd.

The gambler rose and shook down his sleeves. The action convinced Neale that he had held a little gun in each hand. "I saw him draw," he said. "You saved his life. Nevertheless, I appreciate your action. My name is Place Hough, will you drink with me?"

"Sure. . . . My name is Neale."

They approached the bar and drank together.

"A railroad man, I take it?" asked Hough.

"I was. I'm footloose now."

A fleeting smile crossed the gambler's face. "Benton is bad enough, without you being footloose."

"All these camps are tough," replied Neale.

"I was in North Platte, Kearney, Cheyenne, Medicine Bow during their rise," said Hough. "They were tough. But they were not Benton. Benton is hell! And the next camp west, which will be the last . . . it will be Roaring Hell. What will be its name?"

"Why is Benton worse?" inquired Neale.

"The big work is well under way now, with tremendous push from behind. There are three men for every man's work. That lays off two men each day. Drunk or dead! The place is wild . . . far off. There's gold . . . hundreds of thousands of dollars in gold dumped off the trains. Benton has had one pay day. That day was the sight of my life! Then besides time and place and gold . . . there are women."

"I saw a few in the dance hall," replied Neale.

"Then you haven't looked in at Stanton's?"

"Who's he?"

"Stanton is not a man," replied Hough.

Neale glanced inquiringly over his glass.

"Beauty Stanton, they call her," went on Hough. "I saw her in New Orleans years ago when she was a very young woman . . . notorious then, she had the beauty and she led the life . . . did Beauty Stanton."

Neale made no comment and Hough, turning to pay for the drinks, was accosted by several men. They wanted to play poker.

"Gentlemen, I hate to take your money," he said. "But I never refuse to sit in a game. . . . Neale, will you join us?"

They joined a table just vacated. Neale took two of the three strangers to be prosperous merchants or ranchers from the Missouri country. The third was a gambler by profession. Neale found himself in unusually sharp company. He did not have a great deal of money. So in order to keep clear-headed, he did not drink. And he began to win, not by reason of excellent judgment but because he was lucky. He had good cards all the time and part of the time very strong ones. It struck him presently that these remarkable hands came during Hough's deal, and he wondered if the gambler was deliberately manipulating the cards to his advantage. At any rate he won hundreds of dollars.

"Mister Neale, do you always hold such cards?" asked one of the men.

"Why, sure," replied Neale. He could not help being excited and elated.

"Well, he can't be beat," said the other.

"Lucky at cards, unlucky in love," remarked the third of the trio. "I pass."

Hough was looking straight at Neale when this last remark was made. And Neale suddenly lost his smile, his flush. The gambler dropped his glance. "Play the game and don't get personal in your remarks," he said. "This is poker."

Neale continued to win, but his excitement did not return, nor his elation. A random word from a strange man had proven to sting him. Unlucky in love . . . alas . . . what was luck, gold . . . anything to him any more?

By the time the game ended Neale sensed a friendly interest in Hough that was difficult to define or explain, and the conviction gained upon him that the gambler had deliberately dealt him those remarkable cards.

"Let's see," said Hough, consulting his watch. "Twelve o'clock! Stanton's will be humming. We'll go in."

Neale did not want to share his reluctance, yet he did not know just what to say. Then he was drifting. He went.

It seemed that all visitors who had been in the gambling hell gravitated to this other dance hall. The entrance appeared to be through a hotel. At least Neale saw the hotel sign. The building was not made of canvas but painted wood in sections, like the scenes of a stage. Men were coming and going; the hum of music and gaiety came from the rear; there were rugs, pictures, chairs; this place, whatever its nature, made pretensions. Neale did not see any bar.

They entered a big room full of people, apparently doing nothing. From the opposite side, where the dance hall opened, came a hum that seemed at once music and discordance, gaiety and wildness, with a strange carrying undertone, raw and violent.

Hough led Neale across the room to where he could look into the dance hall.

Neale saw a mad colorful flash and whirl of dancers.

Hough whispered in Neale's ear: "Stanton throws the drunks out of here."

No, it appeared the dancers were not drunk with liquor. But there was evidence of other drunkenness than that of the bottle. The floor was crowded. Looking out at the mass, Neale could only see whirling heated faces, white clinging arms, forms swaying around and around, a wild rhythm without grace, a dance in which music was but an instrument, where men and women were lost. Neale had never seen a sight like that. He was stunned. There were no souls here. Only beasts of men—and women for whom there was no name. If death stalked in that camp, as Hough had intimated, and hell was there—then the two could not meet too soon.

If the mass and the spirit and the sense of the scene dismayed Neale, the living beings, the creatures, the women—for the men were beyond him—confounded him with pity, consternation, and stinging regret. He had loved two women—his mother and Allie—so well that he should love all women because they were of the same sex. Yet how impossible! Had these creations any sex? Yet they were—at least many were—young, gay, pretty, wild, full of life. They had swift suppleness, smiles, flashing eyes, a look at once intent and yet vacant. But few onlookers would have seen that. The eyes for which the dance was meant saw the mad whirl, the bare flesh, the brazen glance, the close embrace.

The music ended, the dancers stopped, the shuffling ceased. There were no seats unoccupied so the dancers walked around or formed in groups.

"Well, I see Ruby has spotted you," observed Hough.

Neale did not gather exactly what the gambler meant, yet he associated the remark with a girl dressed in red who had paused at the door with others and looked directly at Neale. At that moment someone engaged Hough's attention. The girl would have been striking in any company. Neale thought her neither beautiful nor pretty, but he kept on looking. Her arms were bare, her dress cut very low. Her face offered vivid contrast to the carmine on her lips. It was a round soft face, with narrow eyes, dark, seductive, bold. She tilted her head on one side and suddenly smiled at Neale. It startled him. It was a smile with the shock of a bullet. It held Neale, so that, when she crossed to him, he could not move. He felt rather than saw Hough return to his side. The girl took hold of the lapels of Neale's coat. She looked up. Her eyes were dark with what seemed red shadows deep in them. She had white teeth. The carmined lips curled in a smile—a smile, impossible to believe, of youth and sweetness that disclosed a dimple in her cheek. She was pretty. She was holding him—pulling him a little toward her.

"I like you!" she exclaimed.

The suddenness of the incident, the impossibility of what was happening made Neale dumb. He felt her, saw her as if he were in a dream. Her face possessed a peculiar fascination. The sleepy, strange, seductive eyes; the provoking half smile, teasing, alluring, the red lips, full and young through the carmine paint; all of her seemed to breathe a different kind of a power than he had ever experienced—unspiritual, elemental, strong as some heady wine. She represented youth, health, beauty terribly linked with evil wisdom, with corrupt and irresistible power, with a base and mysterious affinity for man.

The breath and the charm and the pestilence of her passed over Neale like fire.

"Sweetheart, will you dance with me?" she asked, with her head tilted to one side and her half-open audacious veiled eyes on his.

"No," replied Neale. He put her from him, gently, but coldly.

She showed slow surprise. "Why not? Can't you dance? You don't look like a gawk."

"Yes, I can dance," replied Neale.

"Then will you dance with me?" she retorted, and red spots showed through the white on her cheek.

"I told you no," replied Neale, with cold courtesy.

His reply transported her into a sudden fury. She swung her hand viciously. Hough caught it, saving Neale from a sounding slap in the face.

"Ruby, don't lose your temper," remonstrated the gambler.

"He insulted me!" she cried passionately.

"He did not. Ruby, you're spoiled. . . ."

"Spoiled! Hell! Didn't he look at me . . . flirt with me? That's why I asked him to dance. Then he insulted me. I'll make Cordy shoot him up for it!"

"No you won't," replied Hough, and he pulled her toward his companion, a tall woman with golden hair. "Stanton, shut her up."

The woman addressed spoke a few words in Ruby's ear. Then the girl flounced away. But she turned with withering scorn. "What in hell did you come in here for? You big handsome stiff!" With that she was lost amid her mirthful companions.

Hough turned to Neale. "The girl's a favorite. You ruffled her vanity. . . . You see! That's Benton. If you had happened to be alone, you would have had gun play. Be careful after this."

"But I didn't flirt with her," protested Neale. "I only looked at her . . . curiously, of course. And I said I wouldn't dance."

Hough laughed. "You're young in Benton. . . . Neale, let me introduce you to the lady who saved you some inconvenience. . . . Miss Stanton . . . Mister Neale."

And that was how Neale met Beauty Stanton. It seemed she had done him a service. He thanked her. Neale's manner with women was courteous and deferential. It showed strangely here, by contrast. The Stanton woman was superb, not more than thirty years old, with a face that must have been lovely once and held the haunting ghost of beauty still. Her hair was dead gold; her eyes were large and blue, with dark circles under them, and her features had a clear-cut classic regularity.

"Where's Ancliffe?" asked Hough, addressing Stanton.

She pointed and Hough left them. "Neale, you're new here," affirmed the woman rather curiously.

"Didn't I look like it? I can't forget what that girl said," replied Neale.

"Tell me."

"She asked me what in the hell I came in here for? And she called me. . . ."

"Oh, I heard what Ruby called you. It's a wonder it wasn't worse. She can swear like a trooper. The men are mad over Ruby. It'd be just like her to fall in love with you for snubbing her."

"I hope she doesn't," replied Neale constrainedly.

"May I ask . . . what did you come here for?"

"You mean here to your dance hall? Why, Hough brought me. I met him, we played cards, and. . . ."

"No. I mean what brought you to Benton?"

"To Benton. . . . I don't know," said Neale frankly.

"No work? No intentions? You're no spiker or capper or boss. I know that sort. And I can spot a gambler a mile! The whole world meets out here in Benton. But not many young men like you wander into my place."

"Like me? How so?"

"The men here are wolves . . . on the scent for flesh . . . and like bandits on the trail of gold. . . . But you . . . you're like my friend Ancliffe?"

"*Who* is he?" asked Neale politely.

"Who is he? God only knows. But he's an Englishman and a gentleman. It's a pity men like Ancliffe and you drift out here." She spoke seriously. She had the accent and manner of breeding.

"Why, Miss Stanton?" inquired Neale. He was finding another woman here interesting to him.

"Because it means wasted life. You don't work. You're not crooked. You can't do any good. And only a knife in the back or a bullet from some drunken bully's gun awaits you."

"That isn't a very hopeful outlook, I'll admit," replied Neale thoughtfully.

At this point Hough returned with a pale slender man whose clothes and gait were not American. He introduced him as Ancliffe. Neale felt in the introduction a stimulus to an accumulating interest. Benton might be hell, but he was meeting new types of men and women. Ancliffe was fair; he had a handsome face that held a story, and tired blue eyes that looked out wearily and mildly, without curiosity or hope. The Englishman of broken fortunes.

"Just arrived, eh?" he said to Neale. "Rather jolly here, don't you think?"

"A fellow's not going to stagnate in Benton," replied Neale.

"Not while he's alive," interposed Stanton.

"Miss Stanton, that idea seems to persist with you . . . the brevity of life," said Neale, smiling. "What are the average days for a mortal in this bloody Benton?"

"Days! You mean hours. I call the night blessed that someone is not dragged out of my place. And I don't sell drinks! I've saved Ancliffe's life nine times I know of. Either he hasn't any sense or he wants to get killed."

"I assure you . . . it's the former," said the Englishman.

"But my friends, I'm serious," she returned earnestly. "This awful place is getting on my nerves. . . . Mister Neale here, he would have had to face a gun already but for me."

"Miss Stanton, I appreciate your thought of such good for nothing fellows as I am," replied Neale. "But it doesn't follow that, if I had to face a gun, I'd be sure to go down."

"You can throw a gun?" questioned Hough.

"I had a cowboy gun-thrower for a partner for years . . . out on the surveying of the road."

"Boy, you're courting death!" exclaimed Stanton.

Then the music started up again. Conversation was scarcely worthwhile during the dancing. Neale watched as before. Twice while he gazed at the whirling couples, he caught the eyes of the girl Ruby upon him. They were expressions of pique, resentment, curiosity. Neale did not look that way any more. Besides his attention was otherwise attracted. Hough yelled in his ear to watch the fun. A fight had started. A strapping fellow wearing a belt containing gun and Bowie knife had jumped upon a table just as the music stopped. He was drunk. He looked like a young workman ambitious to be a desperado.

"Ladies an' gennelmen!" he bawled. "I been . . . requested t'sing."

Yells and hoots answered him. He glared ferociously around, trying to pick out one of his insulters. Trouble was brewing. Something was thrown at him from behind and it struck him. He wheeled, unsteady upon his feet. Then several men, bareheaded and evidently attendants of the hall, made a rush for him. The table was upset. The would-be singer went down in a heap, and he was pounced upon, handled like a sack, and thrown out. The crowd roared its glee.

"The worst of that is . . . those fellows 'most always come back, drunk and ugly," said Stanton. "Then we all begin to run or dodge."

"Your men didn't lose time with that rowdy," remarked Neale.

"I've hired all kinds of men to keep order," she replied. "Laborers, ex sheriffs, gunmen, badmen! The Irish are the best on the job. But they won't stick. I've got eight men here now and they are a tough lot. I'm scared to death of them. I believe they rob my guests. But what can I do? Without somebody I couldn't run the place. It'll be the death of me!"

Neale did not doubt that. A shadow surely hovered over these women. He was surprised at the seriousness with which she spoke. Evidently she tried to preserve order—to avert fights and bloodshed so that licentiousness could go on unrestrained. Neale believed they must go hand in hand. He did not see how

189

it would be possible for a place like this to last long. It could not. The life of the place brought out the worst in men. It created opportunities. Neale watched them pass, seeing the truth in the red eyes, the heavy lids, the open mouths, the look and gait and gesture. A wild frenzy had fastened upon their minds. He found an added curiosity in studying the faces of Ancliffe and Hough. The Englishman had run his race. Any place would suit him for the end. Neale saw this and marveled at the man's ease and grace and amiability. He reminded Neale of Larry Red King—the same cool easy careless air. Ancliffe would die game. Hough was not affected by this sort of debauched life any more than he would have been by another kind. He preyed on men. He looked on with cold gray expressionless face. Possibly he, too, would find an end in Benton sooner or later.

These reflections, passing swiftly, made Neale think of himself. What was true for others must be true for him. The presence of any of these persons—of Hough and Ancliffe, of himself, in Beauty Stanton's gaudy resort was a grim and sad proof of disordered and fallen life.

Someone touched him—interrupted his thought.

"You've had trouble?" asked Stanton, who had turned from the others.

"Yes," he said.

"Well, we've all had that. . . . You seem young to me."

Hough turned to speak to Stanton. "Ruby's going to make trouble."

"No!" exclaimed the woman, with eyes lighting.

Neale then saw that the girl Ruby, with a short bold-looking fellow who packed a gun, and several companions of both sexes, had come in from the dance hall to take up a position near him. Stanton went over to them. She drew Ruby aside and talked to her. The girl showed none of the passion that had marked her manner a little while before. Presently Stanton returned.

"Ruby's got over her temper," she said, with evident relief, to Neale. "She asked me to say that she apologized. It's just what I told you. She'll fall madly in love with you for what you did. . . . She's of good family, Neale. She has a sister she talks of . . . and a home she could go back to if she wasn't ashamed."

"That so?" replied Neale thoughtfully. "Do we talk to her?"

At some slight sign Ruby joined the group.

"Ruby, you've already introduced yourself to this gentleman, but not so nicely as you might have," said Stanton.

"I'm sorry," replied Ruby. A certain wistfulness changed her.

"Maybe I was rude," said Neale. "I didn't intend to be. I couldn't dance with anyone here . . . or anywhere. . . ." Then he spoke to her in an aside. "But I'll tell you what I will do. I won a thousand dollars tonight. I'll give you half of it if you'll go home."

The girl shrank as if she had received a stab. Then she stiffened. "Why don't *you* go home?" she retorted. "We're all going to hell out here. And the gamest get there soonest!" She glared at Neale an instant, white-faced and hard, and then, rejoining her companions, she led them away.

Beauty Stanton seemed to have received something of the check that had changed the girl Ruby. Presently she leaned toward Neale and whispered to him. "Boy, you're courting death. Someone . . . something has hurt you. But you're young. . . . *Go home!*" Then she bade him good night and left the group.

He looked on in silence after that. When Ancliffe departed, he was glad to follow Hough out into the street. There the same confusion held. A loud throng hurried by, as if bent on cramming into a few hours the life that would not last long.

Neale was interested to inquire more about Ancliffe. And the gambler replied that the Englishman had come from no one knew where—that he did not go to extremes in drinking or betting—that he evidently had become attached to Beauty Stanton—that he surely must be a ruined man of class who had left all behind him and had become like so many men out there—a leaf in the storm.

"Stanton took to you," went on Hough. "I saw that. . . . And poor Ruby! I'll tell you, Neale, I'm sorry for some of these women."

"Who wouldn't be?"

"Women of this class are strange to you, Neale. But I've mixed with them for years. Of course, Benton sets a pace no man ever saw before. Still, the harder and vilest of these scullions sometimes shows an amazing streak of good. And women like Ruby and Beauty Stanton whose early surroundings must have been refined . . . they are beyond understanding. They will cut your heart out for a slight, and sacrifice their lives for a courteous word. It was your manner that cost Ruby and won Beauty Stanton. They meet with neither coldness nor courtesy out here. It must be bitter as gall for a woman like Stanton to be treated as you treated her . . . with respect. Yet see how it got her!"

"I didn't see anything in particular," replied Neale.

"You were too excited and disgusted with the whole scene," said Hough as they reached the roaring lights of the gambling hell. "Will you go in and play again? There are always open games."

"No, I guess not . . . unless you think. . . ."

"Boy, I think nothing except that I liked your company and that I owe you a service. Good night."

Neale walked to his lodgings, tired and thoughtful and moody. Behind him the roar lulled and swelled. It was 3:00 in the morning. He wondered when these night hawks slept. As for himself, he found slumber not easily gained. Dawn was lighting the east when he at last fell asleep.

# CHAPTER SIXTEEN

Neale slept until late the next day and awoke with the pang a new day always gave him now. He arose slowly, gloomily with the hateful consciousness that he had nothing to do. He had wanted to be alone, and now loneliness was bad for him. Almost he regretted that he had refused to let Larry Red King come with him. He had begun to acquire the habits of the vicious.

"If I were half a man I'd have done with it all . . . quick," he muttered in scorn, and he thought of the broken Englishman, serene and at ease, settled with himself. And he thought of the girl Ruby who had flung the taunt at him that the "gamest get there soonest." Not for long should he forget that. He was a kind of a coward. Certainly that abandoned girl was not one. She was lost, but she was magnificent.

"I guess I'll leave Benton," he soliloquized. But the place . . . the wildness fascinated him. "No. I guess I'll stay."

It angered him that he could still be ashamed of himself. He was victim to many moods—and underneath every one of them was the steady ache, the dull pain, the pang in his breast, deep in the bone.

As he left his lodgings, he heard the whistle of a train. The scene down the street was similar to the one that had greeted him the day before, only the dust was not blowing so thickly. He went into a hotel for his meal and fared better, watching the hurry and scurry of men. After he had finished he strolled toward the station.

193

Benton had two trains each day now. This one, just in, was long and loaded to its utmost capacity. Neale noticed an Indian arrow sticking fast over a window of one of the coaches. There were flat cars loaded with sections of houses and boxcars full of furniture. Benton was growing every day. At least a thousand persons got off that train, adding to the dusty jostling mêlée.

Suddenly Neale came face to face with Larry Red King.

"Red!" he yelled, and actually made at the cowboy.

"I'm sure glad to see you," drawled King. "What in hell busted loose 'round heah?"

Neale drew him out of the crowd. The cowboy had not changed. He carried a small pack done up in a canvas. "Red, your face looks like home to a man in a strange land," declared Neale. "But I forbid you to follow me."

"Who followed you?" blustered King.

"How about your job?"

"Wal, thet man Lee come along . . . seen me . . . had a little palaver with my boss."

"Lee!" exclaimed Neale. "Oh, I remember. So he had you fired?"

"Mebbe. Anyway, I give it to thet boss . . . good an' hard."

"Where are your horses?"

King looked less at his ease.

"Wal, I sold them."

"Sold them? Those great horses? Oh, Red, you didn't."

"Hell! It costs money to ride on this heah U.P.R. thet we built, an' I had no money."

"But what did you come for? Red, I told you to cut loose from me. I'm on the downgrade. And you had a good job. . . . I . . . I cared for those horses."

"Will you shut up aboot my horses?"

Neale had never before seen the tinge of gray in that red-bronze face. "But I told you not to follow me."

"Wal, who followed you?" retorted King.

"You did. Now, didn't you? Don't lie."

"If you put it that way, yes, I did. Now what're you-all goin' to do aboot it?"

"I'll lick you good," declared Neale hotly. He was angry at King, but angrier at himself that he had been the cause of the cowboy's loss of work and of his splendid horses.

"Lick me?" ejaculated King. "You mean beat me up?"

"Yes. You deserve it."

King took him in earnest and seemed very much concerned. Neale could almost have laughed at the cowboy's serious predicament.

"Wal, I reckon I ain't much of a fighter with my fists," said King soberly. "So come on an' get it over."

"Oh, damn you, Red! I wouldn't lay a hand on you. And I *am* sick. I'm glad to see you. But why . . . why did you follow me?" Neale's voice grew full and trembling.

King became confused and his red face grew redder and the keen blue flash of his eyes softened. "Wal, you see . . . I heard what a tough place this heah Benton was . . . an' I reckoned as how you'd be gettin' wilder an' wilder . . . so I jest throwed up an' come." King ended this long speech lamely, but the way he hitched at his belt was conclusive.

Neale felt too deeply touched to reply. He had to accept King's loyalty whether he ought to or not, and he was half ashamed of his gladness. A warmth stirred in his heart.

"Wal, by Gawd! Look who's heah!" exclaimed the cowboy.

Neale wheeled with a start. He saw a scout—in buckskin—a tall form with the stride of a mountaineer, strangely familiar. "Slingerland!" he cried.

The trapper bounded at them, his tanned face glowing, his gray eyes glad.

"Boys, it's come at last! I knowed I'd run into you someday," he said, and he gripped them with horny hands.

Neale tried to speak, but a terrible cramp in his throat choked him. He appealed with his hands to Slingerland. The trapper lost his smile and the iron set returned to his features.

King choked over his utterance. "Al-lie. . . . What aboot . . . her?"

"Boys, it's broke me down," replied Slingerland hoarsely. "I swear to you I never left Allie alone fer a year . . . an' then . . . the fust time . . . when she made me go . . . I come back an' finds the cabin burnt. . . . She's gone! Gone! No redskin job. Them damned riff-raff out of Californy! I tracked 'em. Then a hell of a storm comes up. No tracks left. . . . All's lost! An' I goes back to my traps in the mountains."

"What . . . become . . . of . . . her?" whispered Neale.

Slingerland looked away from him. "Son . . . you remember Allie. . . . She'd die . . . quick . . . wouldn't she, Red?"

"Shore. Thet girl . . . couldn't . . . hev lived a day," replied King thickly.

Neale plunged blindly away from his friends. Then the torture in his breast seemed to burst. The sobs came—heavy—racking. He sank upon a box and bowed his head. There King and Slingerland found him.

The cowboy looked down with helpless pain. "*Aw,* pard . . . don't take it . . . so hard," he implored.

But he knew and Slingerland knew that sympathy could do no good here. There was no hope, no help. Neale was stricken. They stood there, the elder man looking all the sadness and inevitableness of that wild life, and the younger—the cowboy— slowly changing to iron.

"Slingerland, you-all said some Californy outfit got Allie?" he queried.

"I'm sure an' sartin," replied the trapper. "Them days there wasn't any travelin' west . . . so early after winter. You recollect them four bandits as rode on us one day? They was from Californy."

"Wal, I'll be lookin' fer men with thet Californy brand," drawled King, and in his slow easy cool speech there was a note deadly and terrible.

Neale slowly ceased his sobbing. "My nerves's gone," he said shakily.

"No. It jest broke you all-up to see Slingerland. An' it shore did me, too," replied King.

"It's hard, but. . . ." Slingerland could not finish his thought.

"Slingerland, I'm glad to see you, even if it did cut me," said Neale more rationally. "I'm surprised, too. Are you here with a load of pelts?"

"No. Boys, I hed to give up trappin'. I couldn't stand the loneliness . . . after . . . after. . . . An' now I'm killin' buffalo meat for the soldiers an' the construction gangs. Jes' got in on thet train with a carload of fresh meat."

"Buffalo meat," echoed Neale. His mind wandered.

"Son, how's your work goin'?"

Neale shook his head.

The cowboy answering for him said: "We kind of chucked the work, Slingerland."

"What? Are you hyar in Benton doin' nothin'?"

"Shore. Thet's the size of it."

The trapper made a vehement gesture of disapproval and he bent more of a scrutinizing gaze upon Neale.

"Son, you're not gone an' . . . an'. . . ."

"Yes!" replied Neale, throwing out both hands. "I quit. I couldn't work. I *can't* work! I *can't* rest or stand still! Yes, I've gone. I'm done . . . ruined . . . dead on my feet!"

A spasm of immense regret contracted the trapper's face. And King, looking away over the sordid dusty passing throng, cursed under his breath. Neale was the first to recover his composure.

"Let's say no more. What's done is done," he said. "Suppose you take us on one of your buffalo hunts."

Slingerland grasped at straws. "Wal, now, thet ain't a bad idee. I can use you," he replied eagerly. "But it's hard an' dangerous work. We git chased by redskins often. An' you'd hev to ride. I reckon, Neale, you're good enough on a hoss. But our cowboy friend hyar . . . he can't ride, as I recollect your old arguments."

"My job was hosses," drawled King.

"An' besides, you've got to shoot straight, which Red hasn't hed experience of," went on Slingerland.

"I seen you was packin' a Winchester all shiny an' new," replied King. "Shore, I'm in fer anythin' with ridin' an' shootin'."

"You'll both go, then?"

Neale and King accepted his proposition then and there.

"You'll need to buy rifles an' shells, thet's all," said Slingerland. "I've hosses an' outfit over at Medicine Bow. An' I've been huntin' east of thar. Come on, we'll go to a store. Thet train's goin' back soon."

"Wal, I come in on thet train an' now I'm leavin' on it," drawled King. "Shore is funny. Without lookin' over this heah Benton."

On the ride to Medicine Bow Slingerland inquired if Neale and King had ever gone back to the scene of the massacre of the caravan where Horn had buried his gold.

Neale had absolutely forgotten the buried gold. Probably when he and King had scoured the Black Hills for trace of Allie they had passed down the valley where the treasure had been hidden. Slingerland gave the same reason for his oversight. They talked about the gold and planned, when the railroad reached the foothills, to go after it.

Both Indians and buffalo were sighted from the train windows before the trio got to Medicine Bow.

"I reckon I don't like thet," declared Slingerland. "I was friendly with the Sioux. But now thet I've come down hyar to kill off their buffalo fer the whites, they're ag'in' me. I know thet. An' I allus regarded them buffalo as Injun property. If it wasn't thet I seen this railroad means the end of the buffalo an' the Injuns, too, I'd never hev done it. Thet I'll swar."

It was night when they reached Medicine Bow. How quiet and dark after Benton! Neale was glad to get there. He wondered if he could conquer his unrest. Would he go wandering on again? He doubted himself and dismissed the thought. Perhaps the companionship of his old friends and anticipation of action would effect a change in him.

Neale and King spent the night in Slingerland's tent. Next morning the trapper was ready with horses at an early hour, but, owing to the presence of Sioux in the vicinity, it was thought best to wait for the work train and ride out on the plains under its escort.

By and by the train, with its few cars and half a hundred workmen, was ready, and the trapper and his comrades rode out alongside. Some few miles from camp the train halted at a place where stone work and filling awaited the laborers. Neale was again interested, in spite of himself. His love for that railroad was quite as hopeless as other things in his life. These laborers were picked men, all soldiers, and many Irish, and they stacked their guns before taking up shovels and bars.

"Domn me, if it ain't me ould friend Neale!" exclaimed a familiar voice.

And there stood Casey, with the same old grin, the same old black pipe! Neale's first feeling of pleasure at seeing the old flagman was counteracted by one of dismay at the possibility of coming in contact with old acquaintances. It would hurt him to meet General Lodge or any of the engineers who had predicted a future for him.

Shane and McDermott were also in this gang, and they slouched forward.

"It's that gun-throwin' cowboy as wuz oncet goin' to kill Casey!" exclaimed McDermott, at sight of King.

Neale, during the few moments of reunion with his old comrades of the survey, received a melancholy insight into himself and a clearer view of them. The great railroad had gone on, growing, making men change. He had been passed by. He was no longer a factor. Along with many, many other men he had retrograded. The splendid spirit of the work had gone from him. Only the wild and the violent and the base attracted him now. He had ceased to grow. But those uncouth Irishmen—they had changed in other ways. They were the same slow loquacious quarreling trio as before, but they showed the shock of the years of toil, of fight, of growth under the great movement and its spirit—the thing that great minds had embodied and the laborers were no longer ordinary men. Something shone out of them. Neale saw it. He felt an inexplicable littleness in their presence. They had gone on; he had been left. They would toil and fight till they filled nameless graves. He, too, would find a nameless grave, he thought, but he would not lie in it as one of these. The moment was poignant for Neale, exceedingly bitter, and revealing.

Slingerland was not long in sighting buffalo. After making a careful survey of the rolling country for hiding Indians, he rode out with Neale, King, and two other men—Brush and an Irishman named Pat—who were to skin the buffalo that the hunters killed and help load the meat into wagons that would follow.

"It ain't no trick to kill buffalo," Slingerland was saying to his friends. "But I don't want old bulls an' old cows killed. An' when you're ridin' fast an' the herd is branded, it's hard to tell the difference. You boys stick close to me an' watch me first. An' keep one eye peeled fer Injuns."

Slingerland approached the herd without alarming it, until some little red calves on the outskirts of the herd became frightened. Then the herd lumbered off, raising a cloud of dust. The roar of hoofs was thunderous.

"Ride!" yelled Slingerland.

But the least interesting sight to Neale was King riding away from them. He was wheeling the buffalo on the rumps with his bare hand before Slingerland and Neale got near enough to shoot.

At the trapper's first shot the herd stampeded. Thereafter it took riding to keep up, to choose the level ground, and to follow Slingerland's orders. Neale got up in the thick of the rolling din and dust. The pursuit liberated something fierce within him that gave him a measure of freedom from his constant pain. All before him spread the great black bobbing herd. The wind whistled, the dust choked him, the gravel stung his face, the stray even action of his horse was exhilarating. He lost track of King. But he stuck close to Slingerland. The trapper kept shooting at intervals. Neale saw the puffs of smoke, but in the thundering din he could not hear a report. It seemed impossible for him to select the kind of buffalo Slingerland wanted shot. Neale could not tell one from the other. He rode right upon their flying heels, however, finally unable to restrain himself from shooting, he let drive, and saw a beast drop and roll over. Neale rode on.

Presently out of a lane in the dust he thought he saw Slingerland pass. He reined toward the side. King was riding furiously at him and Slingerland's horse was stretched out, heading straightaway. The trapper madly waved his arms. Neale spurred toward them. Something was amiss. King's face flashed in the sun. He whirled his horse to take Neale's course, and then he pointed.

Neale thrilled as he looked. A few hundred rods in the rear rode a band of Sioux, coming swiftly. A cloud of dust rose behind them. They had no doubt been hiding in the vicinity of the grazing buffalo, lying in wait. As Neale closed in on King, he saw the cowboy's keen glance measuring distance and speed.

"We shore got to ride!" was what King apparently yelled, although the sound of words drifted as a faint whisper to Neale. But the roar of buffalo hoofs was rapidly diminishing.

Then Neale realized what it meant to keep close to the cowboy. Every moment King turned around both to watch the Indians and to have a glance at his comrade; they began to gain on Slingerland. Brush was riding for dear life off to the right, and the Irishman Pat, still farther in that direction, was in the most perilous situation.

Already the white skipping streaks of dust from bullets whipped up in front of him. The next time Neale looked back the Sioux had split up; some were riding hard after Brush and Pat; the majority were pursuing the other three hunters, cutting the while a little to the right, for Slingerland was working around toward the work train. Neale saw the smoke of the engine and then the train. It seemed far away. And he was sure the Indians were gaining. What incomparable riders! They looked half naked, dark, gleaming, low over their mustangs, feathers and trappings flying in the wind—a wild and panic-provoking sight.

"Don't ride so close!" yelled King. "They're spreadin'!"

Neale gathered that the Indians were riding farther apart because they soon expected to be in range of bullets, and King wanted Neale to ride farther from him for the identical reason.

Neale saw the first white puff of smoke from a rifle of the leader. The bullet hit far behind—more shots kept raising the dust—the last time still a few yards short.

"Gawd! Look!" yelled King.

"The devils hit Pat's hoss!"

Neale saw the Irishman go down with his horse, plunge in the dust, and roll over and lie still. "They got him!" he yelled at King.

"Ride thet hoss!" came back grimly and appealingly from the cowboy.

Neale rode as he had never before ridden. Fortunately his horse was fresh and fast, and that balanced the driving the cowboy was giving his mount. For a long distance they held their own with the Sioux. They gained a straight-away course for the work train, so that, with the Sioux behind, they had only to hold out for a few miles. Brush appeared as well off as they were. Slingerland lead by perhaps a hundred feet, far over to the left, and he was wholly out of range.

It took a very short time at that pace to cover a couple of miles. And then the Indians began to creep up closer and closer. Again they were shooting. Neale heard the reports and each one made him flinch in expectation of feeling the burn of a bullet. Brush was now turning to fire his rifle.

Neale bethought himself of his own Winchester that he was carrying in his hand. Dropping the rein over the horn of his saddle, he turned half around. How close, how red, how fierce these Sioux were! He felt his hair rise stiffly under his hat. And at the same instant a hot wrath rushed over him, a madness to fight, to give back blow for blow. Just then several of the Indians fired. He heard the sharp *cracks*, then the *spats* of bullets striking the ground; he saw the little streaks of dust in front of him. Then the whistle of lead! That made him shoot in return. His horse lunged forward, almost throwing him, and ran the faster for his fright. Neale heard King begin to shoot. It became a running duel then, with the Indians scattering wide, riding low, yelling like demons, and keeping up a continuous volley. They were well armed with white men's guns. Neale worked the level of his rifle while he looked ahead for an instant to see where his horse was running, then he wheeled quickly and took a snap shot at the nearest Indian, no more than three hundred yards distant now. He saw where his bullet, going wide, struck up the dust. It was desperately hard to shoot from the back of a scared horse. Neale did not notice that King's shots were any more effective than his. He grew certain the Sioux were gaining faster now. But the work train was not far away. He saw the workmen on top of the cars waving their arms. Rough ground, though, the last stretch.

King was drawing ahead. He had used all the shells in his rifle and now with hand and spur was goading his horse.

Suddenly Neale heard the soft *thud* of lead striking flesh. His horse leaped with a piercing snort of terror. Neale thought he was going down. But he recovered and went plunging on, still swift and game, although with uneven gait. King yelled. His red face flashed over his shoulder. He saw something was wrong with Neale's horse and he pulled his even.

"Save your own life!" yelled Neale fiercely. It enraged him to see the cowboy holding back to let him come up. But he could not prevent it.

"He's hit!" shouted King.

"Yes. But not badly!" shouted Neale in reply. "Spread out!"

The cowboy now swerved a foot. He watched Neale's horse with keen sure eyes.

"He's breakin'! Mebbe he can't last!"

Bullets whistled all around Neale now. He heard them strike the stones on the ground and sing away; he saw them streak through the scant grass; he felt the tug at his shoulder where one cut through his coat, stinging at the skin. That touch, light as it was, stung the panic out of him. The strange darkness before his eyes, hard to see through, passed away. He wheeled to shoot again, and with deliberation he aimed as best he could. Yet he might as well have tried to hit flying birds. He emptied the Winchester.

Then, hunching low in the saddle, Neale hung on. Slingerland was close to the train; Brush, on his side, appeared to be about out of danger; the pursuit had narrowed down to Neale and King. Now anger and the grimness faded from Neale. He did not want to go plunging down in front of those lean wild mustangs, to be ridden over and trampled and mutilated. The thought sickened him. The roar of pursuing hoofs grew distinct, but Neale did not look back.

Another roar broke on his ear—the clamor of the Irish soldier-laborers as they yelled and fired.

"Pull him! Pull him!" came the piercing cry from King.

Neale was about to ride his frantic horse straight into the work train. Desperately he hauled the horse up and leaped off. King was down, waiting, and his mount went plunging away. Bullets were pattering against the sides of the cars from which puffed streaks of flame and smoke.

"Up wid yez, lads!" sang out a cheery voice, and Casey's grin and black pipe appeared over the rim of the car, and his big hands reached down.

One quick and straining effort and Neale was up, over the side, to fall on the floor in a pile of sand and gravel. All whirled down around him for a second. His heart labored. He was wet and hot and shaking.

"Shore yez ain't hit now!" exclaimed Casey.

King's nervous hands began to slide and press over Neale.

"No . . . I'm . . . all . . . safe," panted Neale.

The engine whistled shrilly, as if in defiance of the Indians, and with a jerk and *rattle* the train started.

Neale recovered to find himself in a novel and thrilling situation. The car was of a gondola type, being merely a flat car, with sides about four feet high; it had thick oak planking that bullets did not penetrate. Besides himself and King, there were half a dozen soldiers, all kneeling at little portholes. Neale peeped over the rim. In a long thinned out line the Sioux were circling around the train, hiding on the offside of their mustangs, shooting from those difficult positions. They were going at full speed, working in closer. A bullet, striking the rim of the car and showering splinters in Neale's face, attested to the fact that the Sioux were still to be feared, even from a moving fort. Neale dropped back and, reloading his rifle, found a hole from which to shoot. He emptied his magazine before he realized it. But what with his trembling hands and the jerking of the train and the swift motion of the Indians, he did not do any harm to the foe.

Suddenly with a jolt the train halted.

"Blocked again, b'gorra," said Casey calmly. "Me pipe's out. Sandy, gimme a match."

The engine whistled two shrill blasts.

"What's that for?" asked Neale quickly.

"Them's for the men in the first car to pull over the engine an' remove obstructions from the track," replied Casey.

Neale dared to risk a peep over the top of the car. The Sioux were circling closer to the front of the train. All along the half dozen cars ahead of Neale puffs of smoke and jets of flame shot out. Heavy volleys were being fired. The attack of the savages seemed to be concentrating up forward, evidently to derail the engine or kill the engineer.

Casey pulled Neale down. "Risky fer yez," he said. "Use a porthole an' foight."

"My shells are gone," replied Neale. He lay well down in the car, then, and listened to the uproar and waited for the Irish trio. When the volleys and the fiendish yells mingled, he could not hear anything else. There were intervals, however, when the uproar lulled for a moment.

Casey got his black pipe well lit, puffed a cloud of smoke, and picked up his rifle. "Drill, ye terriers, drill . . . drill, ye terriers, drill!" he sang, and shoved his weapon through a porthole. He squinted over the breech. "Mac, it's the same bunch as attacked us day before yesterday," he observed.

"It shure ain't," replied McDermott. "There's a million of them today." He aimed his rifle, as if following a moving object, and fired.

"Mac, you get excited in a fight. Now I never do. An' I've seen that pinto hoss an' that domn' redskin a lot of times. I'll kill him yet."

Casey kept squinting and aiming, and then, just as he pressed the trigger, the train started with a sudden lurch.

"Spiled me aim. That engineer's savin' of the Sooz tribe! Drill, ye terriers, drill . . . drill, ye terriers, drill. . . . Shane, I don't hear yez shootin'."

"How'n hell can I shoot when me eye is full of blood?" demanded Shane.

Neale then saw blood on Shane's face. He crawled quickly to the Irishman. "Man, are you shot? Let me see."

"Jist a bullet hit me, loike," replied Shane.

Neale found that a bullet, perhaps glancing from the wood, had cut a gash over Shane's eye, from which the blood poured. Shane's hands and face and shirt were bloody. Neale bound a scarf tightly over the wound. "Let me take the rifle now," he said.

"Thanks, lad. I ain't hurted. An' hev Casey make me loife miserable foriver. Not much. He's a harrd mon, that Casey." Shane crouched back to his porthole, with his bloody bandaged face and his bloody hands. And just then the train stopped with a rattling *crash*.

"When we get beyond them ties as was scattered along here, mebbe we'll go on in," remarked McDermott.

"Mac, yez looks on the gloomy side," replied Casey. Then quickly he aimed and shot. "I loike it better when we ain't movin'," he soliloquized with satisfaction. "That redskin won't niver scalp a soldier of the U.P.R. . . . Drill, ye terriers, drill . . . drill, ye terriers, drill!"

The engine whistle shrilled out and once more the din of conflict headed to the front. Neale lay there, seeing the reality of what he had dreamed. These old soldiers, these toilers with rail and sledge and shovel, these Irishmen with the rifles—they were the builders of the great U.P.R. Glory might never be theirs, but they were the battle-scarred heroes. They were as used to fighting as working. They dropped their sledges or shovels to run for their guns.

Again the train started up and had scarcely gotten under way when with jerk and bump it stopped once more. The conflict grew fiercer as the Indians became more desperate. But evidently they were kept from closing in, for during the thick of the heaviest volleying the engine again began to puff and the wheels to grind. Slowly the train moved on. Like hail the bullets *pattered* against the car. Smoke drifted away on the wind.

Neale lay there watching these cool men who fought off the savages. No doubt Casey and Shane and McDermott were merely three of many thousands engaged in building and defending the U.P.R. This trio liked the fighting, perhaps better than the toiling. Casey puffed his old black pipe, grinned and aimed, shot and reloaded, sang his quaint song and joked with his comrades, all in the same cool quiet way. If he knew that the shadow of death hung over the team, he did not show it. He was not a thinker. Casey was a man of action. Only once he yelled, and that was when he killed the Indian on the pinto mustang.

Shane grew less loquacious and he drooped and fumbled over his rifle, but he kept on shooting. Neale saw him feel the hot muzzle of his gun, and shake his bandaged head. The blood trickled down his cheek.

McDermott plied his weapon, and ever and anon he would utter some pessimistic or gloomy word, or presage dire disaster, or remind Casey that his scalp was destined to dry in a Sioux's lodge, or call on Shane to hit something to save his life, or declare that the engine was off the track. He rambled on. But it was all talk. The man had gray hairs and he was a born fighter.

This time the train gained more headway and evidently had passed the point where the Indians could find obstructions to place on the track. Neale saw through a porthole that the Sioux were dropping back from the front of the train and were no longer circling. Their firing had become desultory. Medicine Bow was in sight. The engine gathered headway.

"We'll get the rest of the day off," remarked Casey complacently. "Shane, yez are domn' quiet betoimes. An', Mac, I shure showed yez up today."

"Ye *did* not," retorted McDermott. "I kilt jist twenty-nine Sooz!"

Casey grinned. "Jist thirty was moine. An', Mac, as they wuz only about fifty of them, yez must be a liar."

The train drew on toward Medicine Bow. Firing ceased. Neale stood up to see the Sioux riding away. Their ranks did not seem noticeably depleted.

"Drill, ye terriers, drill!" sang Casey as he wiped his sweaty and begrimed rifle. "Mac, how many Sooz did Shane kill?"

"B'gorra, he ain't said yet," replied McDermott. "Say Shane. . . . *Casey!*"

Neale whirled at the sharp change of tone.

Shane lay face down on the floor of the car, his bloody hands gripping his rifle. His position was inert, singularly expressive.

209

Neale strode toward him. But Casey reached him first. He laid a hesitating hand on Shane's shoulder.

"Shane, old mon," he said, but the cheer was not in his voice. Casey dropped his pipe. Then he turned his comrade over. Shane had done his best and his last for the U.P.R.!

# CHAPTER SEVENTEEN

Neale and King decided to return to Benton. Slingerland saw them off and said that when it became practical to hunt buffalo again, he would send for them. Also, they planned to go into the Black Hills late in the fall, visit Slingerland's old camp, and then try to locate the gold buried by Horn.

The trapper's last words to Neale were interesting: "Son, there's a feller hyar in Medicine Bow who says as how he thought your pard Red was a bad cowpuncher from the Panhandle of Texas."

"Bad?" queried Neale. "Red's as good as gold."

"Wal, he meant a gun-throwin' bad man, I take it."

"Don't let Red overhear you say it," replied Neale, "and advise your informant to be careful. I've always had a hunch Red was really somebody."

"Benton'll work on the cowboy," continued Slingerland earnestly. "An', son, I ain't so all-fired sure of you."

"I'll take what comes," returned Neale shortly. "Good bye, old friend. Look me up when you come to Benton. And if you can use us for buffalo hunting without the 'domn' Sooz,' as Casey says, why, we'll come."

As the train pulled out, Neale carried with him the memory of Slingerland's reluctant and wistful good bye. It made Neale think: where were he and King going? Friendships in this Wild West were stronger ties than he had known elsewhere.

The train arrived at Benton after dark. And the darkness

seemed a windy gulf out of which roared yellow lights and excited men. The tents, with the dim lights through the canvas, gleamed pale and obscure, like so much of the life they hid. The throngs hurried, the dust blew, the band played, the barkers clamored for their trade.

Neale found the more pretentious hotels overcrowded and he was compelled to go to his former lodgings, where he and King were accommodated.

"Now we're here . . . what'll we do?" queried Neale, more to himself. He felt as if driven. And the mood he hated and feared was impinging upon his mind.

"Shore, we'll eat," replied King.

"Then what?"

"Wal, I reckon, see what's goin' on in this heah Benton."

As a matter of fact, Neale reflected, there was nothing to do that he wanted to do.

"You-all air gettin' the blues," said King with solicitude.

"Red, I'm never free of them."

King put his hand on Neale's shoulder. Demonstration of this kind was rare with the cowboy. "Pard, are we goin' to see this heah Benton . . . an' then brace an' go back to work?"

"No. I can't hold a job," replied Neale bitterly.

"You're showin' a yellow streak? You're done, as you told Slingerland? Nothin' ain't no good? Life's over, fer all thet's sweet an' right? Is thet your stand?"

"Yes, it must be Red," said Neale with scorn of himself. "But you . . . it needn't apply to you. Let me alone. You go your way."

"I reckon I'm sorry," rejoined King, ignoring Neale's last words. "I always hoped you'd get over Allie's loss. . . . You had so much to live fer."

"Red, I wish the bullet that hit Shane today had hit me instead. You needn't look like that. I mean it. Today when the

Sioux chased up, my hair went stiff and my heart was in my mouth. I ran for my life as if I loved it. But that was my miserable cowardice. I'm sick of the game . . . and almost through."

"Are you in daid earnest?" asked King huskily.

Neale nodded gloomily. He did not ever regret the effect of his speech upon the cowboy. He divined that somehow the moment was critical and fateful for King, but he did not care. The black spell was enfolding him. All seemed hard, cold, monstrous within his breast. He could not love anything. He was lost. He realized the magnificent loyalty of this simple Texan, who was his true friend.

"Red, for God's sake, don't make me ashamed to look you in the eyes," appealed Neale. "I want to go on . . . you know?"

"Wal, I reckon I'll stick," drawled King. He had changed when he said that. He had aged. The dry humor of the cowboy, the amiable ease, was wanting.

"Oh, hell, forgive my selfish rottenness!" burst out Neale. "I'm not the man I was. But don't think I don't love you."

They went out together, and the hum of riotous Benton called them and the lights beckoned and the melancholy night engulfed them.

Next morning late, on the way to breakfast, Neale encountered a young man whose rough bronzed face somehow seemed familiar.

At sight of Neale this young fellow brightened, and he lunged forward. "Neale! Findin' you was like huntin' for a needle in a haystack."

Neale could not place him, and he did not try hard for recognition, for that surely would recall his former relation to the railroad.

"I don't remember you," replied Neale.

"I'll bet Red does," said the stranger, with a grin at the cowboy.

"Shore. Your name's Campbell, an' you was a lineman for Baxter," returned King.

"Right you are," said Campbell, offering his hand to Neale, and then to King. He appeared both glad and excited.

"I guess I recall you now," said Neale thoughtfully. "You said . . . you were hunting me?"

"Well, I should smile," returned Campbell, and handed Neale a letter.

Neale tore it open and hastily perused its contents. It was a brief urgent request from Baxter that Neale return to work. The words, almost like an order, made Neale's heart swell for a moment. He stood there staring at the paper. King read the letter over his shoulder.

"Pard, shore I was expectin' jist thet there, an' I say go!" exclaimed King.

Neale slowly shook his head.

Campbell made a quick, nervous movement. "Neale, I was to say . . . tell . . . there's more'n your old job waitin' for you."

"What do you mean?" queried Neale.

"That's all, except the corps has struck a snag out there, west of Benton. It's a bad place. You an' Henney were west in the hills when this survey was made. It's a deep wash . . . bad grade an' curves. The gang's stuck. An' Baxter swore, saying . . . 'We've got to have Neale back on the job!' "

"Where's Henney?" asked Neale rather thickly. Campbell's words affected him powerfully.

"Henney had to go to Omaha. Boone is sick at Fort Fetterman. Baxter has only a new green hand out there, an' they've sure struck a snag."

"That's too bad," replied Neale still thoughtfully. "Is . . . the chief . . . is General Lodge there?"

"Yes. There's a trooper camp. Colonel Dillon an' some of the officers have their wives out on a little visit to see the work. They couldn't stand Benton."

"Will you thank Baxter and tell him I'm sorry. I must refuse," said Neale.

"You won't come!" ejaculated Campbell.

Neale shook his head.

King reached out with big eager hand. "See heah, pard, I reckon you will go."

Campbell acted strangely, as if he wanted to say more, but did not have authority. He looked dismayed. Then he said: "All right, Neale. I'll take your message. But you can expect me back." Then he went his way.

"Neale, shore's there's somethin' in the wind," said King. "Wal, it jist tickles me. They can't build the railroad without you."

"Would you go back to work?" queried Neale.

"Shore I would if they'd have me. But I'd reckon thet little run-in of mine with Smith has made bad feelin'. An' come to think of thet, if I did go back, I'd only have to fight some of Smith's friends. An' I reckon I'd better not go. It'd only make trouble for you."

"Me! You heard me refuse."

"Shore, I heerd you," drawled King softly. "But you're goin' back if I have to hawg-tie you . . . an' pack you out there on a horse."

Neale said no more. If he had said another word, he would have betrayed himself to his friend. He yearned for his old work. To think that the engineer corps needed him filled him with joy. But at the same time he knew what an effort it would take to apply himself to any task. He hated to attempt it. He doubted himself. He was morbid. All that day he wandered around at King's heels, half oblivious of what was going on. After dark he slipped away from his friend to be alone. And being alone in the dark quietness brought home to him the truth of a strange strong growth, out of the depths of him, that was going to overcome his morbid craving to be idle, to drift, to waste his life on a haunting memory.

He could not sleep that night, and so was awake when King lounged in, slow and heavy. The cowboy was half drunk. Neale took him to task, and they quarreled. Finally King grew silent and fell asleep. After that Neale likewise dropped into slumber.

In the morning King was again his old cool, easy, reckless self, and had apparently forgotten Neale's sharp words. Neale, however, felt a change in himself. This was the first morning for a long time that he had not hated the coming of daylight.

When he and King went out, the sun was high. For Neale there seemed something more than the sunshine in the air. At sight of Campbell, waiting in the same place they had encountered him yesterday, Neale's pulse quickened.

Campbell greeted him with a bright smile. "I'm back," he said.

"So I see," replied Neale constrainedly.

"I've a message for you from the chief," announced Campbell.

"The chief!" exclaimed Neale.

King edged closer to them, with the characteristic hitch at his belt, and his eyes flashed.

"He asks as a personal favor that you come out to see him," replied Campbell.

Neale flushed. "General Lodge asks that?" he echoed. There was a slow heat stirring all through him.

"Yes. . . . Will you go?"

"I . . . I guess I'll have to," replied Neale. He did not feel that he was deciding. He had to go. But this did not prove that he must take up his old work.

King swung his hand on Neale's shoulder, almost staggering

him. The cowboy beamed. "Go in to breakfast," he said. "Order for me, too. I'll be back."

"You want to hurry," rejoined Campbell. "We've only a half hour to eat an' catch the work train."

King strode back toward the lodging house. And it was Campbell who led Neale into the restaurant and ordered the meal. Neale's mind was not in a whirl, nor dazed, but he did not get much further in thought than the remarkable circumstance of General Lodge's sending for him personally. Meanwhile Campbell rapidly talked about masonry, roadbeds, washouts, and other things that Neale heard, but did not clearly understand. Then King returned. He carried Neale's bag, which he deposited carefully on the bench.

"I reckon you might as well take it along," he drawled.

Neale felt himself being forced.

They indulged in little further conversation while hurriedly eating breakfast. That finished, they sallied forth toward the station. Campbell clambered aboard the work train. "Come on, Red," he said.

And Neale joined him in like speech.

"Wal, seein' as how I want you-all to get on, an' the railroad built, I reckon I'd better not go," drawled King. His blue eyes shone warm upon his friend.

"Red, I'll be back in a day or so," said Neale.

"*Aw*, now, pard, you stay. Go back on the job an' stick," appealed the cowboy.

"No. I quit, and I'll stay quit. I might help out . . . for a day . . . just as a favor. But. . . ." Neale shook his head.

"I reckon . . . if you care anythin' aboot me . . . you'll shore stick."

"Red, you'll go to the bad if I leave you here alone," protested Neale.

"Wal, if you stay, we'll both go," replied King sharply. He had changed subtly. "It's in me to go to hell . . . I reckon I've gone . . . but thet ain't so for you."

"Two's company," said Neale, with an attempt at lightness. But it was pretend. King worried him.

"Listen. If you go back on the job . . . then it'll be all right for you to run in heah to see me once in a while. But if you throw up this chance, I'll. . . ." King paused. His ruddy tan had faded slightly.

Neale eyed him, aware of a hard and tense contraction of the cowboy's throat. "Well, what'll you do?" queried Neale shortly.

King threw back his head and the subtle fierce tensity seemed to leave him.

"Wal, the day you come back I'll clean out Stanton's place . . . jest to start entertainin' you," he replied, with his slow drawl as marked as ever it was.

A stir of anger in Neale's breast subsided with the big warm realization of this wild cowboy's love for him, and the melancholy certainty that King would do exactly as he threatened.

"Suppose I come back and beat you-all up," suggested Neale.

"Wal, thet won't make a damn' bit of difference," replied King seriously.

Whereupon Neale soberly bade his friend good bye and boarded the train.

The ride appeared slow and long, dragged out by innumerable stops. All along the line laborers awaited the train to unload supplies. At the end of the line there was a congestion Neale had not observed before in all the work. Freight cars, loaded with stone and iron beams and girders for bridge work, piles of ties and piles of rails, and gangs of idle men, attested to the delay caused by an obstacle to progress. The sight aggressively stimulated Neale. He felt very curious to learn the cause of the setback, and his old scorn of difficulties flashed up.

The camp Neale's guide led him to was back some distance from the construction work. It stood in a little valley through which ran a stream. There was one large building, low and flat, made of boards and canvas, adjoining a substantial old log cabin, and clustered around, although not close together, were a considerable number of tents. Troopers were in evidence, some on duty and many idle. In the background the slopes of the valley were dark green with pine and cedar.

At the open door of the building Neale met Baxter face to face, and that worthy's greeting left Neale breathless and aghast, yet thrilling with sheer gladness.

"What're . . . you . . . up against?" asked Neale.

"The boss'll talk to you. Get in there," Baxter replied, and pushed Neale inside. It was a big room, full of smoke, noise, men, tables, papers. There were guns stacked under portholes. Someone spoke to Neale, but he did not see who. All the faces he saw so swiftly appeared vague, yet curious, interested. Then Baxter halted him at a table. Once again Neale faced his chief. Baxter announced something—Neale did not hear what.

General Lodge looked older, sterner, more worn. He stood up. "Hello, Neale," he said, offering his hand, and a flash of a smile changed his face.

Neale replied to the greeting with a dignity that was not true to his feelings

"Come in here," said the chief, and he led Neale into another room, of different aspect. It was small; the walls were of logs; new boards had been recently put in the floor; new windows cut, and it contained Indian blankets, chairs, a couch.

Here General Lodge bent a stern and piercing gaze upon his former lieutenant. "Neale, you failed me when you quit your job," he said. "You were my right-hand man. You quit me in my hour of need."

"General, I . . . I was furious at that rotten commissioner

219

deal," replied Neale, choking. What he had done now seemed so little—an offense to his chief. "My work was ordered done over!"

"Neale, that was nothing to what I've endured. You should have grit your teeth . . . and gone on. That five miles of reconstruction was nothing . . . nothing."

In his chief's inflexible voice, in the worn and shadowed face Neale saw the great burden, and somehow he was reminded of Lincoln. And a passion of remorse seized Neale. Why had he not been faithful to this steadfast man who had needed him?

"It seemed . . . so much to me," faltered Neale.

"Why did you not look at that as you have looked at so many physical difficulties . . . the running of a survey, for instance?"

"I . . . I guess I have a yellow streak."

"Why didn't you come to me?" went on the chief. Evidently he had been disappointed in Neale.

"I might have come . . . only Red, my friend . . . he got into it, and I was afraid he'd kill somebody," replied Neale.

"That cowboy . . . he was a great fellow, but gone wrong. He shot one of the bosses . . . Smith."

"Yes, I know. Did . . . did Smith die?"

"No, but he'll never be any more good for the U.P.R., that's certain. Where is your friend now?"

"I left him in Benton."

"Benton!" exclaimed the chief bitterly. "I am responsible for Benton. This great work of my life is a hell on wheels, moving on and on. . . . Your cowboy friend has no doubt found his place . . . and his match . . . in Benton."

"Red has broken loose from me . . . from any last restraint."

"Neale, what have you been doing?"

And at that Neale dropped his head.

"Idling in the camps . . . drifting from one place to the next . . . drinking, gambling, eh?"

"I'm ashamed to say, sir, that of late I have been," replied

Neale, and he raised his gaze to his chief's.

"But . . . you haven't been . . . associating with those camp women!" exclaimed General Lodge, with his piercing eyes dark on Neale.

"No!" cried Neale. The speech had hurt him.

"I'm glad to hear that . . . gladder than you can guess. I was afraid . . . but no matter. . . . What you did do is bad enough. You ought to be ashamed. A young man with your intelligence, your nerve, your gifts! I haven't had a single man whose chances compared with yours. If you had stuck, you'd be at the head of my engineer corps right now. Baxter is played out. Boone is ill. Henney had to take charge of the shops in Omaha. . . . And you, with fortune and fame awaiting you, throw up your job to become a bum. . . . To drink and gamble away your life in these rotten camps!"

General Lodge's scorn flayed Neale. "Sir, you may not know I . . . I lost someone . . . very dear to me. After that I didn't seem to care." Neale turned to the window. He was ashamed of what blurred his eyes. "If it hadn't been for that . . . I'd never have failed you."

The chief strode to Neale and put a hand on his shoulder. "Son, I believe you. Maybe I've been a little hard. Let's forget it." His tone had softened and there was a close pressure of his hand. "The thing is now . . . will you come back on the job?"

"Baxter's note . . . Campbell said they'd struck a snag here. You mean help them get by that?"

"Snag! I guess it is a snag. It bids fair to make all our labor and millions of dollars . . . wasted. . . . But I'm not asking you to come back, just to help us over this snag. I mean, will you come back for good . . . and stick?"

Neale was lifted out of the gloom into which memory had plunged him. He turned to his chief, and strangely found him apparently another person. There was a light on his face, an eagerness on his lips, and the keen stern eyes were soft.

"Son, will you come back . . . stand by me till the finish?" repeated General Lodge, his voice deep and full. There was more here than just the relation of employer to his lieutenant. More, seemingly, than to see a keen hope and faith, at last after bitter disappointment, justified in the end!

"Yes, sir, I'll come back," replied Neale in low voice.

Their hands met.

"Good!" exclaimed the chief. Then he deliberately took out his watch and studied it. His hand trembled slightly. He did not raise his eyes again to Neale's face. "I'll call you . . . later," he said. "You stay here. I'll send someone in." With that he went out.

Neale remained standing, his eyes fixed on the gray-green slope, seen through the window. He seemed a trifle unsteady on his feet and braced himself with a knee against the couch. His restraint, under extreme agitation, began to relax. A flooding splendid thought filled his mind—his chief had called him back to the great work.

Presently the door behind him opened and closed very softly. Then he heard a low quick gasp. Someone had entered. Suddenly the room seemed strange, full, charged with terrible portent. And he turned as if a giant hand had heavily swung him around.

It was not light at the other end of the room, yet he saw a slight figure of a girl backed against the door. Her outline was familiar. Haunting ghost of his dreams! Bewildered and stultified he stared, trembling all over. The figure moved, swayed. A faint sweet voice called, piercing his heart like a keen blade. All of a sudden he had gone mad, he thought; this return to his old work had disordered his mind. The tremor of his body succeeded to a dizziness; his breast seemed about to burst.

*"Neale!"* called the sweet voice. She was coming toward him

swiftly. *"It's Allie . . . alive and well!"*

Neale felt lifted, as if by invisible wings. His limbs were use-less—had lost strength and feeling. The room whirled around him, and in that whirl appeared Allie Lee's face. Alive—flushed—radiant! Recognition brought a maddening check—a shock—and Neale's sight darkened. Tender, fluttering hands caught him; soft strong arms strained him convulsively. Then sense vaguely failed him.

# CHAPTER EIGHTEEN

Neale's recovery seemed a rebirth into another world—a paradise. His eyes opened on the window to see azure blue—fleecy cloud—golden sunshine.

There was a warm wet cheek pressed close to his, bright chestnut strands of hair over his face, tight little hands clutching his breast. He scarcely breathed until he lay there long enough to realize Allie Lee lived. Then he was so weak he could hardly move.

"Allie . . . you're not dead?" he whispered.

With a start she raised her head. She was kneeling beside the couch where he lay. It was absolutely the face of Allie Lee that bent over him.

"I'm the livest girl you ever saw," she replied, with a little low laugh of joy.

"Allie . . . then you're actually alive . . . safe . . . here!" he exclaimed in wild assurance.

"Yes . . . yes. . . . With you again! Isn't it glorious? But, oh! I gave you a shock. You frightened me so. . . . Neale, are you well?"

"I wasn't . . . but I am now." He trembled as he gazed up at her. Yes—it was Allie's face—incomparable, unforgettable. She might have been a little thin and strained. But time, and whatever she had endured, had only enhanced her loveliness. No harm had befallen her—that was written in the white glow of her face, in the violet eyes, dark and beautiful, with the brave soul shining through their haunting shadows, in the perfect lips, tremulous and tender with love.

"Neale, they told me you gave up your work . . . were going to the bad," she said, with an eloquence of distress changing voice and expression.

"Yes. Allie Lee, I loved you . . . I cared for nothing."

"You gave up. . . ."

"Allie," he interrupted passionately. "Don't talk of *me!* You haven't kissed me!"

Allie blushed. "I haven't? That's all you know!"

"Have you?"

"Yes, I have . . . I have. . . . I was afraid I'd strangled you!"

"I never felt it. I don't know that I fainted, but I lost all sense of feeling. . . . Kiss me now. Prove you're alive and love me still!"

And then presently when Neale caught his breath again it was to whisper: "Precious Allie."

"Am I alive? Do I love you?" she whispered, bending over him, her eyes like purple stars, her face flooded with a dark rose color.

"I'm forced to believe it, but you must prove it often," he replied. Then he sat up and drew her to a seat beside him. "I've had many dreams of you, yet not one like this. . . . How is it you *are* alive? By what Providence? I shall pray to that Providence all my life. . . . How do you come to be here? Tell me quick."

She leaned, close against him. "That's easy," she replied. "Only some time I want to tell you all . . . everything. . . . Do you remember the four ruffians who visited Slingerland's cabin one day when we were all there? Well, they came back one day . . . the first time Slingerland ever left me alone. They fired the cabin and carried me off. Then they fought among themselves. Two were killed. I made up my mind to get on a horse and run. Just as I was ready I spied Indians riding down. I had to shoot the ruffian Frank. But didn't kill him. Then I got on a horse and tried to ride away. The Indians captured me . . . took me to their camp. There an Indian girl freed me . . . led me away at night. I found a trail and walked . . . oh, nights and days, it seemed. Then I fell in with a caravan. I thought I was saved. But the leader of that caravan turned out to be Durade."

"*Durade!*" echoed Neale intensely.

"Yes. He was traveling east. He treated me well, but threatened me. When we reached the construction camp, somewhere back there, he started his gambling place. One night I escaped. I walked all that night . . . all the next day. And I was about ready to drop when I found this camp. It was night again. I saw the lights. They took me in. Missus Dillon and the other women were so kind, so good to me. I told very little about myself. I only wanted to be hidden here and have them send for you. Then they brought General Lodge, your chief, to see me. He was kind, too. He promised to get you here. It has been a whole terrible week of waiting. . . . But now. . . ."

"Allie," burst out Neale, "they never told me a word about you . . . never gave me a hint. They sent for me to come back to my job. I could have come a day sooner . . . the day Campbell found me. . . . Oh!"

"I knew they did not find you at once. And I learned yesterday they had located you. That eased my mind. A day more or less . . . what was that? . . . but they were somehow strange about you. Then Missus Dillon told me how the chief had been disappointed in you . . . how he had needed you . . . how he must have you back."

"Good Lord! Getting me back would have been easy enough if they had only told me!" exclaimed Neale impatiently.

"Dear, maybe that was just it. I suspect General Lodge cared enough for you to want you to come back to your job for your sake . . . for his sake . . . for sake of the railroad. And not for me."

"Aha," breathed Neale softly. "I wonder? Allie, how cheap, how little I felt a while ago, when he talked to me. I never was so ashamed in my life. He called me. . . . But that's over. . . . You said Durade had you. Allie, that scares me to death."

"It scares me, too," she replied. "For I'm in more danger hidden here than when he had me."

"Oh, no! How can that be?"

"He would kill me for running away," she shuddered, paling. "But while I was with him, obedient . . . I don't think he would have done me harm. I'm more afraid now than when I was his prisoner."

"I'll take a bunch of soldiers and go after Durade," said Neale grimly.

"No. Don't do that. Let him alone. Just get me away safely . . . far out of his reach."

"But, Allie, that's not possible now," declared Neale. "I'm certainly not going to lose sight of you, now I've got you again. And I must go back to work. I promised."

"I can stay here . . . or go along with you to other camps . . . and be careful to veil myself and hide."

"But that's not safe . . . not the best plan," protested Neale. Then he gave a start; his face darkened. "I'll put Red on Durade's trail."

"Oh, no, Neale! Don't do that! Please don't do that. Reddy would kill him."

"I rather guess he would. And why not?"

"I don't want Durade killed. It would be dreadful. He never hurt me. Let him alone. After all, he seems the only father I ever knew. . . . Oh, I don't care for him. I despise him. . . . But, let him live. . . . He will soon forget me. He is mad to gamble. This railroad of gold is a rich stake for him. He will not last long, nor will any of his kind."

Neale shook his head doubtfully. "It doesn't seem wise to me . . . letting him go. . . . Allie, does he use his right name, Durade?"

"No."

"What does he look like? You described him once to me, but I've forgotten."

Allie resolutely refused to tell him and once more entreated Neale to let well enough alone, to keep her hidden from the mob, and not to seek Durade.

"He has a bad gang," she added. "They might kill you. And do you . . . you think I'd . . . ever be . . . able to live longer without you?"

Whereupon Neale forgot all about Durade and vengeance, and everything but the nearness and sweetness of this girl.

"When shall we get married?" he asked presently.

This simple question caused Allie to avert her face. And just at that moment there came a knock on the door. Allie made a startled movement.

"Come in!" called Neale.

It was his chief who entered. General Lodge's face wore the smile that softened it. Then it showed surprise. "Neale, you're transfigured!"

Neale's laugh rang out. "Behold cause . . . even for that," he replied, and indicated the blushing Allie.

"Son, I didn't have to play my trump card to fetch you back to work," said the general.

"If you only had!" exclaimed Neale.

Allie got up, shyly and with difficulty disengaged her hand from Neale's. "You . . . you must want to talk," she said, then she fled.

"A wonderful girl, Neale. We're all in love with her," declared the chief. "She dropped down on me one night . . . asked for

228

protection, and you! She does not talk much. All we know is that she is the girl you saved back in the hills . . . and has been kept a prisoner. Here she hides, by day and night. She will not talk. But we know she fears someone."

"Yes, indeed she does," replied Neale seriously. And then briefly he told General Lodge Allie's story as related by her.

"Well!" ejaculated the chief. "If that doesn't beat me! What are you going to do?"

"I'll keep her close. Surely she will be safe here . . . hidden . . . with the soldiers about."

"Of course. But you can never tell what's going to happen. If she could be gotten to Omaha . . . now. . . ."

"No . . . no," replied Neale almost violently. He could not bear the thought of parting with Allie, now, just when he had found her. Then the chief's suggestion had reminded Neale of the possibility of Allie's father materializing. And the idea was attended by a vague dread.

"We're stuck. It's an engineering problem, that I hope . . . and expect you to solve."

"Who ran this survey in the first place?"

"It's Baxter's work . . . with the men he had under him then," replied the chief. "Somebody blundered. His later surveys made over one hundred feet grade to the mile. That won't do. We've got to get down to ninety feet. Baxter's stuck. The new surveyor is floundering. Oh, it's bad business, Neale. . . . I don't sleep of nights."

"No wonder," returned Neale, and he felt suddenly the fiery grip of his old state of mind towards all the engineering obstacles. "I'm going out to look over the ground."

"I'll send Baxter . . . and some of the men with you."

"No, thanks," replied Neale. "I'd rather take up my job all alone out there."

The chief's acquiescence was silent and eloquent.

Neale strode outdoors. The color of things, the feel of wind, the sounds of men and horses—all about him had remarkably changed—as he himself had incalculably changed. General Lodge had said—transfigured.

He walked down to the construction line and went among the idea men, and the strings of cars, and piles of rails, and piles of ties. He seemed to absorb them again. Then he walked the loose, unspiked ties down to where they ended, and so on along the graded roadbed to the point where his quick eyes recognized the trouble. They swiftly took in what had been done, and what had been attempted. How much needless work begun and completed in the building of the railroad! He clambered around in the sand, up and down the ravine, over the rocks, along the stream for half a mile, and it was laborious work. But how good to pant and sweat once more! He retraced his steps. Then he climbed the long slope of the hill. The wind up there blew him a welcome, and the sting and taste of dust were sweet. His step was swift. And then again he loitered with keen roving glance studying the lay of the ground. Neale's was the deduction method of arriving at conclusions. Today he was inspired. And at length there blazed suddenly his solution to the problem.

Then he gazed over the rolling hills with contemplative and dreamy eyes. They were beautiful, strong, changeless—and he divined now how they might have helped him, if he had only looked with seeing eyes.

Late that afternoon, tired and dusty, he tramped into the big office room. General Lodge was pacing the floor, chewing at his cigar; Baxter sat over blueprint papers and his face was weary; Colonel Dillon, Campbell, and several other young men also were there.

Neale saw that his manner of entrance, or the look of him, or both struck these men singularly. He laughed. "It was great . . . going back to my job!" he exclaimed.

Baxter sat up. General Lodge threw away his cigar with an action that suggested a sudden utilizing of a weary but indomitable spirit.

"Did you find the snag we've struck?" asked Baxter slowly.

"No," replied Neale.

"Aha! Well, I'll have to take you out tomorrow and show you."

The chief's keen eyes began to shine as they studied Neale.

"No, couldn't find any snag, Baxter, old boy. . . . And the reason is because there's no snag to find."

Baxter stared and his warm face reddened. "Boy, somethin's gone to your head," he retorted.

"Wal, I should smile, as Red would say."

Baxter pounded the table. "Neale, it's no smiling matter," he said harshly. "You come back here . . . your eye and mind fresh . . . but even so . . . it can't be you make light of this difficulty. You can't . . . you can't. . . ."

"But, I do!" cried Neale, his manner subtly changing.

Baxter got up. His shaking hand rustled a paper he held. "I know you . . . of old. You've tormented me often. You're a boy. . . . But here . . . this . . . this thing has stumped me. I've had no one to help. . . . And I'm getting old . . . this damned railroad has made me old. If . . . if you saw a way out . . . tell me. . . ." Baxter faltered. Indeed he had aged.

Neale saw the growth of the great railroad with its great problems in the face and voice of the old engineer. "Listen," he said swiftly. "A half mile down from where you struck your snag, we'll change the course of that stream! We'll change the line . . . set a compound curve by intersections . . . and we'll get much less than a ninety-foot grade to the mile." Then he turned to General Lodge. "Chief, Baxter had so many problems . . . so much on his mind that he couldn't think. . . . The work will go on tomorrow."

"But, Neale, you went out without any instrument," protested the chief.

"I didn't need one."

"Son, are you sure? This has been a stumper. What you say . . . seems too good . . . too. . . ."

"Am I sure?" cried Neale gaily. "Look at Baxter's face!"

Indeed one look at the old engineer was confirmation enough.

Neale was made much of that night. The chief and his engineers, the officers and their wives, all vied with one another in their efforts to celebrate Neale's return to work. The dinner party was merry, yet earnest, too. Baxter made a speech, his fine old face alight with gladness as he extolled youth and genius, and the inspiring power of bright eyes. Neale had to answer. His voice was deep and full as he said that Providence had returned him to his work and to a happiness he had believed lost. He denied the genius attributed to him, but not the inspiring power of bright eyes, and he paid as fine a tribute to Baxter.

Through all this gaiety and earnestness Allie's lips were mute, and her cheeks flushed and pale by turns. It was an ordeal for her, both confusing and poignant. At last she and Neale got away alone to the cabin room where they had met earlier in the day.

They leaned at the open window, close together, hands locked, gazing out over the quiet valley. The moon was full, and broad belts of silver light lay in strong contrast to black shadows. The hour was late. The sentries paced their beats.

Allie stirred and lifted her face to Neale's. "What they said about you makes me al-almost as happy as to see you again," she said.

"They said! Who? What?" asked Neale dreamily.

"Oh, I heard, I remember! For instance, Mister Baxter said you had genius."

"He was just eulogizing me," replied Neale. "What he said about your bright eyes was more to the point, I think."

"It's sweet to believe I could inspire you. But I know . . . and you know . . . that if I had not been here, you would have seen through the engineering problem just the same. . . . Now, be honest."

"Yes, I would," replied Neale frankly. "Though, perhaps, not so swiftly. I could see through stone today."

"And that proves your worth, your duty it always has been . . . to stand by your chief. Oh, I love him! He seems so much younger today. You have encouraged them all. . . . Oh, dear Neale, there is something noble in what you can do for him. Can't you see it?"

"Yes, Allie, indeed I do."

"Promise me . . . never to fail him again."

"I promise."

"No matter what happens to me! I am alive, safe, well . . . and I'm yours. But something might happen . . . you can never tell. I don't refer particularly to Durade and his gang. I mean life and everything is uncertain out here. So promise me . . . no matter what happens, that you'll stand by your work."

"I promise that, too," replied Neale huskily. "But you frighten me. You fear . . . for yourself?"

"No, I don't," she protested.

"Fate could not be so brutal . . . to take you from me . . . anyway. I'll not think of it."

"Do not. Nor will I. . . . I wouldn't have asked you . . . why this night has shown me your opportunity. I'm so proud . . . so proud. You'll be great someday."

"Well, if you're so proud . . . if you think I'm so wonderful, why haven't you rewarded me for that little job today?"

"Reward you? How?"

"How do you suppose?"

She was pale, eloquent, grave. But he was low-voiced, gay, intense.

"Dear Neale . . . what . . . what can I do? I have nothing. . . . So big a thing as you did today!"

"Child! You can kiss me."

Allie's secret gravity changed. She smiled. "I shore can, as Reddy used to say. That's my privilege. But you spoke of a reward. My kisses . . . they are yours . . . and as many as the . . . the grains of sand out there . . . they are not reward."

"No? Listen. For just one kiss . . . if I had to earn it so . . . I would dig that roadbed out there, carry every tie and rail with my bare hands, drive every spike. . . ."

"Neale, you talk like a boy. Something indeed has gone to your head."

"Yes, indeed it has. It's your face . . . in the moonlight."

She hid that for a moment on his breast. "I . . . I want to be serious," she whispered. "I want to thank God for my good fortune. To think of you and your work! The future! And you . . . you only want kisses."

"Well, since your future must be largely made up of kisses suppose you begin *your* work . . . right now."

"Oh, you are teasing. Yet when you ask of me . . . whatever you ask . . . I have no mind . . . no will. Something drags at me. . . . I feel it now . . . as I used to when you made me wade the brook."

"Ah! That is my sweetest memory of you. How it haunted me!"

They stood silent for a while. Now in the moon-blanched space the sentries trod monotonously. A coyote yelped, sharp and wild. The wind moaned low. Suddenly Neale shook himself, as if awakening.

"Allie, it grows late. We must say good night. . . . Today has been blessed! I am grateful to the depths of my heart. . . . But I won't let you go . . . until my reward. . . ."

She raised her face, white and noble in the moonlight.

# CHAPTER NINETEEN

Neale slept in a tent, and, when he suddenly was awakened, it was bright daylight. His ears vibrated to a piercing blast. For an instant he could not distinguish the sound. But when it ceased, then he knew it had been a ringing bugle call. Following that, came the voices and movements of excited troopers.

He rolled out of his blankets to get into boots and coat, and rush out. The troopers appeared all around him in hurried orderly action. Neale asked a soldier what was up.

"Redskins, b'gorra . . . before breakfast," was the disgusted reply.

Neale thought of Allie and his heart contracted. A swift glance on all sides, however, failed to see any evidence of attack on the camp. He espied General Lodge and Colonel Dillon among a group before the engineers' quarters. Neale hurried up.

"Good morning, Neale," said the chief grimly. "You're back on the job all right."

And Colonel Dillon added: "A little action to celebrate your return, Neale!"

"What's happened?" queried Neale shortly.

"We just got a telegraph message," replied Dillon, "or half a message. 'Big force. Sioux. . . .' That's all. The operator says the wire was cut in the middle of that message."

"Big force . . . Sioux," repeated Neale. "Between here and Benton?"

"Of course. We sent a scout on horseback down along the line."

"Neale, you'll find guns inside. Help yourself," said General Lodge. "You'll take breakfast with us in the cabin. We don't know what's up yet. But it looks bad for us . . . having the women here. This cabin is no fort."

"General, we can have all those railroad ties hustled here, and throw up defenses," suggested the officer.

"That's a good idea. But the troopers will have to carry them. That work train won't get out here today."

"It's not likely. But we can use the graders from the camp up the line. . . . Neale, go in and get guns and a bite to eat. I'll have a horse here ready for you. I want you to ride out after those graders."

"All right," replied Neale rapidly. "Have you told . . . do the women know yet what's up?"

"Yes. And that girl of yours has nerve. Hurry, Neale."

Neale rode away on his urgent errand without having seen Allie. His orders had been to run the horse. It was some distance to the next grading camp—how far he did not know. And the possibility of his return being cut off by Indians, which possibility was implied by Dillon, had quickened Neale into a realization of the grave nature of the situation.

He had difficulty climbing down and up the gorge, but once across it, there was the graded roadbed, leading straight to the next camp. This roadbed was soft, and not easy going for a horse. Neale found better ground along the line, on hard ground. And here he urged the fresh horse to a swift and a steady gait.

The distance was farther than he imagined, and probably exceeded ten miles. He rode at a gallop through a wagon train camp, which, from its quiet looks, was not connected with the work on the railroad, straight on into the midst of two hundred or more graders just about to begin the day's work. His advent called a halt to everything. Sharply and briefly Neale communicated the orders given him. Then he wheeled his horse on the return trip.

When he galloped through the wagon train camp, several rough-appearing men hailed him curiously.

"Indians!" yelled Neale as he swept on. He glanced back once to see a tall, dark-faced man wearing a frock coat speak to the others, and then wildly fling his arms.

It was downhill this way. And the horse, now thoroughly heated and excited, ran his swiftest. Far down the line Neale saw columns of smoke rolling upward. They appeared farther on than his camp, yet they caused him apprehension. His cheek blanched at the thought that the camp containing Allie Lee might be surrounded by Indians. His fears, however, were groundless, for soon he saw the white tents and the cabins, with the smoke columns rising far below.

Neale rode into camp from the west in time to see Dillon's scout galloping hard up from the east. Neale dismounted before the waiting officers to give his report.

"Good," replied Dillon. "You certainly made time. We can figure on those graders in an hour or so?"

"Yes. There were horses enough for half the gang," answered Neale.

"Now for Anderson's report," muttered the officer.

Anderson was the scout. He rode up on a foam-lashed mustang, and got off, dark and grimy with dust. His report was that he had been unable to get in touch with any soldiers or laborers along the line, but he had seen enough with his own eyes. Halfway between the camp and Benton a large force of Sioux had torn up the track—halted and fired the work train. A desperate battle was being fought, with the odds against the workmen, for the reason that the train of boxcars was burning. Troops must be rushed to the rescue.

Colonel Dillon sent a trooper with orders to saddle horses.

This sent a cold chill through Neale. "General, if the Sioux rounded us up here in this camp, we'd be hard put to it," he said forcibly.

"Right you are, Neale. The high slopes, rocks, and trees would afford cover . . . whoever picked out this location for a camp wasn't thinking of Indians. . . . But we need scarcely expect an attack here."

"Suppose we got the women away . . . in the hills," suggested Neale.

Anderson shook his head. "They might be worse off. Here you've shelter, water, food, and men coming. That's a big force of Sioux. They'll have look-outs on all the hills."

It was decided to leave a detachment of soldiers under Lieutenant Brady, who was to remain in camp until the arrival of the graders, and then follow hard on Colonel Dillon's trail.

Besides Allie Lee there were five other women in camp, and they all came out to see the troops ride away. Neale heard Colonel Dillon assure his wife that he did not think there was any danger. But the color failed to return to her face. The other women, excepting Allie, were plainly frightened. Neale found new pride in Allie. She had little fear of the Sioux.

General Lodge rode beside Colonel Dillon at the head of the troops. They left camp on a trot, raising a cloud of dust, and quickly disappeared around the curve of the hill. The troopers who were left behind stacked their guns and sallied out after railroad ties with which to build defenses. Anderson, the scout, rode up the slope to a secluded point from which he was to keep watch. The women were instructed to stay inside the log cabin adjoining the flimsy quarters of the engineers. Baxter, with his assistants, overhauled the guns and ammunition left, and Neale gathered up all the maps and plans and drawings, and put them in a bag to keep close at hand.

Time passed swiftly, and in another half hour the graders began to arrive. They came riding on bareback, sometimes two on one horse, flourishing their guns—a hundred or more red-faced Irishmen spoiling for a fight. Their advent eased Neale's dread. Still, a strange feeling weighed upon him, and he could not understand it or shake it. He had no optimism for the moment. He judged it to be over-emotion, a selfish and rather exaggerated fear for Allie's safety.

Lieutenant Brady then departed with his soldiers, leaving the noisy laborers to carry ties and erect bulwarks. The Irish, as ever, growled and voiced their complaints at finding work, instead of fighting.

"Hurry an' fetch us yez domn' Sooz!" was the cry sent after Brady, and that voiced the spirit of the gang.

In an hour they had piled a fence of railroad ties, six feet high, around the engineers' quarters. This task had scarcely been done when Anderson was discovered riding recklessly down the slope.

Baxter threw up his hands. "We're going to have it," he said. "Neale, I'm not so young as I was."

Anderson rode in behind the barricade and dismounted. "Sioux!"

The graders greeted this information with loud hurrahs. But when Anderson pointed out a large band of Sioux filing down from the hilltop the enthusiasm was somewhat checked. It was the largest hostile force of Sioux that Neale had ever seen. Sight of the lean wild figures stirred Neale's blood, and then again sent that cold chill over him. The Indians rode down the higher slope and turned off at the edge of the timber out of rifle range. Here they got off their mustangs and apparently held a council. Neale plainly saw a befeathered chieftain point with long arms.

Then the band moved, disintegrated, and presently seemed to have melted into the ground.

"Men, we're in for a siege!" yelled old Baxter.

At this juncture the women came running out, badly frightened.

"The Indians! The Indians!" cried Mrs. Dillon. "We saw them . . . behind the cabin . . . creeping down through the rocks."

"Get inside . . . stay in the cabin," ordered Baxter.

Allie was the last one crowded in. Neale, as he half forced her inside, was struck with a sudden wild change in her expression.

"There . . . there," she whispered, trying to point.

Just then rifle shots and the spattering of bullets made quick work urgent.

"Go . . . get inside the log walls," said Neale as he shoved Allie in.

Excitement prevailed among the graders. They began to run under cover of the enclosure and some began to shoot aimlessly.

"Anderson, take some men. Go to the back of the cabin!" shouted Baxter.

The scout called for men to follow him and run out. So many of the graders essayed to follow that they blocked the narrow opening between enclosure and house. Suddenly one of them in the rear sheered around so that he looked at Neale. It was but a momentary glance, but Neale saw recognition there. Then the man was gone. And Neale sustained a strange surprise. That face had been familiar, but he could not recall where he had ever seen it. A red leering evil visage, with prominent hard features, grew more vivid in memory as Neale's mind revolved closer to discovery.

"Inside with you, Neale!" yelled Baxter.

Baxter and Neale, with the four young engineers, took to the several rooms of the log cabin, where each selected an aperture between the logs or a window through which to fire upon the Indians. Neale soon ascertained that there was nothing to shoot at, unless it was at white puffs of smoke rising from behind rocks on the slope. There was absolutely not a sign of an Indian. The graders were firing, but Neale believed they would have done little to save their powder. Bullets *pattered* against the logs; now and then a leader pellet sung through a window to *thud* into the wall. Neale shut the heavy door leading from the cabin into the engineers' quarters. Four bullets ripped through from one side to the other of this canvas and clapboard structure. Then Neale passed from room to room, searching for Allie. Two of the young engineers were kneeling at a chink between the logs, aiming and firing in great excitement. Campbell had sustained a slight wound, and looked white with rage and fear. Baxter was peeping from behind the rude jamb of a window.

"Nothin' to shoot at, boy," he said in exasperation.

"Wait. Listen to that bunch of Irish shoot. They're wasting powder."

"We've plenty of ammunition. Let 'em shoot. They may not hit any redskins, but they'll scare 'em."

"We can hold on here . . . if the troopers hurry back," said Neale.

"Sure. But maybe they're hard at it, too. I've no doubt this is the same bunch of Sioux that held up the work train."

"Neither have I. And if the troops don't get here before dark. . . ."

Neale halted, and Baxter shook his gray head.

"That would be bad," he said. "But we've squeezed out of narrow places before . . . buildin' this U.P.R."

Neale found the women in the large room, between the corner of the walls and a huge stone fireplace. They were quiet. Allie leaped at sight of Neale. Her hands trembled as she grasped him.

"Neale!" she whispered. "I saw Fresno!"

"Who's he?" queried Neale blankly.

"He's one of Durade's gang."

"No!" exclaimed Neale. He drew Allie aside. "You're scared."

"I'd never forget Fresno," she replied positively. "He was one of the ruffians who burned Slingerland's cabin and made off with me."

Then Neale shook with a violent start. He grasped Allie tight. "I saw him, too. Just before I came in. I saw one of the men that visited us at Slingerland's. . . . Big hulking fellow . . . red angry face . . . bad look."

"That's Fresno. He and the gang must have been camped with these graders you brought here. Oh, I'm more afraid of Fresno's gang than the Indians."

"But Allie . . . they don't know you're here. You're safe. The troops will be back soon and drive these Indians away."

Allie clung to Neale, and again he felt something of the terror these ruffians had inspired in her. He reassured her, assuming a confidence he was far from feeling, and cautioned her to stay there in that protected corner. Then he went in the other room of his station. It angered Neale, and alarmed him, that another peril perhaps menaced Allie, and he prayed for the return of the troops.

But the day passed swiftly, in intense watchfulness on the part of the defenders, and in a waiting game on part of the besiegers. They kept up a desultory firing all afternoon. Now and then a reckless grader, running from post to post, drew a volley from the Sioux, and likewise something that looked like an Indian called forth shots from the defenders. But there was no real fighting.

It developed that the Sioux were waiting for night. A fiery arrow, speeding from a bow in the twilight, left a course of sparks in the air, like a falling rocket. It appeared to be a signal for demoniacal yells on all sides. Rifle shots ceased to come from the slopes. As darkness fell, gleams of little fires shot up from all around. The Sioux were preparing to shoot volleys of burning arrows down into the camp.

Anderson hurried in to consult with Baxter. "We're surrounded," he said tersely. "The redskins are goin' to try burnin' us out. We're in a mighty tight place."

"What's to be done?" asked Baxter.

Anderson shook his head.

In the instant there was a dull *spat* of an object striking the roof over their heads. This sound was followed by a long shrill yell.

"That was a burnin' arrow," declared Anderson.

The men, as of one accord, ran out through the engineers' quarters to the open. It was now dark. Little fires dotted the hillsides. A dull red speck, like an ember, showed over the roof, darkened, and disappeared. Then a streak of fire shot out from the black slope and sped on clear over the camp.

"Sooner or later they'll make a go of that," muttered Anderson.

Neale heard the scout's horse that had been left there in the enclosure.

"Anderson, suppose I jump your horse. It's dark as pitch. I could run through . . . reach the troops. I'll take the chance."

"I had that idee myself," replied Anderson. "But it seems to me if them troopers wasn't havin' hell they'd've been here long ago. I'm lookin' for them every minnit. They'll come. An' we've got to fight fire now 'afore they get here."

"But there's no fire yet," said Baxter.

"There will be," replied Anderson. "But mebbe we can put it out as fast as they start it. Plenty of water here. An' it's dark. What I'm afraid of is they'll fire the tents out there . . . an' then it'll be light as day. We can't risk climbin' over the roofs."

"Neale, go inside . . . call the boys out," said Baxter.

Neale had to feel his way through the rooms. He called to his comrades, and then to the women to keep up their courage—that surely the troops would soon return.

When he went out again, the air appeared full of fiery streaks. Shouts of the graders defiantly answered the yells of the savages. Showers of sparks were dropping upon the camp. The Sioux had ceased shooting their rifles for the present, and, judging from their yells, they had crawled down closer under the cover of night.

Presently a bright light flared up outside of the enclosure. One of the tents had caught fire. The Indians yelled triumphantly. Neale and his companions crouched back in the shadow. The burning tent set fire to the tent adjoining. They blazed up like paper, lighting the camp and slopes. But not an Indian was visible. They stopped yelling. Then Neale heard the *thudding* of arrows. Almost at once the roof of the engineers' quarters, which was merely strips of canvas over a wooden frame, burst into flames. The Sioux did not need then to shoot any more burning arrows at the cabin, and they were well aware of that fact. In a single moment the roof of the cabin was blazing. More tents ignited, flared up, and the scene was almost as light as day. Rifles again began to crack. The crafty Indians poured a hail of bullets into the enclosure and the walls of the buildings. Still not an Indian was visible for the defenders to shoot at.

Anderson, Neale, and Baxter were in grim consultation. They agreed with the scout's: "Reckon the game's up. Hustle the women out."

Neale crawled along the enclosure to the opening. On that side of the buildings there was dark shadow. But it was lifting. He ran along the wall, and he heard the whistle of bullets. Back of the cabin the Indians appeared to have gathered in force. Neale got to the corner and peered around. The blazing tents lighted up this end. He saw the graders break and run, more on his side of the cabin, some on the other, while others crowded into the door and window. Neale ran back to the window on the dark side of the cabin. He clambered in. A door of this room was open, and, through it, Neale saw the roof of the engineers' quarters blazing. He heard the women screaming. Suddenly they, too, were running out to the enclosure. Neale hurried into the room where he had left Allie. He called. There was no answer, but a growing roar outside apparently drowned his voice. It was dark in this room. He felt along the wall, the fireplace, the corner. Allie was not there. The room was empty. His hands, groping low along the floor, came in contact with the bag he had left in Allie's charge. It contained the papers he had taken the precaution to save. Probably in her flight to escape from the burning cabin she had dropped it. But that was not like Allie; she would have clung to the bag while strength and sense were hers. Perhaps she had not gotten out of the cabin.

Neale searched again, growing more and more aware of the strife outside. He heard the *crackling* of wood over his head. Evidently the cabin was burning like tinder. There were men in the back room fighting, yelling, crowding. Neale could see only dim burly forms and the flashes of guns. Smoke floated thick, there. Someone, on the inside or outside, was beating at the door with an axe. He decided quickly that whatever Allie might have done, she would not have gone into that room. He retraced his steps, groping, feeling everywhere in the dark.

Suddenly the *crackling,* the shots, the yells ceased, or had been drowned in volume of greater sound. Neale ran to the window. The flare from the burning tents was dying down. But into the edge of the circle of light he saw loom a line of horsemen. "Troopers!" he cried joyfully. A great black pressing weight seemed lifted off his mind. The troops would soon rout that band of sneaking Sioux.

Neale ran to the back room, where, above the din outside, he made himself heard. But for all he could see or hear, his tidings of rescue did not at once affect the men there. Then he forgot them and the fight outside in his search for Allie. The cabin was on fire and he did not mean to leave it until he was absolutely sure she was not hidden or lying in a faint in some corner. And he had not made sure of that until the burning roof began to fall in. Then he leaped out the window and ran back to the enclosure.

The blaze here was no longer bright, but Neale could see distinctly. Some of the piles of ties were burning. The heat had begun to drive the men out. Troopers were everywhere. And it appeared the rattle of rifles was receding up the valley. The Sioux had retreated.

Here Neale continued his search for Allie. He found Mrs. Dillon and three of her companions, but Allie was not with them. All he could learn from the frightened women was that Allie had been with them when they started to run from the cabin. They had not seen her since.

Still Neale did not despair, although his heart sank. Allie was hiding somewhere. Frantically he searched the enclosure, questioned every man he met, rushed back to the burning cabin, where the fire drove him out. But there was no trace of Allie.

Then the conviction of calamity settled upon him. While the cabin burned, and the troopers and graders watched, Neale now searched for the face of the man he had recognized—the ruffian Allie called Fresno. This search was likewise fruitless.

The following hours were a hideous slow nightmare for Neale. He had left one hope—that daylight would disclose Allie somewhere.

★ ★ ★ ★ ★

Day eventually dawned. It disclosed many facts. The Sioux had departed, but if they had suffered any loss, there was no evidence of it. The engineers' quarters, cabin, and tents had burned to the ground. Utensils, bedding, food, grain, tools, and instruments—everything of value except the papers Neale had saved had gone up in smoke. The troopers, who had rescued the work team, must now depend on that train for new supplies. Many of the graders had been wounded, some seriously, but none fatally. Nine of them were missing, as was Allie Lee.

The blow was terrible for Neale. Yet he did not sink under it. He did not consider the opinion of his sympathetic friends that Allie had wildly run out of the burning cabin to fall into the hands of the Sioux. He returned with the graders to their camp, and it was no surprise to him to find the wagon train, that had tarried near, gone in the night. He trailed that wagon train to the next camp, where on the busy road he lost the wheel tracks. Next day he rode horseback all the way in to Benton. But all his hunting and questioning availed nothing. Gloom, heart-sickness, and despair seized upon him. Those fiends had gotten her again. It was fate that she be taken away from him once more. He believed now all that she had said, and there was something of hope in the thought that, if Durade had found her again, she would at least not be at the mercy of ruffians like Fresno. But this was a forlorn hope. Still it upheld Neale, and determined him to seek her during that time his work did not occupy him.

And thus it came about that Neale plodded through his work along the line during the day, and late in the afternoon rode back with the laborers to Benton. If Allie Lee lived, she was in Benton.

# CHAPTER TWENTY

Neale took up lodgings with his friend Larry Red King. He did not at first tell the cowboy about his recovery of Allie Lee and then her loss, and when finally he could not hold the revelation any longer, he regretted that he had been compelled to tell.

King took the news hard. He inclined to the idea that she had run out, fell into the hands of the Indians. Nevertheless he grew at once terribly bitter against men of the Fresno stamp, and in fact against all the outlaw, ruffian, desperado class so numerous in Benton.

Neale begged King to be cautious, to go slow, to ferret out things, and so help him, instead of making it harder to locate Allie.

"Pard, I reckon Allie's done for," he said gloomily.

"No . . . No! Red, I feel she's alive . . . well. If she were dead or . . . or . . . wouldn't I know?" protested Neale.

But King was not convinced. He had seen the hard side of border life; he knew the odds against Allie.

"Reckon I'll look fer that Fresno," he said. And deeper than before he plunged in Benton's wild life.

One morning in the early hours, Neale, on returning to his lodgings, found the cowboy there. In the dim light King looked strange. He had his gun belt in his hands. Neale turned up the lamp.

"Hello, Red, what's the matter? You look pale and sick,"

249

queried Neale.

"They wanted to throw me out of that dance hall," said King.

"Which one?"

"Stanton's."

"Well, did they?" inquired Neale.

"Wal, I reckon not. I walked. An' some night I'll shore clean out that hall."

Neale did not know what to make of King's appearance. The cowboy seemed to be relaxing. His lips that had been tight began to quiver and his hands shook. Then he swung the heavy gun belt with somber and serious air, as if he were undecided about leaving it off even when he went to bed.

"Red, you've thrown a gun!" exclaimed Neale.

King glanced at him and Neale sustained a shock.

"Shore," he drawled.

"By heaven, I knew you would!" declared Neale excitedly, and he clenched his fist. "Did you . . . you kill someone?"

"Pard, I reckon he's daid," mused the cowboy. "I didn't look to see. . . . Fust gun I've throwed fer long. . . . It'll come back now, shore'n hell!"

"What'll come back?" queried Neale. King did not answer this. "Who'd you shoot?" Neale went on.

"Pard, I reckon it ain't my way to gab a lot," replied King.

"But you'll tell *me*," insisted Neale passionately. He jerked the gun and belt from King and threw them on the bed.

"All right," drawled King, taking a deep breath. "I went into Stanton's hall the other night. An' a pretty girl made eyes at me. Wal, I shore asked her to dance. I reckon we'd been good pards if we'd been let alone. But there's a heap of fellers runnin' her, an' some of them didn't cotton to me. One they called Cordy . . . he shore did get offensive. He's the four-flush loud kind. I didn't want to make any trouble fer the girl Ruby . . . thet's her name . . . so I was mighty good-natured. . . . I dropped in Stanton's early tonight. Ruby spotted me first off an' she asked me to dance. Shore I'm no dandy dancer, but I tried to learn. We was gettin' along powerful nice when in come Cordy, hoppin' mad. He had a feller with him, an' both had been triflin' with red liquor. You oughta seen the crowd get back. Made me think Cordy an' his pard had blowed a lot 'round heah an' got a rep. Wal, I knowed they was bluff. Jest mean ugly four-flushers. Shore they didn't an' couldn't know nothin' of me. I reckon I was only that long-legged red-bearded galoot from Texas. Anyhow, I was made to understand it might get hot sudden-like, if I didn't clear out. I left it to the girl. An' some of them girls is full of hell. Ruby jest stood there scornful an' sassy, with her haid leanin' to one side, her eyes half shut, an' a little smile on her face. I'd call her more'n hell. A nice girl gone wrong. Them kind shore is the dangerest. . . . 'Wal,' she says, 'Reddy, are you goin' to let them run you out of heah? They haven't any strings on me.' So I slapped Cordy's face an' told him to shut up. He let out a roar an' got wild with his hands, like them four-flush fellars do who wants to look real bad. I says, pretty sharp-like . . . 'Don't make any moves now.' . . . an' the darned fool went for his gun! Wal, I caught his hand, twisted the gun away from him, poked him in the ribs with it, an' then shoved it back in his belt. He was crazy. But pretty pale an' surprised. Shore I acted sudden-like. Then I says . . . 'My festive gent, if you think of that move again, you'll be stiff before you start it.' Guess he believed me."

King paused in his narrative and wiped his face and moistened his lips. Evidently he was considerably shaken.

"Well, go on," said Neale impatiently.

"Thet was all right so far as it went," resumed King. "But the pard of Cordy's . . . he was half drunk an' a big brag anyhow. He took up Cordy's quarrel. He hollered so, he stopped the music an' drove 'most everybody out of the hall. They were peepin' in at the door. But Ruby stayed. There's a game kid, an' I'm a-goin' to see her tomorrow."

"You are not," declared Neale. "Hurry up. Finish your story."

"Wal, the big bloke swaggered all over me, an' I seen right off thet he didn't have sense enough to be turned. Then I got cold. I always used to . . . but thet's neither heah nor there. . . . He says . . . 'Are you goin' to keep away from Ruby?' An' I says very polite . . . 'I reckon not.' Then he throws hisself in shape, like he meant to leap over a hoss, an' hollers . . . 'Pull yer gun!' I asks very innocent . . . 'What for, mister?' An' he bawls fer the crowd . . . ' 'Cause I'm a-goin' to bore you an' I never kill a man till he goes fer his gun.' To thet I replies more considerate . . . 'But it ain't fair. You'd better get the first shot.' Then the fool hollers . . . 'Redhead!' Thet settled him. I leaps over *quick*, slugged him one . . . left-handed. He staggered, but he didn't fall. . . . Then he straightens up an' goes fer his gun."

King halted again. He looked as if he had been insulted and a bitter irony sat upon his lips.

"I seen . . . when he dropped, thet he never got his hand to his gun at all. . . . Jest as I'd reckoned. Wal, what made me sick was . . . my bullet went through some of them thin walls . . . an' hit a girl in another house. She's bad hurt. . . . They oughta have walls thet'd stop a bullet."

Next day Neale heard the same narrative from the lips of Ancliffe, and it differed only in the essential details of the cowboy's consummate coolness. Ancliffe, who was an eyewitness of the encounter, disclosed that drink or passion or bravado had no part in determining King's conduct. Ancliffe talked at length about the cowboy. Evidently he had been struck with King's singular manner and look and action. Ancliffe had all an Englishman's intelligent and phlegmatic observing powers, and the conclusion he drew was that King had reacted to a situation familiar to him.

Neale took more credence in what Slingerland had told him at Medicine Bow. That night Hough and their many other acquaintances halted Neale to gossip about Larry Red King.

The cowboy had been recognized by Texans visiting Benton. They were cattle barons and they did not speak freely of King until ready to depart from the land. King's right name was Fisher. He had a brother—a famous Texas outlaw called King Fisher. King had always been Red Fisher, and, when he left Texas, he was on the way to become as famous as his brother. Texas had never been too hot for Red until he killed a sheriff. He was a born gunfighter, and was well known on all the ranches from the Panhandle to the Río Grande. He had many friends; he was a great horseman, a fine cowman. He had never been remarkable for bad habits or ugly temper. Only he had an itch to throw a gun and he was unlucky in always running into trouble. Trouble gravitated to him. His redhead was a target for abuse and he was sensitive and dangerous because of that. Texas, the land of gunfighters, had seen few who were his equal in cool nerve and keen eye and swift hand.

Neale did not tell King what he had heard. The cowboy changed subtly, not in his attitude toward Neale, but toward all else. Benton and its wildness might have been his proper setting. So many rough and bad men, inspired by the time and place, essayed to be equal to Benton. But they lasted a day and were forgotten. The great compliment paid to Larry Red King was the change in the attitude of this wild camp. He had been one among many—a stranger. The time came when the dance halls grew quiet as he entered and the gambling hells suspended their games. His fame increased as from lip to lip his story passed, always gaining something. Jealousy, hatred, and fear grew with his fame. It was hinted that he was always seeking some man or men from California. He had been known to question new arrivals: "Might you-all happen to be from California? Have you ever heered of an outfit thet made off with a girl out heah in the Black Hills?"

Neale drifted. Gambling became a habit. Drinking did not get such a hold upon him, because liquor made him sick. He became a friend and companion of Place Hough. Ancliffe sought him, also, and he was often in the haunts of these men. They did not take so readily to King. The cowboy had become a sort of nervous factor to any community. His presence was not conducive to a comfortable hour. For King, although he still drawled his talk and sauntered around, looked the name the Texas visitors had left him. His flashing blue eyes, cold and intent and hard in his flaming red face, his blazing red hair, his stalking form and his gun swinging low—these were so striking as to make his presence always felt. Beauty Stanton claimed the cowboy had ruined her business and that she had a terror of him. But Neale doubted the former statement. All business, good and bad, grew in Benton.

It was strange that as this attractive and notorious woman conceived a terror of King she formed an infatuation for Neale. He would have been blind to it but for the dry humor of Place Hough and the amiable indifference of Ancliffe, who had anticipated a rival in Neale. Their talk, like most talk, drifted through Neale's ears. What did he care? He liked these men, not for what they did or what they were, but because there was a terrible need in him of something to make him forget himself. Both Hough and Ancliffe began to loom largely to Neale. They wasted every day, every hour, and yet, underneath the one's cold passionless pursuit of gold, and the other's serene and gentle quest for effacement, there was something finer left of other years. Neale began to look at himself in the light in which he saw his friends. Benton was full of gamblers and broken men who had once been gentlemen. Neale met them every day—gambled with them—watched them. He measured them all by what he might have been himself. They had given up, but within him there was a continued struggle. He swore to himself, as he had to King, that he was hopeless, yet there was never a sleeping or a waking hour that his better nature did not rise up to flay and accuse and exhort. Drink did not help him, since before he could take enough to make him drunk, a cold and hateful nausea prohibited his further indulgence. The excitement and allurement of the dance halls, although he admired their power, were impossible for him, because while there, in the presence of these pretty and abandoned women, he remembered the past more vividly than elsewhere.

Gambling, then, seemed the only medium by which he could extract a few hours of oblivion from his tortured life. And since he could not play games of chance alone, he had to go to the gambling hells to bear as best he could the baseness that attached itself to him there. Women had free run of all the places in Benton.

At first Neale was flirted with and importuned. Then he was scorned. Then he was let alone. Finally, as day by day he went on, always courteous, even considerate of the women who happened in his way, but blind and cold to the meaning of them there, he was at last respected and admired.

In the afternoons there was always a game in the big gambling place, and in fact the greatest stakes were played for by gamblers like Hough, pitted against each other. Night time was reserved for the fleecing of the builders of the U.P.R., the wage earners whose gold was the lure and the magnet. Neale won large sums of money in those games in which he played with Place Hough. His winnings he scattered or lost in games where he was outpointed or cheated. It was all one to him, for what he cared for was the game, not the result.

One day a number of Eastern capitalists visited Benton. The fame of the town drew crowds of the curious and greedy. And many of these transient visitors seemed to want to have their fling at the gambling hells and dancing halls. There was a contagion in the wildness that affected even the selfish. It would be something to remember and boast of when Benton with its life was a thing of the past.

Place Hough met old acquaintances among some St. Louis visitors who were out to see the road and Benton, and perhaps to find investments, and he assured them blandly that their visit would not be memorable unless he relieved them of surplus cash. So a game with big stakes was begun. Neale, with Hough and five of the visitors, made up the table.

Eastern visitors worked bitterly upon Neale's mood, but he did not betray it. He was always afraid he would come face to face with some of the directors or some of the engineers who he knew so well. That was why, while gambling, he seldom looked up from his cards. The crowd came and went, but he never saw it.

This big game attracted watchers. The visitors were noisy; they drank a good deal; they lost with an equanimity that excited interest, even in Benton. The luck for Neale see-sawed back and forth. Then he lost steadily until he had to borrow from Hough.

About this time Beauty Stanton, with Ruby and another woman, entered the room, and were at once attracted by the game, to the evident pleasure of the visitors. And then unexpectedly Larry Red King stalked in and lounged forward, cool, easy, careless, his cigarette half smoked, his blue eyes keen.

"Hey, is that *him?*" whispered one of the visitors, indicating King.

"That's Red," replied Hough. "Hope he's not looking for one of your gentlemen."

They laughed, but not spontaneously.

"I've seen his like in Dodge City," said one.

"Ask him to set in the game," said another.

"No. Red's a cardsharp," replied Hough. "And I'd hate to see him catch one of you pulling a crooked deal."

They lapsed back into the intricacies and fascination of poker.

Neale, however, found the game unable to hold his undivided attention. King was there, looking and watching, and he made Neale's blood run cold. The girl Ruby was there across from him, with her half-closed eyes, mysterious and sweet, upon him. And Beauty Stanton was there, behind him, as she had often stood to watch a game.

"Neale, I'll bring you luck," she said, and put her hand on his shoulder.

Neale's luck did change. Fortune faced about abruptly, with its fickle inconsistency, and Neale had a run of cards that piled the gold and bills before him, and brought a crowd ten deep around the table. When the game broke up, Neale had now $10,000.

"See. I brought you luck," whispered Beauty Stanton in his ear. And across the table Ruby smiled hauntingly and mockingly.

Neale waved the crowd toward the bar. Only the women and King refused the invitation. Ruby gravitated irresistibly toward the cowboy.

"Aren't you connected with the road?" inquired one of the visitors, drinking next to Neale.

"I am," replied Neale.

"Saw you in Omaha at the office of the company. My name's Blair. I sell supplies to Commissioner Lee. He has growing interests along the road."

Neale's lips closed and he set down his empty glass. Excusing himself, he went back to the group he had left. King sat on the edge of the table. Ruby stood close to him and she was talking;

Stanton and the other woman had taken chairs.

"Wal, I reckon you made a rake-off," drawled King as Neale came up. "Lend me some money, pard."

Neale glanced at King and from him to the girl. She dropped her eyes. "Ruby, do you like Red?" he queried.

"Sure do," replied the girl.

"Red, do you like Ruby?" went on Neale.

Beauty Stanton smiled her interest. The other woman came back from nowhere to watch Neale.

King regarded his friend in mild surprise. "I reckon it was a terrible case of love at first sight," he drawled.

"I'll call your bluff," flashed Neale. "I've just won ten thousand dollars. I'll give it to you. . . . Will you take it and leave Benton . . . go back . . . no! . . . go on west . . . begin life over again?"

"Together . . . you mean!" exclaimed Beauty Stanton as she rose with a glow on her faded face. No need then to wonder why she had been named Beauty!

"Yes, together," replied Neale in swift steadiness. "You've started bad. But you're young. It's never too late. This money can buy you a ranch . . . begin all over again."

"Pard, haven't you seen too much red liquor?" drawled King.

The girl shook her head. "Too late," she said softly.

"Why?"

"Red is bad, but he's honest. I'm both bad and dishonest."

"Ruby, I wouldn't call you dishonest," returned Neale bluntly. "Bad? Yes. And wild. But if you had a chance. . . ."

"No," she said.

"You're both slated for hell. What's the sense of it?"

"I don't see that you're slated for heaven," retorted Ruby.

"Wal, I shore say echo," drawled King as he rolled a cigarette. "Pard, you're drunk this heah minnit!"

258

"I'm not drunk. I appeal to you, Miss Stanton," protested Neale.

"You certainly are not drunk," she replied. "You're just. . . ."

"Crazy!" interrupted Ruby.

They laughed.

"Maybe I do have crazy impulses," replied Neale, and he felt his face grow white. "Every once in a while I see a flash . . . of . . . of I don't know what. I could do something big . . . even now . . . if my heart wasn't dead."

"Mine's in its grave," said Ruby bitterly. "Come, Stanton, let's get out of this. Find me men who talk of drink and women."

Neale deliberately reached out and stopped her as she turned away. He faced her. "You're no four-flush," he said. "You're game. You mean to play this out to the finish. . . . But you're no . . . no maggot like the most. You can think. You're afraid to talk to me."

"I'm afraid of no man. But you . . . you're a fool . . . a sky pilot. You're. . . ."

"The thing is . . . it's not too late."

"It *is* too late!" she cried, with trembling lips.

Neale saw and felt less dominance over her. "It is *never* too late!" he responded with all his force. "I can prove that."

She looked at him mutely. The ghost of another girl stood there instead of the wild Ruby of Benton.

"Pard, you're drunk shore!" ejaculated King as he towered over them, and gave his belt a hitch. The cowboy sensed events.

"I've annoyed you more than once," said Neale. "This's the last. . . . So tell me the truth. . . . Could *I* take you away from this life?"

"Take me? How . . . man?"

"I'm wasting my own life. I know that. I could hardly do worse. But I'd hold it . . . as worthy . . . to save a girl like you . . . *any* girl . . . from hell."

"But . . . how?" she faltered. The bitterness, the irony, the wrong done her by life was not manifest now.

"You refused my plan . . . with Red. . . . Come with me, then."

"My God . . . he's not in earnest!" gasped the girl to her women friends. How cruel it was to have this thought forced upon her, to rise by it, to lose some of her hate of men, to feel softened once more—all in vain! She could not believe. She received no help from her friends.

"I am in earnest," said Neale.

Then the tension of the girl relaxed. Her face showed a rebirth of soul. "I can't accept," she replied. If she thanked him, it was with a look. Assuredly her eyes had never before held that gaze for Neale. Then she left the room, and presently Stanton's companion followed her. But Beauty Stanton remained. She appeared amazed at something, in dismay with something.

King lighted his cigarette. "Shore I'd call thet a square kid," he said. "Neale, if you get any drunker, you'll lose all thet money."

"I'll lose it anyhow," replied Neale absent-mindedly.

"Wal, stake me right heah an' now."

At that Neale generously and still absent-mindedly delivered to King gold and notes that he did not count.

"Hell! I ain't no bank!" protested the cowboy.

Hough and Ancliffe joined them, and with amusement watched King try to find pockets enough for his small fortune.

"Easy come, easy go in Benton," said the gambler with a smile. Then his glance, alighting upon the quiet Stanton, grew a little puzzled. "Beauty, what ails you?"

She was pale and her expressive eyes were fixed upon Neale. Hough's words startled her. "What ails me? Place, I've had a forgetful moment . . . a happy one . . . and I'm deathly sick."

Ancliffe stared in wild surprise. He took her literally.

Beauty Stanton looked at Neale again. "Will you come to see me?" she asked with sweet directness.

"Thank you . . . no," replied Neale. He was amazed. She had asked him that before, and he had coldly but courteously repelled what he thought were her advances. This time he was scarcely courteous.

The woman flushed. She appeared about to make a quick and passionate reply, in anger and wounded pride, but she controlled the impulse. She left the room with Ancliffe.

"Neale, do you know Stanton is infatuated with you?" asked Hough thoughtfully.

"Nonsense," replied Neale.

"She is, though. These women can't fool me. I told you days ago I suspected that. Now I'll gamble on it. And you know how I play my cards!"

"She saw me win a pile of money," said Neale, with scorn.

"I'll bet you can't make her take a dollar of it. Any amount you want and any odds."

Neale would not accept the wager. What was he talking about anyway? What was his drift of things? His mind did not seem right. Perhaps he had drunk too much. The eyes of both Ruby and Beauty Stanton troubled him. What had he done to these women?

"Neale, you're more than usually excited today," observed Hough. "Probably was the run of luck. And then you spouted to the women."

Neale confessed his offer to Ruby and King, and then his own impulse. "Ruby called me a fool . . . crazy . . . a sky pilot. Maybe. . . ."

"Sky pilot! Well, the little devil." Hough laughed. "I'll gamble she called you that before you declared yourself."

"Before, yes. I tell you, Hough, I have crazy impulses. They've grown on me out here. They burst like lightning out of a clear sky. I would have done just that thing for Ruby. . . . Mad, you say? Why, man, she's no worse than I am. It would have given me respect for myself. There was something deep behind that impulse. Strange . . . not understandable. I'm at the mercy of every hour here. What could be worse? Benton has got into my blood. And I see how Benton is a product of this great advance of progress . . . of civilization . . . the U.P.R. We're only atoms in a force no one can understand. . . . Look at Red King. That cowboy was set . . . fixed like stone in his character. But Benton has called to the worst and wildest in him. He'll do something terrible. Mark what I say. We'll all do something terrible. You . . . Place Hough, with all your cold implacable control! The moment will come, born out of this abnormal time. I can't explain, but I feel. There's a workshop in this hell of Benton. Invisible, monstrous, and nameless! Nameless like the new graves dug every day out here on the desert. How few of the honest toilers dream of the spirit that is working on them. That Irishman Shane . . . think of him! He fought while his brains oozed from a hole in his head. I saw, but I didn't know, then. I wanted to take his place. He said . . . no . . . he wasn't hurt . . . and Casey would laugh at him. Aye . . . Casey would have laughed! They are men. There are thousands of them. The U.P.R. goes on! It can't be stopped. It has the momentum of a great nation rolling on from behind. . . . And I, who have fallen, and you, who are a drone among the bees, and Ruby and Stanton with their kind . . . poor creatures sucked into the vortex! And the mob of leeches. . . . Why, we all are so stung by that nameless spirit that we are stirred beyond ourselves, and dare both height and depth of impossible things!"

The gambler showed strong response to Neale's passion.

"You must be drunk," he said gravely. "And yet what you say hits me hard. I'm a gambler. But sometimes . . . there are moments when I might be less or more. There's mystery in the air.

This Benton is a chaos. Those hairy toilers of the rails! I've watched them hammer and lift and dig and fight. By day, they sweat and they bleed and sing and joke and quarrel . . . and go on with the work. By night they are seized by the furies. They fight among themselves while being plundered and murdered by Benton's wolves. Heroic by day . . . hellish by night! And so, spirit or what . . . they set the pace."

Next afternoon, when parasitic Benton awoke, it found the girl Ruby dead in her bed.

Her door had to be forced. She had not been murdered. She had destroyed much of the contents of a trunk. She had dressed herself in simple garments no one in Benton had ever seen. It did not appear what means she had employed to take her life. She was only one of many. More than one girl of Benton's throng had sought the same short road, and cheated life of further pain.

When Neale heard about it, late that afternoon, Ruby was in her grave. It suited him to walk out in the twilight and stand a while in the silence beside the bare sandy mound. No stone—no mark. Another nameless grave! She had been a child once, with dancing eyes and smiles, loved by someone, surely, and perhaps mourned by someone living. The low hum of Benton's awakening night life was borne faintly on the wind. The sand seeped; the coyotes wailed, and yet there was silence. Twilight lingered. Out in the desert the shadows deepened.

By some chance the grave of the scarlet woman adjoined that of a laborer who had been killed by a blast. Neale remembered the spot. He had walked out there before. A morbid fascination often drew him to view that ever-increasing row of nameless graves. As the workman had given his life to the road, so had the woman. Neale saw a significance in the parallel.

Neale returned to the town troubled in mind. He remembered

the last look Ruby had given him. Had he awakened conscience in her? Upon questioning Hough, he learned that Ruby had absented herself from the dancing hall and had denied herself to all that last night of her life.

There was to be one more incident relating to this poor girl before Benton in a mad rush should forget her.

Neale divined it before it came to pass, and he was present and as powerless to prevent it as any other spectator in Beauty Stanton's hall. King reacted in his own peculiar way to the news of Ruby's suicide and the rumored cause. He stalked into that dancing hall where his voice stopped the music and the dancers.

"Come out heah!" he shouted to the pale Cordy.

And King spun the man into the center of the hall, where he called him every vile name known to the camp, scorned and slapped and insulted him, shamed him before that breathless crowd, goaded him at last into a desperate reaching for his gun, and killed him as he drew it.

# CHAPTER TWENTY-ONE

Benton slowed and quieted down a few days before pay day to get ready for the great rush. Only the saloons and dance halls and gambling hells were active, and even here the difference was manifest. The railroad yard was the busiest place in the town, for every train brought huge loads of food, merchandise, and liquor, the transporting of which taxed the teamsters to their utmost.

The day just before pay day saw the beginning of a singular cycle of change. Gangs of laborers rode in on the work trains from the grading camps and the camps at the head of the rails, now miles west of Benton. A rest of several days inevitably followed the visit of the pay car. It was difficult to keep enough men at work to feed and water the trains, and they would have sorry protection from the Indians had not the troops been on duty. Pay days were not off days for the soldiers.

Steady streams of men flowed toward Benton from east and west, and that night the hum of Benton was merry, subdued, waiting.

Bright and early the town with its added thousands awoke. The morning was clear, rosy, fresh. On the desert the colors changed from soft gray to red and the whirls of dust riding the wind resembled little clouds with sunset lines. Silence and solitude and unbroken level reigned outside, in infinite contrast to the seething town. Benton resembled an ant heap at break of day. A thousand songs arose, crude and coarse and loud, but full of joy. Pay day and vacation were at hand!

> Then drill, my paddies, drill,
> Drill, my heroes, drill,
> Drill all day,
> No sugar in your tay,
> Workin' on the U.P. Railway

Casey was one Irish trooper of thousands who varied the song and tune to suit his taste. The content alone they all held. Drill! They were laborers who would turn into regiments at a word.

They showed their stubby beards and donned their best—a bronzed sturdy cheery army of wild boys. The curse that lurked up under the canvas tents rested but lightly upon their broad shoulders.

Strangely the morning began without the gusty wind so common to that latitude. And the six inches of powdery white dust did not rise. The wind, too, waited. The powers of heaven smiled in the clear quiet morning, but the powers of hell waited for the hours to come—the night and darkness.

At 9:00 a mob of five thousand men had congregated around the station, most of them out in the open, on the desert side of the track. They were waiting for the pay train to arrive. This hour was the only orderly one that Benton ever saw. There was laughter, profanity, play—a continuous hum, but compared to Benton's usual turmoil it was pleasant. The workmen talked in groups and, like all crowds of men sober and unexcited, were given mostly to badinage and idle talk.

"Wot was ut I owed ye, Moike?" asked a strapping grader.

Mike scratched his head. "Wos it thirty dollars this toime?"

"It war," replied the other. "Moike, yez hev a memory."

A big Negro pushed out his huge jaw and blustered at his fellows: "I'se a gwine to bust thet yaller nigger's haid," he declared.

"Bill, he's your fren'. Cool down, man, cool down," replied a comrade.

A teamster was writing a letter in lead pencil, using a board over his knees.

"Jim, you goin' to send money home?" queried a fellow laborer.

"I am that, an' first thing when I get my pay," was the reply.

"Reminds me, I owe for this suit I'm wearin'. I'll drop in an' settle."

A group of spikers held forth on a little bank above the railroad track, at a point where a few weeks before they had fastened those very rails with lusty blows.

"Well, boys, I think I see the smoke of our pay dirt . . . 'way down the line," said one.

"Bandy, your eyes are pore," replied another.

"Yep, she's comin'," said another. " 'Bout time for I haven't two-bits to my name."

"Boys, no buckin' the tiger for me today," declared Bandy.

He was laughed at by all, except the quiet comrade who gazed thoughtfully eastward, back over the vast and rolling country. He was thinking of home, of wife and little girl, of what pay day meant for them.

Bandy gave him a friendly slap on the shoulder. "Frank, you got drunk an' laid out all night, last pay day."

Frank remembered, but he did not say what he had forgotten that last pay day.

A long and gradual slope led from Benton down across the barren desert toward Medicine Bow. The railroad track split it and narrowed to a mere thread upon the horizon. The crowd of watching, waiting men saw smoke rise over that horizon line and a dark, flat, creeping object. Through the big throng ran a restless murmur. The train was in sight. It might have been a harbinger of evil for a subtle change—nervous, impatient, brooding—visited that multitude. A slow movement closed the disintegrated crowd and a current of men worked forward to encounter resistance and like currents. They had begun to crowd for advantageous position closer to the pay car to be the first in line.

A fight started somewhere and loud curses and dull blows, and then a jostling mass tried the temper of the slow-marching men. Some boss yelled for order from a boxcar and he was hooted. There was no order. When the train whistled for Benton, a hoarse and sustained shout ran through the mob, not from all lips, not from any massed group, but taken up from man to man—a strange sound, the first note of calling Benton.

The train arrived. Troops alighting preserved order near the pay car, and out of the dense mob a slow stream of men flowed into the car at one end and out at the other.

Bates, a giant digger and a bully, was the first man in the line, the first to get his little share of the fortune in gold passing out of the car that day. Long before half of that mob had received its pay, Bates lay dead upon a sanded floor, killed in a drunken brawl.

And the Irishman Mike had received his $30.

And the big Negro had broken the head of his friend.

And the teamster had forgotten to send money home.

And his comrade had neglected to settle for the suit of clothes he was wearing.

And Bandy for all his vows had gone straight to bucking the tiger.

And Frank, who had gotten drunk last pay day, had been mindful of wife and little girl far away—and had done his duty, which Benton that day made his last!

As the spirit of the gangs changed with the coming of gold, so did that of the day. The wind began to blow, the dust began to fly, the sun began to burn, and the freshness and serenity of the morning passed.

Main Street in Benton became black-streaked with men, white-sheeted with dust. There was a whining whistle in the wind as it swooped down. It complained; it threatened; it strengthened, and from the heating desert it blew in hot. A steady *tramp, tramp, tramp* rattled the lone boards as the army marched down upon Benton. It moved slowly, the first heave of a great mass getting under way, with increasing momentum. Stores and shops, restaurants and hotels and saloons took toll from these first comers. Benton swallowed up the builders as fast as they marched from the pay train. It had an insatiable maw. The bands played martial airs, and soldiers who had lived through the Rebellion felt the thrill and the quick-step and the call of other days.

Toward afternoon Benton began to hurry. The hour was approaching when crowded halls and tents must make room for fresh and unspent gangs. The swarms of men still marched up the street. Benton was gay and noisy and busy then. White shirts and blue and red and plaid held their brightness despite the dust. Gaudily dressed women passed in and out of the halls. All was excitement, movement, color, merriment, and dust and wind and heat. The crowds moved on because they were pushed on. Music, laughter, shuffling feet, and *clinking* glass, a steady tramp, voices low and voices loud, the hoarse band of the bawl of the barker—all merged into a roar—a roar that started merry and wore strangely different and swelled to nameless din.

The sun set, the twilight fell, the wind went down, the dust settled—and night mantled Benton. The roar of the day became subdued. It resembled the purr of the gorging hyena. The yellow and glaring torches, the bright lamps, the dim pale lights behind tent walls, all accentuated the blackness of the night and filled space with shadows, like specters. Benton's streets were full of drunken men, staggering back along the way they had marched in. No woman showed herself. The darkness seemed a cloak, cruel yet pitiful. It hid the flight of a man running from fear; it softened the sounds of brawling and deadened the pistol shot. Under its cover soldiers slunk away sobered and ashamed, and murderous bandits waited in ambush, and brawny porters dragged men by the heels, and young gamblers in the flush of success hurried to new games, and broken wanderers sought some place to rest, and a long line of the vicious, of mixed dialect and different color, filed down in the dark to the tents of lust.

Life indoors that night in Benton was monstrous, wonderful, and hideous.

Every saloon was packed, and every dive and room, with a hoarse violent mob of furious men. Furious in mirth—furious for drink—furious with wildness, insane and lecherous, spilling gold and blood!

The gold that did not flow over the bars flowed into the greedy hands of the cold swift gamblers, or into the clutching fingers of wild-eyed women. The big gambling hell had extra lights, extra attendants, extra tables, and there around the great glittering mirror-blazing bar struggled and laughed and shouted a drink-beset mass of humanity. And all through the rest of the big room groups and knots of men stood and bent and sat around tables, intent, absorbed, obsessed, listening with strained ears, watching with wild eyes, reaching with shaking hands— only to grasp and throw down cards and push rolls of gold toward cold-faced gamblers, and lurch up with curse and glare. This was the night of golden harvest for the black-garbed, steel-nerved, cold-eyed cardsharps. They knew the brevity of time and hour and life.

In the dancing halls there was a maddening whirl, an immense and incredible hilarity, a wild fling of unleashed burly men, an honest drunken spree, and the hideous red-eyed drunkenness that did not spring from drink, and the unveiled passion, the brazen lure, the silent obscenity, the raw, corrupt, and terrible presence of bad women in absolute license at a wild and baneful hour. In the madness of that night, which produced sights no sober eye could recall, there was written finality—the end. Benton reached its greatest, wildest, blackest, vilest. But not its deadliest! That must come—later—as an effect. But the height or the depth was reached.

The scene at midnight was unreal, hard, medieval. No savage dance ever equaled that. Dance of cannibals, dance of sun-worshippers, dance of Apaches on the warpath, dance of cliff-dwellers wild over the massacre of a dreaded foe—these might have been comparable to that dance of gold and lust in Beauty Stanton's parlors.

Benton seemed breathing hard, laboring under its load of evil, dancing toward its close.

Night wore on, and the hour of dawn approached.

The lamps were dead; the tents were dark; the music was stilled, and the low soft roar was a hollow mockery of its earlier strength.

Like specters men staggered slowly and wanderingly through the gray streets. Gray ghosts! All was gray. A vacant laugh pealed out and a strident curse, and then again the low murmur prevailed. Benton was going to rest. Weary, drunken, spent nature sought oblivion—on disordered beds, hard floors, and in dusty corners. An immense and hovering shadow held the tents and halls and streets in obscurity. Through the opaque gloom the silent and the mumbling revelers reeled along. Louder voices broke the spell only for an instant. Death lay in the middle of the main street, in the dust—and no passing man halted. It lay as well down the side streets, in sandy ditches, and on tent

271

floors, and behind the bar of the gambling hell, and in a corner of Beauty Stanton's parlor. Likewise death had his counterpart in hundreds of prostrate men, who lay in drunken stupor, asleep, insensible to the dust in their faces. No one answered the low moans of the man, who, stabbed and robbed, had crawled so far and could crawl no farther.

But the dawn would not stay back to hide Benton's hideousness. The gray lifted out of the streets, the shadows lightened, the east kindled, and the sweet soft freshness of a desert dawn came in on the gentle breeze.

And when the sun arose, splendid and golden, with its promise and beauty, it shone upon a ghastly silent motionless Benton asleep.

# CHAPTER TWENTY-TWO

To Allie Lee again a prisoner in the clutches of Durade, the days in Benton had been mysterious, the nights dreadful. She listened with throbbing ears in fear and trembling. Footsteps and low voices, ceaseless, as of a passing army—and the strange muffled roar, rising and swelling and dying.

Durade's caravan had entered Benton in the dark. Allie had gotten an impression of wind and dust, lights and many noisy hurried men, and a crowded jumble of tents. She had lived in a back room of a canvas house. A door opened out into a little yard, fenced high with heavy planks over or through which she could not see. Here she had been allowed to walk. She had seen Durade once, the morning after Fresno and his gang had brought her to Benton, when he had said meals would be brought her and she must stay there until he had secured better quarters. He had blazed with excitement. Allie might have scaled the high fence, but she was afraid of Durade, and more afraid of the unknown peril outside than she was of him.

She listened to the mysterious life of Benton, wondering and fearful, and through the hours there came to her a nameless certainty of something tremendous and terrible that was to happen to her. But spirit and hope were unquenchable. Not prayer nor reason nor ignorance was the source of her sustained and inexplicable courage. A star shone over her destiny, or a good angel hovered near. She sensed in a vague and perplexing way that she must be the center of a mysterious cycle of events. The hours were fraught with strain and suspense, yet they passed fleetingly. A glorious and saving moment was coming—a meeting that would be as terrible as sweet. Her lover Neale was nearby at the railroad compound and she felt his nearness. It was that which kept her alive. She knew with her heart. And while she thrilled at the sound of every step, she also shuddered. For there was Durade with his desperadoes! Blood would be spilled. Somewhere, somehow that meeting would come. Neale would find her. And the cowboy! Allie remembered the red blaze of his face—the singular piercing blue of his eye, his cool easy careless air, his drawling speech—and underneath all his lazy gentleness, a deadliness of blood and iron.

So Allie Lee listened to all sounds, particularly to all footsteps, waiting for that which was to make her heart stand still.

Someone had entered the room adjoining hers—was now fumbling at the rude door that had always been barred from the other side. It opened. Stitt, the mute who attended and guarded her, appeared carrying bundles. Entering, he deposited these upon Allie's bed. Then he made signs for her to change the garb she wore to what evidently was in the bundles. Further, he gave her to understand she was to hurry—that she was to be taken away. With that he went out, shutting and barring the door after him.

Allie's hands shook as she opened the packages. The very next hour might bring her freedom! She was surprised to find a complete outfit of women's apparel of well made and fine material. Benton then had stores and women! Hurriedly she made the change, which was very welcome. The dress did not fit her as well as it might have, but the bonnet and cloak were satisfactory, as were the little boots. She found a long dark veil and wondered if she was expected to put that on.

A knocking at the door preceded a call: "Allie, are you ready?"

"Yes," she replied.

The door opened. Durade entered. He appeared thinner than she had ever seen him, with more white in or beneath his olive complexion, and there were strain and passion in his face. Allie knew he labored under some strong suppressed excitement. More and more he seemed to lose something of his old character of the Spanish manner.

"Put that veil on," he said. "I'm not ready for Benton to see you."

"Are you . . . taking me away?" she asked.

"Only down the street. I've a new place," he replied. "Come. Stitt will bring your things."

Allie could not see very well through the heavy veil and she stumbled over the rude thresholds. Durade took hold of her arm and presently led her out into the light. The air was hot, windy, dusty. The street was full of hurrying and lounging men. Allie heard different snatches of speech as she and Durade went on. Some stared and leered at her, at which times Durade's hold tightened on her arm and his step quickened. She was certain no one looked at Durade. Some man jostled her—another pinched her arm. Her ears tingled with unfamiliar and coarse speech.

They walked through heavy sand and dust, then along a boardwalk, to turn wide before what was apparently a new brick structure. But a closer view showed it to be painted wood. The place rang hollow with a sound of hammers. It looked well, but did not feel stable underfoot. Durade led her through two large hall-like rooms into a small one, light and newly furnished.

"The best Benton afforded," said Durade, waving his hand. "You'll be comfortable. There are books . . . newspapers. . . . Here's a door opening into a little room. It's dark, but there's a bathtub, water, towels, soap . . . and you've a mirror. . . . Allie, this is luxury to what you've had to put up with."

"It is, indeed," she replied, removing her veil, and then the cloak and bonnet. "But . . . am I to be shut up here?"

"Yes. Sometimes at night, early, I'll take you out to walk. But Benton is. . . ."

"What?" she asked as he paused.

"Benton will not last long," he finished, with a shrug of his shoulders. "There'll be another one of these towns out along the line. We'll go there. And then to Omaha." More than once he had hinted at going on eastward. "I'll find your mother . . . someday," he added darkly. "If I didn't believe that, I'd do differently by you."

"Why?"

"I want her to see you as good as she left you. Then. . . . Are you ever going to tell me how she gave me the slip?"

"She's dead, I told you."

"Allie, that's a lie. She's hiding in some trapper's cabin or among the Indians. I should have hunted all over that country where you met my caravan. But the scouts feared the Sioux. The Sioux! We had to run. And so I never got the truth of your strange appearance on that trail."

Allie had learned that reiteration of the fact of her mother's death only convinced Durade the more that she was living. While he had this hope, she was safe as long as she obeyed him. A dark and sinister meaning lay covert in his words. She doubted not that he had the nature and the power to use her to be revenged upon her mother. That and gambling appeared to be all for which he lived.

Suddenly he seized her fiercely in his arms. "You're the picture of *her!*" Then slowly he released her and the corded red of his neck subsided. His action had been that of a man robbed of all he loved, who remembered in a fury of violent longing, hate, and despair, and who found that the mother's daughter did not suffice.

Allie was left alone. She gazed around the room that she expected to be her prison for an indefinite time. Walls and ceiling were sections locking together, and in some places she could see through the cracks between. One side opened upon a tent wall, the other into a house of canvas. When Allie put her hand against any part of her room, she found that it swayed and *creaked.* She grasped then that this house had been made in sections, transported to Benton by train, and hurriedly thrown together.

She looked next at the newspapers. How strange to read news of the building of the U.P.R.! The name of General Lodge, chief engineer, made Allie tremble. He had predicted a fine future for Warren Neale. She read that General Lodge now had a special train and contemplated an inspection trip out as far as the rails were laid. She read that the Pacific Construction Company was reported to be crossing the Sierra Nevada—that there were ten thousand Chinamen at work on the road—and the day when East and West were to meet was sure to come. Eagerly she searched, her heart thumping, for the name of Neale, but she did not find it. She read in one paper that the Sioux were active along the line between Medicine Bow and Kearney. Every day the workmen would sight a band of Indians, and, growing accustomed to the sight, they would become careless, and so many lost their lives. A massacre had occurred out in the western end of the road where the construction gangs were working. Day after day the Sioux had prowled around, without attacking, until the hardy and reckless laborers lost fear and caution. Then, one day, a grading gang working a mile from the troops, was set upon by a band of Sioux and, before they could raise a gun in defense, were killed and scalped in their tracks.

Allie read on. She devoured the news. Manifestly the world was awakening to the reality of the great railroad. How glad

Neale must be! Always he had believed in the greatness and the reality of the U.P.R. Somewhere along that line he was working—perhaps every night he rode into Benton. Her emotions overwhelmed her as she thought of him so near and for a moment she could not see the print. He was working hard, because he meant to earn an important place someday, and of course he probably thought she was dead. Strangest of all was that she did live! She breathed—she was well, strong, palpitating, right there in Benton, reading about the building of the railroad—and all the time Neale and his friends believed her dead. It was terrible. She wondered with a pang what her disappearance would mean to Neale. Once he had said his life would be over if he lost her. She shivered. What could hold him there in Benton if he no longer had her to think of?

Suddenly her eye rested on a printed letter, familiar somehow, startling her. Allison Lee!

"Allison Lee," she breathed very low. *"My father!"* And she read that Allison Lee, commissioner of the U.P.R., and contractor for big jobs along the line, would shortly lease his home in Council Bluffs, to meet some of the directors in New York City in the interests of the railroad. "If Durade and he ever meet," she whispered. "They *will* meet."

And in that portent she saw loom on the gambler's horizon another cloud. In his egotism and passion and despair he was risking more than he knew. He could not hope to keep her a prisoner this way for very long. Allie felt again the gathering surety of an approaching climax in this dire situation.

"My danger is . . . he may harm me . . . use me for his gambling lure . . . or kill me," she murmured. And her prevision of salvation contended with the dark menace of the hour. But as always she rose beyond hopelessness. Her thought was interrupted here by the entrance of the mute, Stitt, who brought her a few effects left at the former place, and then a tray holding her dinner.

That day passed swiftly.

Darkness came, bringing a strange augmentation of the sounds with which Allie had become familiar. She did not use her lamp, for she had become accustomed to being without one, and she seemed to be afraid of a light. Only a dim pale glow came in at her window. But the sound of Benton—that grew as night fell. She had heard something similar in the gold camps where Durade had lingered; this was at once the same and yet vastly different. She lay listening and thinking. The low roar was that of human beings and any one of its many constituents seemed difficult to distinguish. Voices—footsteps—movements—music—mirth—dancing—*clink* of gold and glasses—the high shrill laugh of a woman—the loud vacant laugh of a man—and the gust of dust-laden wind sweeping overhead—all these blended in the mysterious sound that seemed the strife and agony of Benton. For hours it kept her awake, and, when she did fall asleep, it was so late in the night that when she awakened next day, she thought it must be noon or later.

That day passed and another night came. It brought a change in that the house she was in became alive and roaring. Durade had gotten his establishment under way. Allie lay in sleepless suspense. Rough, noisy, thick-voiced men appeared to be close to her, in one of the rooms adjoining hers, and outside in the tents. The room, however, into which hers opened was not entered. Dawn had come before Allie fell asleep.

Thus several days passed during which she saw only the attendant Stitt, and Allie began to feel a strain that she believed would be harder on her than direct contact with Benton life. While she was shut up there what chance had she of ever seeing Neale or Reddy if they were in Benton? Durade had said he would take her outdoors occasionally, but she had not seen him. Restlessness and gloom began to weigh upon her, and she was in continual conflict with herself. She began to think of disobeying Durade. Something would happen to him sooner or later, and in that event she would be no better off than if she tried to escape. Whatever the evil of Benton it was possible that she might not fall into evil hands. Anything would be better than her confinement here, with no sight of the sun, no one to speak to, nothing to do but brood and fight her fancies and doubts, and listen to that ceaseless soft mysterious din. Allie believed she could not long bear that. Now and then occurred a change in her mind that frightened her. It was a regurgitation of the old tide of somber horror that had been her madness after the murder of her mother.

She was working herself into a frenzied state when unexpectedly Durade came to her room. At first glance she hardly knew him. He looked thin and worn; his eyes glittered; his hands shook, and the strange radiance that emanated from him when his passion for gambling had been crowned with success shone stronger than Allie had ever seen it.

"Allie, the time's come," he said. He seemed to be looking back into the past.

"What . . . time?" she asked.

"For you to do for me . . . as your mother did before you."

"I . . . I . . . don't understand."

"Make yourself beautiful!"

"Beautiful? How?" Allie had an inkling of what he meant, but all her mind repudiated the thought.

Durade laughed. He had indeed changed. He seemed a weaker man. Benton was acting powerfully upon him. "How little vanity you have! Allie, you are beautiful now . . . any time. You'll be so when you're old or dead. . . . I mean for you to show more of your beauty. . . . Let down your hair. Braid it a little. Put on a white waist. Open it at the neck. . . . You remember how your mother did."

Allie stared at him, slowly paling. She could not speak. It had come—what she had dreaded.

"You look like a ghost!" Durade exclaimed. "Like she did . . . years ago when I told her . . . this . . . the first time!"

"You mean to use me . . . as you used her?" faltered Allie.

"Yes. But you needn't be afraid or sick. You'll only be looked at. I'll always be with you."

"What am I to do?"

"Be ready in the afternoon when I call you. You can serve drinks . . . and be looked at."

"I know now why my mother hated you!" burst out Allie. For the first time she too hated him, and felt the stronger for it.

"She'll pay for that hate and so will you," he replied passionately. His physical reaction seemed involuntary—a shrinking as if from a stab. Then followed swift violence. He struck Allie across the mouth with his open hand, a hard blow, almost upsetting her. "Don't let me hear that from you again!" he continued furiously. With that he left the room, closing but not barring the door.

Allie put her hand to her lips. They were bleeding. She tasted her own warm and salty blood. Then there was born in *her* something that burned and throbbed and swelled and drove out all that had been kind and pitying toward this man, and all her vacillations. That blow was what she had needed. There was a certainty now as to her peril, just as there was imperious call for her to help herself and save herself.

"Neale or Reddy will visit Durade's," she soliloquized, with her pulses beating fast. "And if they do not come . . . someone will come. Some man I can trust."

Therefore she welcomed Durade's intention. She paid more heed to the brushing and arranging of her hair, and to her appearance than ever before in her life. The white of her throat and neck mantled red with a blush of shame as she exposed them, intentionally, for the gaze of men. Her beauty was to be used as had been her mother's. And she prayed that if she must submit to bold gaze and indignity from many roisterers that there might be one, attracted as the others, who would see through her beauty to her soul, and know that she was not what she seemed.

She had not long to sit down and meditate and wait. She heard the heavy steps and voices of men entering the room next to hers. Presently Durade called her. With a beating heart Allie rose and pushed open the door. From that moment there would never be any more monotony for her—nor peace—nor safety. Yet she was glad, and faced the room bravely, for Neale or Reddy might be there.

Durade had furnished this larger place luxuriously, and evidently intended to use it for a private gambling den, where he would bring picked gamesters. Allie saw about eight or ten men who resembled miners or laborers.

Durade led her to a table that had been placed under some shelves, which were littered with bottles and glasses. He gave her instructions what to do when called upon, saying that Stitt would help her, and then, motioning her to a chair, he went back to the men. It was difficult for her to raise her eyes and she could not at once do so.

"Durade, who's the girl?" asked a man.

The gambler vouchsafed for reply only a mysterious smile.

"Bet she's from California," said another. "They bloom like that out there."

"Now ain't she your daughter?" queried a third.

But Durade chose to be mysterious. In that he left his guests license for covert glances without the certainty that would permit boldness.

They gathered around a table to play faro. Then Durade called for drinks. This startled Allie and she hesitated to comply with his demand. When she lifted her eyes and met the glances of these men, she had a strange feeling that somehow recalled the California days. Her legs were weak under her; a hot anger labored under her breast; she had to drag her reluctant feet across the room. Her spirit sank, and then leaped. It whispered that looks and words and touches could only hurt and shame her for this hour of her evil plight. They must rouse her resistance and cunning and wit. It was a fact that she was there, helpless for the present. But she lived—her love was infinite—and through these she trusted herself to her fate.

Fresno was there, throwing dice with ten soldiers. To his ugliness had been added something that robbed his face of bronze and health—the tinge of outdoor life—and gave it red and swollen lines and shades, and beastly greed. Benton had made a bad man worse.

Mull was there, heavier than when he had ruled the grading camp, sodden with drink, thick-lipped and red-cheeked, burly, brutal, and still showing in every action and loud word the bully. He was whirling a wheel and rolling a ball and calling out in his heavy voice. With him was a little sallow-faced man, like a wolf, with sweaty downcast eyes and restless hands. He answered to the name of Andy. These two were engaged in fleecing several blue-shirted half-drunken spikers.

Durade was playing faro with four other men, or at least there were that number seated with him. One, whose back was turned toward Allie, wore black and looked and seemed different from the others. He did not talk or drink. Evidently his winning aggravated Durade. Presently Durade called the man Jones.

Then there were several others standing around, dividing their attention between Allie and the gamblers. The door opened occasionally, and each time a different man entered to hold a moment's whispered conversation with Durade, and then went out. These men were of the same villainous aspect that characterized Fresno. Durade had surrounded himself with lieutenants and comrades who might be counted upon to do anything.

Allie was not long in gathering this fact, not that there were subtle signs of suspicion among the gamesters. Most of them had gotten under the influence of drink that Durade kept ordering. Evidently he furnished this liquor free and with a purpose.

The afternoon's play ended shortly. As far as Allie could see, Jones, the man in black, a pale, thin-lipped, cold-eyed gambler, was the only guest to win. Durade's manner was not pleasant while he paid over evident debts. Durade always had been a poor loser.

"Jones, you'll sit in tomorrow?" said Durade.

"Maybe," replied the other.

"Why not? You're winnin'," retorted Durade, hot-headed in an instant.

"Winners are choosers," returned Jones, with an enigmatic smile. His hard cold eyes shifted to Allie, and seemed to pierce her, then went back to Durade and Mull and Fresno. Plain it was to Allie, with her woman's intuition, that if Jones returned, it would not be because he trusted that trio. Durade apparently made an effort to swallow his resentment or whatever irritated him. The gambling pallor of his face had never been more marked. He went out with Jones, and the others slowly followed.

Fresno approached Allie. "Hello, gurly! You sure look purtier than in that buckskin outfit." He leered.

Allie got up, ready for flight or defiance, anything. Durade had forgotten her.

Fresno saw her glance at the door. "He's goin' to the bad," he went on, with his big hand indicating the door. "Benton's too hot fer his kind. He'll not git up some fine mornin'. . . . An' you'd better cotton to me. You ain't his kin . . . an' he hates you an' you hate him. I seen that. I'm no fool. I'm sorta gone on you."

"Fresno, I'll tell Durade," replied Allie, forcing her lips to be firm. If she expected to intimidate him, she was disappointed.

Fresno leered wisely. "You'd better not. Fer I'll kill him, an' then you'll be a sweet little chunk of meat among a lot of wolves." He laughed and lurched up his huge frame. He wore a heavy gun and a knife in his belt. Also, there protruded the butt of a pistol from the inside of his open vest.

Allie felt the heat from his huge body and she smelled the whiskey upon him and sensed the base faithless malignant animalism of the desperado. Assuredly if he had any fear, it was not of Durade.

"I'm sorta gone on you myself," repeated Fresno. "An' Durade's a greaser. He's runnin' a crooked game. All these games are crooked. But Benton won't stand for a polite greaser who talks sweet an' gambles crooked. Mebbe no one's told you what this place Benton is."

"I haven't heard. Tell me," replied Allie. She might learn from anyone.

Fresno appeared at fault for speech. "Benton's a beehive," he replied presently. "An' when the bees come home with their honey, why the red ants an' scorpions an' centipedes an' rattlesnakes get busy. I've seen some places in my time, but Benton beats 'em all. . . . Say, I'll sneak you out at night to see what's goin' on. An' I'll treat you handsome. I'm sorta. . . ."

The entrance of Durade cut short Fresno's further speech.

"What are you saying to her?" demanded Durade in anger.

"I was jest tellin' her about what a place Benton is," replied Fresno.

"Allie, is that true?" queried Durade sharply.

"Yes," she replied.

"Fresno, I did not like your looks."

"Boss, if you don't like 'em, you know what you can do," rejoined Fresno impudently, and he lounged out of the room.

"Allie, these men are all bad," said Durade. "You must avoid them when my back's turned. I cannot run my place without them, so I am compelled to endure much."

Allie's attendant came in then with her supper and she went to her room.

Thus began Allie Lee's life as an unwilling and innocent accomplice of Durade in his retrogression from a gambler to a criminal. In California he had played the game, diamond cut diamond. But he had broken. His hope, spirit, luck, nerve were gone. The bottle and Benton had magnifying and terrible influence upon his passion for gambling.

The days passed swiftly. Every afternoon Durade introduced a new company to his private den. Few ever came twice. Yet Allie knew that all who entered to gaze at her had heard of her. This was sickening, although it had a grain of hope, for if all the men in Benton or out on the road could only pass through Durade's hall, the time would come when she would meet Neale or Reddy. She lived for that. She was constantly on the look-out for a man she could trust with her story. Honest-faced laborers were not wanting in that stream of visitors Durade ushered into her presence, but either they were drunk or obsessed by gambling, or no opportunity afforded to give a hint to one that might bring him back again. Durade did not want any visitors of this kind to return. Many who had been there tried, but failed, to gain admittance. Durade and his dealers worked deliberately.

These afternoons grew to be hideous for Allie. She had been subjected to every possible attention, annoyance, indignity, and insult, except direct violence. She could only shut her eyes and ears and lips. Fresno found many opportunities to approach her, sometimes with Durade there, blind to all but the cards and gold. At such times Allie wished she were sightless and deaf and feelingless. But after she was safely in her room again, she told herself nothing had happened. She was still the same as she had always been. And sleep obliterated what she had suffered. Every day was one nearer to that fateful and approaching moment. And when that moment did come, what would all this horror amount to? It would fade—be as nothing. She would not let words and eyes harm her. They were not tangible—they had no substance for her. They made her sick with rage and revolt at the moment, but they had no power, no taint, no endurance. They were evil passing winds.

As she saw Durade's retrogression, so she saw the changes in all about him. His winnings were large and his strong passion for play increased with them. The free gold that enriched Fresno and Mull and Andy augmented the wildness that claimed them. There were Durade's other helpers—Black, his swarthy doorkeeper, and a pallid fellow called Dayos, who always glanced behind him, and Grist, a short lame bullet-headed silent man—all of them subtly changed till the change was great. Their usefulness to Durade was not in gambling among themselves, but they would do it. He could not control them. Violence threatened many times to be enacted in the private den, yet always held off, until the second visit of the gambler, Jones. With Durade's success had come the craze for bigger stakes, and these could only be played for with other gamblers. So the black-frocked cold-faced sharps became frequent visitors at Durade's. Jones won on that second visit—a fatal winning for him. Allie saw the giant Fresno suddenly fling himself upon Jones and bear him to the floor. Then Allie fled to her room. But she heard curses—a shot—a groan—Durade's loud voice proclaiming that the gambler had cheated—and then the scraping of a heavy body being dragged out.

This murder horrified Allie, yet sharpened her senses. She had seen the light of the days. Providence had protected her. Durade had grown rich—wild—vain—mad to pit himself against the coolest and more skillful gamblers in Benton—and therefore his end was imminent. Allie lay in the dark, listening to Benton's strange wailing roar, sad yet hideous, and out of what she had seen and heard, and from the mournful message on the night wind, she realized how closely associated were gold and evil and men, and inevitably they must lead to wildness and to blood and to death.

# CHAPTER TWENTY-THREE

Following Ruby's death and Larry Red King's wildness, Neale resumed his work with the railroad. He kept alive his hope of finding Allie Lee. More and more, as the work progressed, Neale was entrusted with important inspections.

Long since he had discovered his talent for difficult problems, and with experience had come new confidence in his powers. He had been sent from place to place, in each case with favorable results. General Lodge consulted him, Baxter relied upon him, the young engineers learned from him. And when Baxter and his assistants were sent on ahead into the Rockies, Neale had an enormous amount of work on his hands. Still he usually managed to get back to Benton at night.

Whereupon at once he became a seeker, a searcher, and he believed there was not a tent or a hut or a store or a hall in the town that he had not visited. But he found no clue of Allie; he never encountered the well-remembered face of the bandit, Fresno. He saw more than one Spaniard and many Mexicans, not one of whom could have been the gambler Durade. But Benton was too full, too changeful, too secret to be thoroughly searched in little time. Neale bore his burden, although it grew heavier each day. And his growing work on the railroad was his salvation.

One morning he went to the telegraph station expecting orders from General Lodge. He found the chief's special train at the station headed east.

"Neale, I'm off for Omaha," said Lodge. "Big pow-wow. The directors roaring again."

"What about?" queried Neale, always alive to interest of that nature.

"Cost of the construction. What else? Neale, there are two kinds of men building the U.P.R.. . . . Men who see the meaning of the great work . . . and men who see only the gold in it."

"And they conflict. . . . That's what you mean?"

"Exactly. We've been years on the job now . . . and the nearer the meeting of rails from west to east . . . the harder our problems. Kenney played out . . . Boone is ill . . . and Baxter won't last much longer. If I was not an old soldier I would be done up now."

"Chief, I can see only success," replied Neale, with spirit.

"Assuredly. We see with the same eyes," said General Lodge, smiling. "Neale, I've a job for you that will make you gray-headed."

"Hardly that," returned Neale, laughing.

"Do you remember the survey we made out there in the Black Hills for Number Ten bridge? Made over two years ago."

"I'm not likely to forget it."

"Well, the rails are within twenty miles of Number Ten. There'll be there presently . . . and no piers to cross on."

"How's that?"

"I don't know. The report came in only last night. It's a queer document. Here it is. Study it at your leisure. . . . It seems a big force of men have been working there for months. Piers have been put in . . . only to sink!"

"Sink!" ejaculated Neale. "*Whew!* That's a stumper. . . . Chief, the survey is mine. . . . I'll never forget how I worked on it."

"Could you have made a mistake?"

"Of course," replied Neale readily. "But I'd never believe that unless I saw it. A tough job it was . . . but just the kind of work I eat up."

"Well, you can go out and eat it up some more."

"That means I'll have to camp out there. I can't get back to Benton."

"No, you can't. And isn't that just as well?" queried the chief, with his keen dark glance on Neale. "Son, I've heard your name coupled with gamblers . . . and that Stanton woman."

"No doubt. I know them. I've been . . . seeking some trace of . . . Allie."

"You still hope to find her? You still imagine some of this riff-raff Benton gang made off with her?"

"Yes."

"Son . . . it's scarcely possible," said Lodge earnestly. "Anderson claims the Sioux got to her. We're all inclined to that. . . . Oh, it's hard, Neale. . . . Love and life are only atoms under the iron heel of the U.P.R.. . . . It's too late now. You can't forget . . . no . . . but you must not risk your life . . . your opportunities . . . your reputation."

Neale turned away his face a moment and was silent. An engine whistled; a bell began to ring; some train official called to General Lodge.

The chief held up his hand for a little more delay. "I'm off," he said rapidly. "Neale, you'll go out to Number Ten and take charge."

That surprised and thrilled Neale into eagerness. "Who are the engineers?"

"Blake and Coffee. I don't know them. Henney sent them out from Omaha. They're well recommended. But that's no matter. Something is wrong. You're to have full charge of engineers, bosses, masons. In fact I've sent word out to that effect."

"Who's the contractor?" asked Neale.

"I don't know. But whoever he is, he has made a pile of money out of this job. . . . And the job's not done. That's what galls me."

"Well, chief, it *will* be done," said Neale, sharp with determination.

"Good! Neale, I'll start east with another load off my shoulders. . . . And, son . . . if you throw up a bridge so there'll be no delay, something temporary for the rails and the work train . . . and then plan piers right for Number Ten . . . well . . . you'll hear from it, that's all."

They shook hands.

"I may be gone a week or a month, I can't tell," went on the chief. "But when I do come, I'll probably have a train load of directors, commissioners, stockholders."

"Bring them on," said Neale. "Maybe if they saw more of what we're up against, they wouldn't holler so."

"Right. . . . Remember you've full charge and that I trust you implicitly. Good bye and good luck!"

The chief boarded his train as it began to move. Neale watched it leave the station and with a swelling heart he realized that he had been placed high, that his promotion of advancement had not been without warrant.

The work train was backing into the station, and would depart westward in short order. Neale hurried to his lodgings to pack his few belongings. King was lying on his cot, fully dressed and asleep. Neale shook him.

"Wake up, you lazy son-of-a-gun!" shouted Neale.

King opened his eyes.

"Wal, what's wrong? Is it last night or tomorrow?"

"Red, I'm off. Got charge of a big job."

"Is thet all?" drawled King sleepily. "Why, shore I always knowed you'd be chief engineer someday."

"Pard . . . sit up," said Neale unsteadily. "Will you stay

sober . . . and watch . . . and listen for some news of Allie. . . . Till I come back to Benton?"

"Neale, air you still dreamin'?" asked King incredulously.

"No. . . . Will you do that much for me?"

"Shore."

"Thank you, old friend. Good bye now . . . I've got to rustle."

He left King sitting on his cot, staring at nothing. Neale had to run to catch the work train.

A brawny Irishman extended a red-sleeved arm to help him up. "Up wid yez. . . . Thar!"

Neale found himself with bag and rifle and blanket sprawling on the gravel-covered floor of a flat car. Casey, the old lineman, grinned at him over the familiar short black pipe.

"B'gorra, it's me ould friend Neale!"

"It sure is. How're you, Casey?"

"Pretty good for an ould soldier. . . . An' it's news I hear of yez, me boy!"

"What news?"

"Shure yez hed a boost. General Lodge hisself was tellin' Grady, the boss, that yez had been given charge of Number Ten."

"Yes, that's correct."

"I'm domn' glad to hear ut," declared the Irishman. "But yez hev a hell of a job in that Number Ten."

"So I've been told. What do you know about it, Casey?"

"Shure, ut ain't much. A friend of mine was mixin' mortar over there. An' he sez when the crick was dry ut hed a bottom, but whin wet ut shure hed none."

"Then I have got a job on my hands," replied Neale grimly.


These days, it took the work train several hours to reach the end of the rails. Neale rode by some places with a profound satisfaction in the certainty that, but for him, the track would not yet have been spiked there. Construction was climbing fast into the Black Hills. He wondered when and where would be the long looked-for meeting of the rails connecting East with West. Word had drifted over the mountains that the Pacific division of the construction was already in Utah.

At the camp Colonel Dillon offered Neale an escort of troopers out to Number Ten, but Neale decided he could make better time alone. There had been no late sign of the Indians in that locality and he knew both the road and the trail.

Early next morning, mounted on a fast horse, he set out. It was a melancholy ride. For several times he had been over that ground, once traveling west with King, full of ardor and joy at the prospect of soon seeing Allie Lee, and again on the return, in despair at loss of her.

He rode the twenty miles in three hours. The camp of dirty tents was clustered in a hot dusty valley surrounded by hills sparsely fringed with trees. Neale noted the timber as a lucky augury to his enterprise. It was an idle camp, full of lolling laborers.

As Neale dismounted a Mexican came forward.

"Look after the horse," said Neale, and, taking his luggage, he made for a big tent with a fly extended in front. Several men sat on camp chairs around a table. One of them got up, and stepped out.

"Where's Blake and Coffee?" inquired Neale.

"I'm Blake," was the reply. "And there's Coffee. Are you Mister Neale?"

"Yes."

"Coffee, here's our new boss!" called Blake, as he took part of Neale's baggage.

Coffee appeared to be a sunburned, middle-aged man, rather bluff and hearty in his greeting. The younger engineer, Blake, was a tanned, thin-faced individual, with a shifty gaze and constrained manner. The third fellow they introduced as a line-man named Somers. Neale had not anticipated a cordial reception and felt disposed to be generous.

"Have you got quarters for me here?" he inquired.

"Sure. There's lots of room and a cot," replied Coffee.

They carried Neale's effects inside the tent. It was large and spare, containing table and lamp, boxes for seats, several cots and bags.

"It's hot. Got any drinking water?" asked Neale, taking off his coat. Next he opened his bag to take things out, then drank thirstily of the water offered him. He did not care much for this part of his new task. These engineers might be sincere and competent, but he had been sent on to judge of their work, and the situation was not pleasant. Neale had observed many engineers come and go during his experience on the road, and that fact, with the authority given him and his loyalty to the chief, gave him cause for worry. He hoped, and he was ready to believe these engineers had done their best on an extremely knotty problem.

"We got Lodge's telegram last night," said Coffee. "Kinda sudden. It jarred me."

"No doubt. I'm sorry. What was the message?"

"Lodge never wastes words," replied the engineer shortly. But he did not vouchsafe the information Neale asked.

Then Neale threw his notebook upon the dusty table, and, sitting down on a box, he looked up at the men. Both engineers were studying him intently, almost eagerly, Neale imagined.

"Number Ten's a tough nut to crack, eh?" he inquired.

"We've been here three months," replied Blake.

"Wait till you see that quicksand hole," added Coffee.

"Quicksand! It was a dry solid streambed when I run the line through here and drew the plans for Number Ten," declared Neale.

295

Coffee and Blake stared blankly at him. So did the lineman, Somers.

"You! Did *you* draw the plans we . . . we've been working on?" asked Coffee.

"Yes, I did," answered Neale slowly. It struck him that Blake had paled slightly. Neale sustained a slight shock of surprise and antagonism. He bent over his notebook, opening it to a clean page. Fighting his first impressions, he decided they had arisen from the manifest dismay of the engineers and their consciousness of a blunder.

"Let's get down to notes," Neale went on, taking up his pencil. "You've been here three months?"

"Yes."

"With what force?"

"Two hundred men on and off."

"Who's the gang boss?"

"Colohan. He's had some of the biggest contracts along the line."

Neale was about to inquire the name of the contractor, but he refrained, governed by one of his peculiar impulses.

"Anybody working when you got here?" he supplemented.

"Yes. Masons had been cutting stone for six weeks."

"What's been done?"

Coffee laughed harshly. "We got the three piers in . . . good and solid on dry bottom. Then along comes the rain . . . and our work melts into the quicksand. Since then we've been try-ing to do it over."

"But why did this happen in the first place?"

Coffee spread wide his arms. "Ask me something easy. Why was the bottom dry and solid? Why did it rain? Why did solid earth turn into quicksand?"

Neale slapped the notebook shut and rose to his feet. "Gentle-men, that is not the talk of engineers," he said deliberately.

"The hell you say! What is it then?" burst out Coffee, his face blushing redder.

"I'll tell you later," replied Neale, turning to the lineman. "Somers, tell this gang boss, Colohan, I want him." Then Neale left the tent. He had started to walk away when he heard Blake speak in a fierce undertone.

"Didn't I tell you? We're up against it!"

And Coffee growled a reply Neale could not understand. But the tone of it was conclusive. These men had made a serious blunder and were blaming each other, hating each other for it. Neale was conscious of anger. This section of line came under his survey, and he had been proud to be given such important and difficult work. Incompetent or careless engineers had bungled Number Ten. Neale strode among the idle and sleeping laborers, between the tents, and then past the blacksmith's shop and the feed corrals down to the river.

A shallow stream of muddy water came murmuring down from the hills. It covered the wide bed that Neale remembered had been a dry, sand-and-gravel waste. On each side the abutment piers had been undermined and washed out. Not a stone remained in sight. The banks were hollowed inward, and shafts of heavy boards were sliding down. In the middle of the stream stood a coffer dam in course of building and near it another that had collapsed. These frameworks almost hid the top of the middle pier, which had evidently slid over, and was sinking on its side. There was no telling what had been sunk in that hole. All the surroundings—the tons of stone, cut and uncut, the piles of moldy lumber, the platforms and rafts, the manifestations in the worn shores up and down both sides—all attested to the long weeks of fruitless labor, and to the engulfing mystery of that shallow murmuring stream.

Neale returned thoughtfully to camp. Blake and Coffee were sitting under the fly in company with a stalwart Irishman.

"Fine sinkhole you picked out for Number Ten, don't you think?" queried Blake.

Neale eyed his interrogator with somewhat of a penetrating glance. Blake did not frankly meet that gaze. The young man seemed to be laboring with what Neale took to be a bitterness difficult to conceal.

"Yes, it's a sinkhole, all right, and no mistake," replied Neale. "It's just what I calculated when I run the plans. . . . Did you follow those plans?"

Blake appeared about to reply when Coffee cut him short. "Certainly we did," he snapped.

"Then where are the breakwaters?" asked Neale sharply.

"Breakwaters?" ejaculated Coffee. His surprise was sincere.

"Yes, breakwaters," retorted Neale. "I drew plans for breakwaters to be built upstream, so that in high water the rapid current would be directed equally between the piers, and not against them."

"Oh, yes . . . why . . . we must have got . . . it mixed," replied Coffee. "Thought they were to be built last. Wasn't that it, Blake?"

"Sure," replied his colleague, but his tone lacked something.

"Ah . . . I see," said Neale slowly.

Then the big Irishman got up to extend a huge hand. "I'm Colohan," he boomed.

Neale liked the bronzed rough face, good-natured and intelligent. And he was aware of a shrewd pair of gray eyes taking his measure. Why these men seemed to want to look through Neale might have been natural enough, but began to be strange to him. He had come there to help them, not to discharge them. Colohan, however, did not rouse Neale's antagonism as the others had begun to.

"Colohan, are you sick of this job?" queried Neale, after greeting the boss.

"Yes . . . an' no," replied Colohan.

"You want to quit, then?" went on Neale bluntly.

The Irishman evidently took this curt query as a foreword of the coming dismissal. He looked shamed, crestfallen, at a loss to reply.

"Don't misunderstand me," continued Neale. "I'm not going to fire you. But if you are sick of the job, you can quit. I'll boss the gang myself. . . . The rails will be here in ten days. And I'm going to have a trestle over that hole so the rails can cross. No holding up the work at this stage of the game! There's near five thousand men in the gangs back along the line . . . coming fast. They've all become imbued with one idea . . . success. The U.P.R. is going through. Soon out here the rails will meet! Colohan, make it a matter of your preference. Will you stick?"

"You bet!" he replied heartily. A ruddy glow emanated from his face. Neale was quick to sense that this Irishman, like Casey, had an honest love for the railroad, whatever he might feel for the labor.

"Get on the job then," ordered Neale cheerily. "We'll hustle while there's daylight. We'll have that trestle ready when the rails get here."

Coffee laughed scornfully. "Neale, that sounds fine, but it's impossible, until the trains get here with piles and timbers, iron, etcetera. We meant to run up a trestle then."

"I daresay," replied Neale. "But the U.P.R. did not start that way, and never would finish that way."

"Well, you'll have your troubles," declared Coffee.

"Troubles! Do you imagine I'm going to think of *myself?*" retorted Neale. These fellows were beginning to get on his nerves. Coffee grew sullen, Blake shifted uneasily from foot to foot, Colohan beamed upon Neale.

"Come on with them orders," Colohan said.

"Right! Send men up on the hills to cut and trim trees for

piles and beams. . . . Find a way or make one for horses to snake down these timbers. Haul that pile driver down to the river and set it up. . . . Have the engineer start up steam and try out. . . . Look the blacksmith shop over to see if there's iron enough. If not, telegraph Benton for more . . . for whatever you want . . . and send wagons back to the end of the rails. . . . That's all for this time, Colohan."

"All right, chief," replied the boss, and he saluted. Then he turned sneeringly to Blake and Coffee. "Did you hear them orders? I'm not takin' none from you again. They're from the chief."

Colohan's manner or tone or the word "chief" annoyed Coffee. He looked nasty. "Go on and work, then, you big Irish paddy," he said violently. "Your chief blarney doesn't fool us. You're only working to get on the right side of your new boss. . . . Let me tell you . . . you're in this Number Ten deal as deep as we are."

It had developed that there was hatred between these men. Colohan's face turned fiery red, and, looming over Coffee, he looked the quick-tempered and dangerous nature of his class.

"Coffee, I'm sayin' this to your face . . . right now. I ain't deep in this Number Ten deal. . . . I obeyed orders . . . an' darn' strange ones, some of them."

Neale intervened and perhaps prevented a clash. "Don't quarrel, men. Sure there's bound to be a little friction for a day or so. But we'll soon get to working smooth."

Colohan strode away without another word. His brawny shoulders were expressive of a doubt.

"Get me my plans for Number Ten construction," said Neale pleasantly. The situation appeared disagreeable, but he meant to do his share at making the best of it.

Blake brought the plans and spread them out on the table.

"Will you both go over them with me?" queried Neale.

"What's the use?" returned Coffee disgustedly. "Neale, you're thick-headed."

"Yes, I guess so," rejoined Neale constrainedly. "That's why General Lodge sent me up here . . . over your clear heads."

No retort was forthcoming from the two disgruntled engineers. Neale went into the tent and drew a seat up to the table in there. He wanted to be alone—to study his plans—to think about the whole matter. He found his old figures and drawings as absorbing as a good story; still there came breaks in his attention. Blake walked into the tent several times, as if to speak, and each time he retired silently. Again some messenger brought a telegram to one of the engineers outside, and it must have caused a whispered colloquy that followed. Finally they went away, and Neale, getting to work in earnest, was not disturbed until called for supper.

Neale ate at a mess table with the laborers, and enjoyed his meal. The paddies always took to him. One thing he gathered early was the fact that Number Ten bridge was a joke with the men. This sobered Neale and he left the cheery bantering company for a quiet walk alone.

It was twilight down in the valley, while still daylight up on the hilltops. A faint glow remained from the sunset, but it faded as Neale looked. He walked a goodly distance from camp, so as to be out of earshot. The cool night air was pleasant after the hot day. It fanned his face. And the silence, the darkness, the stars calmed him. A lonely wolf mourned from the heights, and the long wail brought to mind Slingerland's cabin. Then it was only a quick stop to memory of Allie Lee, and Neale drifted from the perplexities and problems of his new responsibility to haunting memories, hopes, doubts, fears.

When he returned to the tent, he espied a folded paper on the table in the yellow lamp light. It was a telegram addressed to him. It said that back salaries and retention of engineers were at his discretion, and was signed by Lodge. This message nonplussed Neale. What was there that he had not found out? The chief meant that Blake and Coffee would not be paid for past work nor kept for future work unless Neale decided otherwise. While he was puzzling over this message, the engineers came in.

"Say, what do you make of this?" demanded Neale, and he shoved the telegram across the table toward them.

Both men read it. Coffee threw his coat over on his cot, and then lit his pipe. "What I make of that is . . . I lose three months back pay. Nine hundred dollars," he replied, puffing a cloud of smoke.

"And I lose six hundred," supplemented Blake.

Neale leaned back and gazed up at his subordinates. He felt a subtle change in them. Something had been decided for them.

"But this message reads at my discretion," said Neale. "It's a plain surprise to me. I've no intention of making you lose your back pay, or of firing you, either."

"You'll probably do both . . . unless we can get together," assented Coffee.

"That remains to be seen," was the enigmatic reply. "I'll need you both," went on Neale thoughtfully. "We've a big job. We've got to put a force of men on the piers while we're building the trestle. . . . Maybe I'll fall down myself. . . . Heavens, I've made blunders. I can't condemn you fellows. I'm willing to call off all talk about past performances and begin over again."

Neale felt that this proposition should have put another light on the question and should have been received appreciatively if not enthusiastically. But he was somewhat taken aback by the fact that it was not.

"*Ahem!* Well, we can talk it over tomorrow." Coffee yawned.

Neale made no more overtures, busied himself with his notes

for an hour, and then sought his cot.

Next morning, bright and early, Neale went down to the river to make his close inspection of what had been done toward building Number Ten. From Colohan he ascertained the number of shafts and coffer dams sunk; from the masons he learned the amount of stone cut to patterns. And he was not only amazed and astounded, but overwhelmed, and incensed beyond expression. The labor had been prodigious. Hundreds of tons of material had been sunk there, and that meant that hundreds of thousands of dollars also had been sunk.

Upon investigation Neale found that as often as cribbings had been sunk for the piers, they had never been sunk deep enough. Coffer dams that did not dam at all had been useless, senseless wastes of time and material, not to say wages. His plans called for fifty thirty-foot piles driven to bedrock, which, according to the excavations he had had made at the time of survey, was forty feet below the surface. Not a pile had been driven! There had been no solid base for any of the cribbings! No foundations for the piers!

At the discovery a bursting gush of blood burned hotly in Neale's face and neck. "No blunder. No incompetence. No misreading of my plans. But a rotten deliberate deal. Work done over and over again! Oh, I see it all now. General Lodge knew it without ever coming here. The same old story. That black stain . . . that dishonor on the great work! Graft! Graft!"

He clambered out of the wet and muddy hole and up the bank. Then he saw Blake sauntering across the flat toward him. Neale sat down abruptly to hide his face and fury, giving himself the task of scraping mud from his boots. When Blake got there, Neale had himself fairly well in hand as to exterior appearances.

"Hello, Neale," said Blake suavely. "Collected some mud, I see. It's sure a dirty job."

"Yes, it's been dirty in more ways than mud, I guess," replied Neale. The instant his voice sounded in his ears it unleashed his temper.

"Sure has been a pile of money . . . dirty government money . . . sunk in there," rejoined Blake. He had assurance that surprised Neale into a desire to see how far he would go.

"Blake, it's an ill wind that blows nobody good."

A moment of silence passed before Blake spoke again. "Sure. And it'll blow you good, too," he said, breathing hard.

"Every man has his price," replied Neale lightly. Then he felt a big soft roll of bills stuffed into his hand. He took it, trembling all over. He wanted to spring erect—to fling that bribe in its giver's face. But he could control himself a moment longer. "Blake, who's the contractor on this job?" he queried rapidly.

"Don't you know?"

"I don't."

"Well, we supposed you knew. It's Lee."

Neale started as if he had received a stab; the name hurt him in one way and was a shock in another. "Allison Lee . . . the commissioner?" he asked thickly.

"Sure. Oh, we're in right, Neale," replied Blake, with a laugh of relief.

Swift as an Indian, and as savagely, Neale sprang up. He threw the roll of bills into Blake's face. "You try to bribe me! *Me!*" burst out Neale passionately. "You think I'll take your dirty money . . . cover up your crooked job? Why, you sneak! You thief! You dog!" He knocked Blake down.

"Hold . . . on . . . Neale!" gasped Blake. He raised himself on his elbow, half stunned.

"Pick up that money," ordered Neale, and he threatened Blake again. "Hurry! Now march for camp!"

Neale dragged the young engineer into the presence of his superior. Coffee sat at his table under the fly, with Somers and another man. Colohan appeared on the moment, and there were excited comments from others approaching. Coffee stood up. His face turned yellow. His lips snarled.

"Coffee, here's your side partner!" called Neale, and his voice was biting. "I've got you both dead to rights, you liars! You never even tried to work on my plans for Number Ten."

"Neale, what in the hell do you suppose we're out here for?" demanded Coffee harshly. "They're all getting a slice of this money. There's barrels of it. The directors of the road are crooked. They play both ends against the middle. They borrow the money from the government and they pay it out to themselves. You're one of these dreamers. You're Lodge's pet. But you can't scare me."

"Coffee, if there was any law out here for stealing, you'd go to jail," declared Neale. "You're a thief, same as this pup who tried to bribe me. You're worse. You've held up the line. You've ordered your rotten work done over and over again. This is treachery to General Lodge . . . to Henney, who sent you out here. And to me it's . . . it's . . . there's no name low enough. I surveyed the line through here. I drew the plans for Number Ten. And I'm going to prove you both cheats. You and your contractor!"

"Neale, there's more than us in the deal," said Coffee sullenly.

Colohan strode close, big and formidable. "If you mean me, you're a liar," he declared. "An' don't you say it." Coffee was intimidated, and then Colohan turned to Neale. "Boss, I swear I wasn't in on this deal. Lately I guessed it was all wrong. But all I could do was obey orders."

"Neale, you can't prove anything." Coffee sneered. "If you have any sense, you'll shut up. I tell you this is only a *little* deal. I'm on the inside. I know financiers commissioners, Congressmen and Senators . . . and I told you before the directors . . . all in on this U.P.R. pickings . . . you're a fool!"

"Maybe. But I'm no thief," retorted Neale.

"Shut up, will you?" shouted Coffee, who plainly did not take kindly to that epithet before the gathering crowd. "I'm no thief. . . . Men get shot at for saying less than that."

Neale laughed. He read Coffee's mind. That worthy, responding to the wildness of the time and place, meant to cover his tracks one way or another. And Neale had not lived long with Larry Red King for nothing. "Coffee, you *are* a thief," declared Neale, striding forward. "The worst kind! Because you stole without risk. You can't be punished. . . . But I'll carry this deal higher than you." And quick as a flash Neale snatched some telegrams from Coffee's vest pocket. The act infuriated Coffee. His face went purple.

"Hand 'em back!" he yelled, his arm swinging back to his hip.

"I'll bet there's a telegram here from Lee and I'm entitled to keep them," responded Neale, cool and slow.

Then as Coffee furiously jammed his hand back for his gun, Neale struck him. Coffee fell with the overturned table out in the sand. His gun dropped as he dropped. Neale was there light and quick. He snatched up the gun.

"Coffee . . . you and Blake are to understand you're fired," said Neale. "Fired off the job and out of camp, just as you are!"

Fifteen days later the work train crossed Number Ten on a trestle, and the construction progressed with new impetus.

Not many days later a train of different character crept slowly foot by foot over that temporary bridge. It carried passenger coaches, a private car containing the directors of the railroad, and General Lodge's special car. The engine was decorated with flags and the engineer whistled a piercing blast as he rolled out upon the structure. Number Ten had been the last big obstacle.

As fortune would have it, Neale happened on the moment to be standing in a significant and thrilling position, for himself, and for all who saw him. And that happened to be in the middle of the stream opposite the trestle on the masonry of the middle pier now two feet above the coffer dam. He was as wet and muddy as the laborers with him.

Engineer, foreman, brakeman, and passengers cheered him. For Neale, the moment was unexpected and simply heart-swelling. Never in his life had he felt so proud. And yet, stinging amongst these sudden sweet emotions, was a nameless pang.

Presently Neale espied General Lodge leaning out of a window of his car. He was waving. Neale pointed down at his feet, at the solid masonry, and then circling his mouth with his hands he yelled with all his might: "Bedrock!"

His chief yelled back: "You're a soldier!"

That perhaps in the excitement and joy of the moment was the greatest praise the Army officer could render. Nothing could have pleased Neale more.

The train passed over the trestle and on out of sight. Upon its return, about the middle of the afternoon, it stopped in camp. A messenger came with word for Neale to report at once to the directors. He hurried to his tent to secure his papers, and then, wet and muddy, he entered the private car of the directors.

It contained only four men—General Lodge, and Warburton, Rogers, and Rudd. All except the tall white-haired Warburton were comfortable in shirt sleeves, smoking, with a table between them. The instant Neale entered their presence, he divined that he faced a big moment in his life.

The chief's manner, like King's when there was something in the wind, seemed quiet, easy, potential. His searching glance held warmth, and a gleam that thrilled Neale. But he was ceremonious, not permitting himself his old familiarity before these dignitaries of the great railroad.

"Gentlemen, you remember Mister Neale," said Lodge.

They were cordial—pleasant.

Warburton vigorously shook Neale's hand, and leaned back, after the manner of matured men, to look Neale over. "Young man, I'm glad to meet you again," he declared in his big voice. "Remember him! Well, I do . . . though he's thinner, older."

"Small wonder," interposed the chief. "He's been doing a man's work."

"Neale, back there in Omaha you got sore . . . you quit us," went on Warburton reprovingly. "That was bad business. I cottoned to you . . . and I might have. . . . But no matter. You're with us again."

"Mister Warburton, I'm ashamed of that," replied Neale hastily. "But I was hot-headed. . . . Am so still, I fear."

"So am I. So is Lodge. So is any man worth a damn," replied the director.

"Mister Neale, you look cool enough now," observed Rogers, smiling. "Wish I was as wet and cool as you are. It's hot in this desert."

Warburton took off his frock coat. "You gentlemen aren't going to have any but the best of me. . . . And, now Neale tell us things."

Neale looked at his papers, and then at his chief.

"For instance," said Lodge, "tell us about Blake and Coffee."

"Haven't you seen them . . . heard from them?" inquired Neale.

"No. . . . Henney has not, either. And they were his men."

"Gentlemen, I'm afraid I lost my head in regard to them."

"Explain, please," said Warburton. "We will judge your conduct."

It was a rather difficult moment for Neale, because his actions regarding the two engineers now appeared to have been a result of violent temper, instead of an exercise of authority. But then as he remembered Blake's offer and Coffee's threat, the heat thrilled along his nerves, and that stirred him to forceful expression.

"I drove them both out of this camp."

"Why?" queried Warburton sharply.

"Blake tried to bribe me and Coffee. . . ."

"One at a time," interrupted Warburton, and he thrust a strong hand through his hair, ruffling it. He began to scent battle. "What did Blake try to bribe you to do?"

"He didn't say. But he meant me to cover their tracks."

"So! And what did Coffee do?"

"He tried to pull a gun on me."

"Why? Be explicit, please."

"Well, he threatened me. And I laughed at him . . . called him names. . . ."

"What names?"

"Quite a lot, if I remember. The one he objected to was thief. . . . I repeated that, and snatched some telegrams from his pocket. He tried to draw his gun on me . . . and then I drove them both out of camp. . . . They got through safely, for they were seen in Benton."

"Sir, it appears to me you lost your head to good purpose," said Warburton. "Now just what were the tracks they wanted you to cover?"

"I drew the original plans for Number Ten. They had not followed them. To be exact they did not drive piles to hold the cribbings for the piers. They did not go deep enough. They sank shafts . . . they built coffer dams . . . they put in piers over and over again. There was forty feet of quicksand under all their work, and of course it slipped and sank."

Warburton slowly got up. He was growing purple in the face. His hair seemed rising. He doubled a huge fist. "Over and over again!" he roared furiously. "Over and over again! Lodge, do you hear that?"

"Yes. Sounds kind of familiar to me," replied the chief, with one of his rare smiles. He was beyond rage now. He saw the end. He alone, perhaps, had realized the nature of that great work. And that smile had been sad as well as triumphant.

Warburton stamped up and down the car aisle. Manifestly he wanted to smash something or to take out his anger upon his comrades. That was not the quick rage of a moment; it seemed the bursting into flame of a smoldering fire. He used language more felicitous for one of Benton's halls than the private cars of the directors of the Union Pacific Railroad. Once he stooped over Lodge, pounded the table.

"Three hundred thousand dollars sunk in that quicksand hole!" he thundered. "Over and over again! That's what galls me. . . . Work done over and over . . . unnecessary . . . worse than useless . . . all for dirty gold! Not for the railroad, but for gold! God! What a band of robbers we've dealt with! Lodge, why in the hell didn't you send Neale out here at the start?"

A shadow lay dark in the chief's lined face. Why had he not done a million other things? Why indeed! He did not answer the irate director.

"Three hundred thousand dollars sunk in that hole . . . for nothing!" shouted Warburton in a final explosion.

The other two directors laughed.

"*Pooh!*" exclaimed Rogers softly. "What is that? A drop in the bucket. Consult your notebook, Warburton."

And that speech cooled the fighting director. It contained volumes. It evidently struck home. Warburton growled—he mopped his red face—he fell into a seat. "Lodge . . . excuse me," he said apologetically. "You know that . . . what our fine young friend here told me was like someone stepping on my gout. . . . I've been maybe a little too zealous . . . too exacting. Then I'm old and testy. . . . What does it matter? Alas, it's black like that hideous Benton. . . . But we're coming out into the light. Lodge, didn't you tell me this Number Ten bridge was the last obstacle?"

"I did. The rails will go down now fast and straight till they meet out there in Utah. . . . Soon!"

Warburton became composed. The red died out of his face. He looked at Neale. "Young man, can *you* put permanent piers in that sinkhole?"

"Yes. They are started on bedrock," replied Neale.

"Bedrock," he repeated, and remained gazing at Neale fixedly. Then he turned to Lodge. "Do you remember that wild red-headed cowboy . . . Neale's friend? When he said . . . 'I reckon thet's aboot all.'. . . . I'll never forget him. . . . Lodge, say we have Lee and his friend Senator Dunn come in . . . and get it over. An' thet'll be aboot all!"

"Thank heaven," replied the chief fervently. He called to his porter, but as no one replied, General Lodge rose and went into the next car.

Neale had experienced a disturbing sensation in his breast. Lee! Allison Lee! The mere name made him shake. He could not understand, but he felt there was more reason for its effect on him than his relation to Allison Lee as a contractor. Somewhere there was a man named Lee who was Allie's father, and Neale knew he would meet him someday.

Then when the chief walked back into the car with two frock-coated individuals, Neale did recognize on the pale face of one a resemblance to the girl he loved.

There were no greetings. This situation had no formalities. Warburton faced them and he seemed neither cold nor hot. He might have been meeting anyone whose relation with him had passed.

"Mister Lee, as a director of the road, I have to inform you that following the reports of our engineer, here, your present contracts are void and you will not get any more."

A white radiance of rage swiftly transformed Allison Lee. His eyes seemed to blaze purple out of his white face. And Neale knew him to be Allie's father—saw the beauty and fire of her eyes in his.

"Warburton! You'll reconsider. I have great influence. . . ."

"To hell with your influence!" retorted Warburton, the lion in him rising. "The builders . . . the directors . . . the owners of the U.P.R. are right here in this car. Do you understand that? Do you demand I call a spade a spade?"

"I have been appointed by Congress. I will. . . ."

"Congress or no Congress you will never rebuild a foot of this railroad!" thundered Warburton. He stood there glaring, final, assured. "For the sake of your . . . your government connections let us . . . say . . . let well enough alone."

"This upstart boy of an engineer!" burst out Lee in furious resentment. "Who is he? How dare he accuse . . . or report against me?"

"Mister Lee, your name has never been mentioned by him," replied the director.

Lee struggled for self-control. "But, Warburton, it's preposterous!" he protested. "This wild boy . . . the associate of desperadoes . . . his report, whatever it is . . . absurd! Absurd as opposed to my position! A cub surveyor . . . slick with tongue and figures . . . to be thrown in my face. It's outrageous. I'll have him. . . ."

Warburton held up a hand that impelled Lee to silence. In that gesture Neale read what stirred him to his soul. It was coming. He saw it again in General Lodge's fleeting rare smile.

He held his breath. The old pang throbbed in his breastbone.

"Lee, pray let me enlighten you and Senator Dunn," said Warburton sonorously, "and terminate this awkward inter- view. . . . When the last spike is driven out here . . . presently . . . Mister Neale will be chief engineer of maintenance of way of the Union Pacific Railroad!"

# CHAPTER TWENTY-FOUR

So for Neale the wonderful dream had come to pass, and but for the memory that made all hours of life bitter, his cup of joy would have been full.

He made his headquarters in Benton, and spent his days riding east or west over the line, taking up the responsibility he had long trained for, and for which he would soon be accountable—the upkeep, the maintaining of the perfect condition of the railroad.

Toward the end of that month Neale was summoned to Omaha.

The message had been signed *Warburton*. Upon arriving at the terminus of the road, Neale found a marvelous change even in the short time since he had been there. Omaha had become a city. It developed that Warburton had been called back to New York, leaving word for Neale to wait for orders.

Neale availed himself of this period to acquaint himself with the men who he would deal with in the future. Among them, and in the roar of the railroad shops and the bustle of the city, he lost, perhaps temporarily, that haunting sense of loss and pain and gloom. Despite himself the deference shown him was flattering, and his old ambitious habit of making friends reasserted itself. His place was assured now. There were rumors in the air of branch lines for the Union Pacific. He was consulted for advice, importuned for positions, invited here and there. So that the days in Omaha were both profitable and pleasurable.

Then came a telegram from Warburton calling him to Washington, D.C.

It took more than two days to get there, which time dragged slowly for Neale. It seemed to him that his importance grew as he traveled, a fact which was amusing to him. All this resembled a dream.

When he reached the hotel designated in the telegram, it was to receive a warm greeting from Warburton.

"It's a long trip to make for nothing," said the director. "And that's what it amounts to now. I thought I'd need you to answer a few questions for me. But you'll not be questioned officially . . . and so you'd better keep a closed mouth. . . . We've raised the money. The completion of the U.P.R. is assured."

Neale could only conjecture what those questions might have been, for the director offered no explanation. And this circumstance recalled to mind his former impression of the complexity of the financial and political end of the construction. Warburton took him to dinner and later to a club, and introduced him to many men.

For this alone Neale was glad that he had been summoned to the capital. He met Senators, Congressmen, and other government officials, and many politicians and prominent men, all of whom, he was surprised to note, were well informed regarding the Union Pacific. He talked with them, but answered questions guardedly. And he listened to discussions and talk covering every phase of the work, from the Crédit Mobilier to the Chinese coolies that were advancing from the West to meet the paddies of his own division.

How strange to realize that the great railroad had its nucleus, its impetus, and its completion on such a center as this! Here were the frock-coated, soft-voiced, cigar-smoking gentlemen among whom Warburton and his directors had swung the colossal enterprise. What a vast difference between these men and the builders! With the handsome white-haired Warburton, and his associates, as they smoked their rich cigars and drank their wine, Neale contrasted Casey and McDermott, and many another burly spiker or teamster out on the line. Each class was necessary to this task. These Easterners talked of money, of gold as a grade-foreman might have talked of gravel. They smoked and conversed at ease, laughing at sallies, gossiping over what was a tragedy west of North Platte, and about them was an air of luxury, of power, of importance, and a singular grace that Neale felt rather than saw.

Strangest of all to him was the glimpse he got into the labyrinthine plot built around the stock, the finance, the gold that was constructing the road. He was an engineer, with a deductive habit of mind, but he would never be able to trace the intricacy of this monumental aggregation of deals. Yet he was absorbed with interest. Much of the scorn and disgust he had felt out on the line for the mercenaries connected with the work he forgot here among these frock-coated gentlemen.

An hour later Neale accompanied Warburton to the station where the director was to board a train for his return to New York.

"You'll start back tomorrow," said Warburton. "I'll see you soon, I hope . . . out there in Utah where the last spike is to be driven. That will be the day . . . the hour! It will be celebrated all over the States."

Neale returned to his hotel, trying to make out the vital thing that had come to him on this hurried and apparently useless journey. His mind seemed in a whirl. Yet as he pondered, there gradually loomed to him a thought that in the Eastern or constructive end of the great plan there were the same spirit and evil and mystery as there were in the Western or building end. Here big men were interested, involved; out there bigger men sweated and burned and aged and died. The difference was that those toilers gave all for an ideal that to the directors and their partners meant only money—a profit that would precipitate a trip to Europe.

Neale restrained what might have been contempt, and he thought that, if these financiers, or any men, could have seen the life of the diggers and spikers as he knew it, there would have been a nobler motive born. Before he dropped to sleep that night he concluded his trip to Washington and the recognition accorded him by Warburton's circle had fixed a desire in his heart to heave some rails and drive some spikes for the railroad he loved so well. To him the work had been something for which he had striven with all his might and risked his life. He wanted to embody all of it that was possible—to feel that not only his brain had given to the creation, but that his muscle had ached from the toil.

Upon the journey home all the way he seemed steeped in the luxurious and complicated impressions received in Washington. And all these impressions drifted to and fro through a picture of bright-lighted club rooms, richly furnished, where handsome frock-coated gentlemen lounged at their wine and cigars, conversing in softly modulated tones, oblivious to the destinies and lives of common men.

When Neale at last reached Benton it was night. Benton and night! And he had forgotten. A mob of men surged down and up on the train. Neale had extreme difficulty in getting off at all. But the excitement, the hurry, the discordant and hoarse medley of many voices were unusual at that hour around the station, even for strenuous Benton. All these men were carrying baggage. Neale shouted questions into passing ears, until at length some fellow heard and yelled a reply.

The last night of Benton!

He understood then. The great and vile construction camp had reached the end of its career. It was being torn down—

moved away—depopulated. There was an exodus. In another forty-eight hours all that had been Benton, with its accumulated life and gold and toil, would be incorporated in another and a greater and a last camp—Roaring City.

The contrast to the beautiful Washington, the check to his half-dreaming memory of what he had experienced there, the sudden plunge into this dim-lighted, sordid, and roaring hell, all brought about in Neale a revulsion of feeling.

And with the sinking of his spirit there returned the old haunting pangs—the memory of Allie Lee, the despairing doubts of life or death for her. Beyond the camp loomed the dim black hills, mystical, secretive, and unchangeable. If she were out there among them, dead or alive, to know it would be a blessed relief. It was this horror of Benton that he feared.

He walked the street, up and down, up and down, until the hour was late and he was tired. All the halls and saloons were blazing in full blast. Once he heard low, hoarse cries and pistol shots—and then again quick, dull, booming guns. How strange they should make him shiver! But all seemed strange. From these sounds he turned away, not knowing what to do or where to go, since sleep or rest was impossible. Finally he went into a gambling den and found a welcome among players whose faces he knew.

It was Benton's last night, and there was something in the air—a release of compression.

Neale gave himself up to the spirit of the hour and the game. He had almost forgotten himself when a white, jeweled hand flashed over his shoulder, to touch it softly. He heard his name whispered. Looking up, he saw the flushed and singularly radiant face of Beauty Stanton.

# CHAPTER TWENTY-FIVE

The afternoon and night of pay day in Benton, during which Allie Lee was barred in her room, were hideous, sleepless, dreadful hours. Her ears were filled with Benton's roar—whispers and wails and laughs; thick voices of drunken men; the cold voices of gamblers; *clink* of gold and *clink* of glasses; a ceaseless tramp and shuffle of boots; pistol shots muffled and far away, pistol shots ringing and near at hand; the angry hum of brawling men, and strangest of all this dreadful roar were the high-pitched, piercing voices of woman in songs without soul, in laughter without mirth, in cries wild and terrible and mournful.

Allie lay in the dark, praying for the dawn, shuddering at this strife of sound, fearful that any moment the violence of Benton would burst through the flimsy walls of her room to destroy her. But the roar swelled and subsided and died away; the darkness gave place to gray light and then dawn; the sun arose and the wind began to blow. Still Benton slept or it was dead or it was drunk unto exhaustion.

Her mirror told Allie the horror of that night. Her face was white; her eyes were haunted by terrors, with great dark shadows beneath. She could not hold her hands steady.

Late that afternoon there were stirrings and sounds in Durade's hall. The place had awakened. Presently Durade himself brought her food and drink. He looked haggard, worn, yet radiant. He did not seem to note Allie's condition or appearance.

"That deaf and dumb fool who waited on you is gone," said

Durade. "Yesterday was pay day in Benton. . . . Many are gone. . . . Allie, I won fifty thousand dollars in gold!"

"Isn't that enough?" she asked.

He did not hear her, but went on talking of his winnings, of gold, of games, and of big stakes coming. His lips trembled; his eyes glittered; his fingers clawed at the air.

For Allie it was a relief when Durade left her. He had almost reached the apex of his fortunes and the inevitable end. Allie realized that, if she were ever to lift a hand to save herself, she must do so at once. This was a fixed and desperate thought in her mind when Durade called her to her work.

Allie always entered that private den of Durade's with eyes cast down. She had been scorched too often by the glances of men. As she went in this time, she felt the presence of gamblers, but they were quieter than those to whom she had become accustomed. Durade ordered her to fetch drinks, then he went on talking rapidly, in excitement, elated, boastful, almost gay. Others also were talking.

Allie did not look up. As she carried the tray to the large table, she heard a man whisper low: "By jove, Hough, that's the girl." Then she heard a slight, quick intake of breath, and the exclamation: "Good God!"

Both voices thrilled Allie. The former seemed the low, well-modulated, refined, and drawling speech of an Englishman; the latter was keen, quick, soft, and full of genuine emotion.

Allie returned to her chair by the sideboard before she ventured to look up. Durade was playing cards with four men, three of whom were black-garbed, after the manner of professional gamblers. The other player wore gray, and a hat of unusual shape, with wide, loose, cloth band. He removed his hat as he caught Allie's glance, and she associated the act with the fact of her presence. She thought that this must be the man whose voice had proclaimed him English. He had a fair face, lined and shadowed and dissipated, with tired blue eyes and a blond mustache that failed altogether to hide a well-shaped mouth. It was the kindest and saddest face Allie had ever seen there. She read its story. In her extremity she had acquired a melancholy wisdom in the judgment of the faces of the men drifting through Durade's hall. What Allie had heard in this Englishman's voice, she saw in his features. He did not look at her again. He played cards wearily, carelessly, indifferently, with his mind plainly on something else.

"Ancliffe, how many cards?" called one of the black-garbed men.

The Englishman threw down his cards. "None," he said.

The game was interrupted by a commotion in the adjoining room, which was the public gambling hall of Durade's establishment.

"Another fight!" exclaimed Durade impatiently. "And only Mull and Fresno showed up today."

Harsh voices and heavy stamps were followed by a pistol shot. Durade hurriedly arose.

"Gentlemen, excuse me," he said, and went out. One of the gamblers also left the room, and another crossed it to peep through the door. This left the Englishman sitting at the table with the last gambler, whose back was turned toward Allie. She saw the Englishman lean forward to speak. Then the gambler arose and, turning, came directly toward her.

"My name is Place Hough," he said, speaking rapidly and low. "I am a gambler . . . but a gentleman. I've heard strange rumors about you, and now I see for myself . . . you look distressed. Perhaps . . . but can I be of any service to you?"

Allie's heart seemed to come to her throat. She shook all over, and she gazed with piercing intensity at the man. When he had arisen from the table, he had appeared the same black-garbed, hard-faced gambler as any of the others. But looked at closely, he was different. Underneath the cold, expressionless face worked something mobile and soft. His eyes were of crystal clearness and remarkable for a penetrating power. They shone with wonder, curiosity, doubt. Allie instinctively trusted the voice, and then consciously trusted the man. "Oh, sir, I am . . . distressed . . . ill from fright," she faltered. "If I only dared. . . ."

"You dare tell me," he interrupted swiftly. "Be quick. Are you Durade's daughter?"

"Oh, no!"

"What then?"

"Oh, sir . . . you do not think . . . I . . . ?"

"I knew you were good, innocent . . . the moment I laid eyes on you. . . . Who are you?"

"Allie Lee. My father is Allison Lee."

"*Whew!*" The gambler whistled softly and, turning, glanced at the door, then beckoned Ancliffe. The Englishman arose. In the adjoining rooms sounds of strife were abating.

"Ancliffe, this girl is Allie Lee, daughter of Allison Lee . . . a big man of the U.P.R. Something's terribly wrong here. Look at her."

Allie became aware of the Englishman's scrutiny, doubtful, sad, yet kind. She felt a sudden rush of emotion. Her opportunity had come. "I am Allie Lee. My mother ran off with Durade . . . to California. He used her as a lure to draw men to his gambling hells . . . as he uses me now. Two years ago we escaped . . . started East with a caravan. The Indians attacked us. I crawled under a rock . . . escaped the massacre. I. . . ."

"Never mind all your story," interrupted Hough. "We haven't time for that. I believe you. . . . You are held prisoner?"

"Oh, yes . . . locked and barred. I never get out. I have been threatened so . . . that until now I feared to tell anyone. But Durade . . . he is going mad. I . . . I can bear it no longer."

"Miss Lee, you shall not bear it," declared Ancliffe. "We'll take you out of here."

"How?" queried Hough shortly.

Ancliffe was for walking right out with her, but Hough shook his head.

"Listen," began Allie hurriedly. "He would kill me the instant I tried to escape. He loved my mother. He does not believe she is dead. He lives only to be revenged upon her. . . . He has a desperate gang here. Fresno, Mull, Black, Grist, Dayss, a greaser called Mex, and others . . . all the worst of bad men. You cannot get me out of here alive except by some trick."

"How about bringing the troops?"

"Durade would kill me the first thing."

"Could we steal you out at night?"

"I don't see how. They are awake all night. I am barred in, watched. . . . Better work on Durade's weakness. Gold! He's mad for gold. When the fever's on him, he might gamble me away . . . or sell me for gold."

Hough's cold eyes shone like fire in ice. He opened his lips to speak—then quickly motioned Ancliffe back to the table. They had just seated themselves when the two gamblers returned, followed by Durade. He was rubbing his hands in satisfaction.

"What was the fuss about?" queried Hough, tipping the ashes off his cigar.

"Some drunks after money they lost."

"And got thrown out for their pains?" inquired Ancliffe.

"Yes. Mull and Fresno know what to do."

The game was taken up again. Allie sensed a different note in it. The gambler Hough now faced her in his position at the table, and behind every card he played, there seemed to be intense purpose and tremendous force. But he appeared fascinated where formerly he had been indifferent. Soon it developed that Hough, by his spirit and skill, was driving his opponents, inciting their passion for play, working upon their feelings. Durade seemed the weakest gambler, although he had the best luck. Good luck balanced his excited play. The two other gamblers pitted themselves against Hough.

The shadows of evening had begun to darken the room when Durade called for lights. A slim, sloe-eyed, pantherish-moving Mexican came in to execute the order. He wore a belt with a knife in it and looked like a brigand. When he had lighted the lamps, he approached Durade and spoke in Spanish. Durade replied in the same tongue. Then the Mexican went out. One of the gamblers lost and arose from the table.

"Gentlemen, may I go out for more money and return to the game?" he asked.

"Certainly," replied Hough.

Durade assented with bad grace.

The game went on and grew in interest. Probably the Mexican had reported the fact of its possibilities, or perhaps Durade had sent out word of some nature. For one by one his villainous lieutenants came in, stepping softly, gleaming-eyed.

"Durade, have you stopped play outside?" queried Hough.

"Suppertime. Not much going on," replied Mull.

Hough eyed this speaker with keen coolness. "I did not address you," he said.

Durade, catching the drift, came out of his absorption of play long enough to say that with a big game at hand he did not want to risk any interruption. He spoke sincerely, but he did not look sincere.

Presently the second gambler announced that he would consider it a favor to be allowed to go out and borrow money. Then he left hurriedly. Durade, Hough, and Ancliffe played alone, and the luck see-sawed from one to the other until both the other players returned. They did not come alone. Two more black-frocked, black-sombreroed, cold-faced individuals accompanied them.

"May we sit in?" they asked.

"With pleasure," replied Hough.

Durade frowned and the glow left his face. Although the luck was still with him, it was evident that he did not favor added numbers. Yet the man's sensitiveness to any change immediately manifested itself when he won the first large stake. His radiance returned and, also, his vanity.

Hough interrupted the game by striking the table with his hand. The sound seemed hard, metallic, yet his hand was empty. Any attentive observer would have become aware that Hough had a gun up his sleeve. But Durade did not catch the significance. "I object to that man leaning over the table," said Hough, and he pointed to the lounging Fresno.

"Thet so?" leered the ugly giant. He looked bold and vicious.

"Do not address me," ordered Hough.

Fresno backed away silently from the cold-faced gambler.

"Don't mind him, Hough," protested Durade. "They're all excited. Big stakes always work them up."

"Send them out so we can play without annoyance."

"No," replied Durade sharply. "They can watch the game."

"Ancliffe," said Hough, just as sharply, "fetch some of my friends to watch this game! Don't forget Neale and Red King."

Allie, who was watching and listening with strained faculties, nearly fainted at the sudden mention of her lover Neale and her friend Reddy. She went blind for a second; the room turned around and around; she thought her heart would burst with joy.

The Englishman hurried out.

Durade looked up with a passionate and wolfish swiftness. "What do you mean?"

"I want some of my friends to watch the game," replied Hough.

"But I don't allow that red-headed cowboy gunfighter to come into my place."

"That is regrettable, for you will make an exception this time. . . . Durade, you don't stand well in Benton. I do."

The Spaniard's eyes glittered. "You insinuate . . . *señor.* . . ."

"Yes," interposed Hough, and his cold, deliberate voice dominated the explosive Durade. "Do you remember a gambler named Jones? He was shot in this room. . . . If I should happen to be shot here . . . in the same way . . . you and your gang would not last long in Benton."

Durade's face grew livid with rage and fear. And in that moment the mask was off. The nature of the Spaniard stood forth. Another manifest fact was that Durade had not before matched himself against a gambler of Hough's caliber.

"Well, are you only a bluff or do we go on with the game?" inquired Hough.

Durade choked back his rage and signified with a motion of his hand that play should be resumed.

Allie fastened her eyes upon the door. She was in a tumult of emotion. Despite that, her mind revolved wild and intermittent ideas as to the risk of letting Neale see and recognize her there. Yet her joy was so overpowering that she believed if he entered the door, she would rush to him and trust in God to save her. In God and Reddy King! She remembered the cowboy, and a thrill linked all her emotions. Durade and his gang would face a terrible reckoning if Reddy King ever entered to see her there.

Moments passed. The gambling went on. The players spoke low; the spectators were silent. Discordant sounds from outside disturbed the quiet.

Allie stared fixedly at the door. Presently it opened. Ancliffe entered with several men, all quick in movement, alert of eye. But Neale and Red King were not among them. Allie's heart sank like lead. The revulsion of feeling, the disappointment, was sickening. She saw Ancliffe shake his head, and divined in the action that he had not been able to find the friends Hough wanted particularly. Then Allie felt the incredible strangeness of being glad that Neale was not to find her there—that Reddy was not to throw his guns on Durade's crowd. There might be a chance of her being liberated without violence.

This reaction left her weak and dazed for a while. Still she heard the low voices of the gamesters, the *slap* of cards and *clink* of gold. Her wits had gone from her ever since the mention of Neale. She floundered in a whirl of thoughts and fears and tremblings and thrills until gradually she recovered self-possession. Whatever instinct or love or spirit had guided her had done so rightly. She had felt Neale's presence in Benton. It was stingingly sweet; it was terrible to realize that. Her heart swelled with pangs of fullest measure. Surely he believed her dead. Soon he would come upon her—face to face—somewhere. He would learn she was alive—unharmed—true to him with all her soul. Indians, renegade Spaniards, Benton with its terrors, a host of evil men, not these or anything else could keep her from Neale forever. She had believed that always, but never as now, in the clearness of this beautiful spiritual insight. Behind her belief was something unfathomable and great. Not the movement of progress as typified by those men who had dreamed of the railroad, nor the spirit of the unconquerable engineers as typified by Neale, nor the wildness of wild youth like Red King, nor the heroic labor and simplicity and sacrifice of common men, nor the inconceivable passion of these gamblers for gold, nor the mystery hidden in the mad laughter of these fallen women, strange and sad on the night wind—not these nor all of them, wonderful and incalculable as they were, loomed so great as the thing that upheld Allie Lee.

When she raised her head again, the gambling scene had changed. Only three men played—Hough, Durade, and another. And even as Allie looked, this third player threw his cards into the deck and with silent gesture rose from the table to take a position with the other black-garbed gamblers standing behind Hough. The blackness of their attire contrasted strongly with the whiteness of their faces. They had lost gold, which fact meant little to them. But there was something big and significant in their presence behind Hough. Gamblers leagued against a crooked gambling hell. Durade had lost a fortune, yet not all his fortune. He seemed a haggard, flaming-eyed wreck of the once debonair Durade. His hair was wet and disheveled; his collar was open; his hand wavered. Blood trickled down from his lower lip. He saw nothing except the gold, the cards, and that steel-nerved, gray-faced, implacable Hough. Behind him lined up his gang, nervous, strained, frenzied, with eyes on the gold—hate-filled, murderous eyes.

Allie slipped into her room, leaving the door ajar so she could peep out, and there she paced the floor, waiting, listening for what she dared not watch. The gambler, Hough, would win all that Durade had, and then stake it against her. That was what Allie believed. She had no doubts of Hough's winning her, too, but she doubted if he could take her away. There would be a fight. And if there was a fight, then that must be the end of Durade. For this gambler, Hough, with his unshakable nerve, his piercing eyes, his wonderful white hands, swift as light—he would at the slightest provocation kill Durade.

Suddenly Allie was arrested by a loud, long suspiration—a heave of heavy breaths in the room of the gamblers. A chair scraped noisily, breaking the silence, which instantly clamped down again.

"Durade, you're done!" It was the cold, ringing voice of Hough.

Allie ran to the door, peeped through the crack. Durade sat there like a wild beast bound. Hough stood erect over a huge golden pile on the table. The others seemed stiff in their tracks.

"There's a fortune here," went on Hough, indicating the

gold. "All I had . . . all our gentlemen opponents had . . . all *you* had. . . . I have won it all!"

Durade's eyes seemed glued to that dully glistening heap. He could not even look up at the coldly passionate Hough. "All! All!" echoed Durade.

Then Hough, like a striking hawk, bent toward the Spaniard. "Durade, I'll buy your place. I'll give this gold! *Your place with everything in it!*"

Durade was the only man who moved. Slowly he arose, shaking in every limb, and not till he became erect did he unrivet his eyes from that yellow heap on the table. *Señor* . . . do you . . . mock me?" he gasped hoarsely.

"I offer you my winnings for your gambling house . . . *with all it contains!*"

"You are crazy!" ejaculated the Spaniard.

"Certainly. . . . But hurry. Do you accept?"

"*¡Si, señor!*" he cried, with power and joy in his voice. In that moment, no doubt the greatest in his life of gambling, he unconsciously went back to the use of his mother tongue.

Durade, in one splendid gesture that made the gold give out a ringing clash, swept his winnings across the table. "Gentlemen," he called to his friends, "I call upon you as witnesses to this sale!" Then he faced Durade's gang. "Do you men understand the bargain made here?"

"Sure we do," replied Mull.

Others nodded. Then the giant Fresno lurched forward, with a knowing gleam in his wicked eye. "I'm onto you, Hough. A hell of a lot you want the house . . . ! It's the girl you're after!"

Durade did not seem to gather the content of Fresno's words, or else, dazzled by the fortune he had recovered and which he was drawing toward him with clutching hands, he did not care.

Swiftly Hough stepped to Allie's door. He saw her peering out. "Come . . . Miss Lee," he said.

Allie stepped out, trembling and unsteady on her feet, and kept close to Hough.

"Durade, I'll give you back your gambling hell. The girl is all I want."

The Spaniard seemed compelled to look up from his gold. When he saw Allie, another slow and remarkable transformation came over him. He started slightly, perhaps more at Hough's hand on Allie's arm than at the sudden sight of her. The radiance of his strange passion for gold that had put a leaping glory into his haggard face faded into a dark and mounting surprise. It mounted to amaze—to astonishing realization. A blaze burned away the shadows. His eyes betrayed an unsupportable sense of loss and the spirit that repudiated it. For a single instant he was magnificent—and perhaps in that instant race and blood spoke—then, with bewildering suddenness, surely with the suddenness of a memory, he became a black, turgid, dripping-faced victim of unutterable and unquenchable hate.

Allie recoiled in the divination that Durade saw her mother in her. No memory, no love, no gold, no wager, could ever thwart the Spaniard.

"*Señor,* you tricked me," he whispered.

"No. I bought your house and all in it. My friends and your men heard the deal."

"*Señor,* I would not sell that girl for all the gold of the Indians!"

"You have sold her. . . . Let me warn you, Durade. Be careful . . . once in your life."

Durade shoved back the gold so fiercely that he upset the table, and its contents *jangled* on the floor. The spill and the crash of a fortune, scattered everywhere, released Durade's men from their motionless suspense. They began to pick up the gold.

The Spaniard was halted by the gleam of a Derringer in

Hough's hand. Hissing then like a snake, Durade stood still, momentarily held back by a fear that quickly gave place to insane rage.

"Shoot him!" said Ancliffe, with a coolness that proved his foresight.

One of Hough's friends swung a cane, smashing a lamp, then with like swift action he broke the other lamp, instantly plunging the room into darkness. This appeared to be the signal for Durade's men to break loose into a mad scramble for the gold. Durade began to scream and rush forward.

Allie felt herself drawn backward, along the wall, through her door. It was not so dark in there. She distinguished Hough and Ancliffe. The latter closed the door. Hough whispered to Allie, although the din in the other room made such caution needless.

"Can we get out this way?" he asked.

"There's a window," replied Allie.

"Ancliffe, open it and get her out. I'll stop Durade if he comes in. Hurry!"

While the Englishman opened the window, Hough stood in front of the door with both arms extended. Allie could just see his tall form in the pale gloom. Pandemonium had begun in the other room, with Durade screaming for lights, and his men yelling and fighting for the gold, and Hough's friends struggling to get out. But they did not follow Hough into this room and evidently must have thought he had escaped through the other door.

"Come," said Ancliffe, touching Allie. He helped her get out, and followed laboriously. Then he softly called to Hough. The gambler let himself down swiftly and noiselessly. "Now what?" he muttered.

They appeared to be in a narrow alley between a house of boards and a house of canvas. Excited voices sounded inside this canvas structure and evidently alarmed Hough, for with a motion he enjoined silence and led Allie through the dark passage out into a gloomy square surrounded by low, dark structures. Ancliffe followed close behind.

The night was dark, with no stars showing. A cool wind blew in Allie's face, seeming to refresh her after her long confinement. Hough began groping forward. This square had a rough board floor and a skeleton framework. It had been a house of canvas. Some of the partitions were still standing.

"Look for a door . . . any place to get out," whispered Hough to Ancliffe as they came to the opposite side of this square space. Hough, with Allie close at his heels, went to the right while Ancliffe went to the left. Hough went so far, then, muttering, drew Allie back again to the point whence they had started. Ancliffe was there.

"No place. All boarded up tight," he whispered.

"Same on this side. We'll have to. . . ."

"Listen!" exclaimed Ancliffe, holding up his hand.

There appeared to be noise all around, but mostly on the other side of the looming canvas house, behind which was the alleyway that led to Durade's hall. Gleams of light flashed, low down, in the gloom. Durade's high, quick voice mingled with hoarser and deeper voices. Someone in the canvas house was talking to Durade, who apparently must have been in Allie's room, at her window.

"See hyar, greaser, we ain't harborin' any of your outfit, an' we'll plug the fust gent we see!" boomed a surly voice.

Durade's staccato tones succeeded it. "Did you see them?"

"We heard them gettin' out the winder."

Durade's voice rose high in Spanish curses. "Men! Fresno . . . Mull . . . take men . . . go around the street . . . watch! They can't get away. . . . You, Mex, get down in there with the gang. Kill that gambler!"

Lower voices answered, questioning, eager, but indistinct.

"Gold! Kill him . . . bring her back . . . and you can have it all!" shouted Durade.

Following that came the heavy *tramp* of boots and the low roar of angry men.

Hough leaned toward Ancliffe. "They've got us penned in."

"Yes. But it's pretty dark here. And they'll be slow. You watch while I tear a hole through somewhere," replied Ancliffe. He was perfectly cool and might have been speaking of some casual incident. He extinguished his cigarette, dropped it, then put on his gloves.

Hough loomed tall and dark. His face showed pale in the shadow. He stood with his elbows stiff against his sides, a Derringer in each hand. "I wish I had heavier guns," he said.

Allie's thrill of emotion spent itself in a shudder of realization. Calmly and chivalrously these two strangers had taken a stand against her enemies and with a few cool words and actions had accepted whatever might betide.

"I must tell you . . . oh, I must," she whispered, with her hand on Hough's arm. "I heard you send for Neale and Reddy King. . . . It made my heart stop. Neale . . . Warren Neale is my sweetheart. See, I wear his ring. Reddy King is my dearest friend . . . my brother. And, oh, they both believe me dead."

Hough uttered an amazed exclamation and bent low to peer into Allie's face—to see her ring. Ancliffe showed no excitement.

"Ancliffe, did you hear what she said?" queried Hough hoarsely.

"Yes," replied the Englishman.

"How things work out. . . . I always suspected that was what was wrong with Neale. Now I know. He believed this girl was lost . . . dead. No wonder he's haunted . . . driven. Ancliffe, the minute I saw her face I changed. Do you understand me?"

"By Jove, I do," replied Ancliffe.

"I've never been so glad for anything in my life . . . as this moment," said Hough. "I'll block Durade's gang. Will you save the girl?"

"Assuredly," answered the imperturbable Englishman. "Where shall I take her?"

"Where *can* she be safe? The troop camp? No, too far. . . . Aha! Take her to Stanton. Tell Stanton the truth. Stanton will hide her. Then find Neale and King." Hough turned to Allie. "I'm glad you told me about Neale," he said, and where his voice was not husky it held an exquisite softness. "I owe him a great deal. I like him. . . . Ancliffe will get you out of here . . . and safely back to Neale. May God bless you! May you be happy!"

Allie knew somehow—from something in his tone, his presence—that he would never leave this gloomy enclosure. She heard Ancliffe ripping a board off the wall or fence, and that sound seemed alarmingly loud. The voices no longer were heard behind the canvas house. The wind whipped through the bare framework. Somewhere at a distance were music and revelry. Benton's night roar had begun. Over all seemed to hang a menacing and ponderous darkness, as much of life as it was of night. Suddenly a light appeared moving slowly from the most obscure corner of the square, perhaps fifty paces distant.

Hough drew Allie closer to Ancliffe. "Get behind me," he whispered.

A sharp ripping and splitting of wood told of Ancliffe's progress—also it located the fugitives for Durade's gang. The light vanished; quick voices rasped out; then stealthy feet padded over the boards.

Allie saw or imagined she saw gliding forms black against the pale gloom. She was so close to Ancliffe that he touched her as he worked. Turning, she beheld a ray of light through an aperture he had made. Suddenly the gloom split to a reddish

flare. It revealed dark forms. A gun *cracked*. Allie heard the
heavy *thud* of a bullet against the wall. Then Hough shot. His
Derringer made a small, spiteful report. It was followed by a
cry—a groan. Other guns *cracked*. Bullets *pattered* on the wood.
Allie heard the spat of lead striking Hough. It had a sickening
sound. He moved as if from a blow. A volley followed and Allie
could not distinguish those shots fired by Hough, but she saw
the bright flashes. All about her bullets were whistling and *thudding*. She knew with a keen horror every time Hough was struck.
Hoarse yells and strangling cries mixed with the diminishing
shots.

Then Ancliffe grasped her and pushed her through a vent he
had made. Allie crawled backward and she could see Hough
still standing in front. It seemed that he swayed. Then as she
rose further view was cut off. While not looking about her, she
was aware of a dimly lighted storeroom. Outside the shots had
ceased. She heard something heavy fall suddenly, then a *patter*
of quick, light footsteps.

Ancliffe essayed to get through the aperture feet first. It was a
tight squeeze, or else someone held him back. There came a
*crashing* of the wood; Ancliffe's body whirled in the aperture
and he wrestled. Allie heard hissing, sibilant Spanish utterances.
She stood petrified, certain that Durade had attacked Ancliffe.
Suddenly the Englishman crashed through, drawing a supple,
twisting, slender man with him. He held this man by the throat
with one hand and by the wrist with the other. Allie recognized
Durade's Mexican ally. He gripped a knife and the blade was
bloody.

Once inside, where Ancliffe could move, he handled the
Mexican with deliberate and remorseless ease. Allie saw and
heard him twist and break the arm that held the knife. Not that
sight, but the eyes of the Mexican made Allie close her own.
When she opened them, at a touch, Ancliffe stood beside her

and the Mexican lay quivering. Ancliffe held the bloody knife; he hid it under his coat.

"Come," he said. His voice seemed thin.

"But Hough! We must. . . ."

Ancliffe's strange gesture froze Allie's lips. She followed him—clung close to him. There were voices near—and persons. All seemed to fall back before the Englishman. He strode on. Indeed, his movements appeared unnatural. They went down a low stairway, out into the dark. Lights were there to the right, and hurrying forms. Ancliffe ran with her in the other direction. Only dim, pale lamps shone through tents. Down the side street it was quiet and dark. Allie stumbled, would have fallen but for Ancliffe. Yet sometimes he stumbled, too. He turned a corner and proceeded rapidly toward bright lights. The houses loomed big. Down that way many people passed to and fro. Allie's senses admitted a new sound—a confusion of music, dancing, hilarity, all distinct, near at hand. She could scarcely keep up with Ancliffe. He did not speak or look to right or left.

At the corner of a large house—a long structure that sent out gleams of light—Ancliffe opened a door and pulled Allie into a hallway, dark near at hand, but brilliant at the other end. He drew her along this passage, striding slower now and unsteadily. He turned into another hall lighted by lamps. Music and gaiety seemed to sweep stunningly into Allie's face. But Allie saw only one person there—a Negress. As Ancliffe halted, the Negress rose from her seat. She was frightened.

"Call Stanton . . . quick!" he panted. He thrust a handful of gold at her. "Tell no one else!" Then he opened a door, pushed Allie into a bright elegantly furnished parlor, and, closing the door, staggered to a couch, upon which he fell. His face wore a singular look, remarkable for its whiteness. All its careless indifferent weary shade had vanished. As he lay back, his hands loosed their hold of his coat and fell away, all bloody. The knife slid to the floor. A bloody froth flecked his lips.

"Oh . . . heaven! You were . . . stabbed!" gasped Allie, sinking to her knees.

"If Stanton doesn't come in time . . . tell her what happened . . . and ask her to fetch Neale to you," he said. He spoke with extreme difficulty and a fluttering told of blood in his throat.

Allie could not speak. She could not pray. But her sight and her perception were abnormally keen. Ancliffe's strange, clear gaze rested upon her, and it seemed to Allie that he smiled, not with lips or face, but in spirit. How strange and beautiful!

Then Allie heard a rush of silk at the door. It opened—closed. A woman of fair face, bare of arm and neck, glittering with diamonds, swept into the parlor. She had great, dark-blue eyes full of shadows and they flashed from Ancliffe to Allie and back again.

"What's happened? You're pale as death! Ancliffe! Your hands . . . your breast! *My God!*" She bent over him.

"Stanton, I've been . . . cut up . . . and Hough is . . . dead."

"Oh, this horrible Benton!" cried the woman.

"Don't faint. . . . Hear me. You remember we were curious about a girl . . . Durade had in his place. This is she . . . Allie Lee. She is innocent. Durade held her for revenge. He had loved . . . then hated her mother. . . . Hough won all Durade's gold . . . and bought the girl. But we had to fight. . . . Stanton, this Allie Lee is Neale's sweetheart. . . . He believes her dead. . . . You hide her . . . bring Neale to her."

Quickly she replied: "I promise you, Ancliffe, I promise. . . . How strange . . . what you tell. But not strange for Benton. Ancliffe! Speak to me! Oh, he is fading. . . ."

With her first words a subtle change passed over Ancliffe. It was the release of his will. His whole body sank. Under the intense whiteness of his face a cold gray shade began to creep.

His last conscious instant spent itself in the strange gaze Allie had felt before, and now she had a vague perception that in some way it expressed a blessing and a deliverance. The instant the beautiful light turned inward, as if to illumine the darkness of his soul, she divined what he had once been, his ruin, his secret and eternal remorse—and the chance to die that had made him great.

So, forgetful of the other beside her, Allie Lee watched Ancliffe, sustained by a nameless spirit, feeling with melancholy and tragic pity her duty as a woman—to pray for him, to stay beside him, that he might not be alone when he died. And while she watched, with the fading of that singular radiance, there returned to his face a slow, careless weariness, cold now, fixing bitterly, a mask of death.

"He's gone," murmured Stanton, rising. A dignity had come to her. "Dead! And we know nothing of him . . . not his real name . . . nor his place. But not even Benton could keep him from dying like an English gentleman." She took Allie by the hand, led her out of the parlor and across the hall into a bedroom. Then she faced Allie, wonderingly, with all a woman's sympathy, and something else that Allie sensed as a sweet and poignant wistfulness. "Are you . . . Neale's sweetheart?" she asked, very low.

"Oh . . . please . . . find him . . . for me!" sobbed Allie.

The tenderness in this woman's voice and look and touch was what Allie needed more than anything, and it made her a trembling child. How strangely, hesitatingly, with closing eyes, this woman reached to fold her in gentle arms. What a tumult Allie felt throbbing in the full breast where she laid her head.

"Allie Lee . . . and he thinks you dead," she murmured brokenly. "I will bring him . . . to you."

When she released Allie years and shadows no longer showed in her face. Her eyes were tear-wet and darkening; her lips were tremulous. At that moment there was something beautiful and terrible about her. But Allie could not understand.

"You stay here," Stanton said. "Be very quiet . . . I will bring Neale." Opening the door, she paused on the threshold, to glance down the hall first, and then back at Allie. Her smile was beautiful. She closed the door and locked it. Allie heard the soft swish of silk dying away.

# CHAPTER TWENTY-SIX

Beauty Stanton threw a cloak over her bare shoulders, and, hurriedly leaving the house by the side entrance, she stood a moment, breathless and excited, in the dark and windy street. She had no idea why she halted there, for she wanted to run. But the instant she got out into the cool night air a check came to action and thought. Only sensations poured in upon her—the darkness, somehow lonesome and weird; the wailing wind with its weight of dust; the roar of Benton's main thoroughfare, and the low, strange murmur, neither musical nor mirthful, behind her, from that huge hall she called her home. Stranger than these sensations were the lingering effects of others received just before, and they were a swelling and aching of her heart, the glow and quiver of her flesh, thrill on thrill, deep, like bursting pangs of joy never before experienced, the physical sense of a touch, inexplicable in its power.

On her bare breast a place seemed to flush and throb and glow. "Ah," murmured Beauty Stanton. "That girl laid her face here . . . over my heart." It was this then that had halted her, the touch of purity. Innocence in her arms. Then flashing thoughts, like gleams of lightning, illumined her mind. She had received something—a strange incident had occurred—she had an opportunity to do a service—she had seen a face on her breast—a face all soul, exquisitely lonely, sad as a Madonna's, trustful with a trust that created noble and supreme spirit—she had suddenly stepped out of a place become hideous and mournful—there, in the darkness, a strange presence, not life, nor specter, had met her, and the revelry of her fall rang horror in her ears. Ah, inconceivable and monstrous change.

"What was I to *do?*" she murmured. "Oh, yes . . . to find her sweetheart . . . Neale." Then she set off rapidly, but if she had possessed wings or the speed of the wind, she could not have kept pace with her thoughts. She turned the corner of the main street and glided among the hurrying throng. Men stood in groups, talking excitedly. She gathered that there had been fights. More than once she was addressed familiarly, but she did not hear what was said. The wide street seemed strange, dark, dismal, the lights yellow and flaring, the wind burdened, the dark tide of humanity raw, wild, animal, unstable. Above the lights and the throngs hovered a shadow—not the mantle of night nor the dark desert sky.

Her steps took familiar ground, yet she seemed not to know this Benton.

"Once I was like Allie Lee," she whispered. "Not so many years ago."

And the dark tide of men, the hurry and din, the wind and dust, the flickering lights, all retreated spectral-like to the background of a mind returned to youth, hope, love, home. She saw herself at eighteen—yes, Beauty Stanton even then possessed of a beauty that was her ruin; at school, the favorite of a host of boys and girls; at home, where the stately oaks were hung with silver moss and the old Colonial house rang with song of sister and sport of brother, where a sweet-faced, gentle-voiced mother. . . .

"*Ah . . . Mother!*" And at that word the dark tide of men seemed to rise and swell at her, to trample her sacred memory as inevitably and brutally as it had used her body.

Only the piercing pang of that memory remained with Beauty Stanton. She was a part of Benton. She was treading the loose boardwalk of the great and vile construction camp. She might draw back from leer and touch, but nonetheless was she there, a piece of this dark, bold, obscure life. She was a cog in the wheel, a grain of dust in the whirlwind, a morsel of flesh and blood for the hungry maw of a wild and passing monster of progress.

Her hurried steps carried her on with her errand. Neale! She knew where to find him. Often she had watched him play, always regretfully, conscious that he did not fit there. His indifference had baffled her as it had piqued her professional vanity. Men had never been indifferent to her; she had seen them fight for her mocking smiles. But Neale! He had been stone to her charm, yet kind, gracious, deferential. Always she had felt strangely shamed when he stood, bareheaded, before her. Beauty Stanton had foregone respect. Yet respect was what she yearned for. The instincts of her girlhood, surviving, made a whited sepulcher of the present. She could not bear Neale's indifference and she had failed to change it. Her infatuation, born of that hot-bed of Benton life, had beaten and burned itself to destruction against a higher and better love—the only love of her womanhood. She would have slaved for him. But he had passed her by, absorbed with his own secret, working toward some fateful destiny, lost, perhaps, like all the others there.

And now she learned that the mystery of him—his secret— the thing that drove him, made him a failure, a drinking gambling idler who never rested, a ghost of what must have been his earlier ambitious manhood, the near ruin of him—was loss, the same old agony of love that sent so many on endless, restless roads—Allie Lee—and he believed her dead!

After all the bitterness, life had moments of the sweetest joy. Fate was being a little kind to her—Beauty Stanton. It would be from her lips Neale would hear that Allie Lee was alive—in- nocent—unharmed—faithful to him—waiting for him. Beauty Stanton's soul seemed to soar with the realization of how that news would uplift Neale, craze him with happiness, change his life, save him. He was going to hear the blessed tidings from a woman who he had scorned. Always afterward, then, he would think of Beauty Stanton with a grateful heart. She was to be the instrument of his salvation. Hough and Ancliffe had died to save Allie Lee from the vile clutch of Benton, but to Beauty Stanton, the woman of ill fame, had been given the power. She gloried in it. Allie Lee was safely hidden in her house. Those tigers of Durade's, on the scent of gold, would tear down all places in Benton before they would dare to attack her house. The iniquity of her establishment furnished a haven for the body and life and soul of innocent Allie Lee. Beauty Stanton marveled at the strange ways of life. This affair, somehow, was working upon her heart and mind. If she could have prayed, if she had ever dared to hope for some splendid duty, some atonement to soften the dark, grim hardening of her ending career, it would not have been for so much as fate had now dealt to her. She was overwhelmed with her opportunity.

All at once she reached the end of the street. On each side the wall of lighted tents and houses ceased. Had she missed her way—gone down a side street to the edge of the desert? No. The rows of lights behind assured her this was the main street. Yet she was far from the railroad station. The crowds of men hurried by, as always. Before her reached a leveled space, dimly lighted, full of moving objects, and noise of hammers and wagons, and harsh voices. Then suddenly she remembered.

Benton was being evacuated. Tents and houses were being taken down and loaded on trains to be hauled to the next construction camp. Benton's day was done! This was the last night. She had forgotten that the proprietor of her hall, from whom she rented it, had told her that early on the morrow he would take it down, section by section, and load it on the train, and put it together again for her in the next town. In forty-eight hours Benton would be a waste place of board floors, naked frames, débris, and sand, ready to be reclaimed by the desert. It would be gone like a hideous nightmare, and no man would believe what had happened there.

The gambling hell where she had expected to find Neale had vanished, in a few hours, as if by magic. Beauty Stanton retraced her steps. She would find Neale in one of the other places—the Big Tent, perhaps. This hall was unusually crowded, and the scene had the number of men, although not the women and the hilarity and the gold, that was characteristic of pay day in Benton. All the tables in the gambling room were occupied.

Beauty Stanton stepped into this crowded room, her golden head uncovered, white and rapt and strangely dark-eyed, with all the beauty of her girlhood returned, and added to it that of a woman transformed supreme in her crowning hour. As a bad woman, infatuated and piqued, she had failed to allure and seduce Neale to baseness; now as a good woman, with pure motive, she would win his friendship, his eternal gratitude. Stanton had always been a target for eyes, yet never as now, which she drew like a dazzling light in a dark room.

As soon as she saw Neale, she forgot everyone else in that hall. He was gambling. He did not look up. His brow was somber and dark. She approached—stood behind him. Some of the players spoke to her, familiarly, as was her bitter due. Then Neale turned apparently to bow with his old courtesy. Thrill on thrill coursed over her. Always he had showed her respect, deference. She could always before have done without them, dear as they were, but not at this moment. Her heart was full. She had not had a moment like this. She was about to separate him from the baneful and pernicious life of the camps—to tender him a gift of unutterable happiness.

She put a trembling hand on his shoulder—bent over him. "Neale come with me," she whispered.

He shook his head.

"Yes! Yes!" she returned, her voice thrilling with emotion.

Wearily, with patient annoyance, he laid down his cards and looked up. His dark eyes held faint surprise and something that she thought might be pity. "Miss Stanton . . . pardon me . . . but please understand . . . no." Then he turned and, picking up his cards, resumed the game.

Beauty Stanton suffered a sudden vague check. It was as if a cold thought was trying to enter a warm and glowing mind. She found speech difficult. She could not get off the track of her emotional flight. Her woman's wit, tact, knowledge of men would not operate.

"Neale! Come with . . . me!" she cried brokenly. "There's. . . ."

Some man laughed coarsely. That did not affect Stanton until she saw how it affected Neale. His face flushed red and his hands clenched the cards.

"Say, Neale," spoke up this coarse gamester, with a sneer, "never mind us. Go along with your lady friend. . . . You're ahead of the game . . . as I reckon she sees."

Neale threw the cards in the man's face, then, rising, he bent over to slap him so violently as to knock him off his chair.

The crash stilled the room. Every man turned to watch.

Neale stood up, his right arm down menacingly. The gambler arose, cursing, but made no move to draw a weapon.

Beauty Stanton could not, to save her life, speak the words she wanted to say. Something impending, totally unexpected, seemed to have arisen.

"Neale . . . come with . . . me," was all she could say.

"No!" he declared vehemently, with a gesture of disgust and anger.

That, following the coarse implication of the gambler, conveyed to Stanton what all these men imagined. The fools!

The fools! A hot vibrating change occurred in her emotion, but she controlled it. Neale turned his back upon her. The crowd saw and many laughed. Stanton felt the sting of her pride, the leap of her blood. She was misunderstood, but what was that to her? As Neale stepped away, she caught his arm—held him while she tried to get close to him so she could whisper. He shook her off. His face was black with anger. He held up one hand in a gesture that any woman would have understood and hated. It acted powerfully upon Beauty Stanton. Neale believed she was importuning him. To him, her look, whisper, touch had meant only the same as to these coarse dogs of men gaping and grinning. The sweetest and best and most exalted moment she had ever known was being made bitter as gall, sickening, hateful. But what she felt was not the matter of importance, although it made her witless, almost mute, singularly unable to cope with the situation.

*"Allie Lee! At my house!"* burst out Stanton, and then, as if struck by lightning, she grew cold, stiff-lipped.

The change in Neale was swift, terrible. Not comprehension, but passion transformed him into a gray-faced man, amazed, furious, agonized, acting in seeming righteous and passionate repudiation of a sacrilege.

". . . !" His voice hurled out a heinous name, the one epithet that could inflame and burn and curl Beauty Stanton's soul into hellish revolt. Gray as ashes, fire-eyed, he appeared about to kill her. He struck her—hard—across the mouth. *"Don't breathe that name!"*

Beauty Stanton's fear suddenly broke. Blindly she ran out into the street. She fell once—jostled against a rail. The lights blurred; the street seemed wavering; the noise about her filtered through deadened ears; the stalking figures before her were indistinct and unreal.

"He struck me! He called me . . . !" she gasped. And the

exaltation of the last hour vanished as if it had never been. All the years of her stained and evil career leaped into ascendancy. "Hell and hell! I'll have him knifed . . . I'll see him dying! I'll wet my hands in his blood! I'll spit in his face as he dies!" So she gasped out, staggering along the street toward her house. No flame of hate so sudden and terrible and intense as that of the women of ill fame! Beauty Stanton's blood turned to vitriol. Men had wronged her, ruined her, dragged her down into the mire. One by one, during her dark career, the long procession of men she had known had each taken something of the good and the virtuous in her, only to leave behind something of evil in exchange. She was what they had made her. Her soul was a bottomless gulf, black and bitter as the Dead Sea. Her heart was a volcano, seething, turgid, full of contending fires. Her body was a receptacle into which Benton had poured its dregs. The weight of all the iron and stone used in the construction of the great railroad was the burden upon her shoulders. These dark streams of humanity passing her in the street, these beasts of men, these hairy-breasted toilers, had found in her and her kind the strength or the incentive to endure, to build, to go on. And one of them, stupid, selfish, merciless, a man who she had really loved, who could have made her better, to whom she had gone with only hope for him and glory for herself—he had put a vile interpretation upon her appeal, he had struck her before a callous crowd, he had called her the name for which there was no pardon from her class, a name that evoked all the furies and the powers of hell.

"Oh, to cut him . . . to torture him . . . to burn him alive . . . would not be enough!" she panted.

And into the mind that had been lately fixed in happy consciousness of her power for good, there flashed a thousand scintillating, coruscating gleams of hellish thought. Until, with the genius of evil creation, there flashed a crowning one.

"By God! I'll make of Allie Lee the thing I am! The thing he struck . . . the thing he named!"

The woman in Beauty Stanton ceased to be. All that breathed, in that hour, was what men had made her. Revenge, only a word! Murder, nothing! Life, an implacable, inexplicable, impossible flux and reflux of human passion! Reason, intelligence, nobility, love, womanhood, motherhood—all the heritage of her sex had been warped by false and abnormal and terrible strains upon her physical and emotional life. No tigress, no cannibal, no savage, no man, no living creature except a woman who knew how far she had fallen could have been capable of Beauty Stanton's deadly and immutable passion to destroy. Thus life and Nature avenged her. Her hate was immeasurable. She who could have walked naked and smiling down the streets of Benton or out upon the barren desert to die for the man she loved. She had it in her to arouse the inconceivable and mysterious passion of the fallen woman, to become a flame, a scourge, a fatal wind, a devastation. She was fire to man, to her own sex, ice.

Stanton reached her house and entered. Festivities in honor of the last night of Benton were already riotously in order. She placed herself well back in the shadow and watched the wide door.

"The first man who enters I'll give him this key!" she hissed.

She was unsteady on her feet. All her frame quivered. The lights in the hall seemed to have a reddish tinge. She watched. Several men passed out. Then a tall, stalking form appeared, entering. A ball of fire in Stanton's breast leaped and burst. She had recognized in that entering form the wildest, the most violent, and the most dangerous man in Benton—Larry Red King.

Stanton stepped forward, and for the first time in the cowboy's presence she did not experience that singular chill of gloom that he was wont to inspire in her. Her eyes gloated over King. Tall, lean, graceful, easy, with a strange hovering essence of potential force, with his flushed ruddy face and his flashing blue eyes and the upstanding red hair, he looked exactly what he was—a handsome red devil, fearing no man or thing, hell-bent in his cool, inimical reckless wildness.

He appeared to be half drunk. Stanton was trained to read the faces of men who entered there, and what she saw in King's added the last and crowning throb of joy to her hate. If she had been given her pick of the devils in Benton, she would have selected this stalking, gun-packing cowboy.

"Red, I've a new girl here," she said. "Come."

" 'Evenin', Miss . . . Stanton," he drawled. He puffed slightly, after the manner of men under the influence of liquor, and a wicked, boyish, heated smile crossed his face.

She led him easily. But his heavy gun bumped against her, giving her little cold shudders. The passage opened into a wide room, which in turn opened into her dancing hall. She saw strange, eager, dark faces among the men present, but in her excitement did not note them particularly. She led King across the wide room, up a stairway to another hall, and down this to the corner of an intersecting passageway.

"Take . . . this . . . key," she whispered. Her hand shook. She felt herself to be a black and monstrous creature. All of Benton—and many other places—seemed driving her. She was another woman. This was her fling at a rotten world, her slap in Neale's face. But she could not speak again; her lips failed. She pointed to a door.

She waited long enough to see the stalking, graceful cowboy halt in front of the right door. Then she fled.

# CHAPTER TWENTY-SEVEN

For many moments after the beautiful bare-armed woman closed and locked the door Allie Lee sat in ecstasy, in trembling anticipation of Neale.

Gradually, however, in intervals of happy mind wanderings, other thoughts intruded. This little bedroom affected her singularly and she was at a loss to account for the fact. It did not seem that she was actually afraid to be there, for she was glad. Fear of Durade and his gang recurred, but she believed that the time of her deliverance was close at hand. Possibly Durade, with some of his men, had been killed in the fight with Hough. Then she remembered having heard the Spaniard order Fresno and Mull to go around by the street. They were on her trail at that very moment. Ancliffe had been seen, and not much time could elapse before her whereabouts would be discovered. But Allie bore up bravely. She was in the thick of grim and bloody and horrible reality. Those brave men, strangers to her, had looked into her face, questioned her, then had died for her. It was all so unbelievable. In another room, close to her, lay Ancliffe, dead. Allie tried not to think of him; of the remorseless way in which he had killed the Mexican; of the contrast between this action and his gentle voice and manner. She tried not to think of the gambler Hough—the cold iron cast of his face as he won Durade's gold, the strange, intent look that he gave her a moment before the attack. There was something magnificent in Ancliffe's bringing her to a refuge while he was dying; there was

350

something magnificent in Hough's standing off the gang. Allie divined that through her these two men had fought and died for something in themselves as well as for her honor and life.

The little room seemed a refuge for Allie, yet it was oppressive, as had been the atmosphere of the parlor where Ancliffe lay. But this oppressiveness was not death. Allie had become familiar with death near at hand. This refuge made her flesh creep.

The room was not the home of anyone—it was not inhabited, not livable. It contained the same kind of furniture Durade had bought for her. It was clean, comfortable. Still, Allie shrank from touching anything. Through the walls came the low, strange, discordant din to which she had become accustomed—an intense, compelling blend of music, song, voice, and step actuated by one spirit. Then at times she imagined she heard distant hammering and the slap of a falling board.

Probably Allie had not stayed in this room many moments when she began to feel that she had been there hours. Surely the woman would return soon with Neale. And the very thought drove all else out of her mind, leaving her palpitating with hope, sick with longing.

Footsteps outside distracted her from the nervous, dreamy mood. Someone was coming along the hall. Her heart gave a wild bound—then sank. The steps passed by her door. She heard the thick, maudlin voice of a man and the hollow, trilling laugh of a girl.

Allie's legs began to grow weak under her. The strain, the suspense, the longing grew to be too much for her and occasioned a revulsion of feeling. She had let her hopes carry her too high.

Suddenly the door handle *rattled* and turned. Allie was brought to a stifling expectancy, motionless in the center of the room. Someone was outside at the door. Could it be Neale? It must be! Her sensitive ears caught short, puffing breaths—then the *click* of a key in the lock. Allie stood there in an anguish of suspense, with the lift of her heart almost suffocating her. Like a leaf in the wind she quivered.

Whoever was out there fumbled at the key. Then the lock rasped, the handle turned, the door opened. A tall man swaggered in, with head bent sideways, his hand removing the key from the lock. Before he saw Allie, he closed the door. With that he faced around.

Allie recognized the red face, the flashing eyes, the flaming hair. "Red!" she cried, with bursting heart. She took a quick step, ready to leap into his arms, but his violent start checked her. King staggered back—put a hand out. His face was heated and flushed as Allie had never seen it. A stupid surprise showed there. Slowly his hand moved up to cross his lips, to brush through his red hair, then with swifter movement it swept back to feel the door, as if he wanted the touch of tangible things.

"Reckon I'm seein' 'em again," he muttered to himself.

"Oh, Red . . . I'm Allie Lee!" she cried, holding out her hands. She saw the color fade out of his face. A strong rippling shock seemed to go over his body. He took a couple of dragging strides toward her. His eyes had the gaze of a man who did not believe what he saw. The hand he reached out shook.

"I'm no ghost! Red, don't . . . you . . . know me?" she faltered.

Indeed he must have thought her a phantom. Great clammy drops stood out upon his brow.

"Dear old . . . Reddy," she whispered brokenly, with a smile of agony and joy. He would know her when she spoke that way—called him the name she had tormented him with—the name no one else would have dared to use. Then she saw he believed in her reality. His face began to work. She threw her arms about him—she gave up to a frenzy of long-deferred happiness. Where Red was, there would Neale be.

"Allie . . . it ain't . . . you?" he asked hoarsely as he hugged her close.

"Oh, Reddy . . . yes . . . yes . . . and I'll die of joy," she whispered.

"Then you shore ain't . . . daid?" he went on incredulously.

How sweet to Allie was the old familiar Southern drawl. "Dead? Never. . . . Why, I've kissed you . . . and you haven't kissed me back."

She felt his breast heave as he lifted her off her feet to kiss her awkwardly, boyishly.

"Shore . . . the world's comin' to an end! But mebbe I'm only drunk." He held her close, towering over her, while he gazed around him and down at her, shaking his head, muttering again in bewilderment.

"Reddy dear . . . where, oh, where is Neale?" she breathed, all her heart in her voice.

As he released her, Allie felt a difference. His whole body seemed to gather, to harden, then vibrate as if he had been stung.

"My Gawd," he whispered, in hoarse accents of amaze and horror. "Is it you . . . Allie . . . *here?*"

"Of course it's I," replied Allie blankly. His face turned white to the lips. "Reddy, what in the world is wrong?" she gasped, beginning to wring her hands.

Suddenly he leaped at her. With rude, iron grasp he forced her back, under the light, and fixed piercing eyes upon hers. He bent closer. Allie was frightened, yet fascinated. His gaze hurt with its intensity, its strange, penetrating power. Allie could not bear it. "Allie, look at me," he said, low and hard. "Fer I reckon you mayn't hev very long to live."

Allie struggled weakly onto the bed. He looked so gray, grim, and terrible. But she could resist neither his strength nor his spirit. She lay quietly and met the clear, strange fire of his eyes.

In a few swift moments he had changed utterly.

"Reddy . . . aren't . . . you . . . drunk?" she faltered.

"I was, but now I'm sober. . . . Girl, kiss me again!"

In wonder and fear Allie complied, now flushing scarlet. "I . . . I was never so happy," she whispered. "But Reddy . . . you . . . you frighten me. I. . . ."

"Happy!" ejaculated King. Then he let her go and stood up, breathing hard. "There's a hell of a lie heah somewheres . . . but it ain't in you."

"Reddy, talk sense. I'm weak from long waiting. Oh, tell me of Neale!"

What a strange, curious, incomprehensible glance he gave her.

"Allie . . . Neale's heah in Benton. I can take you to him in ten minutes. Do you want me to?"

"*Want you to?* Reddy! I'll die if you don't take me . . . at once!" she cried in anguish.

Again King loomed over her. This time he took her hands. "How long had you been heah . . . before I came?" he asked.

"Half an hour, perhaps . . . maybe less. But it seemed long."

"Do you . . . know . . . what kind of a house you're in . . . this heah room . . . what it means?" he went on very low and huskily.

"No, I don't," she replied instantly, with sudden curiosity. Questions and explanations rushed to her lips. But this strangely acting Red King dominated her.

"No other man . . . came in heah? I . . . was the first?"

"Yes."

Then King seemed to wrestle with himself—with the hold drink had upon him—with that dark and sinister oppression so thick in the room. Allie thrilled to see his face grow soft and light up with the smile she remembered. Only now it held more of sadness, and, as she watched him, drawn irresistibly, she beheld it transform to a glory. How strange to feel in Larry Red King a spirit of gladness, of gratefulness for something beyond her understanding. Again he drew her close. And Allie, keen to read and feel him, wondered why he seemed to want to hide the sight of his face.

"Wal . . . I reckon . . . I was nigh onto bein' drunk," he said haltingly. "Shore is a bad habit of mine . . . Allie. . . . Makes me think a lot of . . . guff . . . jest the same as it makes me see snakes . . . an' things. . . . I'll quit drinkin', Allie. Never will touch liquor again . . . now if you'll jest forgive. . . ." He spoke gently, huskily, with tears in his voice, and he broke off completely.

"Forgive? Reddy, boy, there's nothing to forgive . . . except your not hurrying me to . . . to *him!*" She felt the same violent start in him. He held her a moment longer. Then, when he let go of her and stepped back, Allie saw the cowboy as of old, cool and easy, yet somehow menacing, as he had been that day the strangers rode into Slingerland's camp.

"Allie . . . thet woman Stanton locked you in heah?" queried King.

"Yes. Then she. . . ."

King's quick gesture enjoined silence. Stealthy steps sounded out in the hall. They revived Allie's fear of Durade and his men. It struck her suddenly that King must be ignorant of the circumstances that had placed her there.

The cowboy unlocked the door—peeped out. As he turned, how clear and cold his blue eyes flashed! "I'll get you out of heah," he whispered. "Come."

They went out. The passage was empty. Allie clung closely to the cowboy. At the corner, where the halls met, he halted to listen. Only the low hum of voices came up.

"Reddy, I must tell you," whispered Allie. "Durade and his gang are after me. Fresno . . . Mull . . . Black . . . Dayss . . . you know them?"

"I . . . reckon," he replied, swallowing hard. "My Gawd, you poor little girl! With that gang after you! An' Stanton! I see all now. . . . She says to me . . . 'Red, I've a new girl heah'. Wal, Beauty Stanton, thet was a bad deal for you . . . damn your soul!"

Trembling, Allie opened her lips to speak, but again the cowboy motioned her to be quiet. He need not have done it, for he suddenly seemed terrible, wild, deadly, rendering her mute.

"Allie, if I call to you, duck behind me an' hold onto me. I'll take you out of heah." Then he put her on his left side and led her down the right-hand passage toward the wide room Allie remembered. She saw on into the dance hall. King did not hurry. He sauntered carelessly, yet Allie felt how intense he was. They reached the head of the stairway. The room was full of men and girls. The woman, Stanton, was there, and, wheeling, she uttered a cry that startled Allie. Was this white, glaring-eyed, drawn-faced woman the one who had gone for Neale? Allie began to shake. She saw and heard with startling distinctness. The woman's cry had turned every face toward the stairway, and the buzz of voices ceased.

Stanton ran to the stairway, started up, and halted, raising a white arm in passionate gesture. "Where are you taking that girl?" she called stridently.

King stepped down, drawing Allie with him. "I'm takin' her to Neale."

Stanton shrieked and waved her arms. Indeed, she seemed another woman from the one upon whose breast Allie had laid her head just a little while before. "No, you won't take her to Neale!" cried Stanton.

The cowboy stepped down slowly, guardedly, but he kept on. Allie saw men run out of the crowded dance hall into the open space behind Stanton. Dark, hateful, well-remembered faces of

Fresno—Mull—Black! Allie pressed the cowboy's arm to warn him, and he, letting go of her, appeared to motion her behind him.

"Stanton! Get out of my way!" yelled King. His voice rang with a wild, ruthless note; it carried far and stiffened every figure except that of the frantic woman. With convulsed face, purple in its fury, and the hot eyes of a beast of prey she ran right up at the cowboy, heedless of the gun he held leveled low down.

He shot her. She swayed backward, uttering a low and horrible cry, and, even as she swayed, her face blanched and her eyes changed. She fell heavily, with her golden hair loosening and her bare white arms spreading wide. Then in the horror-stricken silence she lay there, conscious, with an awful haunted realization in the eyes fixed upon the cowboy, with a great growing splotch of blood darkening the white of her dress.

King did not look at Stanton and kept moving down the steps, faster now, and he drew Allie behind him. The first of that stunned group to awake to action was the giant Fresno, as, with blind, unreasoning passion, he attempted to draw upon the cowboy. The *boom* of King's big gun and the *crash* of Fresno as he fell woke the spellbound crowd into an uproar. Screaming women and shouting men rushed madly back into the dance hall.

King turned toward the hallway leading to the street. Mull and Black began shooting as he turned, and hit him, for Allie, holding fast to him, felt the vibrating shock of his body. With two swift shots King killed both men. Mull fell across the width of the hall. And as Allie stumbled over his body, she looked down to see his huge head, his ruddy face, and the great ox eyes, rolling and ghastly. In that brief glance she saw him die.

The cowboy strode fast now. Allie, with hands clenched in his coat, clung desperately to him. Hollow booms of guns filled the passageway, and hoarse shouts of alarmed men sounded from the street. Burned powder smoke choked Allie. All her force was the instinctive unconscious reaction of self-preservation. The very marrow of her bones seemed curdled. She saw the red belches of fire near and far; she passed a man floundering and bellowing on the floor; she felt King jerk back as if struck, and then something wet whipped on her face and something hot grazed her shoulder. A bullet had torn clear through him, from breast to back. He staggered, but he went on. Another man lay on the threshold of the wide door, his head down the step, and his pallid face blood-streaked. A smoking gun lay near his twitching hand. That pallid face belonged to Dayss.

King staggered out into an empty street, looking up and down. "Wal, I reckon . . . thet's . . . aboot . . . all," he drawled, with low, strangled utterance. Then swaying from side to side, he strode swiftly, almost falling forward, holding tightly to Allie. They drew away from the brighter lights. Allie was dimly aware of moving forms ahead and across the street. Once, fearfully, she looked back, to see if they were followed.

The cowboy halted, tottering against a house. He seemed pale and smiling. "Run . . . Allie," he whispered.

"No . . . no . . . no," she replied, clinging to him. "You're shot! Oh, Reddy . . . come on!"

"*Tell . . . my pard . . . Neale. . . .*"

His head fell back hard against the wood and his body, sagging, lodged there. Life had passed out of the gray face. Larry Red King died standing, with a gun in each hand, and the name of his friend the last word upon his lips.

"Oh, Reddy . . . Reddy!" moaned Allie.

She could not run. She could scarcely walk. Dark forms loomed up. Her strength failed, and as she reeled, sinking down, rude hands grasped her. Above her bent the gleaming face and glittering eyes of Durade.

# CHAPTER TWENTY-EIGHT

Beauty Stanton opened her eyes to see blue sky through the ragged vents of a worn-out canvas tent. An unusual quietness all around added to the strange unreality of her situation. She heard only a low, mournful seeping of wind-blown sand. Where was she? What had happened? Was this only a vivid, fearful dream?

She felt stiff, unable to move. Did a ponderous weight hold her down? Her body seemed immense, full of dull, horrible ache, and she had no sensation of lower limbs except a creeping cold.

Slowly she moved her eyes around. Yes, she was in a tent—an abandoned tent, old, ragged, dirty, and she lay on the bare ground. Through a wide tear in the canvas she saw a stretch of bare, flat ground covered with stakes and boards and denuded frameworks and piles of débris. Then grim reality entered her consciousness. Benton was evacuated. Benton was depopulated. Benton—houses, tents, people—had moved away.

During her unconsciousness—perhaps while she had been thought dead—she had been carried to this abandoned tent. A dressing gown covered her, the one she always put on in the first hours after arising. The white dress she had worn last night—was it last night?—still adorned her, but all her jewelry had been taken. Then she remembered being lifted to a couch and cried over by her girls while awe-struck men came to look at her, and talk low among themselves. But she had heard how the cowboy's shot had downed her—how he had fought his way out, only to fall dead in the street and leave the girl to be taken by Durade. Then Beauty Stanton realized that she had been left alone in an abandoned tent to die. She became more conscious then of dull physical agony. But neither fear of death nor thought of pain occupied her mind. That suddenly awoke to remorse. With the slow ebbing of her life evil had passed out. If she had been given a choice between the salvation of her soul and to have Neale with her in her last moments, to tell him the truth, to beg his forgiveness, to die in his arms, she would have chosen the latter. Would not some trooper come before she died, someone to whom she could entrust a message? Some gravedigger? For the great U.P.R. buried the dead it left in its bloody tracks!

With strange feeling hands Stanton searched the pockets of her dressing gown, to find, at length, a little account book with pencil attached. Then, with stiffened fingers, but acute mind, she began to write to Neale. As she wrote, into each word went something of the pang, the remorse, the sorrow, the love she felt, and, when that letter was ended, she laid the little book on her breast and knew for the first time in many years—peace.

She endured the physical agony that gradually wore away. She did not cry out, or complain, or repent, or pray. Most of the spiritual emotion and life left in her had gone into the letter. Memory called up only the last moments of her life—when she saw Ancliffe die; when she folded innocent Allie Lee to the breast that had always yearned for a child; when Neale in his monstrous stupidity had misunderstood her; when he had struck her before the grinning crowd, and in burning words branded her with the one name unpardonable to her class; when at the climax of a morbid and all-consuming hate, a hate of the ruined woman whose body and mind had absorbed the vile dregs, the dark fire and poison of lustful men, she had inhumanly given

Allie Lee to the man she had believed the wildest, most depraved, and most dangerous brute in all Benton; when this Larry Red King, by some strange fatality, becoming as great as he was wild, had stalked out to meet her like some red and terrible death.

She remembered now that strange, icy gloom and shudder she had always felt in the presence of the cowboy. Within her vitals now was the same cold, deadly, sickening sensation, and it was death. Always she had anticipated it, but vaguely, unrealizingly.

King had lifted the burden of her life. She would have been glad—if only Neale had understood her! That was her last wavering conscious thought.

Then she drifted from human consciousness to the instinctive physical struggle of the animal to live, and that was not strong. There came a moment, the last, between life and death, when Beauty Stanton's soul lingered on the threshold of its lonely and eternal pilgrimage, and then drifted across into the gray shadows, into the unknown, out to the great beyond.

Casey leaned on his spade while he wiped the sweat from his brow and regarded his ally, McDermott. Between them yawned a grave they had been digging, and near at hand lay a long, quiet form wrapped in old canvas.

"Mac, I'll be domn' if I loike this job," said Casey, drawing hard at his black pipe.

"Yez want to be a director of the U.P.R., huh?" replied Mc-Dermott.

"Shure an' I've did iviry job but run an ingine. . . . It's imposed on we are, Mac. Thim troopers niver work. Why couldn't they plant these stiffs?"

"Casey, I reckon no wan's bossin' us. Benton picked up an' moved yisteday. An' we'll be goin' soon wid the gravel train. It's only dacent of us to bury the remains of Benton. An' shure yez ought to be glad to see that orful red-head cowboy go under the ground."

"An' fer why?" queried Casey.

"Didn't he throw a gun on yez oncet an' scare the daylights out of yez?"

"Mac, I wuz as cool as a coocumber. An' as to buryin' Red King, I'm proud an' sorry. He wuz Neale's fri'nd."

"My Gawd, but he wor chain lightnin', Casey. They said he shot the woman Stanton, too."

"Mac, thet wor a domn' lie, I bet," replied Casey. "He shot up Stanton's hall, an' a bullet from some of thim wot was foightin' him must hev hit her."

"Mebbe. But it wor bad bizness. That cowboy hit iviry wan of thim fellars in the same place. Shure, they niver blinked afther."

"An', Mac, the best an' dirtiest job we've had on this U.P. was the plantin' of thim fellars."

Casey's huge hand indicated a row of freshly filled graves over which the desert sand was seeping. Then dropping his spade, he bent to the quiet figure.

"Lay hold, Mac," he said.

They lowered the corpse into the hole. Casey stood up, making a sign of the cross before him. "He wor a man!"

Then they filled the grave.

"Mac, wouldn't it be dacent to mark where Red King's buried? A stone or wooden cross with his name?"

McDermott wrinkled his red brow and scratched his sandy beard. Then he pointed. "Casey, wot's the use? See, the blowin' sand's kivered all the graves."

"Mac, yez wor always hell at shirkin' worrk. Come on, now. Drill, ye terrier, drill!"

They quickly dug another long, narrow hole. Then, taking a rude stretcher, they plodded away in the direction of a dilapidated tent that appeared to be the only structure left of Benton. Casey entered ahead of his comrade.

"Thot's sthrange!"

"Wot?" queried McDermott.

"Didn't yez kiver her face whin we laid her down here?"

"Shure an' I did, Casey."

"An' that face has a different look now! Mac, see here!"

Casey stooped to pick up a little book from the woman's breast. His huge fingers opened it with difficulty. "Mac, there's wroitin' in ut!" he exclaimed.

"Wal, rade, ye baboon."

"Oh, I kin rade ut, though I ain't much of a wroiter meself," replied Casey, and then laboriously began to read. He halted suddenly and looked keenly at McDermott.

"Wot the devil? B'gorra, ut's to me fri'nd Neale . . . an' a love letter . . . an'. . . ."

"Wal, kape it, thin, fer Neale an' be dacent enough to rade no more."

Lifting Beauty Stanton, they carried her out into the sunlight. Her white face was a shadowed and tragic record.

"Mac, she wor shure a handsome woman," said Casey, "an' a loidy."

"Casey, yez are always sorry fer somebody. . . . Thot Stanton wuz a beauty an' she mebbe wuz a loidy. But she wuz domn' bad."

"Mac, I knowed long ago thot the milk of human kindness hed curdled in yez. An' yez hev no brains."

"I'm as intilligint as yez any day," retorted McDermott.

"Thin why hedn't yez seen thot this poor woman was alive whin we packed her out here? She come to an' writ thot letter to Neale . . . thin she doied!"

"My Gawd! Casey, yez ain't meanin' ut!" ejaculated McDermott, aghast.

Casey nodded grimly, and then he knelt to listen at Stanton's breast. "Stone dead now . . . thot's shure."

For her shroud these deliberate men used strippings of canvas from the tent, and then, carrying her up the bare and sandy slope, they lowered her into the grave next to the one of the cowboy.

Again Casey made a sign of the cross. He worked longer at the filling in than his comrade, and patted the mound of sand hard and smooth. When he finished, his pipe was out. He relighted it.

"Wal, Beauty Stanton, shure yez hev a cleaner grave than yez hed a bed. . . . Nice white desert sand. . . . An' prisintly no man will ivir know where yez come to lay."

The laborers shouldered their spades and plodded away.

The wind blew steadily in from the desert, seeping the sand in low, thin sheets. Afternoon waned, the sun sank, twilight crept over the barren waste. There were no sounds but the seep of sand, the moan of wind, the mourn of wolf. Loneliness came with the night that mantled Beauty Stanton's grave. Shadows trooped in from the desert and the darkness grew black. On that slope the wind always blew, and always the sand seeped, dusting over everything, imperceptibly changing the surface of the earth. The desert was still at work. Nature was no respecter of graves. Life was nothing. Radiant, cold stars blinked pitilessly out of the vast blue-black vault of heaven. But there hovered a spirit beside this woman's last resting-place—a spirit like the night, sad, lonely, silent, mystical, immense.

And as it hovered over hers so it hovered over other nameless graves.

In the eternal workshop of Nature, the tenants of these un-named and forgotten graves would mingle dust of good with dust of evil, and by the divinity of death resolve equally into the elements again.

The place that had known Benton knew it no more. Coyotes barked dismally down what had been the famous street of the camp and prowled in and out of the piles of débris and frames of wood. Gone was the low, strange roar that had been neither music nor mirth nor labor. Benton remained only a name.

The sun rose upon a squalid scene—a wide flat area where stakes and floors and frames mingled with all the flotsam and jetsam left by a hurried and profligate populace, moving on to another camp. Daylight found no man there, nor any living creature. And all day the wind blew the dust and sheets of sand over the place where had reigned such strife of toil and gold and lust and blood and death. A train passed that day, out of which engineer and fireman gazed with wondering eyes at what had been Benton. Like a mushroom it had arisen, and like a dust storm on the desert wind it had roared away, bearing its freight of labor, of passion, and of evil. Benton had become a name—a fabulous name.

But Nature seemed more merciful than life. For it began to hide what men had left—the scars of habitations where had roared hell. Sunset came, then night and the starlight. The lonely hours were winged, as if in hurry to resolve back into the elements the flimsy remains of that great camp.

And that spot was haunted.

# CHAPTER TWENTY-NINE

Casey left Benton on the work train. It was composed of a long string of box and flat cars loaded with stone, iron, gravel, ties—all necessaries for the upkeep of the road. The engine was at the rear end, pushing instead of pulling, and at the extreme front end there was a flat car loaded with gravel. A number of laborers rode on this car, among whom was Casey. In labor or fighting this Irishman always gravitated to the fore.

All along the track, from outside of Benton to the top of a long, slow rise of desert were indications of the fact that Indians had torn up the track or attempted to derail trains. The signs of Sioux had become such an everyday matter in the lives of the laborers that they were indifferent and careless. Thus isolated, unprotected groups of men, out some distance from the work train, often were swooped down upon by Indians and massacred.

The troopers had gone on with the other trains that carried Benton's inhabitants and habitations.

Casey and his comrades had slow work of it going westward, as it was necessary to repair the track and, at the same time, to keep vigilant watch for the Sioux. They expected the regular train from the east to overtake them, but did not even see its smoke. There must have been a wreck or telegraph messages to hold it back at Medicine Bow.

Toward sunset the work train reached the height of desert land that sloped in long sweeping lines down to the base of the hills. At this juncture a temporary station had been left in the shape of several boxcars where the telegraph operators and a squad of troopers lived.

As the work train lumbered along to the crest of this heave of barren land Casey observed that someone at the station was excitedly waving a flag. Thereupon Casey, who acted as brakeman, signaled the engineer.

"Domn' coorious thet," remarked Casey to his comrade McDermott. "Thim operators knowed we'd stop, anyway."

"Injins!" exclaimed McDermott.

That was the opinion of the several other laborers on the front car. And when the work train halted, that car had run beyond the station a few rods. Casey and his comrades piled off.

A little group of men awaited them. The operator, a young fellow named Collins, was known to Casey. He stood among the troopers, pale-faced and shaking.

"Casey, who's in charge of the train?" he asked nervously.

The Irishman's grin enlarged, making it necessary for him to grasp his pipe. "Shure the engineer's boss of the train an' I'm boss of the gang."

More of the work train men gathered around the group, and the engineer with his fireman approached.

"You've got to hold up here," said Collins.

Casey removed his pipe to refill it. "Ah-huh," he grunted.

"Wire from Medicine Bow . . . order to stop General Lodge's train . . . three hundred Sioux in ambush near this station . . . Lodge's train between here and Roaring City," breathlessly went on the operator.

"An' the message come from Medicine Bow!" ejaculated Casey, while his men gaped and muttered.

"Yes. It must have been sent here last night. But O'Neil, the night operator, was dead. Murdered by Indians while we slept."

"Thot's hell," replied Casey, seriously, as he lit his pipe.

"The message went through to Medicine Bow. Stacey down there sent it back to me. I tried to get Hills at Roaring City. No go. The wire's cut."

"An' shure the gineral's train has left . . . wot's that new camp . . . Roarin' wot?"

"Roaring City. . . . General Lodge went through two days ago with a private train. He had soldiers, as usual. But no force to stand off three hundred Sioux, or even a hundred."

"Wal, the gineral must hev lift Roarin' Camp . . . else that message niver would hev come."

"So I think. . . . Now what on earth can we do? The engineer of his train can't stop for orders short of this station, for the reason that there are no stations."

"An' thim Sooz is in ambush near here?" queried Casey reflectively. "Shure thot could only be in wan place. I rimimber thot higher, narrer pass."

"Right. It's steep upgrade coming east. Train can be blocked. General Lodge with his staff and party . . . and his soldiers . . . would be massacred without a chance to fight. That pass always bothered us for fear of ambush. Now the Sioux have come west far enough to find it. . . . No chance on earth for a train there . . . not if it carried a thousand soldiers."

"Wal, if the gineral an' company was sthopped somewhere beyond thot pass?" queried Casey shrewdly as he took a deep pull at his pipe.

"Then at least they could fight. They have stood off attacks before. They might hold out for the train following, or even run back."

"Thin, Collins, we've only got to sthop the gineral's train before it reaches that domn' trap."

"But we can't!" cried Collins. "The wire is cut. It wouldn't help matters if it weren't. I thought when I saw your train we might risk sending the engine on alone. But your engine is behind all these loaded cars. No switch. Oh, it is damnable!"

"Collins, there's more domnable things than yez ever heerd of. . . . I'll sthop Gineral Lodge!" The brawny Irishman wheeled and strode back toward the front car of the train. All the crowd, to a man, muttering and gaping, followed him. Casey climbed up on the gravel car.

"Casey, wot in hell would yez be afther doin'?" demanded McDermott.

Casey grinned at his old comrade. "Mac, yez do me a favor. Uncouple the car."

McDermott stepped between the cars and the *rattle* and *clank* of iron told that he had complied with Casey's request.

Collins, with all the men on the ground, grasped Casey's idea. "By God! Casey, *can* you do it? There's downgrade for twenty miles. Once start this gravel car and she'll go clear to the hills. But . . . but. . . ."

"Collins, it'll be aisy. I'll slip through that pass loike oil. Thim Sooz won't be watchin' this way. There's a curve. They won't hear till too late. An' shure they don't niver obsthruct a track till the last minute."

"But, Casey, once through the pass you can't control that gravel car. The brakes won't hold. You'll run square into the general's train . . . wreck it!"

"Naw! I've got a couple of ties, an' if thot wreck threatens, I'll heave a tie off on the track an' derail me private car."

"Casey, it's sure death!" exclaimed Collins. His voice and the pallor of his face and the beads of sweat all proclaimed him new to the U.P.R.

"Me boy, nuthin's shure whin yez are drillin' with the paddies."

Casey was above surprise and beyond disdain. He was a huge, toil-hardened, sun-reddened, hard-drinking soldier of the railroad, a loquacious Irishman whose fixed grin denied him any gravity, a foreman of his gang. His chief delight was to outdo his bosom comrade, McDermott. He did not realize that he represented an unconquerable and unquenchable spirit. Neither did his comrade know. But under Casey's grin shone something simple, radiant, hard as steel.

"Put yer shoulders ag'in' an' shove me off," he ordered.

Like automatons the silent laborers started the gravel car.

"Drill, ye terriers, drill! Drill, ye terriers, drill!" sang Casey as he stood at the wheel brake.

The car gathered momentum. McDermott was the last to let go. "Good luck to yez!" he shouted hoarsely.

"Mac, tell thim yez saw me!" called Casey. Then he waved his hand in good bye to the crowd. Their response was a short, ringing yell. They watched the car glide slowly out of sight.

For a few moments Casey was more concerned with the fact that a breeze had blown out his pipe than with anything else. Skilful as years had made him, he found unusual difficulty in relighting it, and he would not have been beyond stopping the car to accomplish that imperative need. When he had succeeded and glanced back, the station was out of sight.

Casey fixed his eyes upon the curve of the track ahead where it disappeared between the sage-covered sandy banks. Here the grade was scarcely perceptible to any but experienced eyes. And the gravel car crept along as if it would stop any moment. But Casey knew that it was not likely to stop, and, if it did, he could start it again. A heavily laden car like this, once started, would run a long way on a very little grade. What worried him was the *creaking* and *rattle* of wheels sounds that, from where he stood, were apparently very loud.

He turned the curve into a stretch of straight track where there came a perceptible increase in the strength of the breeze against his face. While creeping along at this point, he scooped out a hole in the gravel mound on the car, making a place that might afford some protection from Indian bullets and arrows. That accomplished, he had nothing to do but hold on to the wheel brake, and gaze ahead.

It seemed a long time before the speed increased sufficiently to ensure him against any danger of a stop. The wind began to blow his hair and whip away the smoke of his pipe. And the car began to cover distance. Several miles from the station he entered the shallow mouth of a gully where the grade increased. His speed accelerated correspondingly until he was rolling along faster than a man could run. The track had been built on the right bank of the gully that curved between low bare hills, and that grew deeper and of a rougher character. Casey had spiked many of the rails over which he passed.

He found it necessary to apply the brake so that he would not take the sharp curves at dangerous speed. The brake did not work well and gave indications that it would not stand a great deal. With steady, rattling *creak* and an occasional *clank,* the car rolled on.

If Casey remembered the lay of the land, there was a long, straight stretch of track, ending in several curves, the last of which turned sharply into the narrow cut where the Sioux would ambush and obstruct the train. At this point it was Casey's intention to put off the brake and let his car run wild.

It seemed an endless time before he reached the head of that stretch. Then he let go of the wheel. And the gravel car began to roll on faster.

Casey appeared to be grimly and conscientiously concerned over a piece of difficult work. And he was worried about the outcome. He must get his car beyond that narrow cut. If it jumped the track or ran into an obstruction, or if the Sioux spied him in time, then his work would not be well done. He welcomed the gathering momentum, yet was fearful of the curve he saw a long distance ahead. When he reached that, he would be going at a high rate of speed—too fast to take the curve safely.

A little dimness came to Casey's eyes. Years of hot sun and dust and desert wind had not made his eyes any stronger. The low gray walls, the white bleached rocks, the shallow stream of water, the fringe of brush, and the long narrowing track—all were momentarily indistinct in his sight. His breast seemed weighted. Over and over in his mind revolved the several possibilities that awaited him at the cut, and every rod of the distance now added to his worry. It grew to be dread. Chances were against him. The thing entrusted to him was not in his control. Casey resented this. He had never failed at a job. The U.P.R. had to be built—and who could tell?—if the chief engineer and all his staff and the directors of the road were massacred by the Sioux, perhaps that might be a last and crowning catastrophe.

Casey had his first cold thrill. And his nerves tightened for the crisis, while his horny hands gripped on the brake. The car was running wild, with a curve just ahead. It made an unearthly *clatter*. The Indians would hear that. But they would have to be swift, if he stayed on the track. Almost before he realized it the car lurched at the bend. Casey felt the offside wheels leave the rail, heard the scream of the inside wheels grinding hard. But for his grip on the wheel, he would have been thrown. The wind whistled in his ears. With a sudden lurch the car seemed to rise. Casey thought it had jumped the track. But it banged back, righted itself, rounded the curve.

Here the gully widened—sent off branches. Casey saw hundreds of horses—but not an Indian. He rolled swiftly on, crossed a bridge, and saw more horses. His grim anticipation became a reality. The Sioux were in the ambush. What depended on him and his luck! Casey's red cheek blanched, but it was not with fear for himself. Not yet on this ride had he entertained one thought concerning his own personal relation to its fragile possibilities.

To know the Sioux were there made a tremendous difference. A dark and terrible sternness actuated Casey. He projected his soul into that *clattering* car of iron and wood. And it was certain he prayed. His hair stood straight up. There—the narrow cut in the hill! The curve of the track! He was pounding at it. The wheels shrieked. Looking up, he saw only the rocks and gray patches of brush and the bare streak of earth. No Indian showed.

His gaze strained to find an obstruction on the track. The car rode the curve on two wheels. It seemed alive. It entered the cut with hollow, screeching roar. The shade of the narrow place was gloomy. Here! It must happen! Casey's heart never lifted its ponderous weight. Then, shooting around the curve, he saw an open track and bright sunlight beyond.

Above the roar of wheels sounded *spatting* reports of rifles. Casey forgot to dodge into his gravel shelter. He was living a strange, dragging moment—an age. Out shot the car into the light. Likewise Casey's dark blankness of mind ended. His heart lifted with mighty throb. There shone the gray endless slope, stretching out and down to the black hills in the distance. Shrill wild yells made Casey wheel. The hillside above the cut was colorful and spotted with moving objects. Indians! Puffs of white smoke arose. Casey felt the light impact of lead. Glancing bright streaks darted down. They were arrows. Two *thudded* into the gravel, one into the wood. Then something tugged at his shoulder. Another arrow! Suddenly the shaft was there in his sight, quivering in his flesh. It bit deep. With one wrench he tore it out and shook it aloft at the Sioux.

"Oi bate yez domn' Sooz!" he yelled in fierce defiance. The long screeching clamor of baffled rage and the scattering volley of rifle shots kept up until the car passed out of range.

Casey faced ahead. The Sioux were behind him. He had a free track. Far down the gray valley, where the rails disappeared, were low streaks of black smoke from a locomotive. The general's train was coming.

The burden of worry and dread that had been Casey's was now no more—vanished as if by magic. His job had not yet been completed, but he had won. He never glanced back at the Sioux. They had failed in their first effort at ambushing the cut, and Casey knew the troops would prevent a second attempt. Casey faced ahead. The whistle of wind filled his ears, the dry, sweet odor of the desert filled his nostrils. His car was on a straight track, rolling along downgrade, half a mile a minute. And Casey, believing he might do well to slow up gradually, lightly put on the brake. But it did not hold. He tried again. The brake had broken.

He stood at the wheel, his eyes clear now, watching ahead. The train, down in the valley, was miles away, not yet even a black dot in the gray. The smoke, however, began to lift.

Casey was suddenly struck by a vague sense that something was wrong with him. "Phwat the hell," he muttered. Then his mind, strangely absorbed, located the trouble. His pipe had gone out! Casey stooped in the hole he had made in the gravel, and there, knocking his pipe in his palm, he found the ashes cold. When had that ever happened before? Casey wagged his head. For his pipe to go cold and he not to know! Things were happening on the U.P.R. these days. Casey refilled the pipe, and, with the wind whistling over him, he relit it. He drew deep and long, stood up, grasped the wheel, and felt all his blood change.

"Me poipe goin' cold . . . that wor funny," soliloquized Casey. The phenomenon appeared remarkable to him. Indeed, it stood alone. He measured the nature of this job by that forgetfulness. And memories thrilled him. With his eye clear on the track that split the gray expanse, with his whole being permeated by the soothing influence of smoke, with his task almost done, Casey experienced an unprecedented thing for him—he lived over past performances and found them vivid, thrilling, somehow sweet. Battles of the Civil War; the day he saved a flag, and, better, the night he saved Pat Shane, who had lived only to stop a damned Sioux bullet; many and many an adventure with McDermott, who, just a few minutes past, had watched him with round, shining eyes; the fights he had seen and shared—these things passed swiftly through Casey's mind and left more of pride than he had ever known and vaguely bore their relation on to this day when he had outwitted the Sioux and prevented a massacre.

He was pleased with himself—more pleased with what McDermott would think. Casey's boyhood did not return to him, but his mounting exhilaration and all satisfaction were boyish. It was great to ride this way! There—he saw a long, black dot down in the gray. The train! General Lodge had once shaken hands with Casey.

Somebody had to do these things, since the U.P.R. must go across to the Pacific. A day would come when a splendid passenger train would glide smoothly down this easy grade where Casey jolted along on his gravel car. The fact loomed large in the simplicity of the Irishman. He began to hum his favorite song. Facing westward, he saw the black dot grow into a long train. Likewise, he saw the beauty of the red-gold sunset behind the hills. Casey gloried in the wildness of the scene—in the meaning of his ride—particularly in his loneliness. He seemed strangely alone there on that vast gray slope—a man—somehow accountable for all these things. He felt more than he understood. His long-tried nerve and courage and strength had never yielded this buoyancy and sense of loftiness. He was Casey—Casey who had let all the gang run for shelter from the Sioux while he had remained for one last and final drive at a railroad spike. But the cool, devil-may-care indifference, common to all his comrades as well as to himself, was not the strongest factor in the Casey's state today. Up out of the rugged and dormant soul had burst the spirit of a race embodied in one man. Casey was his own audience, and the light upon him was the glory of the setting sun. A nightingale sang in his heart, and he realized that this was his hour. Here the bloody, hard years found their reward. Not that he had ever wanted one or thought of one, but it had come—out of the toil, the pain, the weariness. So his nerves tingled, his pulses beat, his veins glowed, his heart throbbed, and all the new, sweet, young sensations of a boy wildly reveling in the success of his first great venture, all the vague, strange, deep, complex emotions of a man who has become conscious of what he was giving—these shook Casey by storm, and life had no more to give. He knew that, whatever he was, whatever this incomprehensible driving spirit in him, whatever his unknown relation to man and to duty, there had been given him in the peril just passed, in this wonderful ride, a gift splendid and divine.

Casey rolled on, and the train grew plain in his sight. When perhaps several miles of track lay between him and the approaching engine, he concluded it was time to get ready. Lifting one of the heavy ties, he laid it in front where he could quickly shove it off with his foot.

Then he stood up. It was certain that he looked backward, but at no particular thing, an instinctive glance. With his foot on the tie he steadied himself so that he could push it off and leap instantly after. And at that moment he remembered the little book he had found on Beauty Stanton's breast, and which contained the letter to his friend Neale. Casey deliberated in spite of the necessity for speed. Then he took the book from his pocket.

"B'gorra, yez niver can tell, an' thim U.P.R. throopers hev been known to bury a mon widout searchin' his pockets," he said.

And he put the little book between the teeth that held his pipe. Then he shoved off the tie and leaped.

# CHAPTER THIRTY

Neale's amaze and rage at hearing Allie Lee's name on the lips of the Stanton women had been so great that he was beside himself. When he got out of the hall he was shaking, and wet with sweat.

He tore at the neck of his shirt. There was not enough air to keep him from suffocating. He hated the dark street with its hurrying passers-by, and the dim lights, and its incessant murmur. Benton was being torn down. And he plunged away in the direction of the railroad station.

What had happened? Why was he shaking so? How come the sudden keen pang in an old dull wound? The very air and the dim pale tents seemed whirling about his head. And he strode along a block before all became clear in his mind. Beauty Stanton had been at her old trick of trying to win him, but this time either he had been drunk or she had overstepped a certain restraint in her importunity. And he had cursed her—then struck her! He regretted that. But how dared she speak the name of Allie Lee. Neale's body leaped hot again at the memory of her insidious whisper. What had the poor deluded fool meant anyhow? Where had she ever heard that name—so sacred to him? Beauty Stanton had always appeared to be a woman of good instincts and of refinement. Neale had been sorry for her. He appreciated what must have been the difference between her life once and the horror of it now. It began to be a marvel to him that she could have spoken Allie Lee's name. Why? Had she wished to taunt him with the name of an old love? Neale scarcely credited that, and, when he recalled the strange thrilling sweetness of her voice, he made certain she had not been mocking him. How strange then.

Before he grew aware of the swiftness of his gait, he had reached the station. It was a crowded noisy dark place. A long train of freight and passenger cars was pulling out westward to the new construction camp terminus—Roaring City. Neale swung up between two boxcars and climbed to the top of one, where he sat with legs dangling over.

Dim, pale, flickeringly lighted Benton. He saw the dark splotches where two blocks had already been removed. Another day would see the end of that place of hell and gold and blood. He gloated over the fact. This scene before him was like the scene of failure in his heart. His life that was to have been so bright and useful! What had he not suffered in that hideous flat desert hole? And these last few moments of the last hour there—they had been the worst. He was fleeing like a thief in the night. As one fascinated, he watched the lights of Benton disappear. He left nothing there. Even his baggage was not worth taking away. His friend King would follow him, and so would the drinking, gambling horde. All at once Neale was conscious of a strong impelling desire to leap off the car and go back. He had to hold himself. The impulse was strange, inexplicable, and the wrench he suffered when the last light vanished was so poignant that he fell back flat upon the car; all of which emotions he presently decided to be the result of a shock. And accounting for it in that manner, he returned to wondering about the catastrophe a name had wrought. Allie Lee! His despair was as keen as if he had only lost her yesterday. A whisper of her name had made him strike a woman! But he had struck like the savage beast, involuntarily, in blind pain.

The long train rolled out upon the desert. Neale saw the flare of light from the engine and heard the steady exhaust. The roar of wheel and *clink* of chains and *creak* of wood all meant energy—remorseless action—the business of the railroad to move Benton on to another town. Upon every boxcar Neale espied men, and there were two upon the other end of his car. He had faint stirrings in him of the old love of travel, of movement, of the night and the wild, but these seemed only vague and passed away in bitter memory. Achievement, adventure, life were nothing to him any more. His future seemed as dark as that desert floor with its pale horizon line. There seized upon him the blackest gloom, made up of thoughts of defeat and agony and death. A picture stood out in his mind—a picture of a man pursued by the furies down a bleak and naked shingle of the world—and that tremendous abandon of energy, the fixed and staring eyes of horror, the face of torture—all these were his own and these terrible furies were at him now. Soon this mood would become fixed and stable and he would be lost. His mind seemed to embrace all his old possibilities, his hopes at the same moment that it held all the horrible contrast—his broken heart and ruined life—and the baseness that had made him strike a woman. Self destruction had long abided in Neale's reflections, and all that opposed it now was his innate conviction of its cowardliness. He lay there while the train rolled along, hours and miles on into the night and the desert, and his flesh was cold and damp, his blood sluggish, his spirit faint and low.

The dawn came. And the very fact of daylight and the needs of life and the fellowship of men bound for some common goal helped Neale. He swung down inside the boxcar where he found every companion-traveler ready to share food and drink.

All day the train crept along, making slow time, and the rumor flew in from somewhere that the train ahead was fighting off an Indian attack. Late that afternoon suddenly Neale grew weak with a wild sick pain. He got as far as possible into a corner of the car, and there he lay, living over once more the old battle. But it was not a battle any more. It was a retreat, a rout, and in Neale's mind augmented sinister thoughts. He for once would have welcomed an attack of the Sioux. But nothing of such nature occurred and he went to sleep at last. When he awoke, another day had come; the train had kept on, and somewhere near at hand in the great upland plateau lay the new camp, Roaring City.

It took Neale nearly forty-eight hours to reach the new camp— Roaring City. A bigger town than Benton had gone up and more was going up—tents and clapboard houses, sheds and cabins—the same motley jumble, set under beetling red Utah bluffs.

He found lodgings and bought new articles of clothing and a few necessaries for his bare room. Being without food or bed or wash for two days and night was not helpful to the task he must accomplish—the conquering of depression. He ate and slept long, and the following day he took time to make himself comfortable and presentable before he sallied forth to find the offices of the engineer corps. Then he walked on as directed, and heard men talking of Indian ambushes and troops.

When at length he reached the headquarters of the engineer corps, he was greeted with restraint by his old officers and associates; he was surprised and at a loss to understand their attitude.

Even in General Lodge there was a difference. Neale gathered at once that something had happened to put out of his chief's mind the interest that officer surely must have in Neale's trip to Washington. And after greeting him, the first thing General Lodge said gave warrant to the rumors of trouble with Indians.

"My train was to have been ambushed at Deep Cut yesterday," he explained. "Big force of Sioux. We were amazed to find them so far west. It would have been a massacre . . . but for Casey. . . . We have no particulars yet, for the wire is cut. But we know what Casey did. He ran the gantlet of the Indians through that cut. He was on a gravel car running wild downhill. You know the grade. . . . Of course his intention was to hold up my train . . . block us before we reached the ambushed cut. There must have been a broken brake, for he derailed the car not half a mile ahead of us. My engineer saw the runaway flat car and feared a collision. . . . Casey threw a railroad tie . . . on the track . . . in front of him. . . . We found him under the car . . . crushed . . . dying. . . ."

General Lodge's voice thickened and slowed a little. He looked down. His face appeared quite pale.

Neale began to quiver in the full presaging sense of a revelation.

"My engineer, Tom Daley, reached Casey's side just the instant before he died," said General Lodge, resuming his story. "In fact, Daley was the only one of us who did see Casey alive. . . . Casey's last words were 'ambush . . . Sooz . . . Deep Cut,' and then . . . 'me fri'nd Neale!' We were at a loss to understand what he meant . . . that is, at first. We found Casey with this little notebook and his pipe tight between his teeth."

The chief gave the notebook to Neale, who received it with a trembling hand and wondering eye.

"You can see the marks of Casey's teeth in the leather. It was difficult to extract the book. He held on like grim death. Oh! Casey *was* grim death. . . . We could not pull his black pipe out at all. We left it between his set jaws, where it always had been . . . where it belonged. . . . I ordered him buried that way. . . . So they buried him out there along the track."

The chief's low voice ceased, and he stood motionlessly a moment, his brow knotted, his eyes haunted, yet bright with a glory of tribute to a hero.

Neale heard the *ticking* of a watch and the murmur of the street outside. He felt the soft little notebook in his hand. And the strangest sensation shuddered over him. He drew his breath sharply.

When General Lodge turned again to face him, Neale saw him differently—aloof, somehow removed, indistinct.

"Casey meant the notebook for you," said the general. "It belonged to the woman, Beauty Stanton. It contained a letter, evidently written while she was dying. . . . This developed when Daley began to read aloud. We all heard. The instant I understood it was a letter intended for you, I took the book. No more was read. We were all crowded round Daley . . . curious, you know. There were visitors on my train . . . and your enemy Lee. I'm sorry . . . but, no matter. You see it couldn't be helped. . . . That's all. . . ."

Neale was conscious of ignominy even in his dazed state of conjecture and dread. But he stood perfectly erect and gazed straight into the face of the old chief. "Thank you for you courtesy," he said clearly. "Poor old Casey," he murmured. Then he remembered Stanton dying. What had happened? He could not trust himself to read that message before Lodge, and, bowing, he left the room.

But he had to grope his way through the lobby, so dim had become his sight. By the time he reached the street, he had lost his self-control that he had hidden from his former officers—that realization of his disgrace. Something burned his hand. It was the little leather notebook. He had not the nerve to open it. What had been the implication in General Lodge's strange words?

He gazed with awe at the tooth marks on the little book. How had Casey come by anything of Beauty Stanton's? Could it be true that she was dying? Neale believed nothing, yet his whole nervous organization vibrated to the nearness of shock.

Then again he was accosted in the street. A heavy hand, a deep voice arrested his progress. His eyes, sweeping up from the path, saw fringed and beaded buckskin, a stalwart form, a bronzed and bearded face, and keen, gray eyes warm with the light of gladness. He was gripped in hands of iron.

"Son! Hyar you air . . . an' it's the savin' of me!" exclaimed a deep, familiar voice.

"Slingerland!" cried Neale, and he grasped his old friend as a drowning man at an anchor rope. "My God! What will happen next? Oh, I'm glad to find you! Slingerland, I'm in trouble!"

"Son, I reckon I know," replied the other.

Neale shivered. Why did men look at him so? This old trapper had too much simplicity, too big a heart, to hide his pity.

"Come! Somewhere . . . out of the crowd!" cried Neale, dragging at Slingerland. "Don't talk. Don't tell me anything. Wait! I've a letter here . . . that's going to be hell's fire!"

Neale stumbled along out of the crowded street, he did not know where, and with death in his soul he opened Beauty Stanton's book. And he read:

*You called me that horrible name. You struck me. You've killed me. I lie here dying. Oh, Neale! I'm dying—and I loved you. I came to you to prove it. If you had not been so blind—so stupid! My prayer is that someone will see this I'm writing—and take it to you.*

*Ancliffe brought your sweetheart, Allie Lee, to me—to hide her from Durade. He told me to find you, and then he died. He had been stabbed in saving her from Durade's gang. And Hough, too, was killed.*

*Neale, I looked at Allie Lee, and then I understood your ruin. You fool! She was not dead, but alive. Innocent and sweet like an angel. Ah! The wonder of it in Benton! Neale, she did not know—did not feel the kind of a woman I am. She changed me—crucified me. She put her face on my breast. And I have*

384

*that touch with me now, blessed, softening.*

*I locked her in a room and hurried out to find you. For the first time in years I had a happy moment. I understood why you had never cared for me. I respected you. Then I would have gone to hell for you. It was my joy that you must owe your happiness to me—that I would be the one to give you back Allie Lee and hope, and the old, ambitious life. Oh, I gloried in my power. It was sweet. You would owe every kiss of hers, every moment of pride, to the woman you had repulsed. That was to be my revenge.*

*And I found you, and in the best hour of my bitter life— when I had risen above the woman of shame, above thought of self—then you, with hellish stupidity, imagined I was seeking you—you for myself! Your annoyance, your scorn, robbed me of my wits. I could not tell you. I could only speak her name and bid you come.*

*You branded me before that grinning crowd, you struck me! And the fires of hell—my hell—burst in my heart. I ran out of there—mad to kill your soul—to cause you everlasting torment. I swore I would give that key of Allie Lee's room to the first man who entered my house.*

*The first man was Larry Red King. He was drunk. He looked wild. I welcomed him. I sent him to her room.*

*But Red King was your friend. I had forgotten that. He came out with her. He was sober and terrible. Like the mad woman that I was, I rushed at him to tear her away. He shot me. I see his eyes now. But, oh, thank God, he shot me! It was a deliverance.*

*I fell on the stairs, but I saw that flaming-faced devil kill four of Durade's men. He got Allie Lee out. Later I heard he had been killed and that Durade had caught the girl.*

*Neale, hurry to find her. Kill that Spaniard. No man could tell why he has spared her, but I tell you he will not spare her long.*

*Don't ever forget Hough or Ancliffe or that terrible cowboy. Ancliffe's death was beautiful. I am cold. It's hard to write. All is darkening. I hear the moan of wind. Forgive me! Neale, the difference between me and Allie Lee—is a good man's love. Men are blind to woman's agony. She laid her cheek here—on my breast—I—who always wanted a child. I shall die alone. No—I think God is here. There is someone! After all, I was a woman. Neale I forgive. . . .*

# CHAPTER THIRTY-ONE

"Wor I there?" echoed McDermott as he wiped the clammy sweat from his face. "B'gosh, I wor!"

It was half past five. There appeared to be an unusual number of men on the street, not so hurried and business-like and merry as generally, and given to collecting in groups, low-voiced and excited.

General Lodge drew McDermott inside. "Come. You need a bracer. Man, you look sick," he said.

At the bar McDermott's brown and knotty hand shook us he lifted a glass and gulped a drink of whiskey. "Gineral, I ain't the mon I wuz," complained McDermott. "Casey's gone! An' we had hell wid the Injuns gittin' here. An' thin jest afther I stepped off the train . . . it happened."

"What happened? I've heard conflicting reports. My men are out trying to get news. Tell me, Sandy," replied the general eagerly.

"After hearin' of Casey's finish, I was shure needin' stimulants," began the Irishman. "An' prisintly I drhopped into that Durade's Palace. I had my drink, an' thin went into the big room where the moosic wuz. It shure wuz a palace. A lot of thim swells with frock coats wuz there. B'gorra, they ain't above buckin' the tiger. Some of thim I knew. That Misther Lee, wot wuz once a commissioner of the U.P., he wor there with a party of friends. An' I happened to be close by thim whin the dancin' gurl come out. She was shure purty with her bare arms an' legs.

But thot sad! Her eyes wor turrible hauntin', an' roight off I wanted to start a foight.

"Wal, the minnit that Lee seen the gurl he acted strange. I wuz standin' close an' I went closer. 'Most exthraordinary rezemblance,' he kept sayin'. An' thin he dug into his vest fer a pocketbook, an' out of that he took a locket. He looked at it . . . thin at the little gurl who danced so tired and looked so sad. Roight off he turned the color of a sheet. 'Gintlemen, look!' he sez. They all looked, an' shure wuz sthruck with somethin'. 'Gintlemen,' sez Lee, 'me wife left me years ago . . . ran off West wid a gambler. If she iver hed a child . . . that gurl is thot child. Fer she's the livin' image of me wife nineteen years ago!'

"Some of thim laughed at him . . . some of thim stared. But Lee wuz dead in earnest an' growin' more excited ivery minnit. I heerd him mutter low . . . 'My Gawd, it can't be. Her child . . . in a gamblin' hell! But that face. . . . Ah, where else could I expect the child of such a mother?'

"An' Lee went closer to the platform where the gurl danced. His party follered an' I follered, too. . . . Jest whin the moosic sthopped an' the gurl looked up . . . thin she seen Lee. Roight out he sthepped away from the crowd. He wuz whiter'n a ghost. An' the gurl she seemed paralyzed. Sthrange it wor to see how she an' him looked alike thin.

"The crowd seen somethin' amiss, an' went quiet, starin' an' nudgin'. . . . Gineral, domn me if the gurl's face didn't blaze. I niver seen the loike. An' she sthepped off the platform an' come straight fer Lee. An' whin she sthopped she wuz close enough to touch him. Her eyes wor great burnin' holes an' her face shone somethin' wonderful.

"Lee put up a shakin' hand. 'Gurl,' he sez, 'did yez iver hear of Allison Lee?'

"An' all her body seemed to lift. 'He is my father!' she cried. 'I am Allie Lee!'

"An' thin that crowd wuz split up by a mon wot hurried through. He wuz a greaser . . . one of thim dandies on dress an' diamonds . . . a handsome, wicked-lookin' gambler. Seein' the gurl, he snarled . . . 'Go back there!' . . . an' he pointed. She niver even looked at him.

"Somewan back of me sez thot's Durade. Wal, it wor. An' sudden he seen who the gurl wuz watchin' . . . Lee. Thot Durade turned green an' wild-eyed an' stiff. But thot couldn't hold a candle to Lee. Shure he turned into a fiend. He bit out a Spanish name, nothin' loike Durade. An' loike a hissin' snake Durade sez . . . 'Allison Lee!'

"Thin there wuz a deadlock between thim two men, wid the crowd waitin' fer hell to pay. Life-long inimies, sez I, to meself, an' I hed the whole story.

"Durade began to limber up. Anywan what knows a greaser would have been lookin' fer blood. 'She . . . wint . . . back . . . to yez,' panted Durade.

" 'No . . . thief . . . Spanish dog! I have not seen her for nineteen years,' sez Lee.

"The gurl spoke up. 'Mother is dead! Killed by Injuns!'

"Thin Lee cried out . . . 'Did she leave *him?*'

" 'Yes, she did,' sez the gurl. 'She wuz goin' back. Home! Takin' me home. But the caravan wuz attacked by Injuns. An' all but me wor massacred.'

"Durade cut short the gurl's speech. If I iver seen a reptoile it wuz thin. 'Lee, they both left me,' he hisses. 'I tracked them. I lost the mother, but caught the daughter.'

"Thin thot Durade lost his speech fer a minnit, foamin' at the mouth wid rage. If yez niver seen a greaser mad, thin yez niver seen the rale thin'. His face changed yaller an' ould an' wrinkled, wid spots of red. His lip curled up loike a wolf's, an' his eyes . . . they wint down to little black points of hell's fire. He wuz crazy. 'Look at her!' he yelled. 'Allie Lee! Flesh an'

389

blood yez can't deny! *Her* baby! An' she's been my slave . . . my dog to beat an' kick! She's been through Benton. A bare-legged dancer an' toy fer the riff-raff of the camps! She's as vile an' black an' lost as her treacherous mother!'

"Allison Lee shrunk under thot shame. But the gurl . . . Lord! She niver looked wot she was painted by thot devil. She stood white an' still, loike an angel above judgment. Durade drew one of thim little Derringers. An' sudden he hild it on Lee, hissin' now in his greaser talk. I niver seen sich hellish joy on a human face. Murder was nothin' to thot look.

"Jist thin I seen Neale an' Slingerland, an', by Gawd, I thought I'd drop. They seemed to loom up. The girl screamed, wild-loike, an' she swayed about to fall. Neale leaped in front of Lee. 'Durade!' he spit out, an' domn me if I didn't expect to see the roof fly off."

McDermott wiped his moist face and tipped his empty glass to his lips, and swallowed hard. His light-blue eyes held a glint.

"Gineral," he went on, "yez know Neale. How big he is! Wot nerve he's got! There niver wor a mon his equal on the U.P., 'ceptin' Casey. . . . But me, nor anywan, nor yez, either, ever seen Neale loike he wuz thin. He niver hesitated an inch, but wint roight fer Durade. Any domn' fool, iven a crazy greaser, would hev seen his finish in Neale. Durade changed quick from hot to cold. An' he shot Neale. Neale laughed. Funny ringin' sort of laugh, full of thot same joy Durade hed sung out to Lee. Hate an' love of blood it wor. Yez would hev thought Neale felt wonderful happy to sthop a bullet.

"Thin his hand shot out an' grabbed Durade. . . . He jerked him off his feet an' swung him around. The little Derringer flew, an' Sandy McDermott wuz the mon who picked it up. It'll be Neale's whin I see him. . . . Durade jabbered fer help. But no wan come. Thot big trapper, Slingerland, stood there with two guns, an' shure he looked bad. Neale slung Durade around, spillin' some fellers who didn't dodge quick, an' thin he jerked him up backwards. An' Durade come up with a long knife in the wan hand he had free.

"Neale yelled . . . 'Lee, take the gurl out!'

"I seen thin she hed fainted in Lee's arms. He lifted her . . . moved away . . . an' thin I seen no more of thim. Durade made wild an' wicked lunges at Neale, only to be jerked off his balance. I heerd the bones crack in the arm Neale held. The greaser screamed. Sudden he wuz turned ag'in an' swung backwards so thot Neale grabbed the other arm . . . the wan wot held the knife. It wuz a child in the grasp of a giant. Neale shure looked beautiful. I niver wished so much in me loife fer Casey as thin. He would hev enjoyed thot foight, fer he bragged of his friendship fer Neale. An'. . . ."

"Go on, man, end your story!" ordered the general breathlessly.

"Wal, b'gorra, there wuz more crackin' of bones, an' sich screams as I niver heerd from a mon. Turrible, bloodcurdlin'! Neale held both Durade's hands an' wuz squeezin' thot knife handle so the greaser couldn't let go. Thin Neale drew out thot hand of Durade's . . . the wan wot held the knife . . . an' made Durade jab himself, low down. My Gawd, how thot jenteel Spaniard howled! I seen the blade go in an' come our red.

" 'Dance!' yelled Neale, cold an' hard. Domn me, Gineral, the boy wuz so mad and so powerful that he jigged the greaser over the floor, here an' there, all the time stickin' that long blade in and yellin' . . . 'Dance'! No wan had nerve enough to go near him. No wan wanted to, with that buckskin trapper prancin' around like an Indian.

"Durade danced after he wuz dead, that's domn' certain. He had been made to dance an' cut himself to pieces. Neale dragged him to that platform where the poor little gurl . . . Allison Lee's daughter, b'gorra . . . had been forced to dance. An'

Neale stood him up ag'in' the wall an' left him there, his own knife run clear through him . . . shure the bloodiest an' awfulest sight I iver seen."

McDermott looked at the empty glass. "That's all, Gineral. An' if it's jist the same to yez, I'll have another drink."

# CHAPTER THIRTY-TWO

Sight of Warren Neale had transformed life for Allie Lee.

The shame of being forced to dance before bold men, the pain from Durade's blows, the dread that every hour he would do the worst by her or kill her, the sudden and amazing recognition between her and her father—these became dwarfed and blurred in the presence of the glorious truth that Neale lived.

She had seen him with reeling senses and through darkening eyes. She had seen him leap before her father to confront that glittering-eyed Durade. She had neither fear of him nor pity for the Spaniard.

Sensations of falling, of being carried, of the light and dust and noise of the street, of men around her, of rooms and the murmur of voices, of being worked over and spoken to by a kindly woman, of swallowing what was put to her mouth, of answering questions, of letting other clothes be put upon her— all these sensations were felt by her during a great and overwhelming joy in which it seemed she must only listen and watch for him.

She was as if in a trance, aware of all going on about her, but with consciousness riveted upon one stunning fact. When she was left alone, this state gradually wore away, and there remained a throbbing, quivering suspense of love. Her despair had ended. The spirit that had upheld her through all the long, dark hours had reached its fulfillment.

She lay on a couch in a small room curtained off from

another, the latter large and light, and from which presently came a sound of low voices. She heard the quick tread of men; a door opened.

"Lee, I congratulate you. A narrow escape!" exclaimed a deep voice, with something sharp, authoritative in it.

"General Lodge, it was indeed a narrow shave for me," replied another voice, low and husky.

Allie slowly sat up, with the dreamy waiting abstraction less strong. Her father, Allison Lee, and General Lodge, Neale's chief, who had once been so kind to her, were there in the other room.

"Neale killed Durade! Cut him all to pieces!" said the general, with agitation. "I had it from McDermott, one of my spikers . . . reliable man. . . . Neale was shot . . . perhaps cut, too. . . . But he doesn't seem to know it."

Allie sprang up, transfixed and thrilling.

"Neale killed . . . him?" echoed Allison Lee hoarsely. Then followed a sound of a chair falling.

"Indeed, Allison, it's true," broke in a strange voice. "The street's full of men . . . all talking . . . all stirred up. No wonder . . . I think you'd meet with this other."

Other men entered the room.

"Henney, is Neale here?" queried General Lodge sharply.

"They're trying to hold him up . . . in the office. A gang patting him on the back. . . . Durade was not liked," replied someone.

"Is Neale badly hurt?"

"I don't know. He looked it. He was all bloody."

"Colonel Dillon, did you see Neale?" went on the sharp, eager voice.

"Yes. He seemed dazed . . . wild. Probably badly hurt. Yet he moved steadily. No one could stop him," answered another strange voice.

"Ah, here comes McDermott!" exclaimed General Lodge.

Allie's ears throbbed to a slow, shuffling, heavy tread. Her consciousness received the fact of Neale's injury, but her heart refused to accept it as perilous. God could not mock her faith by a last catastrophe.

"Sandy . . . you've seen Neale?"

Allie loved this sharp, keen voice for its note of dread.

"Shure. B'gorra, yez couldn't hilp seein' him. He's as big as a hill an' his shirt's as red as Casey's red wan. I wint to give him the little gun wot Durade pulled on him. Domn' me, he looked roight at me an' niver seen me," replied the Irishman.

"Lee, you will see Neale?" queried General Lodge.

There was a silence.

"No," presently came a cold reply. "It is not necessary. He saved me . . . injury perhaps. I am grateful. I'll reward him."

"How?" rang General Lodge's voice.

"Gold, of course. I remember Neale. He was a gambler. Probably he had a grudge against this Durade. . . . I need not meet Neale, it seems. I am somewhat . . . overwrought. I wish to spare myself further excitement."

"Lee . . . listen!" returned General Lodge violently. "Neale is a splendid young man . . . the nerviest, best engineer I ever knew. I predict great things for him. But he went to the bad for a while. Have you any idea why?"

"No, and it doesn't interest me."

"You'll hear it, anyhow. He saved the life of this girl who has turned out to be your daughter. He took care of her. He loved her . . . was engaged to marry her. . . . But he lost her somehow. And for a long time after that he was no good. It nearly ruined him."

"I do not credit that. Gambling, drink . . . and bad women ruined him."

"No!"

"But, pardon me, General you just said young Neale went to the bad. If . . . as you intimate . . . there was an attachment between him and my unfortunate child, would he have become an associate of gamblers and vicious women?"

"He would not. Neale must have believed Allie Lee dead. The nature of his fury, the retribution he visited upon this damned Spaniard, proves how wild he was."

"Wild, indeed. But hardly from a sense of loyalty. These camps breed blood-spillers. I heard you say that."

"You'll hear me say something more, presently," retorted the other, with heat scarcely controlled. "But we're wasting time. I don't insist that you see Neale. That's your affair. It seems to me the least you could do would be to thank him. I certainly advise you not to offer him gold. I do insist, however, that you let him see the girl."

"No!"

"But, man. . . . Say, McDermott, go fetch Neale in here."

Allie Lee heard all this strange talk with consternation. An irresistible magnet drew her toward those curtains, which she grasped with trembling hands, ready, but not able, to part them and enter the room. It seemed that in there was a friend of Neale's who she was going to love, and an enemy who she was going to hate. As for Neale seeing her—at once—only death could rob her of that.

"General Lodge, I am surprised at your sympathy for Neale," came the cold voice of Allison Lee.

There was no reply. Someone coughed. Footsteps sounded in the hallway, and a hum of distant voices.

"You forget," continued Lee, "what happened not many hours ago when your train was saved by that daredevil Casey . . . the little book held tight in his locked teeth . . . the letter meant for this Neale from one of Benton's camp women. . . . Your engineer read enough. You heard. I heard. . . . A letter from a dying woman. She accused Neale of striking her . . . of killing her. . . . She said she was dying, but she loved him. . . . Do you remember that, General Lodge?"

"Yes, alas. . . . Lee, I don't deny that. But. . . ."

"There are no buts."

"Lee, you're wooden. Appearances are against Neale. I don't seek to extenuate them. But I know men. Neale might have fallen low, it seems he must have. These are terrible times. The beast in a man. In anger or drink Neale might have struck this woman. . . . But kill her. . . . No!"

A gleam pierced Allie Lee's dark bewilderment. They meant Beauty Stanton, that beautiful, fair woman with such a white, soft bosom and such sad eyes—she who Reddy King had shot. What a tangle of fates and lives! She could tell them why Beauty Stanton had died. Then other words, like springing fire, caught Allie's thought, and a sickening ripple of anguish convulsed her. They believed Beauty Stanton had loved Neale . . . had. . . . Allie would have died before admitting that last thought to her consciousness. For a second the room turned black. Her hold on the curtains kept her from falling. With frantic and terrible earnestness—the old dominance Neale had acquired over her—she clung to the one truth that mattered. She loved Neale—belonged to him—and he was there! That they were about to meet again was as strange and wonderful a thing as had ever happened. What had she not endured? What must he have gone through? The fiery, stinging nature of her new and sudden pain she could not realize.

Again the strong speech became distinct to her.

"You'll stay here . . . and you, Dillon. . . . Don't anyone leave this room. . . . Lee, you can leave, if you want. But we'll see Neale, and so will Allie Lee."

Allie spread the curtains and stood there. No one saw her. All the men faced the door through which sounded slow, heavy tread of boots. An Irishman entered. Then a tall man. Allie's troubled soul suddenly calmed. She saw Neale.

Slowly he advanced a few steps. Another man entered, and Allie recognized Slingerland in his buckskin garb. Neale turned, his face in the light. And a poignant cry leaped up from Allie's heart to be checked on her lips. Was this her young and hopeful and splendid lover? She recognized him, yet now did not know him. He stood bareheaded, and her swift, all-embracing glance saw the gray over his temples, and the eyes that looked with strange, vain joy from across the border of a dark hell, and a face white as death and twitching with spent passion, where ghastly hate was slowly fading.

"Mister . . . Lee," he panted, very low, and the bloody patch on his shirt heaved with his breath, "my only . . . regret . . . is I didn't . . . think to make . . . Durade . . . tell the truth. He lied. . . . He wanted to . . . revenge himself . . . on Allie's mother . . . through Allie. What he said . . . about Allie . . . was a lie . . . as black as his heart. He meant that . . . for her. But . . . somehow she was saved. He was a tiger . . . playing . . . and he waited . . . too long. You must realize . . . her innocence . . . and understand. God has watched over Allie Lee! It was not luck . . . not accident. But innocence! Hough died to save her! Then Ancliffe! Then my old friend . . . Larry Red King! These men . . . broken . . . gone to hell . . . out here . . . felt an innocence that made them . . . mad . . . as I have just been. . . . That is proof . . . if you need it. . . . Men of ruined lives . . . could not rise . . . and die . . . as they did . . . victims of a false impression . . . of innocence. . . . *They knew!*"

Neale paused, in a whisper, his eyes intense with their soul-searching gaze to read belief in the cold face of Allison Lee.

"I thank you, Neale, for your service to me and your defense of her," he said. "What can I do for you?"

"Sir . . . I . . . I. . . ."

"Can I reward you in any way?"

The gray burned out of Neale's face. "I ask . . . nothing . . . except that you believe me."

Lee did not grant this, nor was there any softening of his cold face. "I would like to ask you a few questions," he said "General Lodge here informed me that you saved my . . . my daughter's life long ago. . . . Can you tell me what became of her mother?"

"She was in the caravan . . . massacred by Sioux," replied Neale. "I saw her buried. Her grave is not so many miles from here."

Then a tremor changed Allison Lee's expression. He turned away an instant; his hand closed tight; he bit his lips. This evidence of feeling in him relaxed the stony scrutiny of the watchers, and they shifted uneasily on their feet.

Allie stood watching—waiting, with her heart at her lips.

"Where did you take my daughter?" queried Lee presently.

"To the home of a trapper. My friend . . . Slingerland," replied Neale, indicating the buckskin-clad figure. "She lived there . . . slowly recovering. You don't know that she lost her mind . . . for a while. But she recovered. . . . And during an absence of Slingerland's . . . she was taken away. I don't know who did it . . . or how long Durade had her. I thought her . . . dead."

"Were you and she . . . sweethearts?"

"Yes, sir."

"And engaged to marry?"

"Of course," replied Neale dreamily.

"That cannot be now."

"I understand. I didn't expect . . . I didn't think. . . ."

Allie Lee had believed many times that her heart was breaking, but now she knew it had never broken till then. Why did he not turn to see her waiting there—stricken motionless and voiceless, wild to give the lie to those cold, strange words?

"Then, Neale . . . if you will not accept anything from me, let us terminate this painful interview," said Allison Lee.

"I'm sorry. I only wanted to tell you . . . and ask to see . . . Allie . . . a moment," replied Neale.

"No. It might distress her . . . cause a breakdown. I don't want to risk anything that might prevent my taking the next train with her."

"Going to take her . . . back East?" asked Neale, as if talking to himself.

"Certainly."

"Then . . . I . . . won't see her," Neale murmured dazedly.

At this juncture General Lodge stepped out. His face was dark, his mouth stern.

His action caused a breaking of the strange, vise-like clutch—the mute and motionless spell—that had fallen upon Allie. She felt the gathering of tremendous forces in her; in an instant she would show these stupid men the tumult of a woman's heart.

"Lee, be generous," spoke up General Lodge feelingly. "Let Neale see the girl."

"I said no!" snapped Lee.

"But why not, in heaven's name? He deserves that surely."

"Why? I told you why," declared Lee passionately. "He read that woman's letter!"

"But, Lee, that may not be true," protested General Lodge.

"Ask him? If he doesn't look it, I never saw guilt."

Then the general turned to Neale. "Boy . . . tell me . . . was what we read in Beauty Stanton's letter . . . true?"

Neale faced about like a soldier about to be executed, with a tragic darkening of his face. "To my shame . . . it is true," he said clearly.

Then Allie Lee swept forward. *"Oh, Neale!"*

He seemed to rise and leap at once. And she ran straight into his arms. No man, no trouble, no mystery, no dishonor, no barrier—nothing could have held her back the instant she saw how the sight of her, how the sound of her voice, had transformed Neale. For one tumultuous, glorious, terrible moment she clung to his neck, blind, her heart bursting. Then she fell back with hands seeking her breast.

"I heard!" she cried. "I know nothing of Beauty Stanton's letter. . . . But you didn't shoot her. It was Reddy. I saw him do it."

"Allie," he whispered. At last he had realized her actual presence, the safety of her body and soul, and all that had made him strange and old and grim and sad vanished in a beautiful transfiguration.

"You know Reddy did it!" implored Allie. "Tell them so."

"Yes, I know," he replied. "But I did worse. I. . . ."

She saw him shaken by an agony of remorse, and that agony was communicated to her. "Neale, she loved you?"

He bowed his head.

*"Oh!"* Her cry was almost mute, full of an unutterable realization of tragic fatality for her. *"And you . . . you . . . ?"*

Allison Lee strode between them, facing Neale. "See! She knows . . . and if you would spare her . . . go!" he exclaimed.

"She knows . . . what?" gasped Neale, in a frenzy between doubt and certainty.

Allie felt a horrible, nameless, insidious sense of falsity—a nightmare unreality—an intangible Neale, fated, drifting away from her.

"Good bye . . . Allie! Bless you. I'll be . . . happy . . . knowing . . . you're. . . ." He choked, and the tears streamed down his face. It was a face convulsed by renunciation, not by guilt. Whatever he had done, it was not base.

*"Don't let me . . . go. . . . I . . . forgive you!"* she burst out. She held out her arms. *"There's no one in the world but you!"*

But Neale plunged away, upheld by Slingerland, and Allie's

world grew suddenly empty and black.

The train swayed and *creaked* along through the night with that strain and effort that told of upgrade. The oil lamps beamed dimly in corners of the coach. There were soldiers and open windows peering out. There were passengers asleep sitting up and lying down and huddled over their baggage.

But Allie Lee was not asleep. She lay propped up with pillows and blankets, covered by a heavy coat. Her window was open, and a cool desert wind softly blew her hair. She stared out into the night, and the wheels seemed to be grinding over her crushed heart.

It was late. An old moon, misshapen and pale, shone low down over a dark, rugged horizon. Clouds hid the stars. The desert void seemed weirdly magnified by the wan light, and all that shadowy waste, silent, lonely, bleak, called out to Allie Lee the desolation of her soul. For what had she been saved? The train *creaked* on, and every foot added to her woe. Her unquenchable spirit, pure as a white flame that had burned so wonderfully through the months of her peril, flickered now that her peril ceased to be. She had no strong passion left, else she would have hated this *creaking* train.

It moved on. And there loomed bold outlines of rock and ridge familiar to her. They had been stamped upon her memory by the fright of her lonely wanderings along that very road. She knew every rod of the way, dark, lonely, wild as it was. In the midst of that stark space lay the spot where Benton had been. A spot lost in the immensity of the desert. If she had been asleep, she would have awakened while passing there. There was not a light. Flat patches and pale gleams, a long, wan length of bare street, shadows everywhere—these marked Benton's grave.

Allie stared with strained eyes. They were there—in the blackness—those noble men who had died for her in vain. No—not in vain! She breathed a prayer for them—a word of love for Reddy. Reddy, the waster of life, yet the faithful, the symbol of brotherhood. As long as she lived, she would see him stalk before her with his red, blazing fire, his magnificent effrontery, his supreme will. He, who had been the soul of chivalry, the meekest of men before a woman, the inheritor of a reverence for womanhood, had ruthlessly shot out of his way that wonderful white-armed Beauty Stanton.

She, too, must lie there in the shadow. Allie shivered with the cool desert wind that blew in her face from the shadowy spaces. She shut her eyes to hide the dim passing traces of terrible Benton and the darkness that hid the lonely graves.

The train moved on and on, leaving what had been Benton far behind, and once more Allie opened her weary eyes to the dim, obscure reaches of the desert. Her heart beat very slowly under its leaden weight, its endless pang. Her blood flowed at low ebb. She felt the long-forgotten recurrence of an old, morbid horror, like a poison lichen fastening upon the very spring of life. It passed and came, again, and left her once more. Her thoughts wandered back along the night track she had traversed, until again her ears were haunted by that strange sound that had given Roaring City its name. She had been torn away from hope, love, almost life itself. Where was Neale? He had turned from her, obedient to Allison Lee and the fatal complexity and perverseness of life. The vindication of her spiritual faith and the answer to her prayers lay in the fact that she had been saved, but rather than to be here in this car, daughter of a rich father, but separated from Neale, she would have preferred to fill one of the nameless graves in Benton.

# CHAPTER THIRTY-THREE

The sun set pale-gold and austere as Neale watched the train bear Allie Lee away. No thought of himself entered into that solemn moment of happiness. Allie Lee—alive—safe—her troubles ended—on her way home with her father! The long train wound around the bold bluff and at last was gone. For Neale the moment held something big, final. A phase—a part of his life ended there.

"Son, it's over," said Slingerland, who watched with him. "Allie's gone home . . . back to whar she belongs . . . to come into her own. Thank God! An' you . . . why this day turns you back to whar you was once. . . . Allie owes her life to you an' her father's life. Think, son, of these hyar times . . . how much wuss it might hev been."

Neale's sense of thankfulness was unutterable. Passively he went with Slingerland, silent and gentle. The trapper dressed his wounds, tended him, kept men away from him, and watched by him as if he were a sick child.

Neale suffered only the weakness following the action and stress of great passion. His mind seemed full of beautiful solemn bells of blessing, resonant, ringing the wonder of an everlasting unchangeable truth. Night fell—the darkness thickened—the old trapper kept his vigil—and Neale sank to sleep, and the sweet, low-toned bells claimed him in his dreams.

How strange for Neale to greet a dawn without hatred! He and

Slingerland had breakfast together.

"Son, will you go into the hills with me?" asked the old trapper.

"Yes, someday, when the railroad's built," replied Neale thoughtfully.

Slingerland's keen eyes quickened. "But the railroad's about done . . . an' you need a vacation," he insisted.

"Yes," Neale answered dreamily.

"Son, mebbe you ought to wait a while. You're packin' a bullet somewhar in your carcass."

"It's here," said Neale, putting his hand to his breast, high up toward the shoulder. "I feel it . . . a dull, steady, weighty pain. . . . But that's nothing. I hope I always have it."

"Wal, I don't. . . . An', son, you ain't never goin' back to drink an' cards . . . an' all thet hell? Not now!"

Neale's smile was a promise, and the light of it was instantly reflected on the rugged face of the trapper.

"Reckon I needn't've asked thet. Wal, I'll be sayin' good bye. . . . You kin expect me back someday. . . . To see the meetin' of the rails from East an' West . . . an' to pack you off to my hills."

Neale rode out of Roaring City on the work train, sitting on a flat car with a crowd of hairy-breasted, red-shirted laborers. That train carried hundreds of men, tons of steel rails, thousands of ties, and also it was equipped to feed the workers and to fight Indians. It ran to the end of the rails, about forty miles out of Roaring City.

Neale sought out Reilly, the boss. This big Irishman was in the thick of the start of the day—which was like a battle. Neale waited in the crowd, standing there in his shirt sleeves, with the familiar bustle and color strong as wine to his senses. At last Reilly saw him and shoved out a huge paw.

"Hullo, Neale! I'm glad to see ye. . . . They tell me ye did a domn' foine job."

"Reilly, I need work," said Neale.

"But, mon . . . ye was shot!" ejaculated the boss.

"I'm all right."

"Ye look thot an' no mistake. . . . Shure, now, ye ain't serious about work? You . . . that's chafe of all thim engineer jobs?"

"I want to work with my hands. Let me heave ties or carry rails or swing a sledge . . . for just a few days. I've explained to General Lodge. It's a kind of vacation for me."

Reilly gazed with keen, twinkling eyes at Neale. "Ye can't be drunk an' look sober."

"Reilly, I'm sober . . . and in dead earnest," appealed Neale. "I want to go back . . . be in the finish . . . to lay some rails . . . drive some spikes."

The boss lost his humorous, quizzing expression. "Shure . . . shure," replied Reilly, as if he saw, but failed to comprehend. "Ye're on. . . . An' more power to ye!"

He sent Neale out with the gang detailed to heave railroad ties.

A string of flat cars, loaded with rails and ties, stood on the track where the work of yesterday had ended. Beyond stretched the roadbed, yellow, level, winding as far as the eye could see. The sun beat down hot; the dry, scorching desert breeze swept down from the bare hills, across the waste; dust flew up in puffs; uprooted clumps of sage, like balls, went rolling along, and everywhere the veils of heat rose from the sun-baked earth.

"Drill, ye terriers, drill!" rang out a cheery voice. And Neale remembered Casey.

Neale's gang was put to carrying ties. Neale got hold of the first tie thrown off the car.

"Phwat the hell's ye're hurry!" protested his partner. This fellow was gnarled and knotted, brick-red in color, with face a network of seams, and narrow, sun-burned slits for eyes. He answered to the name of Pat.

They carried the tie out to the end of the rails and dropped it on the level roadbed. Men there set it straight and tamped the gravel around it. Neale and his partner went back for another, passing a dozen couples carrying ties forward. Behind these staggered the rows of men burdened with the heavy iron rails.

So the day's toil began.

Pat had glanced askance at Neale, and then had made dumb signs to his fellow laborers, indicating his hard lot in being yoked to this new wild man on the job. But his ridicule soon changed to respect. Presently he offered his gloves to Neale. They were refused.

"But, fri'nd, ye ain't tough loike me," he protested.

"Pat, they'll put you to bed tonight, if you stay with me," replied Neale.

"The hell ye say! Come on, thin!"

At first Neale had no sensations of heat, weariness, thirst, or pain. He dragged the little Irishman forward to drop the ties— then strode back ahead of him. Neale was obsessed by a profound emotion. This was a new beginning for him. For him the world and life had seemed to cease when yesternight the sun sank and Allie Lee passed out of sight. His motive in working there, he imagined, was to lay a few rails, drive a few spikes along the last miles of the road that he had surveyed. He meant to work this way only a little while, till the rails from East met those from West.

This profound emotion seemed accompanied by a procession of thoughts, each thought in turn, like a sun with satellites, reflecting its radiance upon them and rousing strange, dreamy, full-hearted fancies. . . . Allie lived—as good, as innocent as ever, incomparably beautiful—sad-eyed, eloquent, haunting. From that mighty thought sprang both Neale's exaltation and his activity. He had loved her so well that conviction of her death had broken his heart, deadened his ambition, ruined his life. But since, by the mercy of God and the innocence that had made men heroic, she had survived all peril, all evil, then had begun a colossal overthrow in Neale's soul of the darkness, the despair, the hate, the indifference. He had been flung aloft, into the heights, and he had seen into heaven. He asked for nothing in the world. All-satisfied, eternally humble, grateful with every passionate drop of blood throbbing through his heart, he dedicated all his spiritual life to memory. And likewise there seemed a tremendous need in him of sustained physical action, even violence. He turned to the last stages of the construction of the great railroad.

What fine comrades these hairy-breasted toilers made! Neale had admired them once; now he loved them. Every group seemed to contain a trio like that one he had known so well— Casey, Shane, and McDermott. Then he divined that these men were all alike. They all toiled, swore, fought, drank, gambled. Hundreds of them went to nameless graves. But the work went on—the great, driving, united heart beat on.

Neale had again come under its impulse.

When he lifted a tie and felt the hard, splintering wood, he wondered where it had come from, what kind of a tree it was, who had played in its shade, how many birds had nested in it and animals had grazed beneath it. Between him and that square log of wood there was an affinity. Somehow his hold upon it linked him strangely to a long-past, intangible spirit of himself. He must cling to it, lest he might lose that illusive feeling. Then when he laid it down, he felt regret fade into a realization that the yellow-gravel roadbed also inspirited him. He wanted to feel it, work in it, level it, make it somehow his own.

When he strode back for another load, his magnifying eyes gloated over the toilers in action—the rows of men carrying and laying rails, and the splendid brawny figures of the spikers, naked to the waist, swinging the heavy sledges. The blows rang out *spang—spang—spang!* Strong music, full of meaning! When his turn came to be a spiker, he would love that hardest work of all.

The engine puffed smoke and bumped the cars ahead, little by little as the track advanced; men on the train carried ties and rails forward, filling the front cars as fast as they were emptied; long lines of laborers on the ground passed to and fro, burdened going forward, returning empty-handed; the rails and the shovels and the hammers and the picks all caught the hot gleam from the sun; the dust swept up in sheets; the *ring,* the *crash,* the *thump,* the *scrape* of iron and wood and earth in collision filled the air with a sound rising harshly above the song and laugh and curse of men.

A shifting, colorful, strenuous scene of toil!

Gradually Neale felt that he was fitting into this scene, becoming a part of it, an atom once more in the great whole. He doubted while he thrilled. Clearly as he saw, keenly as he felt, he yet seemed bewildered. Was he not gazing out at this construction work through windows of his soul, once more painted, colored, beautiful, because the most precious gift he might have prayed for had been given him—life and hope for Allie Lee?

He did not know. He could not think.

His comrade, Pat, wiped floods of sweat from his scarlet face. "I'll be domn'd if ye ain't a son-of-a-gun fer worrk!" he complained.

"Pat, we've been given the honor of pace-makers. They've got to keep up with us. Come on," replied Neale.

"Be gad, there ain't a mon in the gang phwat'll trade fer me honor, thin," declared Pat. "Fri'nd, I'd loike to live till next pay day."

"Come on, then, work up an appetite," rejoined Neale.

"Shure I'll die. . . . An' I'd loike to ask, beggin' yer pardon, heven't ye got some Irish in ye?"

"Yes, a little."

"I knowed thot. . . . All roight, I'll die with ye, thin." In half an hour Pat was in despair again. He had to rest. "Phwat's . . . yer . . . name?" he queried.

"Neale."

"It ought to be Casey. Fer there was niver but wan loike ye . . . an' he was Casey. . . . Mon, ye're sweatin' blood roight now!"

Pat pointed at Neale's red, wet shirt. Neale slapped his breast, and drops of blood and sweat spattered from under his hand.

"An' shure yer hands are bladin', too!" ejaculated Pat. They were, indeed, but Neale had not noted that.

The boss, Reilly, passing by, paused to look and grin. "Pat, yez got somewan to kape up with today. We're half a mile ahead of yestidy this time." Then he turned to Neale. "I've seen one in yer class . . . Casey by name. An' thot's talkin'." He went his way.

And Neale, plodding on, saw the red face of the great Casey, with its set grin and the black pipe. Swiftly then he saw it as he had heard of it last, and a shadow glanced fleetingly across the singular radiance of his mind.

The shrill whistle of the locomotive halted the work and called the men to dinner and rest. Instantly the scene changed. The slow, steady, rhythmic motions of labor gave place to a scramble back to the long line of cars. Then the horde of sweaty toilers sought places in the shade, and ate and drank and smoked and rested. As the spirit of work had been merry, so was that of rest, with always a dry, grim earnestness in the background.

Neale slowed down during the afternoon, to the unconcealed

thankfulness of his partner. The burn of the sun, the slippery sweat, the growing ache of muscles, the never-ending thirst, the lessening of strength—these sensations impinged upon Neale's emotion and gradually wore to the front of his consciousness. His hands grew raw, his back stiff and sore, his feet crippled. The wound in his breast burned and bled and throbbed. At the end of the day he could scarcely walk.

He rode in with the laborers, slept twelve hours, and awoke heavy-limbed, slow, and aching. But he rode out to work, and his second day was one of agony.

The third was a continual fight between will and body, between spirit and pain. But so long as he could step and lift, he would work on. From that time he slowly began to mend.

Then came his siege with the rails. That was labor that made carrying ties seem light. He toiled on, sweating thin, wearing hard, growing clearer of mind. As pain subsided, and weariness of body no longer dominated him, slowly thought and feeling returned until that morning dawned when, like a flash of lightning illuminating his soul, the profound and exalted emotion again possessed him. Soon he came to divine that the agony of toil and his victory over weak flesh had added to his strange happiness. Hour after hour he bent his back and plodded beside his comrades, doing his share, burdened as they were, silent, watchful, listening, dreaming, keen to note the progress of the road, yet deep in his own intense abstraction. He seemed to have two minds. He saw every rod of the ten miles of track laid every day, knew, as only an engineer could know, the wonder of such progress, and, likewise, always in his sight, in his mind, shone a face, red-lipped, soulful, lovely like a saint's, with mournful violet eyes, star-sweet in innocence. Life had given Allie Lee back to him—to his love and his memory, and all that could happen to him now must be good. At first he had asked for nothing, so grateful was he to fate, but now he prayed for hours and days and nights to remember.

The day came when Neale graduated into the class of spikers. This division of labor to him had always represented the finest spirit of the building. The drivers—the spikers—the men who nailed the rails—who riveted the last links—these brawny, half-naked wielders of the sledges, bronzed as Indians, seemed to embody both the romance and the achievement. Neale experienced a subtle perception with the first touch and lift and swing of the great hammer. And there seemed born in him a genius for the stroke. He had a free, easy swing, with tremendous power. He could drive so fast that his comrade on the opposite rail, and the carriers and layers, could not keep up with him. Moments of rest seemed earned. During these he would gaze with glinting eyes back at the gangs and the trains, at the smoke, dust, and movement, and beyond toward the east.

One day he drove spikes for hours, with the gangs in uninterrupted labor around him, while back a mile along the road the troopers fought the Sioux, and all this time, when any moment he might be ordered to drop his sledge for a rifle, he listened to the voice in his memory and saw the face.

Another day dawned in which he saw the grading gangs return from work ahead. They were done. Streams of horses, wagons, and men on the return! They had met the graders from the west, and the two lines of roadbed had been connected. As these gangs passed, cheer on cheer greeted them from the rail layers. It was a splendid moment.

From lip to lip then went the word that the grading gangs from East and West had passed each other in plain sight, working on, grading on for a hundred miles farther than necessary. They had met and had passed on, side-by-side, doubling the expense of construction.

This knowledge gave Neale a melancholy reminder of the

dishonest aspect of the road building. And he thought of many things. The spirit of the work was grand, the labor heroic, but, alas! Side-by-side with these splendid and noble attributes stalked the specters of greed and gold and lust of blood and of death.

But neither knowledge such as this, nor peril from Indians, or the toil pangs of a galley slave had power to change Neale's supreme state of joy.

He gazed back toward the east, and then with mighty swing he drove a spike. He loved Allie Lee beyond all conception, and next he loved the building of the railroad.

When such thoughts came, he went back to sensorial feelings, to all about him, pouring into eyes and ears and nerves—the great, bold peaks looming dark, the winding, level roadbed, the smoky desert land reflecting heat, the completed track and gangs of moving men like bright ants in the sunlight, and the exhaust of the engines, the old song, "Drill, ye terriers, drill!", the *ring* and *crash* and *thud* and *scrape* of labor, the whistle of the seeping sand on the wind, the feel of the heavy sledge that he could wield as a toy, the throb of pulse, the smell of dust and sweat, the sense of his being there, his action, his solidarity, his physical brawn—once more manhood.

But at last human instincts encroached upon Neale's superlative detachment from self. It seemed all of a sudden that he stepped toward an eastbound train. When he reached the coach something halted him—a thought—where was he going? The westbound work train was the one he wanted. He laughed a little grimly. Certainly he had grown absent-minded. And straightway he became thoughtful, in a different way. Not many moments of reflection were needed to assure him that he had moved toward the eastbound train with the instinctive idea of going to Allie Lee. The thing amazed him.

"But she . . . she's gone out of my life," he soliloquized. "And

I am . . . I *was* glad!"

The lightning-swift shift to past tense enlightened Neale.

He went out to work. That work still loomed splendid to him, but it seemed not the same. He saw and felt the majesty of common free men, sweating and bleeding and groaning over toil comparable to the building of the pyramids; he felt the best that had ever been in him quicken and broaden as he rubbed elbows with these simple, elemental toilers; with them he had gotten down to the level of truth. His old genius for achievement, the practical and scientific side of him, still thrilled with the effects of strong hands against the natural barriers of the desert. He saw the thousands of plodding, swearing, fighting, blaspheming, joking laborers on the field of action—saw the picture they made, red and bronzed and black, dust-begrimed, and how here with the ties and the rails and the roadbed was the heart of that epical turmoil. What approach could great and rich engineers and directors have made to that vast enterprise without these sons of brawn? Neale now saw what he had once dreamed, and that was the secret of his longing to get down to the earth with these men.

He loved to swing that sledge, to hear the *spang* of the steel ring out. He had a sheer physical delight in the power of his body, long since thinned out, hardened, tough as the wood into which he drove the spikes. He loved his new comrade, Pat, the gnarled and knotted little Irishman who cursed and complained of his job and fought his fellow worker's, yet who never lagged, never shirked, and never failed, though his days of usefulness must soon be over. Soon Pat would drop by the roadside, a victim to toil, and whiskey and sun. And he was great in his obscurity. He wore a brass tag with a number; he signed his wage receipt with a cross; he cared only for drink and a painted hag in a squalid tent; yet in all the essentials that Neale now called great, his friend Pat reached up to them—the spirit to work, to stand his share, to go on, to endure, to fulfill his task.

Neale might have found salvation in this late-developed and splendid relation to labor and to men. But there was a hitch in his brain. He would see all that was beautiful and strenuous and progressive around him, and then, in a flash, that hiatus in his mind would operate to make him hopeless.

Then he would stand as in a trance, with far-away gaze in his eyes, until his fellow spiker would recall him to his neglected work. These intervals of abstraction grew upon him until he would leave off in the act of driving a spike.

And sometimes in these strange intervals he longed for his old friend, brother, shadow—Larry Red King. He held to Red's memory, although with it always would return that low, strange roar of Benton's gold and lust and blood and death. Neale did not understand the mystery of what he had been through. It had been a phase of wildness never to be seen again by his race. His ambition and effort, his fall, his dark siege with hell, his friendship and loss, his agony and toil, his victory, were all symbolical of the progress of a great movement. In his experience lay hidden all that development.

The coming of night was always a relief now, for with the end of the day's work he need no longer fight his battle. It was a losing battle—that he knew. Shunning everybody, he paced to and fro out on the dark, windy desert, under the lonely, pitiless stars.

His longing to see Allie Lee grew upon him. While he had believed her dead, he had felt her spirit hovering near him, in every shadow, and her voice whispered on the wind. She was alive now, but gone away, far distant, over mountains and plains, out of his sight and reach, somewhere to take up a new life alien to his. What would she do? Could she bear it? Never would she forget him—be faithless to his memory! Yet she was young and her life had been hard. She might yield to that cold Allison

Lee's dictation. In happy surroundings her beauty and sweetness would bring a crowd of lovers to her.

"But that's all . . . only natural," muttered Neale, in perplexity. "I want her to forget . . . to be happy . . . to find a home. . . . For her to grow old . . . alone! No! She must love some man . . . marry. . . ." And with the spoken words Neale's heart contracted. He knew that he lied to himself. If she ever cared for another man, that would be the end of Warren Neale. But then, he was ended, anyhow. Jealousy, strange, new, horrible, added to Neale's other burdens, finished him. He had the manhood to try to fight selfishness, but he had failed to subdue it, and he had nothing left to fight his consuming love and hatred of life and terrible loneliness and that fierce thing—jealousy. He had saved Allie Lee! Why had he given her up? He had stained his hands with blood for her sake. And that awful moment came back to him when, maddened by the sting of a bullet, he had gloried in the cracking of Durade's bones, in the ghastly terror and fear of death upon the Spaniard's face, in the feel of the knife blade as he forced Durade to stab himself. Always Neale had been haunted by this final scene of his evil life in the construction camps. A somber and spectral shape, intangible, gloomy-faced, often attended him in the shadow. He justified his deed, for Durade would have killed Allison Lee. But that fact did not prevent the haunting shape, the stir in the dark air, the nameless step upon Neale's trail.

And jealousy, stronger than all except fear, wore Neale out of his exaltation, out of his dream, out of his old disposition to work. He could persist in courage if not in joy. But jealous longing would destroy him—he felt that. It was so powerful, so wonderful that it brought back to him words and movements that until then he had been unable to recall.

And he lived over the past. Much still baffled him, yet gradually more and more of what had happened became clear specifically in his memory. He could not think from the present back over the past. He had to ponder the other way.

One day, leaning on his sledge, Neale's torturing self, morbid, inquisitive, growing by what it fed on, whispered another question to his memory. *What were some of the last words she spoke to me?* And there, limned white on the dark background of his mind, the answer appeared: *Neale, I forgive you!*

He recalled her face, the tragic eyes, the outstretched arms.

"Forgive me! For what?" Neale muttered, dazed and troubled. He dropped his sledge and remained standing there, although the noon whistle called the gang to dinner. Looking out across the hot, smoky, arid desert, he saw also that scene where he had appealed to Allison Lee. Etched out vividly, and his ears throbbed to strong speech.

The room full of men—Lee's cold acceptance of fact—his thanks, his offer, his questions, his refusal—General Lodge's earnest solicitation—the rapid exchange of passionate words between them—the query put to Neale and his answer—the sudden appearance of Allie, shocking his heart with rapture— her sweet, wild words—and so the end! How vivid now—how like flashes of lightning in his mind!

"Lee thought I'd killed Stanton," muttered Neale in intense perplexity. "But she . . . she told them Red did it. . . . What a strange idea Lee had . . . and General Lodge, too. He defended me. . . . Ah!"

Suddenly Neale drew from his pocket the little leather notebook that had been Stanton's, and which contained her letter to him. With trembling hands he opened it. Again this letter was to mean a revelation.

General Lodge had said his engineer had read aloud only the first of that message to Neale, and from this Allison Lee and all the listeners had formed their impressions.

Neale read these first lines.

"No wonder they imagined I killed her!" he exclaimed. "She accuses me. But she never meant what they imagined she meant. Why, that evidence could hang me . . . ! Allie told them she saw Red do it. And it's common knowledge now . . . I've heard it here. . . . What, then, had Allie to forgive . . . to forgive with eyes that will haunt me to my grave? My going to the bad? My killing Durade? No!"

Then the truth burst upon him with merciless and stunning force.

*My God! Allie believed what they all believed . . . what I must have blindly made seem true . . . ! That I was Beauty Stanton's lover!*

# CHAPTER THIRTY-FOUR

The home to which Allie Lee was brought stood in the outskirts of Omaha upon a wooded bank above the river.

Allie watched the broad, yellow Missouri swirling by. She liked best to be alone outdoors in the shade of the trees. In the weeks since her arrival there she had not recovered from the shock of meeting Neale only to be parted from him.

But the comfort, the luxury of her home, the relief from constant dread, such as she had known for years, the quiet at night—these had been so welcome, so saving, that her burden of sorrow seemed endurable. Yet in time she came to see that the finding of a father and a home had only added to her bitterness.

Allison Lee's sister, an elderly woman of strong character, resented the homecoming of this strange, lost daughter. Allie had found no sympathy in her. For a while neighbors and friends of the Lees flocked to the house and were kind, gracious, attentive to Allie. Then somehow her story, or part of it, became gossip. Her father, sensitive, cold, embittered by the past, suffered intolerable shame at the disgrace of a wife's desertion and a daughter's notoriety. Allie's presence hurt him; he avoided her as much as possible; the little kindnesses that he had shown, and his feelings of pride in her beauty and charm, soon vanished. There was no love between them. Allie had tried hard to care for him, but her heart seemed to be buried in that vast grave of the West. She was obedient, dutiful, passive, but she could not care for him. And there came a day when she realized that he did not believe she had come unscathed through the wilds of the gold fields and the vileness of the construction camps. She bore this patiently, although it stung her. But the loss of respect for her father did not come until she heard men in his study, loud-voiced and furious, wrangle over contracts and accuse him of double-dealing.

Later he told her that he had become involved in financial straits, and that, unless he could raise a large sum by a certain date, he would be ruined.

And it was this day that Allie sat on a bench in the little arbor and watched the turbulent river. She was sorry for her father, but she could not help him. Moreover, alien griefs did not greatly touch her. Her own grief was deep and all-enfolding. She was heartsick, and always yearning—yearning for that she dared not name.

The day was hot, sultry; no birds sang, but the locusts were noisy; the air was full of *humming* bees.

Allie watched the river. She was idle because her aunt would not let her work. She could only remember and suffer. The great river soothed her. Where did it come from and where did it go? And what was to become of her? Almost it would have been better. . . .

A servant interrupted her. "Missy, heah's a gennelman to see yo'," announced the Negro girl.

Allie looked. She thought she saw a tall, buckskin-clad man carrying a heavy pack. Was she dreaming or had she lost her mind? She got up, shaking in every limb. This tall man moved; he seemed real; his bronzed face beamed. He approached; he set the pack down on the bench. Then his keen, clear eyes pierced Allie.

"Wal, lass," he said gently.

The familiar voice was no dream, no treachery of her mind.

Slingerland! She could not speak. She could hardly see. She swayed into his arms. Then when she felt the great, strong clasp and the softness of buckskin on her face and the odor of pine and sage and desert dust, she believed in his reality.

Her heart seemed to collapse. All within her was riot. *"Neale,"* she whispered in anguish.

"All right an' workin' hard. He sent me," replied Slingerland, swift to get his message out.

Allie quivered and closed her eyes and leaned against him. A beautiful something pervaded her soul. Slowly the tumult within her breast subsided. She recovered.

"Uncle Al," she called him tenderly.

"Wal, I should smile! An' glad to see you . . . why, Lord, I'd never tell you. . . . You're white an' shaky, lass. . . . Set down hyar . . . on the bench . . . beside me. Thar. . . . Allie, I've a powerful lot to tell you."

"Wait! To see you . . . and to hear . . . of him . . . almost killed me with joy," she panted. Her little hands, once so strong and brown, but now thin and white, fastened tightly in the fringe of his buckskin hunting coat.

"Lass, sight of you sort of makes me young ag'in . . . but . . . Allie, those are not the happy eyes I remember."

"I . . . am very unhappy," she whispered.

"Wal, if thet ain't too bad. Shore it's natural you'd be down-hearted, losin' Neale thet way."

"It's not all . . . that," she murmured, and then she told him.

"Wal, wal!" ejaculated the trapper, stroking his beard in thoughtful sorrow. "But I reckon thet's natural, too. You're strange hyar, an' thet story will hang over you. . . . Lass, with all due respect to your father, I reckon you'd better come back to me an' Neale."

"Did *he* tell you . . . to say that?" she whispered tremulously.

"Lord, no!" ejaculated Slingerland.

"Does he . . . care . . . for me still?"

"Lass, he's dyin' fer you . . . an' I never spoke a truer word."

Allie shuddered close to him, blinded, stormed by an exquisite bittersweet fury of love. She seemed, rising, uplifted, filled with rich, strong joy. "I forgave him," she murmured dreamily low to herself.

"Wal, mebbe you'll be right glad you did . . . presently," said Slingerland, with animation. " 'Specially when thar wasn't nothin' much to forgive."

Allie became mute. She could not lift her eyes.

"Lass, listen," began Slingerland. "After you left Roarin' City, Neale went to work. Began by heavin' ties an' rails, an' now he's slingin' a sledge. . . . This was amazin' to me. I seen him only oncet since, an' thet was the other day. But I heerd about him. I rode over to Roarin' City several times. An' I made it my bizness to find out about Neale. . . . He never came into the town at all. They said he worked like a slave thet first day, bleedin' hard. But he couldn't be stopped. An' the work didn't kill him, though thar was some as swore it would. They said he changed . . . an', when he toughened up, thar was never but one man as could equal him, an' thet was an Irish feller named Casey. I heerd it was somethin' worthwhile to see him sling a sledge. . . . Wal, I never seen him do it, but mebbe I will yet.

"A few days back I met him gettin' off a train at Roarin' City. Lord! I hardly knowed him! He stood like an Injun, with the big muscles bulgin', an' his face was clean an' dark, his eye like fire. . . . He nearly shook the daylights out of me. 'Slingerland, I want you!' he kept yellin' at me. An' I said . . . 'So it 'pears, but what fer?' Then he told me he was goin' after the gold thet Horn had buried along the old Laramie Trail. Wal, I took my outfit, an' we rode back into the hills. You remember them. Wal, we found the gold, easy enough, an' we packed it back to Roarin' City. Thar Neale sent me off on a train to fetch the gold to you. An' hyar I am an' thar's the gold."

Allie stared at the pack, bewildered by Slingerland's story. Suddenly she sat up and she felt the blood rush to her cheeks. "Gold! Horn's gold? But it's not mine! Did Neale send it to me?"

"Every ounce," replied the trapper soberly. "I reckon it's yours. Thar was no one else left . . . an' you recollect what Horn said. Lass, it's yours . . . an' I'm goin' to make you keep it."

"How much is there?" queried Allie, with thrills of curiosity. How well she remembered Horn! He had told her he had no relatives. Indeed, the gold was hers.

"Wal, Neale an' me couldn't calkilate how much, hevin' nothin' to weigh the gold. But it's a fortune."

Allie turned from the pack to the earnest face of the trapper. There had been many critical moments in her life, but never one with the suspense, the fullness, the inevitableness of this.

"Did Neale send anything else?" she flashed.

"Wal, yes, an' I was comin' to thet," replied Slingerland as he unlaced the front of his hunting frock. Presently he drew forth a little leather notebook, which he handed to Allie. She took it while looking up at him. Never had she seen his face radiate such strange emotion. She divined it to be the supreme happiness inherent in the power to give happiness.

Allie trembled. She opened the little book. Surely it would contain a message that would be as sweet as life to dying eyes. She read a name, written in ink, in a clear script: *Beauty Stanton.* Her pulses ceased to beat, her blood to flow, her heart to throb. All seemed to freeze within her except her mind. And that leaped fearfully over the first lines of a letter—then feverishly on to the close—only to fly back and read again. Then she dropped the book. She hid her face on Slingerland's breast. She clutched him with frantic hands. She clung there, her body all held rigid, as if some extraordinary strength or inspiration or joy had suddenly inhibited weakness.

"Wal, lass, hyar you're takin' it powerful hard . . . an' I made sure. . . ."

"Hush," whispered Allie, raising her face. She kissed him. Then she sprang up like a bent sapling released. She met Slingerland's keen gaze—saw him start—then rise as if the better to meet a shock.

"I am going back with you," she said coolly.

"Wal, I knowed you'd go."

"Divide that gold. I'll leave half for my father."

Slingerland's great hands began to pull at the pack. "Thar's a train soon. I calkilated to stay over a day. But the sooner the better. . . . Lass, will you run off or tell him?"

"I'll tell him. He can't stop me, even if he would. . . . The gold will save him from ruin. . . . He will let me go." She stooped to pick up the little leather notebook and placed it in her bosom. Her heart seemed to surge against it. The great river rolled on—rolled on—magnified in her sight. A thick, rich, beautiful light shone under the trees. What was this dance of her blood while she seemed so calm, so cool, so sure?

"Does he have any idea . . . that I might return to him?" she asked.

"None, lass, none! Thet I'll swear," declared Slingerland. "When I left him at Roarin' City the other day, he was . . . wal, like he used to be. The boy come out in him again, not jest the same, but brave. Sendin' thet gold an' thet little book made him happy. . . . I reckon Neale found his soul then. An' he never expects to see you again in this hyar world."

# CHAPTER THIRTY-FIVE

Building a railroad grew to be an exact and wonderful science with the men of the Union Pacific, from engineers down to the laborers who ballasted and smoothed the roadbed. Wherever the work trains stopped, there began a *hum* like a beehive. In short time little flat cars were brought into requisition. Gangs loaded rails to a flat car, and the horses or mules were driven at a gallop to the front. There two men grasped the end of a rail and began to slide it off. In couples, other laborers of that particular gang laid hold, and, when they had it off the car, they ran away with it to drop it in place. While they were doing this, other gangs, followed with more rails. Four rails laid to the minute! When one of the cars was empty, it was tipped off the track to make room for the next one. And as that next one passed, the first was tipped back again to be hauled swiftly for another load of rails.

Four rails down to the minute! It was Herculean toil. The men who fitted the rails were cursed the most frequently because they took time, a few seconds, when there was no time.

Then the spikers! These brawny, half-naked, sweaty giants— what a grand spanging music of labor rang from under their hammers! Three strokes to a spike for most spikers! Only two strokes for such as Casey or Neale! Ten spikes to a rail—four hundred rails to a mile! How many million times had brawny arms swung and sledges *clanged!*

Forward every day the work trains crept westward, closer and

425

closer to that great hour when they would meet the work trains coming east.

The momentum now of the road-laying was tremendous. The spirit that nothing could stop had become embodied in a scientific army of toilers, a mass, a machine, ponderous, irresistible, moving on to the meeting of the rails.

Every day the criss-cross of ties lengthened out along the winding roadbed, and the lines of glistening rails kept pace with them. The sun beat down hot—the dust flew in sheets and puffs—the smoky veils floated up from the desert. Red-shirted toilers, blue-shirted toilers, half-naked toilers, sweat and bled, and laughed grimly, and sucked at their pipes, and bent their broad backs. The pace had quickened to the limit of human endurance. Fury of sound filled the air. In sound and pace was the mighty gathering impetus of a last heave, a last swing.

Promontory Point was the place destined to be famous as the meeting of the rails.

On that summer day in 1869, which was to complete the work, special trains arrived from West and East. The governor of California, who was also president of the western end of the line, met the vice-president of the United States and the directors of the Union Pacific. Mormons from Utah were there in force. The government was represented by officers and soldiers in uniform, and these, with their military band, lent the familiar martial air to the last scene of the great enterprise. Here mingled the Irish and Negro laborers from the East with the Chinese and Mexican from the West. These Eastern paddies laid the last rails on one end, while the Western coolies laid those on the other. The rails joined! Spikes were driven, until the last one remained.

The Territory of Arizona had presented a spike of gold, silver, and iron, Nevada had given one of silver and a railroad tie of laurel wood, and the last spike of all—of solid gold—was presented by California.

The driving of the last spike was to be heard all over the United States. Omaha was the telegraphic center. From here all messages were replied to: *When the last spike is driven at Promontory Point we will say, 'Done!'*

The magic of the wire was to carry that single message abroad over the face of the land.

The President of the United States was to be congratulated, as were the officers of the Army, and the engineers of the work. San Francisco had arranged a monster celebration marked by the booming of cannon and enthusiastic parades. Free railroad tickets into Sacramento were to fill that city with jubilant crowds. At Omaha cannon were to be fired, business abandoned, and the whole city given over to festivity. Chicago was to see a great parade and decorations. In New York a hundred guns were to boom out the tidings. Trinity Church was to have special services, and the famous chimes were to play "Old Hundred". In Philadelphia a ringing of the Liberty Bell in Independence Hall would initiate a celebration. And so it would be in all prominent cities of the Union.

Neale was at Promontory Point that summer day. He stood aloof from the crowd, on a little bank, watching with shining eyes.

To him the scene was great, beautiful, final.

Only a few hundreds of that vast army of laborers were present at the meeting of the rails, but enough were there to represent the whole. Neale's glances were swift and gathering. His comrades, Pat and McDermott, sat near, exchanging lights for their pipes. They seemed reposeful, and for them the matter was ended. Broken hulks of toilers of the rails! Neither would labor any more. A burly Negro, with crinkly, bullet-shaped head, leaned against a post; a brawny spiker, naked to the waist, his wonderful shoulders and arms brown, shiny, knotted, scarred, stood near, sledge in hand; a group of Irishmen, red- and blue-shirted, puffed their black pipes and argued; swarthy, sloe-eyed Mexicans, with huge sombreros on their knees, lolled in the shade of a tree, talking low in their mellow tones and fingering cigarettes; Chinamen, with long pigtails and foreign dress, added strangeness and colorful contrast.

Neale heard the low murmur of voices of the crowd, and the slow puffing of the two engines, head on, only a few yards apart, so strikingly different in shape. Then followed the pounding of hoofs and tread of many feet, the clang of iron as the last rail went down. How clear, sweet, spanging the hammer blows! And there was the old sighing sweep of the wind. Then came a gunshot, the snort of a horse, a loud laugh.

Neale heard all with sensitive, recording ears.

"Mac, yez are so domn' smart . . . now tell me who built the U.P.?" demanded Pat.

"Thot's asy. Me fri'nd Casey did, b'gorra," retorted McDermott.

"Loike hell he did! It was the Irish."

"Shure, thot's phwat I said," McDermott replied.

"Wal, thin, phwat built the U.P.? Tell me thot. Yez knows so much."

McDermott scratched his sun-blistered, stubble-field of a face, and grinned. "Whiskey built the Eastern half, an' cold tay built the Western half."

Pat regarded his comrade with considerable respect. "Mac, shure yez is intilligint," he granted. "The Irish lived on whiskey an' the Chinamons on tay. . . . Wal, yez is so domn' orful smart, mebbe yez can tell me who got the money for thot worrk."

"B'gorra, I know where ivery dollar wint," replied McDermott.

And so they argued on, oblivious to the impressive last stage.

Neale sensed the rest, the repose in the attitude of all the laborers present. Their hour was done. And they accepted that with the equanimity with which they had met the toil, the heat and thirst, the Sioux. A splendid, rugged, loquacious, crude, elemental body of men, unconscious of heroism. Those who had survived the five long years of toil and snow and sun, and the bloody Sioux, and the roaring camps, bore the scars, the furrows, the gray hairs of great and wild times.

A lane opened up in the crowd to the spot where the rails had met.

Neale got a glimpse of his associates, the engineers, as they stood near the frock-coated group of dignitaries and directors. Then Neale felt the stir and lift of emotion, as if he were on a rising wave. His blood began to flow fast and happily. He was to share their triumph. The moment had come. Someone led him back to his post of honor as the head of the engineer corps.

A silence fell then over that larger, denser multitude. It grew impressive, charged, waiting.

Then a man of God offered up a prayer. His voice floated dreamily to Neale. When he had ceased, there were slow, dignified movements of frock-coated men as they placed in position the last spike.

The silver sledge flashed in the sunlight and fell. The sound of the driving-stroke did not come to Neale with the familiar *spang* of iron; it was soft, mellow, golden.

A last stroke! The silence vibrated to a deep, hoarse acclaim from hundreds of men—a triumphant, united hurrah, simultaneously sent out with that final message: *"Done!"*

A great flood of sound, of color seemed to wave over Neale. His eyes dimmed with salt tears, blurring the splendid scene. The last moment had passed—that for which he had stood with all faith, all spirit—and the victory was his. The darkness passed out of his soul.

Then, as he stood there, bareheaded, at the height of this all-satisfying moment, when the last echoing melody of the sledge had blended in the roar of the crowd, a strange feeling of a presence struck Neale. Was it spiritual—was it divine—was it God? Or was it only baneful, fateful—the specter of his accomplished work—a reminder of the long, gray future?

A hand slipped into his—small, soft, trembling, exquisitely thrilling. Neale became still as a stone—transfixed. He knew that touch. No dream, no fancy, no morbid visitation! He felt warm flesh—tender, clinging fingers, and then the pulse of blood that beat of hope—love—life—Allie Lee!

# Chapter Thirty-Six

Slingerland saw Allie Lee married to Neale by that minister of God whose prayer had followed the joining of the rails.

And to the old trapper had fallen the joy and the honor of giving the bride away and of receiving her kiss, as though he had been her father. Then the happy congratulations from General Lodge and his staff; the merry dinner given the couple, and its toasts warm with praise of the bride's beauty and the groom's luck and success with Neale's strange, rapt happiness and Allie's soul shining through her dark-blue eyes—this hour was to become memorable for Slingerland's future dreams.

Slingerland's sight was not clear when, as the train pulled away, he waved a last good bye to his young friends. Now he had no hope, no prayer left unanswered, except to be again in his beloved hills. Abruptly he hurried away to the corrals where his pack train was all in readiness to start. He did not speak to a man. That hour with Allie and Neale, that last look at their wonderful faces—for Slingerland this was to be what he would carry away into the wilderness with him.

He had packed a dozen burros—the largest and completest pack train he had ever driven. The abundance of carefully selected supplies, tools, and traps to last him many years—surely all the years that he would live.

Slingerland did not intend to return to civilization, and he never even looked back at that blotch on the face of the bluff—that hideous Roaring City.

He drove the burros at a good trot, his mind at once busy and absent, happy with the pictures of that last hour, gloomy with the undefined, unsatisfied cravings of his heart. Friendship with Neale, affection for Allie acquainted him with the fact that he had missed something in life—not friendship, for he had had hunter friends, but love, perhaps of a sweetheart, surely love of a daughter. These would be his realized longings, as that splendid Neale and his faithful Allie would be his loved memories.

For the rest the old trapper was glad to see the last of habitations, and of men, and of the railroad. Slingerland hated that great, shining steel band of progress connecting East and West. Every ringing sledge-hammer blow had sung out the death knell of the trapper's calling. This railroad spelled the end of the wilderness. What one group of greedy men had accomplished others would imitate, and the grass of the plains would be burned, the forests blackened, the fountains dried up in the valleys, and the wild creatures of the mountains driven and hunted and exterminated. The end of the buffalo had come—the end of the Indian was in sight—and that of the fur-bearing animal and his hunter must follow soon with the hurrying years.

Slingerland hated the railroad, and he could not see it as Neale did, or any of the engineers or builders. This old trapper had the vision of the Indian—that far-seeing eye cleared by distance and silence, and the force of the great, lonely hills. Progress was great, but nature undespoiled was greater. If a race could not breed all stronger men, through its great movements, it might better not breed any, for the bad over-multiplied the good, and so their needs magnified into greed. Slingerland saw many shining bands of steel across the plains and mountains, many stations and hamlets and cities, a growing and marvelous prosperity from timber, mines, farms, and in the distant end—a gutted West.

He made his first camp on a stream watering a valley twenty miles from the railroad. There were Indian tracks on the trails. But he had nothing to fear from Indians. That night, though all was starry and silent around him as he lay, he still held the feeling that was insupportable.

Next day he penetrated deeper into the foothills, and soon he had gained the fastnesses of the mountains. No longer did he meet trails except those of deer and lion and bear. And so day after day he drove his burros, climbing and descending the rocky ways, until he had penetrated to the very heart of the great wild range.

In all his roaming over untrodden lands he had never come into such a wild place. No foot, not even an Indian's, had ever desecrated this green valley with its clear, singing stream, its herds of tame deer, its curious beaver, its pine-covered slopes, its looming, gray, protective peaks. And at last he was satisfied to halt there—to build his cabin and his corral.

Discontent and longing, and then hate, passed into oblivion. These useless passions could not long survive in such an environment. By and by the old trapper's only link with the past was memory of a stalwart youth, and of a girl with violet eyes, and of their sad and wonderful romance, in which he had played a happy part.

The rosy dawn, the days of sun and cloud, the still, windy nights, the solemn stars, the moon-blanched valley with its grazing herds, the beautiful wild mourn of the hunting wolf and the whistle of the stag, and always and ever the murmur of the stream—in these, and in the solitude and loneliness of their haunts, he found his goal, his serenity, the truth and best of remaining life for him.

# Chapter Thirty-Seven

A band of Sioux warriors rode out upon a promontory of the hills, high above the great expanse of plain. Long, lean arms were raised and pointed.

A chief dismounted and strode to the front of his band. His warbonnet trailed behind him; there were unhealed scars upon his bronze body; his face was old, full of fine, wavy lines, stern, craggy, and inscrutable; his eyes were dark, arrowy lightnings.

They beheld, far out and down upon the plain, a long low, moving object leaving a trail of smoke. It was a train on the railroad. It came from the east and crept toward the west. The chief watched it, and so did his warriors. No word was spoken, no sign made, no face changed.

But what was in the mind and the heart and the soul of that great chief?

This beast that puffed smoke and spat fire and shrieked like a devil of an alien tribe—that split the silence as hideously as the long track split the once smooth plain—that was made of iron and wood—this thing of the white man's, coming from out of the distance where the Great Spirit lifted the dawn, meant the end of the hunting grounds and the doom of the Indian. Blood had flowed; many warriors lay in their last sleep under the trees, but the iron monster that belched fire had come more and more. These white men were as many as the needles of the pines. They fought and died, but always others came.

This chief was old and wise, taught by sage and star and

434

mountain and wind, and the loneliness of the prairie land. He recognized a superior race, but not a nobler one. White men would glut the treasures of water and earth. An Indian had been born to little labor, to hunt his meat, to repel his red foes, to watch the clouds and serve his gods. But these white men would come like a great flight of grasshoppers to cover the length and breadth of the prairie land. The buffalo would roll away, like a dust cloud, in the distance, and never return. No meat for the Indian—no grass for his mustang—no place for his home. The Sioux must fight till he died or be driven back into waste places where grief and hardship would end him.

Red and dusky, the sun was setting beyond the desert. The old chief swept aloft his arm, and then in his acceptance of the inevitable bitterness he stood in magnificent austerity, somber as death, seeing in this railroad train creeping, fading into the ruddy sunset, a symbol of the destiny of the Indian—vanishing—vanishing—vanishing. . . .

# ABOUT THE AUTHOR

**Zane Grey** was born Pearl Zane Gray at Zanesville, Ohio in 1872. He was graduated from the University of Pennsylvania in 1896 with a degree in dentistry. He practiced in New York City while striving to make a living by writing. He married Lina Elise Roth in 1905 and with her financial assistance he published his first novel himself, Betty Zane (1903). Closing his dental office, the Greys moved into a cottage on the Delaware River, near Lackawaxen, Pennsylvania. Grey took his first trip to Arizona in 1907 and, following his return, wrote *The Heritage of the Desert* (1910). The profound effect that the desert had had on him was so vibrantly captured that it still comes alive for a reader. Grey couldn't have been more fortunate in his choice of a mate. Trained in English at Hunter College, Lina Grey proofread every manuscript Grey wrote, polished his prose, and later she managed their financial affairs. Grey's early novels were serialized in pulp magazines, but by 1918 he had graduated to the slick magazine market. Motion picture rights brought in a fortune and, with 109 films based on his work, Grey set a record yet to be equaled by any other author. Zane Grey was not a realistic writer, but rather one who charted the interiors of the soul through encounters with the wilderness. He provided characters no less memorable than one finds in Balzac, Dickens, or Thomas Mann, and they have a vital story to tell. "There was so much unexpressed feeling that could not be entirely portrayed," Loren Grey, Grey's younger son and a noted psychologist, once recalled, "that, in later years, he would weep when re-reading one of his own books." Perhaps, too, closer to the mark, Zane Grey may have wept at how his attempts at being truthful to his muse had so often been essentially altered by his editors, so that no one might ever be able to read his stories as he had intended them. It may be said of Zane Grey that, more than mere adventure tales, he fashioned psycho-dramas about the odyssey of the human soul. If his stories seem not always to be of the stuff of the mundane world, without what his stories do touch, the human world has little meaning— which may go a long way to explain the hold he has had on an enraptured reading public ever since his first Western novel in 1910. His next Five Star Western will be *Desert Heritage*, the fully restored *The Heritage of the Desert*.